Stephen King is the author of more than fifty books, all of them worldwide bestsellers. Many of them have been turned into celebrated films and television series, including *Misery* and *The Shawshank Redemption*. King was the recipient of both America's prestigious 2014 National Medal of Arts and the 2003 National Book Foundation Medal for distinguished contribution to American Letters. In 2007 he also won the Grand Master Award from the Mystery Writers of America. He lives with his wife Tabitha in Maine.

Visit his website at www.stephenking.com

Facebook: www.facebook.com/OfficialStephenKing

END OF WATCH

Bill Hodges, who now runs a two-person agency called Finders Keepers with partner Holly Gibney, is intrigued by the letter Z written with a marker at a crime scene. As similar cases mount up, Hodges is stunned to discover that the evidence points to Brady Hartsfield, the notorious 'Mercedes Killer.' It should be impossible: Brady is confined to a hospital room in a seemingly unresponsive state. But Brady Hartsfield has lethal new powers. And he's planning revenge not just on Hodges and his friends, but on an entire city. The clock is ticking in unexpected ways . . .

Books by Stephen King
Published by Ulverscroft:

FIRESTARTER
CUJO
THE DEAD ZONE
EVERYTHING'S EVENTUAL
FROM A BUICK 8
CELL
FINDERS KEEPERS

STEPHEN KING

END OF WATCH

Complete and Unabridged

CHARNWOOD
Leicester

First published in Great Britain in 2016 by
Hodder & Stoughton
London

First Charnwood Edition
published 2018
by arrangement with
Hodder & Stoughton
An Hachette UK company
London

The line by T.S. Eliot is from *The Love Song of
J. Alfred Prufrock*

A catalogue record for this book is available
from the British Library.

ISBN 978–1–4448–3835–0

Published by
F. A. Thorpe (Publishing)
Anstey, Leicestershire

Set by Words & Graphics Ltd.
Anstey, Leicestershire
Printed and bound in Great Britain by
T. J. International Ltd., Padstow, Cornwall

This book is printed on acid-free paper

For Thomas Harris

Get me a gun
Go back into my room
I'm gonna get me a gun
One with a barrel or two
You know I'm better off dead than
Singing these suicide blues.

APRIL 10, 2009
MARTINE STOVER

It's always darkest before the dawn.

This elderly chestnut occurred to Rob Martin as the ambulance he drove rolled slowly along Upper Marlborough Street toward home base, which was Firehouse 3. It seemed to him that whoever thought that one up really got hold of something, because it was darker than a wood-chuck's asshole this morning, and dawn wasn't far away.

Not that this daybreak would be up to much even when it finally got rolling; call it dawn with a hangover. The fog was heavy and smelled of the nearby not-so-great Great Lake. A fine cold drizzle had begun to fall through it, just to add to the fun. Rob clicked the wiper control from intermittent to slow. Not far up ahead, two unmistakable yellow arches rose from the murk.

'The Golden Tits of America!' Jason Rapsis cried from the shotgun seat. Rob had worked with any number of paramedics over his fifteen years as an EMT, and Jace Rapsis was the best: easygoing when nothing was happening, unflappable and sharply focused when everything was happening at once. 'We shall be fed! God bless capitalism! Pull in, pull in!'

'Are you sure?' Rob asked. 'After the object lesson we just had in what that shit can do?'

1

The run from which they were now returning had been to one of the McMansions in Sugar Heights, where a man named Harvey Galen had called 911 complaining of terrible chest pains. They had found him lying on the sofa in what rich folks no doubt called 'the great room,' a beached whale of a man in blue silk pajamas. His wife was hovering over him, convinced he was going to punch out at any second.

'Mickey D's, Mickey D's!' Jason chanted. He was bouncing up and down in his seat. The gravely competent professional who had taken Mr Galen's vitals (Rob right beside him, holding the First In Bag with its airway management gear and cardiac meds) had disappeared. With his blond hair flopping in his eyes, Jason looked like an overgrown kid of fourteen. 'Pull in, I say!'

Rob pulled in. He could get behind a sausage biscuit himself, and maybe one of those hash brown thingies that looked like a baked buffalo tongue.

There was a short line of cars at the drive-thru. Rob snuggled up at the end of it.

'Besides, it's not like the guy had a for-real heart attack,' Jason said. 'Just OD'd on Mexican. Refused a lift to the hospital, didn't he?'

He had. After a few hearty belches and one trombone blast from his nether regions that had his social X-ray of a wife booking for the kitchen, Mr Galen sat up, said he was feeling much better, and told them that no, he didn't think he needed to be transported to Kiner Memorial. Rob and Jason didn't think so, either, after listening to a recitation of what Galen had put

2

away at Tijuana Rose the night before. His pulse was strong, and although his blood pressure was on the iffy side, it probably had been for years, and was currently stable. The automatic external defibrillator never came out of its canvas sack.

'I want two Egg McMuffins and two hash browns,' Jason announced. 'Black coffee. On second thought, make that three hash browns.'

Rob was still thinking about Galen. 'It was indigestion this time, but it'll be the real thing soon enough. Thunderclap infarction. What do you think he went? Three hundred? Three-fifty?'

'Three twenty-five at least,' Jason said, 'and stop trying to spoil my breakfast.'

Rob waved his arm at the Golden Arches rising through the lake-effect fog. 'This place and all the other greasepits like it are half of what's wrong with America. As a medical person, I'm sure you know that. What you just ordered? That's nine hundred calories on the hoof, bro. Add sausage to the Egg McMuffdivers and you're riding right around thirteen hundred.'

'What are *you* having, Doctor Health?'

'Sausage biscuit. Maybe two.'

Jason clapped him on the shoulder. 'My man!'

The line moved forward. They were two cars from the window when the radio beneath the in-dash computer blared. Dispatchers were usually cool, calm, and collected, but this one sounded like a radio shock jock after too many Red Bulls. 'All ambulances and fire apparatus, we have an MCI! I repeat, MCI! This is a high-priority call for all ambulances and fire apparatus!'

3

MCI, short for mass casualty incident. Rob and Jason stared at each other. Plane crash, train crash, explosion, or act of terrorism. It almost had to be one of the four.

'Location is City Center on Marlborough Street, repeat City Center on Marlborough. Once again, this is an MCI with multiple deaths likely. Use caution.'

Rob Martin's stomach tightened. No one told you to use caution when heading to a crash site or gas explosion. That left an act of terrorism, and it might still be in progress.

Dispatch was going into her spiel again. Jason hit the lights and siren while Rob cranked the wheel and pulled the Freightliner ambo into the lane that skirted the restaurant, clipping the bumper of the car ahead of him. They were just nine blocks from City Center, but if Al-Qaeda was shooting the place up with Kalashnikovs, the only thing they had to fire back with was their trusty external defibrillator.

Jason grabbed the mike. 'Copy, Dispatch, this is 23 out of Firehouse 3, ETA just about six minutes.'

Other sirens were rising from other parts of the city, but judging from the sound, Rob guessed their ambo was closest to the scene. A cast iron light had begun creeping into the air, and as they wheeled out of McDonald's and onto Upper Marlborough, a gray car knitted itself out of the gray fog, a big sedan with a dented hood and badly rusted grille. For a moment the HD headlights, on high beam, were pointed straight at them. Rob hit the dual

4

air-horns and swerved. The car — it looked like a Mercedes, although he couldn't be sure — slewed back into its own lane and was then nothing but taillights dwindling into the fog.

'Jesus Christ, that was close,' Jason said. 'Don't suppose you got the license plate?'

'No.' Rob's heart was beating so hard he could feel it pulsing on both sides of his throat. 'I was busy saving our lives. Listen, how can there be multiple casualties at City Center? God isn't even up yet. It's gotta be closed.'

'Could've been a bus crash.'

'Try again. They don't start running until six.'

Sirens. Sirens everywhere, beginning to converge like blips on a radar screen. A police car went bolting past them, but so far as Rob could tell, they were still ahead of the other ambos and fire trucks.

Which gives us a chance to be the first to get shot or blown up by a mad Arab shouting allahu akbar, he thought. *How nice for us.*

But the job was the job, so he swung onto the steep drive leading up to the main city administration buildings and the butt-ugly auditorium where he'd voted until moving out to the suburbs.

'*Brake!*' Jason screamed. '*Jesus-fuck, Robbie, BRAKE!*'

Scores of people were coming at them from the fog, a few sprinting nearly out of control because of the incline. Some were screaming. One guy fell down, rolled, picked himself up, and ran on with his torn shirttail flapping beneath his jacket. Rob saw a woman with shredded hose, bloody shins, and only one shoe. He came to a

5

panic stop, the nose of the ambo dipping, unsecured shit flying. Meds, IV bottles, and needle packs from a cabinet left unsecured — a violation of protocol — became projectiles. The stretcher they hadn't had to use for Mr Galen bounced off one wall. A stethoscope found the pass-through, smacked the windshield, and fell onto the center console.

'Creep along,' Jason said. 'Just creep, okay? Let's not make it worse.'

Rob feathered the gas and continued up the slope, now at walking pace. Still they came, hundreds, it seemed, some bleeding, most not visibly hurt, all of them terrified. Jason unrolled the passenger window and leaned out.

'What's going on? Somebody tell me what's going on!'

A man pulled up, red-faced and gasping. 'It was a car. Tore through the crowd like a mowing machine. Fucking maniac just missed me. I don't know how many he hit. We were penned in like hogs because of the posts they set up to keep people in line. He did it on purpose and they're laying around up there like . . . like . . . oh man, dolls filled with blood. I saw at least four dead. There's gotta be more.'

The guy started to move on, plodding now instead of running as the adrenaline faded. Jason unhooked his seatbelt and leaned out to call after him. 'Did you see what color it was? The car that did it?'

The man turned back, pale and haggard. 'Gray. Great big gray car.'

Jason sat back down and looked at Rob.

Neither of them had to say it out loud: it was the one they had swerved to avoid as they came out of McDonald's. And that hadn't been rust on its snout, after all.

'Go, Robbie. We'll worry about the mess in back later. Just get us to the prom and don't hit anyone, yeah?'

'Okay.'

By the time Rob arrived in the parking lot, the panic was abating. Some people were leaving at a walk; others were trying to help those who had been struck by the gray car; a few, the assholes present in every crowd, were snapping photos or making movies with their phones. Hoping to go viral on YouTube, Rob assumed. Chrome posts with yellow DO NOT CROSS tape trailing from them lay on the pavement.

The police car that had passed them was parked close to the building, near a sleeping bag with a slim white hand protruding. A man lay sprawled crossways on top of the bag, which was in the center of a spreading bloodpuddle. The cop motioned the ambo forward, his beckoning arm seeming to stutter in the swinging blue glare of the lightbar atop his cruiser.

Rob grabbed the mobile data terminal and got out while Jason ran around to the rear of the ambo. He emerged with his First In Bag and the external defibrillator. The day continued to brighten, and Rob could read the sign flapping over the main doors of the auditorium: **1000 JOBS GUARANTEED!** *We Stand With the People of Our City!* — **MAYOR RALPH KINSLER.**

Okay, that explained why there had been such a crowd, and so early in the morning. A job fair. Times were tough everywhere, had been since the economy had its own thunderclap infarction the year before, but they had been especially tough in this little lakefront city, where the jobs had started bleeding away even before the turn of the century.

Rob and Jason started toward the sleeping bag, but the cop shook his head. His face was ashen. 'This guy and the two in the bag are dead. His wife and baby, I guess. He must have been trying to protect them.' He made a brief sound deep in his throat, something between a burp and a retch, clapped a hand over his mouth, then took it away and pointed. 'That lady there might still be with us.'

The lady in question was sprawled on her back, her legs twisted away from her upper body at an angle that suggested serious trauma. The crotch of her dressy beige slacks was dark with urine. Her face — what remained of it — was smeared with grease. Part of her nose and most of her upper lip had been torn away. Her beautifully capped teeth were bared in an unconscious snarl. Her coat and half of her roll-neck sweater had also been torn away. Great dark bruises were flowering on her neck and shoulder.

Fucking car ran right over her, Rob thought. Squashed her like a chipmunk. He and Jason knelt beside her, snapping on blue gloves. Her purse lay nearby, marked by a partial tire-track. Rob picked it up and heaved it into the back of

8

the ambo, thinking the tire print might turn out to be evidence, or something. And of course the woman would want it.

If she lived, that was.

'She's stopped breathing, but I got a pulse,' Jason said. 'Weak and thready. Tear down that sweater.'

Rob did it, and half the bra, straps shredded, came with it. He pushed the rest down to get it out of the way, then began chest compressions while Jason started an airway.

'She going to make it?' the cop asked.

'I don't know,' Rob said. 'We got this. You've got other problems. If more rescue vehicles come steaming up the drive like we almost did, someone's gonna get killed.'

'Ah, man, there are people laying hurt everywhere. It's like a battlefield.'

'Help the ones you can.'

'She's breathing again,' Jason said. 'Get with me, Robbie, let's save a life here. Hop on the MDT and tell Kiner we're bringing in a possible neck fracture, spinal trauma, internal injuries, facial injuries, God knows what else. Condition critical. I'll feed you her vitals.'

Rob made the call from the mobile data terminal while Jason continued squeezing the Ambu bag. Kiner ER answered immediately, the voice on the other end crisp and calm. Kiner was a Level I trauma center, what was sometimes called Presidential Class, and ready for something like this. They trained for it five times a year.

With the call-in made, he got an O_2 level

(predictably lousy) and then grabbed both the rigid cervical collar and the orange backboard from the ambo. Other rescue vehicles were arriving now, and the fog had begun to lift, making the magnitude of the disaster clear.

All with one car, Rob thought. Who would believe it?

'Okay,' Jason said. 'If she ain't stable, it's the best we can do. Let's get her onboard.'

Careful to keep the backboard perfectly horizontal, they lifted her into the ambo, placed her on the stretcher, and secured her. With her pallid, disfigured face framed by the cervical collar, she looked like one of the ritual female victims in a horror movie . . . except those were always young and nubile, and this woman looked to be in her forties or early fifties. Too old to be job-hunting, you would have said, and Rob only had to look at her to know she would never go job-hunting again. Or walk, from the look of her. With fantastic luck, she might avoid quadriplegia — assuming she got through this — but Rob guessed that her life from the waist down was over.

Jason knelt, slipped a clear plastic mask over her mouth and nose, and started the oxygen from the tank at the head of the stretcher. The mask fogged up, a good sign.

'Next thing?' Rob asked, meaning What else can I do?

'Find some epi in that junk that flew around, or get it out of my bag. I had a good pulse for awhile there, but it's gone thready again. Then fire this monkey up. With the injuries she's sustained, it's a miracle she's alive at all.'

Rob found an ampoule of epinephrine under a tumbled box of bandages and handed it over. Then he slammed the back doors, dropped into the driver's seat, and got cranking. First to the scene at an MCI meant first to the hospital. That would improve this lady's slim chances just a little bit. Still, it was a fifteen-minute run even in light morning traffic, and he expected her to be dead by the time they got to Ralph M. Kiner Memorial Hospital. Given the extent of her injuries, that might be the best outcome.

But she wasn't.

★ ★ ★

At three o'clock that afternoon, long after their shift was over but too wired to even think about going home, Rob and Jason sat in the ready-room of Firehouse 3, watching ESPN on mute. They had made eight runs in all, but the woman had been the worst.

'Martine Stover, that was her name,' Jason said at last. 'She's still in surgery. I called while you were in the can.'

'Any idea what her chances are?'

'No, but they didn't just let her crater, and that means something. Pretty sure she was there looking for an executive secretary's position. I went in her purse for ID — got a blood type from her driver's license — and found a whole sheaf of references. Looks like she was good at her job. Last position was at the Bank of America. Got downsized.'

11

'And if she lives? What do you think? Just the legs?'

Jason stared at the TV, where basketball players were running fleetly up the court, and said nothing for a long while. Then: 'If she lives, she's gonna be a quad.'

'For sure?'

'Ninety-five percent.'

A beer ad came on. Young people dancing up a storm in a bar. Everyone having fun. For Martine Stover, the fun was over. Rob tried to imagine what she would be facing if she pulled through. Life in a motorized wheelchair that she moved by puffing into a tube. Being fed either pureed gluck or through IV tubes. Respirator-assisted breathing. Shitting into a bag. Life in a medical twilight zone.

'Christopher Reeve didn't do so bad,' Jason said, as if reading his thoughts. 'Good attitude. Good role model. Kept his chin up. Even directed a movie, I think.'

'Sure he kept his chin up,' Rob said. 'Thanks to a cervical collar that never came off. And he's dead.'

'She was wearing her best clothes,' Jason said. 'Good slacks, expensive sweater, nice coat. Trying to get back on her feet. And some *bastard* comes along and takes it all.'

'Did they get him yet?'

'Not the last I heard. When they do, I hope they string him up by the nutsack.'

★ ★ ★

12

The following night, while delivering a stroke victim to Kiner Memorial, the partners checked on Martine Stover. She was in the ICU, and showing those signs of increasing brain function that signal the imminent recovery of consciousness. When she did come back, someone would have to give her the bad news: she was paralyzed from the chest down.

Rob Martin was just glad it wouldn't have to be him.

And the man the press was calling the Mercedes Killer still hadn't been caught.

Z

JANUARY 2016

1

A pane of glass breaks in Bill Hodges's pants pocket. This is followed by a jubilant chorus of boys, shouting *'That's a HOME RUN!'*

Hodges winces and jumps in his seat. Dr Stamos is part of a four-doctor cabal, and the waiting room is full this Monday morning. Everyone turns to look at him. Hodges feels his face grow warm. 'Sorry,' he says to the room at large. 'Text message.'

'And a very loud one,' remarks an old lady with thinning white hair and beagle dewlaps. She makes Hodges feel like a kid, and he's pushing seventy. She's hip to cell phone etiquette, though. 'You should lower the volume in public places like this, or mute your phone entirely.'

'Absolutely, absolutely.'

The old lady goes back to her paperback (it's *Fifty Shades of Grey*, and not her first trip through it, from the battered look of the thing). Hodges drags his iPhone out of his pocket. The text is from Pete Huntley, his old partner when Hodges was on the cops. Pete is now on the verge of pulling the pin himself, hard to believe but true. End of watch is what they call it, but Hodges himself has found it impossible to give up watching. He now runs a little two-person firm called Finders Keepers. He calls himself an independent skip-tracer, because he got into a little trouble a few years back and can't qualify for a private investigator's license. In this city you have to be bonded. But a PI is what he is, at least some of the time.

Call me, Kermit. ASAP. Important.

Kermit is Hodges's actual first name, but he goes by the middle one with most people; it keeps the frog jokes to a minimum. Pete makes a practice of using it, though. Finds it hilarious.

Hodges considers just pocketing the phone again (after muting it, if he can find his way to the DO NOT DISTURB control). He'll be called into Dr Stamos's office at any minute, and he wants to get their conference over with. Like most elderly guys he knows, he doesn't like doctors' offices. He's always afraid they're going to find not just something wrong but something *really* wrong. Besides, it's not like he doesn't know what his ex-partner wants to talk about: Pete's big retirement bash next month. It's going to be at the Raintree Inn, out by the airport. Same place where Hodges's party took place, but this time he intends to drink a lot less. Maybe not at all. He had trouble with booze when he was active police, it was part of the reason his marriage crashed, but these days he seems to have lost his taste for alcohol. That's a relief. He once read a science fiction novel called *The Moon Is a Harsh Mistress*. He doesn't know about the moon, but would testify in court that whiskey is a harsh mistress, and that's made right here on earth.

He thinks it over, considers texting, then rejects the idea and gets up. Old habits are too strong.

The woman behind the reception desk is Marlee, according to her nametag. She looks about seventeen, and gives him a brilliant cheerleader's smile. 'He'll be with you soon, Mr Hodges, I promise. We're just running a teensy bit behind. That's Monday for you.'

'Monday, Monday, can't trust that day,' Hodges says.

She looks blank.

'I'm going to step out for a minute, okay? Have to make a call.'

'That's fine,' Marlee says. 'Just stand in front of the door. I'll give you a big wave if you're still out there when he's ready.'

'That works.' Hodges stops by the old lady on his way to the door. 'Good book?'

She looks up at him. 'No, but it's very energetic.'

'So I've been told. Have you seen the movie?'

She stares up at him, surprised and interested. 'There's a *movie?*'

'Yes. You should check it out.'

Not that Hodges has seen it himself, although Holly Gibney — once his assistant, now his partner, a rabid film fan since her troubled childhood — tried to drag him to it. Twice. It was Holly who put the breaking pane of glass/home run text alert on his phone. She found it amusing. Hodges did, too . . . at first. Now he finds it a pain in the ass. He'll look up how to change it on the Internet. You can find anything on the Internet, he has discovered. Some of it is helpful.

19

Some of it is interesting. Some of it is funny.

And some of it is fucking awful.

2

Pete's cell rings twice, and then his old partner is in his ear. 'Huntley.'

Hodges says, 'Listen to me carefully, because you may be tested on this material later. Yes, I'll be at the party. Yes, I'll make a few remarks after the meal, amusing but not raunchy, and I'll propose the first toast. Yes, I understand both your ex and your current squeeze will be there, but to my knowledge no one has hired a stripper. If anyone has, it would be Hal Corley, who is an idiot, and you'd have to ask hi — '

'Bill, stop. It's not about the party.'

Hodges stops at once. It's not just the intertwined babble of voices in the background — police voices, he knows that even though he can't tell what they're saying. What stops him dead is that Pete has called him Bill, and that means it's serious shit. Hodges's thoughts fly first to Corinne, his own ex-wife, next to his daughter Alison, who lives in San Francisco, and then to Holly. Christ, if something has happened to Holly . . .

'What is it about, Pete?'

'I'm at the scene of what appears to be a murder-suicide. I'd like you to come out and take a look. Bring your sidekick with you, if she's available and agreeable. I hate to say this, but I think she might actually be a little smarter than you are.'

Not any of his people. Hodges's stomach muscles, tightened as if to absorb a blow, loosen. Although the steady ache that's brought him to Stamos is still there. 'Of course she is. Because she's younger. You start to lose brain cells by the millions after you turn sixty, a phenomenon you'll be able to experience for yourself in another couple of years. Why would you want an old carthorse like me at a murder scene?'

'Because this is probably my last case, because it's going to blow up big in the papers, and because — don't swoon — I actually value your input. Gibney's, too. And in a weird way, you're both connected. That's probably a coincidence, but I'm not entirely sure.'

'Connected how?'

'Does the name Martine Stover ring a bell?'

For a moment it doesn't, then it clicks in. On a foggy morning in 2009, a maniac named Brady Hartsfield drove a stolen Mercedes-Benz into a crowd of job-seekers at City Center, downtown. He killed eight and seriously injured fifteen. In the course of their investigation, Detectives K. William Hodges and Peter Huntley interviewed a great many of those who had been present on that foggy morning, including all the wounded survivors. Martine Stover had been the toughest to talk to, and not only because her disfigured mouth made her all but impossible to understand for anyone except her mother. Stover was paralyzed from the chest down. Later, Hartsfield had written Hodges an anonymous letter. In it he referred to her as 'your basic head on a stick.' What made that especially cruel was the

21

radioactive nugget of truth inside the ugly joke.

'I can't see a quadriplegic as a murderer, Pete . . . outside an episode of *Criminal Minds*, that is. So I assume — ?'

'Yeah, the mother was the doer. First she offed Stover, then herself. Coming?'

Hodges doesn't hesitate. 'I am. I'll pick up Holly on the way. What's the address?'

'1601 Hilltop Court. In Ridgedale.'

Ridgedale is a commuter suburb north of the city, not as pricey as Sugar Heights, but still pretty nice.

'I can be there in forty minutes, assuming Holly's at the office.'

And she will be. She's almost always at her desk by eight, sometimes as early as seven, and apt to be there until Hodges yells at her to go home, fix herself some supper, and watch a movie on her computer. Holly Gibney is the main reason Finders Keepers is in the black. She's an organizational genius, she's a computer wizard, and the job is her life. Well, along with Hodges and the Robinson family, especially Jerome and Barbara. Once, when Jerome and Barbie's mom called Holly an honorary Robinson, she lit up like the sun on a summer afternoon. It's a thing Holly does more often than she used to, but still not enough to suit Hodges.

'That's great, Kerm. Thanks.'

'Have the bodies been transported?'

'Off to the morgue as we speak, but Izzy's got all the pictures on her iPad.' He's talking about Isabelle Jaynes, who has been Pete's partner since Hodges retired.

22

'Okay. I'll bring you an éclair.'

'There's a whole bakery here already. Where are you, by the way?'

'Nowhere important. I'll get with you as soon as I can.'

Hodges ends the call and hurries down the hall to the elevator.

3

Dr Stamos's eight-forty-five patient finally reappears from the exam area at the back. Mr Hodges's appointment was for nine, and it's now nine thirty. The poor guy is probably impatient to do his business here and get rolling with the rest of his day. She looks out in the hall and sees Hodges talking on his cell.

Marlee rises and peeks into Stamos's office. He's sitting behind his desk with a folder open in front of him. **KERMIT WILLIAM HODGES** is computer-printed on the tab. The doctor is studying something in the folder and rubbing his temple, as though he has a headache.

'Dr Stamos? Shall I call Mr Hodges in?'

He looks up at her, startled, then at his desk clock. 'Oh God, yes. Mondays suck, huh?'

'Can't trust that day,' she says, and turns to go.

'I love my job, but I hate this part of it,' Stamos says.

It's Marlee's turn to be startled. She turns to look at him.

'Never mind. Talking to myself. Send him in. Let's get this over with.'

Marlee looks out into the hall just in time to see the elevator door closing at the far end.

4

Hodges calls Holly from the parking garage next to the medical center, and when he gets to the Turner Building on Lower Marlborough, where their office is located, she's standing out front with her briefcase planted between her sensible shoes. Holly Gibney: late forties now, tallish and slim, brown hair usually scrooped back in a tight bun, this morning wearing a bulky North Face parka with the hood up and framing her small face. You'd call that face plain, Hodges thinks, until you saw the eyes, which are beautiful and full of intelligence. And you might not really see them for a long time, because as a rule, Holly Gibney doesn't do eye contact.

Hodges slides his Prius to the curb and she jumps in, taking off her gloves and holding her hands up to the passenger-side heating vent. 'It took you a very long time to get here.'

'Fifteen minutes. I was on the other side of town. I caught all the red lights.'

'It was *eighteen* minutes,' Holly informs him as Hodges pulls into traffic. 'Because you were speeding, which is counterproductive. If you keep your speed to exactly twenty miles an hour, you can catch almost all the lights. They're timed. I've told you that several times. Now tell me what the doctor said. Did you get an A on your tests?'

Hodges considers his options, which are only two: tell the truth or prevaricate. Holly nagged him into going to the doctor because he's been having stomach issues. Just pressure at first, now some pain. Holly may have personality problems, but she's a very efficient nagger. Like a dog with a bone, Hodges sometimes thinks.

'The results weren't back yet.' This is not quite a lie, he tells himself, because they weren't back to *me* yet.

She looks at him doubtfully as he merges onto the Crosstown Expressway. Hodges hates it when she looks at him that way.

'I'll keep after this,' he says. 'Trust me.'

'I do,' she says. 'I do, Bill.'

That makes him feel even worse.

She bends, opens her briefcase, and takes out her iPad. 'I looked up some stuff while I was waiting for you. Want to hear it?'

'Hit me.'

'Martine Stover was fifty at the time Brady Hartsfield crippled her, which would make her fifty-six as of today. I suppose she could be fifty-seven, but since this is only January, I think that's very unlikely, don't you?'

'Odds are against, all right.'

'At the time of the City Center event, she was living with her mother in a house on Sycamore Street. Not far from Brady Hartsfield and *his* mother, which is sort of ironic when you think of it.'

Also close to Tom Saubers and his family, Hodges muses. He and Holly had a case involving the Saubers family not long ago, and that one

25

also had a connection to what the local newspaper had taken to calling the Mercedes Massacre. There were all sorts of connections, when you thought about it, perhaps the strangest being that the car Hartsfield had used as a murder weapon belonged to Holly Gibney's cousin.

'How does an elderly woman and her severely crippled daughter make the jump from the Tree Streets to Ridgedale?'

'Insurance. Martine Stover had not one or two whopping big policies, but three. She was sort of a freak about insurance.' Hodges reflects that only Holly could say that approvingly. 'There were several articles about her afterward, because she was the most badly hurt of those who survived. She said she knew that if she didn't get a job at City Center, she'd have to start cashing her policies in, one by one. After all, she was a single woman with a widowed, unemployed mother to support.'

'Who ended up taking care of her.'

Holly nods. 'Very strange, very sad. But at least there was a financial safety net, which is the purpose of insurance. They even moved up in the world.'

'Yes,' Hodges says, 'but now they're out of it.'

To this Holly makes no reply. Up ahead is the Ridgedale exit. Hodges takes it.

5

Pete Huntley has put on weight, his belly hanging over his belt buckle, but Isabelle Jaynes is as smashing as ever in her tight faded jeans and blue blazer. Her misty gray eyes go from Hodges to Holly and then back to Hodges again.

'You've gotten thin,' she says. This could be either a compliment or an accusation.

'He's having stomach problems, so he had some tests,' Holly says. 'The results were supposed to be in today, but — '

'Let's not go there, Hols,' Hodges says. 'This isn't a medical consultation.'

'You two are more like an old married couple every day,' Izzy says.

Holly replies in a matter-of-fact voice. 'Marriage to Bill would spoil our working relationship.'

Pete laughs and Holly shoots him a puzzled glance as they step inside the house.

It's a handsome Cape Cod, and although it's on top of a hill and the day is cold, the house is toasty-warm. In the foyer, all four of them put on thin rubber gloves and bootees. How it all comes back, Hodges thinks. As if I was never away.

In the living room there's a painting of big-eyed waifs hung on one wall, a big-screen TV hung on another. There's an easy chair in front of the tube with a coffee table beside it. On the table is a careful fan of celebrity mags like *OK!* and scandal rags like *Inside View*. In the middle of the room there are two deep grooves in the rug. Hodges thinks, This is where they sat in the evenings to watch TV. Or maybe all day long. Mom in her easy chair, Martine in her wheelchair. Which must have weighed a ton, judging by those marks.

27

'What was her mother's name?' he asks.

'Janice Ellerton. Husband James died twenty years ago, according to . . . ' Old-school like Hodges, Pete carries a notebook instead of an iPad. Now he consults it. 'According to Yvonne Carstairs. She and the other aide, Georgina Ross, found the bodies when they arrived this morning shortly before six. They got paid extra for turning up early. The Ross woman wasn't much help — '

'She was gibbering,' Izzy says. 'Carstairs was okay, though. Kept her head throughout. Called the police right away, and we were on-scene by six forty.'

'How old was Mom?' Hodges asks.

'Don't know exactly yet,' Pete says, 'but no spring chicken.'

'She was seventy-nine,' Holly says. 'One of the news stories I searched while I was waiting for Bill to pick me up said she was seventy-three when the City Center Massacre happened.'

'Awfully long in the tooth to be taking care of a quadriplegic daughter,' Hodges says.

'She was in good shape, though,' Isabelle says. 'At least according to Carstairs. Strong. And she had plenty of help. There was money for it because — '

' — of the insurance,' Hodges finishes. 'Holly filled me in on the ride over.'

Izzy gives Holly a glance. Holly doesn't notice. She's measuring the room. Taking inventory. Sniffing the air. Running a palm across the back of Mom's easy chair. Holly has emotional problems, she's breathtakingly literal, but she's

28

also open to stimuli in a way few people are.

Pete says, 'There were two aides in the morning, two in the afternoon, two in the evening. Seven days a week. Private company called' — back to the notebook — 'Home Helpers. They did all the heavy lifting. There's also a housekeeper, Nancy Alderson, but apparently she's off. Note on the kitchen calendar says *Nancy in Chagrin Falls*. There's a line drawn through today, Tuesday, and Wednesday.'

Two men, also wearing gloves and bootees, come down the hall. From the late Martine Stover's part of the house, Hodges assumes. Both are carrying evidence cases.

'All done in the bedroom and bathroom,' one of them says.

'Anything?' Izzy asks.

'About what you'd expect,' the other says. 'We got quite a few white hairs from the tub, not unusual considering that's where the old lady highsided it. There was also excrement in the tub, but just a trace. Also as you would expect.' Off Hodges's questioning look, the tech adds, 'She was wearing continence pants. The lady did her homework.'

'Oough,' Holly says.

The first tech says, 'There's a shower chair, but it's in the corner with extra towels stacked on the seat. Looks like it's never been used.'

'They would have given her sponge baths,' Holly says.

She still looks grossed out, either by the thought of continence pants or shit in the bathtub, but her eyes continue to flick everywhere. She may ask a question or two, or drop a comment, but mostly she'll remain silent, because people intimidate her, especially in close quarters. But Hodges knows her well — as well as anyone can, at least — and he can tell she's on high alert.

Later she will talk, and Hodges will listen closely. During the Saubers case the year before, he learned that listening to Holly pays dividends. She thinks outside the box, sometimes way outside it, and her intuitions can be uncanny. And although fearful by nature — God knows she has her reasons — she can be brave. Holly is the reason Brady Hartsfield, aka Mr Mercedes, is now in the Lakes Region Traumatic Brain Injury Clinic at Kiner Memorial. Holly used a sock loaded with ball bearings to crush in his skull before Hartsfield could touch off a disaster much greater than the one at City Center. Now he's in a twilight world the head neuro guy at the Brain Injury Clinic refers to as 'a persistent vegetative state.'

'Quadriplegics can shower,' Holly amplifies, 'but it's difficult for them because of all the life-support equipment they're hooked up to. So mostly it's sponge baths.'

'Let's go in the kitchen, where it's sunny,' Pete says, and to the kitchen they go.

The first thing Hodges notices is the dish drainer, where the single plate that held Mrs Ellerton's last meal has been left to dry. The countertops are sparkling, and the floor looks clean enough to eat on. Hodges has an idea that

30

her bed upstairs will have been neatly made. She may even have vacuumed the carpets. And then there's the continence pants. She took care of the things she could take care of. As a man who once seriously considered suicide himself, Hodges can relate.

6

Pete, Izzy, and Hodges sit at the kitchen table. Holly merely hovers, sometimes standing behind Isabelle to look at the collection of photos on Izzy's iPad labeled ELLERTON/STOVER, sometimes poking into the various cupboards, her gloved fingers as light as moths.

Izzy takes them through it, swiping at the screen as she talks.

The first photo shows two middle-aged women. Both are beefy and broad-shouldered in their red nylon Home Helpers uniforms, but one of them — Georgina Ross, Hodges presumes — is crying and gripping her shoulders so that her forearms press against her breasts. The other one, Yvonne Carstairs, is apparently made of sterner stuff.

'They got here at five forty-five,' Izzy says. 'They have a key to let themselves in, so they don't have to knock or ring. Sometimes Martine slept until six thirty, Carstairs says. Mrs Ellerton is always up, gets up around five, she told them, had to have her coffee first thing, only this morning she's not up and there's no smell of coffee. So they think the old lady overslept for once, good for her. They tiptoe into Stover's bedroom, right down the hall, to see if *she's* awake yet. This is what they find.'

Izzy swipes to the next picture. Hodges waits for another *oough* from Holly, but she is silent and studying the photo closely. Stover is in bed with the covers pulled down to her knees. The damage to her face was never repaired, but what remains looks peaceful enough. Her eyes are closed and her twisted hands are clasped together. A feeding tube juts from her scrawny abdomen. Her wheelchair — which to Hodges looks more like an astronaut's space capsule — stands nearby.

'In Stover's bedroom there *was* a smell. Not coffee, though. Booze.'

Izzy swipes. Here is a close-up of Stover's bedside table. There are neat rows of pills. There's a grinder to turn them to powder, so that Stover could ingest them. Standing among them and looking wildly out of place is a fifth of Smirnoff Triple Distilled vodka and a plastic syringe. The vodka bottle is empty.

'The lady was taking zero chances,' Pete says. 'Smirnoff Triple Distilled is a hundred and fifty proof.'

'I imagine she wanted it to be as quick for her daughter as possible,' Holly says.

'Good call,' Izzy says, but with a notable lack of warmth. She doesn't care for Holly, and Holly doesn't care for her. Hodges is aware of this but has no idea why. And since they rarely see Isabelle, he's never bothered to ask Holly about it.

Have you got a close-up of the grinder?' Holly asks.

'Of course.' Izzy swipes, and in the next photo, the pill grinder looks as big as a flying saucer. A dusting of white powder remains in the cup. 'We won't be sure until later this week, but we think it's oxycodone. Her scrip was refilled just three weeks ago, according to the label, but that bottle is as empty as the vodka bottle.'

She goes back to Martine Stover, eyes closed, scrawny hands clasped as if in prayer.

'Her mother ground up the pills, funneled them into the bottle, and poured the vodka down Martine's feeding tube. Probably more efficient than lethal injection.'

Izzy swipes again. This time Holly *does* say 'Oough,' but she doesn't look away.

The first photo of Martine's handicap-equipped bathroom is a wide shot, showing the extra-low counter with its basin, the extra-low towel racks and cabinets, the jumbo shower-tub combination. The slider in front of the shower is closed, the tub in full view. Janice Ellerton reclines in water up to her shoulders, wearing a pink nightgown. Hodges guesses it would have ballooned around her as she lowered herself in, but in this crime scene photo it clings to her thin body. There is a plastic bag over her head, secured by the kind of terrycloth belt that goes with a bathrobe. A length of tubing snakes from beneath it, attached to a small canister lying on the tile floor. On the side of the canister is a decal that shows laughing children.

'Suicide kit,' Pete says. 'She probably learned

how to make it on the Internet. There are plenty of sites that explain how to do it, complete with pix. The water in the tub was cool when we got here, but probably warm when she climbed in.'

'Supposed to be soothing,' Izzy puts in, and although she doesn't say *oough*, her face tightens in a momentary expression of distaste as she swipes to the next picture: a close-up of Janice Ellerton. The bag had fogged with the condensation of her final breaths, but Hodges can see that her eyes were closed. She also went out looking peaceful.

'The canister contained helium,' Pete says. 'You can buy it at any of the big discount stores. You're supposed to use it to blow up the balloons at little Buster's birthday party, but it works just as well to kill yourself with, once you have a bag over your head. Dizziness is followed by disorientation, at which point you probably couldn't get the bag off even if you changed your mind. Next comes unconsciousness, followed by death.'

'Go back to the last one,' Holly says. 'The one that shows the whole bathroom.'

'Ah,' Pete says. 'Dr Watson may have seen something.'

Izzy goes back. Hodges leans closer, squinting — his near vision isn't what it once was. Then he sees what Holly saw. Next to a thin gray power cord plugged into one of the outlets, there's a Magic Marker. Someone — Ellerton, he presumes, because her daughter's writing days were long over — drew a single large letter on the counter: **Z**.

'What do you make of it?' Pete asks.

Hodges considers. 'It's her suicide note,' he says at last. 'Z is the final letter of the alphabet. If she'd known Greek, it might have been omega.'

'That's what I think, too,' Izzy says. 'Kind of elegant, when you think of it.'

'Z is also the mark of Zorro,' Holly informs them. 'He was a masked Mexican cavalier. There have been a great many Zorro movies, one starring Anthony Hopkins as Don Diego, but it wasn't very good.'

'Do you find that relevant?' Izzy asks. Her face expresses polite interest, but there's a barb in her tone.

'There was also a television series,' Holly goes on. She's looking at the photo as though hypnotized by it. 'It was produced by Walt Disney, back in the black-and-white days. Mrs Ellerton might have watched it when she was a girl.'

'Are you saying she maybe took refuge in childhood memories while she was getting ready to off herself?' Pete sounds dubious, which is how Hodges feels. 'I guess it's possible.'

'Bullshit, more likely,' Izzy says, rolling her eyes.

Holly takes no notice. 'Can I look in the bathroom? I won't touch anything, even with these.' She holds up her small gloved hands.

'Be our guest,' Izzy says at once.

In other words, Hodges thinks, buzz off and let the adults talk. He doesn't care for Izzy's 'tude when it comes to Holly, but since it seems to bounce right off her, he sees no reason to make an issue of it. Besides, Holly really is a bit skitzy this morning, going off in all directions. Hodges supposes it was the pictures. Dead people never look more dead than in police photos.

She wanders off to check out the bathroom. Hodges sits back, hands laced at the nape of his neck, elbows winged out. His troublesome gut hasn't been quite so troublesome this morning, maybe because he switched from coffee to tea. If so, he'll have to stock up on PG Tips. Hell, *buy* stock. He's really tired of the constant stomachache.

'Want to tell me what we're doing here, Pete?'

Pete raises his eyebrows and tries to look innocent. 'Whatever can you mean, Kermit?'

'You were right when you said this would make the paper. It's the kind of sad soap-opera shit people love, it makes their own lives look better to them — '

'Cynical but probably true,' Izzy says with a sigh.

' — but any connection to the Mercedes Massacre is casual rather than causal.' Hodges isn't entirely sure that means what he thinks it means, but it sounds good. 'What you've got here is your basic mercy killing committed by an old lady who just couldn't stand to see her daughter suffer anymore. Probably Ellerton's last thought when she turned on the helium was I'll be with you soon, honey, and when I walk the streets of heaven, you'll be walking right beside me.'

Izzy snorts at that, but Pete looks pale and

thoughtful. Hodges suddenly remembers that a long time ago, maybe thirty years, Pete and his wife lost their first child, a baby daughter, to SIDS.

'It's sad, and the papers lap it up for a day or two, but it happens somewhere in the world every day. Every hour, for all I know. So tell me what the deal is.'

'Probably nothing. Izzy says it *is* nothing.'

'Izzy does,' she confirms.

'Izzy probably thinks I'm going soft in the head as I approach the finish line.'

'Izzy doesn't. Izzy just thinks that it's time you stop letting the bee known as Brady Hartsfield buzz around in your bonnet.'

She switches those misty gray eyes to Hodges.

'Ms Gibney there may be a bundle of nervous tics and strange associations, but she stopped Hartsfield's clock most righteously, and I give her full credit for it. He's zonked out in that brain trauma clinic at Kiner, where he'll probably stay until he catches pneumonia and dies, thereby saving the state a whole potful of money. He's never going to stand trial for what he did, we all know that. You didn't catch him for the City Center thing, but Gibney stopped him from blowing up two thousand kids at Mingo Auditorium a year later. You guys need to accept that. Call it a win and move on.'

'Whew,' Pete says. 'How long have you been holding that in?'

Izzy tries not to smile, but can't help it. Pete smiles in return, and Hodges thinks, They work as well together as Pete and I did. Shame to break up that combination. It really is.

'Quite awhile,' Izzy says. 'Now go on and tell him.' She turns to Hodges. 'At least it's not little gray men from *The X-Files*.'

'So?' Hodges asks.

'Keith Frias and Krista Countryman,' Pete says. 'Both were also at City Center on the morning of April tenth, when Hartsfield did his thing. Frias, age nineteen, lost most of his arm, plus suffered four broken ribs and internal injuries. He also lost seventy percent of the vision in his right eye. Countryman, age twenty-one, suffered broken ribs, a broken arm, and spinal injuries that resolved after all sorts of painful therapy I don't even want to think about.'

Hodges doesn't, either, but he's brooded over Brady Hartsfield's victims many times. Mostly on how the work of seventy wicked seconds could change the lives of so many for years . . . or, in the case of Martine Stover, forever.

'They met in weekly therapy sessions at a place called Recovery Is You, and fell in love. They were getting better . . . slowly . . . and planned to get married. Then, in February of last year, they committed suicide together. In the words of some old punk song or other, they took a lot of pills and they died.'

This makes Hodges think of the grinder on the table beside Stover's hospital bed. The grinder with its residue of oxycodone. Mom dissolved all of the oxy in the vodka, but there must have been plenty of other narcotic medications on that table. Why had she gone to all the trouble of the plastic bag and the helium when she could have swallowed a bunch of Vicodin, chased it with a bunch of Valium, and called it good?

'Frias and Countryman were the sort of youngster suicides that also happen every day,' Izzy says. 'The parents were doubtful about the marriage. Wanted them to wait. And they could hardly run off together, could they? Frias could barely walk, and neither of them had jobs. There was enough insurance to pay for the weekly therapy sessions and to kick in for groceries at their respective homes, but nothing like the kind of Cadillac coverage Martine Stover had. Bottom line, shit happens. You can't even call it a coincidence. Badly hurt people get depressed, and sometimes depressed people kill themselves.'

'Where did they do it?'

'The Frias boy's bedroom,' Pete says. 'While his parents were on a day trip to Six Flags with his little brother. They took the pills, crawled into the sack, and died in each other's arms, just like Romeo and Juliet.'

'Romeo and Juliet died in a tomb,' Holly says, coming back into the kitchen. 'In the Franco Zeffirelli film, which is really the best — '

'Yes, okay, point taken,' Pete says. 'Tomb, bedroom, at least they rhyme.'

Holly is holding the *Inside View* that was on the coffee table, folded to show a picture of Johnny Depp that makes him look either drunk, stoned, or dead. Has she been in the living room, reading a scandal sheet all this time? If so, she really is having an off day.

Pete says, 'Have you still got the Mercedes, Holly? The one Hartsfield stole from your cousin Olivia?'

'No.' Holly sits down with the folded newspaper in her lap and her knees primly together. 'I traded it last November for a Prius like Bill's. It used a great deal of gas and was not eco-friendly. Also, my therapist recommended it. She said that after a year and a half, I had surely exorcised its hold over me, and its therapeutic value was gone. Why are you interested in that?'

Pete sits forward in his chair and clasps his hands together between his spread knees. 'Hartsfield got into that Mercedes by using an electronic gizmo to unlock the doors. Her spare key was in the glove compartment. Maybe he knew it was there, or maybe the slaughter at City Center was a crime of opportunity. We'll never know for sure.'

And Olivia Trelawney, Hodges thinks, was a lot like her cousin Holly: nervy, defensive, most definitely not a social animal. Far from stupid, but hard to like. We were sure she left her Mercedes unlocked with the key in the ignition, because that was the simplest explanation. And because, on some primitive level where logical thinking has no power, we *wanted* that to be the explanation. She was a pain in the ass. We saw her repeated denials as a haughty refusal to take responsibility for her own carelessness. The key in her purse, the one she showed us? We assumed that was just her spare. We hounded her, and when the press got her name, *they* hounded her. Eventually, she started to believe she'd done what we believed she'd done: enabled a monster with mass murder on his mind. None of us considered the idea that a computer geek might have cobbled together that unlocking gizmo. Including Olivia Trelawney herself.

'But we weren't the only ones who hounded her.'

Hodges is unaware that he's spoken aloud until they all turn to look at him. Holly gives him a small nod, as if they have been following the exact same train of thought. Which wouldn't be all that surprising.

Hodges goes on. 'It's true that we never believed her, no matter how many times she told us she took her key and locked her car, so we bear part of the responsibility for what she did, but Hartsfield went after her with malice aforethought. That's what you're driving at, isn't it?'

'Yes,' Pete says. 'He wasn't content with stealing her Mercedes and using it as a murder weapon. He got inside her head, even bugged her computer with an audio program full of screams and accusations. And then there's you, Kermit.'

Yes. There was him.

Hodges had received an anonymous poison pen letter from Hartsfield when he was at an absolute low point, living in an empty house, sleeping badly, seeing almost no one except Jerome Robinson, the kid who cut his grass and did general repairs around the place. Suffering from a common malady in career cops: end-of-watch depression.

Retired police have an extremely high suicide

41

rate, Brady Hartsfield had written. This was before they began communicating by the twenty-first century's preferred method, the Internet. *I wouldn't want you to start thinking about your gun. But you are thinking about it, aren't you?* It was as if Hartsfield had sniffed out Hodges's thoughts of suicide and tried to push him over the edge. It had worked with Olivia Trelawney, after all, and he'd gotten a taste for it.

'When I first started working with you,' Pete says, 'you told me repeat criminals were sort of like Turkish rugs. Do you remember that?'

'Yes.' It was a theory Hodges had expounded to a great many cops. Few listened, and judging by her bored expression, he guessed Isabelle Jaynes would have been one of those who did not. Pete had.

'They create the same pattern, over and over. Ignore the slight variations, you said, and look for the underlying sameness. Because even the smartest doers — like Turnpike Joe, who killed all those women at rest stops — seem to have a switch inside their brains that's stuck on Repeat. Brady Hartsfield was a connoisseur of suicide — '

'He was an *architect* of suicide,' Holly says. She's looking down at the newspaper, her brow furrowed, her face paler than ever. It's hard for Hodges to relive the Hartsfield business (at least he's finally managed to quit going to see the son of a bitch in his room in the Brain Injury Clinic), but it's even harder for Holly. He hopes she won't backslide and start smoking again, but it wouldn't surprise him if she did.

42

'Call it what you want, but the pattern was there. He goaded his own mother into suicide, for Christ's sake.'

Hodges says nothing to this, although he has always doubted Pete's belief that Deborah Hartsfield killed herself when she discovered — perhaps by accident — that her son was the Mercedes Killer. For one thing, they have no proof that Mrs Hartsfield ever did find out. For another, it was gopher poison the woman ingested, and that had to be a nasty way to go. It's possible that Brady murdered his mother, but Hodges has never really believed that, either. If he loved anyone, it was her. Hodges thinks the gopher poison might have been intended for someone else . . . and perhaps not for a person at all. According to the autopsy, it had been mixed in with hamburger, and if there was anything dogs liked, it was a ball of raw ground meat.

The Robinsons have a dog, a loveable floppy-eared mutt. Brady would have seen him many times, because he was watching Hodges's house and because Jerome usually brought the dog along when he cut Hodges's lawn. The gopher poison could have been meant for Odell. This is an idea Hodges has never mentioned to any of the Robinsons. Or to Holly, for that matter. And hey, it's probably bullshit, but in Hodges's opinion, it's as likely as Pete's idea that Brady's mom offed herself.

Izzy opens her mouth, then shuts it when Pete holds up a hand to forestall her — he is, after all, still the senior member of their partnership, and by quite a few years.

'Izzy's getting ready to say Martine Stover was murder, not suicide, but I think there's a very good chance that the idea came from Martine herself, or that she and her mother talked it over and came to a mutual agreement. Which makes them both suicides in my book, even though it won't get written up that way in the official report.'

'I assume you've checked on the other City Center survivors?' Hodges asks.

'All alive except for Gerald Stansbury, who died just after Thanksgiving last year,' Pete says. 'Had a heart attack. His wife told me coronary disease runs in his family, and that he lived longer than both his father and brother. Izzy's right, this is probably nothing, but I thought you and Holly should know.' He looks at each of them in turn. '*You* haven't had any bad thoughts about pulling the pin, have you?'

'No,' Hodges says. 'Not lately.'

Holly merely shakes her head, still looking down at the newspaper.

Hodges asks, 'I don't suppose anyone found a mysterious letter Z in young Mr Frias's bedroom after he and Ms Countryman committed suicide?'

'Of course not,' Izzy says.

'That you know of,' Hodges corrects. 'Isn't that what you mean? Considering you just found this one today?'

'Jesus please us,' Izzy says. 'This is silly.' She looks pointedly at her watch and stands.

Pete gets up, too. Holly remains seated, looking down at her filched copy of *Inside View*.

Hodges also stays put, at least for the moment. 'You'll go back to the Frias-Countryman photos, right, Pete? Check it out, just to be sure?'

'Yes,' Pete says. 'And Izzy's probably right, I was silly to get you two out here.'

'I'm glad you did.'

'And . . . I still feel bad about the way we handled Mrs Trelawney, okay?' Pete is looking at Hodges, but Hodges has an idea he's really speaking to the thin, pale woman with the junk newspaper in her lap. 'I never once doubted that she left her key in the ignition. I closed my mind to any other possibility. I promised myself I'd never do that again.'

'I understand,' Hodges says.

'One thing I believe we all can agree on,' Izzy says, 'is that Hartsfield's days of running people down, blowing people up, and architecting suicides are behind him. So unless we've all stumbled into a movie called *Son of Brady*, I suggest we exit the late Ms Ellerton's house and get on with our lives. Any objections to that idea?'

There are none.

7

Hodges and Holly stand in the driveway for a moment before getting into the car, letting the cold January wind rush past them. It's out of the north, blowing straight down from Canada, so the usually present smell of the large, polluted lake to the east is refreshingly absent. There are

45

only a few houses at this end of Hilltop Court, and the closest has a FOR SALE sign on it. Hodges notices that Tom Saubers is the agent, and he smiles. Tom was also badly hurt in the Massacre, but has come almost all the way back. Hodges is always amazed by the resilience of which some men and women are capable. It doesn't exactly give him hope for the human race, but . . .

Actually, it does.

In the car, Holly puts the folded *Inside View* on the floor long enough to fasten her seatbelt, then picks it up again. Neither Pete nor Isabelle objected to her taking it. Hodges isn't sure they even noticed. Why would they? To them, the Ellerton house isn't really a crime scene, although the letter of the law may call it that. Pete was uneasy, true, but Hodges thinks that had little to do with cop intuition and was a quasi-superstitious response instead.

Hartsfield should have died when Holly hit him with my Happy Slapper, Hodges thinks. That would have been better for all of us.

'Pete *will* go back and look at the pictures from the Frias-Countryman suicides,' he tells Holly. 'Due diligence, and all that. But if he finds a Z scratched somewhere — on a baseboard, on a mirror — I will be one surprised human being.'

She doesn't reply. Her eyes are far away.

'Holly? Are you there?'

She starts a little. 'Yes. Just planning how I'll locate Nancy Alderson in Chagrin Falls. It shouldn't take too long with all the search programs I've got, but you'll have to talk to her.

46

I can do cold calls now if I absolutely have to, you know that — '

'Yes. You've gotten good at it.' Which is true, although she always makes such calls with her trusty box of Nicorette close at hand. Not to mention a stash of Twinkies in her desk for backup.

'But I can't be the one to tell her that her employers — her *friends*, for all we know — are dead. You'll have to do it. You're good at things like that.'

Hodges feels that nobody is very good at things like that, but doesn't bother saying so. 'Why? The Alderson woman wouldn't have been there since last Friday.'

'She deserves to know,' Holly says. 'The police will get in touch with any relatives, that's their job, but they're not going to call the housekeeper. At least I don't think so.'

Hodges doesn't, either, and Holly's right — the Alderson woman deserves to know, if only so she doesn't turn up to find an X of police tape on the door. But somehow he doesn't think that's Holly's only interest in Nancy Alderson.

'Your friend Pete and Miss Pretty Gray Eyes hardly did *anything*,' Holly says. 'There was fingerprint powder in Martine Stover's bedroom, sure, and on her wheelchair, and in the bathroom where Mrs Ellerton killed herself, but none upstairs where she slept. They probably went up long enough to make sure there wasn't a body stashed under the bed or in the closet, and called it good.'

'Hold on a second. You went upstairs?'

'Of course. *Somebody* needed to investigate thoroughly, and those two sure weren't doing it. As far as they're concerned, they know exactly what happened. Pete only called you because he was spooked.'

Spooked. Yes, that was it. Exactly the word he was looking for and hadn't been able to find.

'I was spooked, too,' Holly says matter-of-factly, 'but that doesn't mean I lost my wits. The whole thing was wrong. Wrong wrong wrong, and you need to talk to the housekeeper. I'll tell you what to ask her, if you can't figure it out for yourself.'

'Is this about the Z on the bathroom counter? If you know something I don't, I wish you'd fill me in.'

'It's not what I know, it's what I saw. Didn't you notice what was *beside* that Z?'

'A Magic Marker.'

She gives him a look that says *you can do better.*

Hodges calls on an old cop technique that comes in especially handy when giving trial testimony: he looks at the picture again, this time in his mind. 'There was a power cord plugged into the wall beside the basin.'

'Yes! At first I thought it must be for an e-reader and Mrs Ellerton left it plugged in there because she spent most of her time in that part of the house. It would be a convenient charging point, because all the plugs in Martine's bedroom were probably in use for her life-support gear. Don't you think so?'

'Yeah, that could be.'

'Only I have both a Nook and a Kindle — '

Of course you do, he thinks.

' — and neither of them has cords like that. Those cords are black. This one was gray.'

'Maybe she lost the original charging cord and bought a replacement at Tech Village.' Pretty much the only game in town for electronic supplies, now that Discount Electronix, Brady Hartsfield's old employer, has declared bankruptcy.

'No. E-readers have prong-type plug-ins. This one was wider, like for an electronic tablet. Only my iPad also has that kind, and the one in the bathroom was much smaller. That cord was for some kind of handheld device. So I went upstairs to look for it.'

'Where you found . . . ?'

'Just an old PC on a desk by the window in Mrs Ellerton's bedroom. And I mean *old*. It was hooked up to a modem.'

'Oh my God, no!' Hodges exclaims. 'Not a modem!'

'This is *not* funny, Bill. Those women are *dead*.'

Hodges takes a hand from the wheel and holds it up in a peace gesture. 'Sorry. Go on. This is the part where you tell me you powered up her computer.'

Holly looks slightly discomfited. 'Well, yes. But only in the service of an investigation the police are clearly not going to make. I wasn't *snooping*.'

Hodges could argue the point, but doesn't.

'It wasn't password protected, so I looked at Mrs Ellerton's search history. She visited quite a

49

few retail sites, and lots of medical sites having to do with paralysis. She seemed very interested in stem cells, which makes sense, considering her daughter's condi — '

'You did all this in ten minutes?'

'I'm a fast reader. But you know what I *didn't* find?'

'I'm guessing anything to do with suicide.'

'Yes. So how did she know about the helium thing? For that matter, how did she know to dissolve those pills in vodka and put them in her daughter's feeding tube?'

'Well,' Hodges says, 'there's this ancient arcane ritual called reading books. You may have heard of it.'

'Did you see any books in that living room?'

He replays the living room just as he did the photo of Martine Stover's bathroom, and Holly is right. There were shelves of knick-knacks, and that picture of big-eyed waifs, and the flatscreen TV. There were magazines on the coffee table, but spread in a way that spoke more to decoration than to voracious reading. Plus, none of them was exactly *The Atlantic Monthly.*

'No,' he says, 'no books in the living room, although I saw a couple in the photo of Stover's bedroom. One of them looked like a Bible.' He glances at the folded *Inside View* in her lap. 'What have you got in there, Holly? What are you hiding?'

When Holly flushes, she goes totally Defcon 1, the blood crashing to her face in a way that's alarming. It happens now. 'It wasn't stealing,' she says. 'It was *borrowing.* I never steal, Bill. Never!'

50

'Cool your jets. What is it?'

'The thing that goes with the power cord in the bathroom.' She unfolds the newspaper to reveal a bright pink gadget with a dark gray screen. It's bigger than an e-reader, smaller than an electronic tablet. 'When I came downstairs, I sat in Mrs Ellerton's chair to think a minute. I ran my hands between the arms and the cushion. I wasn't even hunting for something, I was just doing it.'

One of Holly's many self-comforting techniques, Hodges assumes. He's seen many in the years since he first met her in the company of her overprotective mother and aggressively gregarious uncle. In their company? No, not exactly. That phrase suggested equality. Charlotte Gibney and Henry Sirois had treated her more like a mentally defective child out on a day pass. Holly is a different woman now, but traces of the old Holly still remain. And that's okay with Hodges. After all, everyone casts a shadow.

'That's where it was, down on the right side. It's a Zappit.'

The name chimes a faint chord far back in his memory, although when it comes to computer chip-driven gadgetry, Hodges is far behind the curve. He's always screwing up with his own home computer, and now that Jerome Robinson is away, Holly is the one who usually comes over to his house on Harper Road to straighten him out. 'A whatsit?'

'A Zappit Commander. I've seen advertisements online, although not lately. They come pre-loaded with over a hundred simple electronic games like Tetris, Simon, and SpellTower. Nothing complicated like Grand Theft Auto. So tell me what it was doing there, Bill. Tell me what it was doing in a house where one of the women was almost eighty and the other one couldn't turn a light switch, let alone play video games.'

'It seems odd, all right. Not downright bizarre, but on the odd side, for sure.'

'And the cord was plugged in right next to that letter Z,' she says. 'Not Z for the end, like a suicide note, but Z for Zappit. At least that's what I think.'

Hodges considers the idea.

'Maybe.' He wonders again if he has encountered that name before, or if it's only what the French call *faux souvenir* — a false memory. He could swear it has some connection to Brady Hartsfield, but he can't trust that idea, because Brady is very much on his mind today.

How long has it been since I've gone to visit him? Six months? Eight? No, longer than that. Quite a bit longer.

The last time was not long after the business having to do with Pete Saubers and the cache of stolen money and notebooks Pete discovered, practically buried in his backyard. On that occasion, Hodges found Brady much the same as ever — a gorked-out young man dressed in a plaid shirt and jeans that never got dirty. He was sitting in the same chair he was always sitting in when Hodges visited Room 217 in the Brain Injury Clinic, just staring out at the parking garage across the way.

The only real difference that day had been outside Room 217. Becky Helmington, the head nurse, had moved on to the surgical wing of Kiner Memorial, thereby closing Hodges's conduit to rumors about Brady. The new head nurse was a woman with stony scruples and a face like a closed fist. Ruth Scapelli refused Hodges's offer of fifty dollars for any little tidbits about Brady and threatened to report him if he ever offered her money for patient information again. 'You're not even on his visitors list,' she said.

'I don't want information about him,' Hodges had said. 'I've got all the information about Brady Hartsfield I'm ever going to need. I just want to know what the staff is saying about him. Because there have been rumors, you know. Some of them pretty wild.'

Scapelli favored him with a disdainful look. 'There's loose talk in every hospital, Mr Hodges, and always about patients who are famous. Or infamous, as is the case with Mr Hartsfield. I held a staff meeting shortly after Nurse Helmington moved from Brain Injury to her current situation, and informed my people that the talk about Mr Hartsfield was to stop immediately, and if I caught wind of more rumors, I would trace them to their source and see that the person or persons spreading them was dismissed. As for you . . . ' Looking down her nose at him, the fist of her face tightening even more. 'I can't believe that a former police officer, and a decorated one at that, would resort to bribery.'

Not long after that rather humiliating encounter, Holly and Jerome Robinson cornered him and staged a mini-intervention, telling Hodges that his visits to Brady had to end. Jerome had been especially serious that day, his usual cheerful patter nowhere to be found.

'There's nothing you can do in that room but hurt yourself,' Jerome had said. 'We always know when you've been to see him, because you go around with a little gray cloud over your head for the next two days.'

'More like a week,' Holly added. She wouldn't look at him, and she was twisting her fingers in a way that made Hodges want to grab them and make her stop before she broke something. Her voice, however, was firm and sure. 'There's nothing left inside him, Bill. You need to accept that. And if there was, he'd be happy every time you showed up. He'd see what he's doing to you and be happy.'

That was the convincer, because Hodges knew it was the truth. So he stays away. It was kind of like quitting smoking: hard at first, easier as time went by. Now whole weeks sometimes pass without thoughts of Brady and Brady's terrible crimes.

There's nothing left inside him.

Hodges reminds himself of that as he drives back into the heart of the city, where Holly will kick her computer into high gear and start hunting down Nancy Alderson. Whatever happened in that house at the end of Hilltop Court — the chain of thoughts and conversations, of tears and promises, all ending in the dissolved pills injected into the feeding tube and the tank of helium with the laughing children decaled on the side — it can have nothing to do with Brady Hartsfield, because Holly literally bashed his brains out. If Hodges sometimes doubts, it's because he can't stand the idea that Brady has somehow escaped punishment. That in the end, the monster eluded him. Hodges didn't even get to swing the ball bearing-loaded sock he calls his Happy Slapper, because he was busy suffering a heart attack at the time.

Still, a ghost of memory: Zappit.

He *knows* he has heard that before.

His stomach gives a warning twinge, and he remembers the doctor's appointment he blew off. He'll have to take care of that, but tomorrow should be soon enough. He has an idea that Dr Stamos is going to tell him he has an ulcer, and for that news he can wait.

8

Holly has a fresh box of Nicorette by her telephone, but doesn't need to use a single chew. The first Alderson she calls turns out to be the housekeeper's sister-in-law, who of course wants to know why someone from a company called Finders Keepers wants to get in touch with Nan.

'Is it a bequest, or something?' she asks hopefully.

'One moment,' Holly says. 'I have to put you on hold while I get my boss.' Hodges is not her boss, he made her a full partner after the Pete

55

Saubers business last year, but it's a fiction she often falls back on when she's stressed.

Hodges, who has been using his own computer to read up on Zappit Game Systems, picks up the phone while Holly lingers by his desk, gnawing at the neck of her sweater. Hodges hovers his finger over the hold button on his phone long enough to tell Holly that eating wool probably isn't good for her, and certainly not for the Fair Isle she's wearing. Then he connects with the sister-in-law.

'I'm afraid I have some bad news for Nancy,' he says, and fills her in quickly.

'Oh my God,' Linda Alderson says (Holly has jotted the name on his pad). 'She's going to be devastated to hear that, and not just because it means the end of the job. She's been working for those ladies since 2012, and she really likes them. She had Thanksgiving dinner with them just last November. Are you with the police?'

'Retired,' he says, 'but working with the team assigned to the case. I was asked to get in touch with Ms Alderson.' He doesn't think this lie will come back to haunt him, since Pete opened the door by inviting him to the scene. 'Can you tell me how to get in touch with her?'

'I'll give you her cell number. She went to Chagrin Falls for her brother's birthday party on Saturday. It was the big four-oh, so Harry's wife made a fuss about it. She's staying until Wednesday or Thursday, I think — at least that was the plan. I'm sure this news will bring her back. Nan lives alone since Bill died — Bill was my husband's brother — with only her cat for company. Mrs Ellerton and Ms Stover were sort of a surrogate family. This will just make her so sad.'

Hodges takes the number down and calls immediately. Nancy Alderson picks up on the first ring. He identifies himself, then gives her the news.

After a moment of shocked silence, she says, 'Oh, no, that can't be. You've made a mistake, Detective Hodges.'

He doesn't bother to correct her, because this is interesting. 'Why do you say that?'

'Because they're *happy*. They get along so well, watching TV together — they love movies on the DVD player, and those shows about cooking, or where women sit around talking about fun things and having celebrity guests. You wouldn't believe it, but there's a lot of laughter in that house.' Nancy Alderson hesitates, then says, 'Are you *sure* you're talking about the right people? About Jan Ellerton and Marty Stover?'

'Sorry to say I am.'

'But . . . she had accepted her condition! Marty, I'm talking about. Martine. She used to say that getting used to being paralyzed was actually easier than getting used to being a spinster. She and I used to talk about that all the time — being on our own. Because I lost my husband, you know.'

'So there was never a Mr Stover.'

'Yes there was, Janice had an earlier marriage. Very short, I believe, but she said she never regretted it because she got Martine. Marty did have a boyfriend not long before her accident,

57

but he had a heart attack. Carried him right off. Marty said he was very fit, used to exercise three days a week at a health club downtown. She said it was being so fit that killed him. Because his heart was strong, and when it backfired, it just blew apart.'

Hodges, a coronary survivor, thinks, Reminder to self: no fitness club.

'Marty used to say that being alone after someone you love passes on was the worst kind of paralysis. I didn't feel exactly the same way about my Bill, but I knew what she meant. Reverend Henreid came in to see her often — Marty calls him her spiritual adviser — and even when he didn't, she and Jan did daily devotions and prayers. Every day at noon. And Marty was thinking about taking an accounting course online — they have special courses for people with her kind of disability, did you know that?'

'I didn't,' Hodges says. On his pad he prints STOVER PLANNING TO TAKE ACCOUNTING COURSE BY COMPUTER and turns it so Holly can read it. She raises her eyebrows.

'There were tears and sadness from time to time, of course there was, but for the most part they were *happy*. At least . . . I don't know . . .'

'What are you thinking about, Nancy?' He makes the switch to her first name — another old cop trick — without thinking about it.

'Oh, it's probably nothing. *Marty* seemed as happy as ever — she's a real love-bug, that one, you wouldn't believe how spiritual she is, always sees the good side of everything — but Jan did seem a little withdrawn lately, as if she had something weighing on her mind. I thought it might be money worries, or maybe just the after-Christmas blues. I never *dreamed* . . . ' She sniffles. 'Excuse me, I have to blow.'

'Sure.'

Holly grabs his pad. Her printing is small — constipated, he often thinks — and he has to hold the. pad almost touching his nose to read ASK HER ABOUT ZAPPIT!

There's a honking sound in his ear as Alderson blows her nose. 'Sorry.'

'That's all right. Nancy, would you know if Mrs Ellerton happened to have a small handheld game console? It would have been pink.'

'Goodness sakes, how did you know that?'

'I really don't know anything,' Hodges says truthfully. 'I'm just a retired detective with a list of questions I'm supposed to ask.'

'She said a man gave it to her. He told her the game gadget was free as long as she promised to fill out a questionnaire and send it back to the company. The thing was a little bit bigger than a paperback book. It just sat around the house awhile — '

'When was this?'

'I can't remember exactly, but before Christmas, for sure. The first time I saw it, it was on the coffee table in the living room. It just stayed there with the questionnaire folded up beside it until after Christmas — I know because their little tree was gone — and then I spied it one day on the kitchen table. Jan said she turned it on just to see what it would do, and found out there were solitaire games on it, maybe as many as a dozen different kinds, like Klondike and Picture and Pyramid. So, since she was using it, she filled out the questionnaire and sent it in.'

'Did she charge it in Marty's bathroom?'

'Yes, because that was the most convenient place. She was in that part of the house so much, you know.'

'Uh-huh. You said that Mrs Ellerton became withdrawn — '

'A *little* withdrawn,' Alderson corrects at once. 'Mostly she was the same as always. A love-bug, just like Marty.'

'But something was on her mind.'

'Yes, I think so.'

'*Weighing* on her mind.'

'Well . . . '

'Was this around the same time she got the handheld game machine?'

'I guess it was, now that I think about it, but why in the world would playing solitaire on a little pink tablet depress her?'

'I don't know,' Hodges says, and prints DEPRESSED on his pad. He thinks there's a significant jump between being withdrawn and being depressed.

'Have their relations been told?' Alderson asks. 'There aren't any in the city, but there are cousins in Ohio, I know that, and I think some in Kansas, too. Or maybe it was Indiana. The names would be in her address book.'

'The police will be doing that as we speak,' Hodges says, although he will call Pete later on to make sure. It will probably annoy his old partner, but Hodges doesn't care. Nancy

Alderson's distress is in every word she utters, and he wants to offer what comfort he can. 'May I ask one more question?'

'Of course.'

'Did you happen to notice anyone hanging around the house? Anyone without an obvious reason to be there?'

Holly is nodding vigorously.

'Why would you ask that?' Alderson sounds astonished. 'Surely you don't think some *outsider* — '

'I don't think anything,' Hodges says smoothly. 'I'm just helping the police because there's been such a staff reduction in the last few years. City-wide budget cuts.'

'I know, it's awful.'

'So they gave me this list of questions, and that's the last one.'

'Well, there was nobody. I'd have noticed, because of the breezeway between the house and the garage. The garage is heated, so that's where the pantry and the washer-dryer are. I'm back and forth in that breezeway all the time, and I can see the street from there. Hardly anyone comes all the way up Hilltop Court, because Jan and Marty's is the last house. It's just the turnaround after that. Of course there's the postman, and UPS, and sometimes FedEx, but otherwise, unless someone gets lost, we've got that end of the street to ourselves.'

'So there was no one at all.'

'No, sir, there sure wasn't.'

'Not the man who gave Mrs Ellerton the game console?'

'No, he approached her in Ridgeline Foods. That's the grocery store at the foot of the hill, down where City Avenue crosses Hilltop Court. There's a Kroger about a mile further on, in the City Avenue Plaza, but Janice won't go there even though things are a little cheaper, because she says you should always buy locally if you . . . you . . . ' She gives a sudden loud sob. 'But she's done shopping *anywhere*, isn't she? Oh, I can't believe this! Jan would never hurt Marty, not for the world.'

'It's a sad thing,' Hodges says.

'I'll have to come back today.' Alderson now talking to herself rather than to Hodges. 'It may take awhile for her relatives to come, and someone will have to make the proper arrangements.'

A final housekeeping duty, Hodges thinks, and finds the thought both touching and obscurely horrible.

'I want to thank you for your time, Nancy. I'll let you go n — '

'Of course there was that elderly fellow,' Alderson says.

'What elderly fellow was that?'

'I saw him several times outside 1588. He'd park at the curb and just stand on the sidewalk, looking at it. That's the house across the street and down the hill a little way. You might not have noticed it, but it was for sale.'

Hodges did notice, but doesn't say so. He doesn't want to interrupt.

'Once he walked right up the lawn to look in the bay window — this was before the last big

62

snowstorm. I think he was window shopping.' She gives a watery laugh. 'Although my mother would have called it window *wishing*, because he surely didn't look like the sort who could afford a house like that.'

'No?'

'Uh-uh. He was dressed in workman's clothes — you know, green pants, like Dickies — and his parka was mended with a piece of masking tape. Also, his car looked very old and had spots of primer on it. My late husband used to call that poor man's polish.'

'You don't happen to know what kind of car it was, do you?' He flips his pad to a fresh sheet and writes, FIND DATE OF LAST BIG SNOWSTORM. Holly reads it and nods.

'No, I'm sorry. I don't know cars. I don't even remember the color, just those spots of primer paint. Mr Hodges, are you sure there hasn't been some mistake?' She's almost begging.

'I wish I could tell you that, Nancy, but I can't. You've been very helpful.'

Doubtfully: 'Have I?'

Hodges gives her his number, Holly's, and the office number. He tells her to call if anything occurs to her that they haven't covered. He reminds her that there may be press interest because Martine was paralyzed at City Center in 2009, and tells her she isn't obliged to talk to reporters or TV news people if she doesn't want to.

Nancy Alderson is crying again when he breaks the connection.

9

He takes Holly to lunch at Panda Garden a block down the street. It's early and they have the dining room almost to themselves. Holly is off meat and orders vegetable chow mein. Hodges loves the spicy shredded beef, but his stomach won't put up with it these days, so he settles for Ma La Lamb. They both use chopsticks, Holly because she's good with them and Hodges because they slow him down and make a post-lunch bonfire in his guts less likely.

She says, 'The last big storm was December nineteenth. The weather service reported eleven inches in Government Square, thirteen in Branson Park. Not exactly huge, but the only other one so far this winter dropped just four inches.'

'Six days before Christmas. Around the same time Janice Ellerton was given the Zappit, according to Alderson's recollection.'

'Do you think the man who gave it to her was the same one looking at that house?'

Hodges snares a piece of broccoli. It's supposed to be good for you, like all veggies that taste bad. 'I don't think Ellerton would have accepted *anything* from a guy wearing a parka mended with masking tape. I'm not counting the possibility out, but it seems unlikely.'

'Eat your lunch, Bill. If I get any further ahead of you, I'll look like a pig.'

Hodges eats, although he has very little appetite these days even when his stomach isn't giving him the devil. When a bite sticks in his throat, he washes it down with tea. Maybe a good idea, since tea seems to help. He thinks about those test results he is yet to see. It occurs to him that his problem could be worse than an ulcer, that an ulcer might actually be the best-case scenario. There's medicine for ulcers. Other things, not so much.

When he can see the middle of his plate (but Jesus, so much food left around the edges), he sets his chopsticks aside and says, 'I found something out while you were hunting down Nancy Alderson.'

'Tell me.'

'I was reading about those Zappits. Amazing how these computer-based companies pop up, then disappear. They're like dandelions in June. The Commander didn't exactly corner the market. Too simple, too expensive, too much sophisticated competition. Zappit Inc. stock went down and they got bought out by a company called Sunrise Solutions. Two years ago *that* company declared bankruptcy and went dark. Which means Zappit is long gone and the guy giving out Commander consoles had to be running some kind of scam.'

Holly is quick to see where that leads. 'So the questionnaire was bullpoop just to add a little whatdoyoucallit, verisimilitude. But the guy didn't try to get money out of her, did he?'

'No. At least not that we know of.'

'Something weird is going on here, Bill. Are you going to tell Detective Huntley and Miss Pretty Gray Eyes?'

Hodges has picked up the smallest piece of

65

lamb left on his plate, and here is an excuse to drop it. 'Why don't you like her, Holly?'

'Well, she thinks I'm crazy,' Holly says matter-of-factly. 'There's that.'

'I'm sure she doesn't — '

'Yes. She does. She probably thinks I'm dangerous, too, because of the way I whopped Brady Hartsfield at the 'Round Here concert. But I don't care. I'd do it again. A thousand times!'

He puts a hand over hers. The chopsticks she's holding in her fist vibrate like a tuning fork. 'I know you would, and you'd be right every time. You saved a thousand lives, and that's a conservative estimate.'

She slides her hand from beneath his and starts picking up grains of rice. 'Oh, I can deal with her thinking I'm crazy. I've been dealing with people thinking that all my life, starting with my parents. But there's something else. Isabelle only sees what she sees, and she doesn't like people who see more, or at least look for more. She feels the same way about you, Bill. She's jealous of you. Over Pete.'

Hodges says nothing. He's never considered such a possibility.

She puts down her chopsticks. 'You didn't answer my question. Are you going to tell them what we've learned so far?'

'Not quite yet. There's something I want to do first, if you'll hold down the office this afternoon.'

Holly smiles down at the remainder of her chow mein. 'I always do.'

66

10

Bill Hodges isn't the only one who took an instant dislike to Becky Helmington's replacement. The nurses and orderlies who work in the Traumatic Brain Injury Clinic call it the Bucket, as in Brain Bucket, and before long Ruth Scapelli has become known as Nurse Ratched. By the end of her third month, she has gotten three nurses transferred for various small infractions, and one orderly fired for smoking in a supply closet. She has banned certain colorful uniforms as 'too distracting' or 'too suggestive.'

The doctors like her, though. They find her swift and competent. With the patients she is also swift and competent, but she's cold, and there's an undertone of contempt there, as well. She will not allow even the most cataclysmically injured of them to be called a gork or a burn or a wipeout, at least not in her hearing, but she has a certain *attitude*.

'She knows her stuff,' one nurse said to another in the break room not long after Scapelli took up her duties. 'No argument about that, but there's something missing.'

The other nurse was a thirty-year veteran who had seen it all. She considered, then said one word . . . but it was *le mot juste*. 'Mercy.'

Scapelli never exhibits coldness or contempt when she accompanies Felix Babineau, the head of Neuro, on his rounds, and he probably wouldn't notice if she did. Some of the other doctors *have* noticed, but few pay any mind; the doings of such lesser beings as nurses — even head nurses — are far below their lordly gaze.

It is as if Scapelli feels that, no matter what is wrong with them, the patients of the Traumatic Brain Injury Clinic must bear part of the responsibility for their current condition, and if they only tried harder, they would surely regain at least *some* of their faculties. She does her job, though, and for the most part she does it well, perhaps better than Becky Helmington, who was far better liked. If told this, Scapelli would have said she was not here to be liked. She was here to care for her patients, end of story, full stop.

There is, however, one long-term patient in the Bucket whom she hates. That patient is Brady Hartsfield. It isn't because she had a friend or relative who was hurt or killed at City Center; it's because she thinks he's shamming. Avoiding the punishment he so richly deserves. Mostly she stays away and lets other staff members deal with him, because just seeing him often infuses her with a daylong rage that the system should be so easily gamed by this vile creature. She stays away for another reason, too: she doesn't entirely trust herself when she's in his room. On two occasions she has done something. The kind of thing that, were it discovered, might result in *her* being the one fired. But on this early January afternoon, just as Hodges and Holly are finishing their lunch, she is drawn down to Room 217 as if by an invisible cable. Only this morning she was forced to go in there, because Dr Babineau insists she accompany him on rounds, and Brady is his star patient. He marvels at how far Brady has come.

'He should never have emerged from his coma at all,' Babineau told her shortly after she came on staff at the Bucket. He's a cold fish, but when he speaks of Brady he becomes almost jolly. 'And look at him now! He's able to walk short distances — with help, I grant you — he can feed himself, and he can respond either verbally or with signs to simple questions.'

He's also prone to poking himself in the eye with his fork, Ruth Scapelli could have added (but doesn't), and his verbal responses all sound like *wah-wah* and *gub-gub* to me. Then there's the matter of waste. Put a Depends on him and he holds it. Take it off, and he urinates in his bed, regular as clockwork. Defecates in it, if he can. It's as if he knows. She believes he *does* know.

Something else he knows — of this there can be no doubt — is that Scapelli doesn't like him. This very morning, after the exam was finished and Dr Babineau was washing his hands in the en suite bathroom, Brady raised his head to look at her and lifted one hand to his chest. He curled it into a loose, trembling fist. From it his middle finger slowly extended.

At first Scapelli could barely comprehend what she was seeing: Brady Hartsfield, giving her the finger. Then, as she heard the water go off in the bathroom, two buttons popped from the front of her uniform, exposing the center of her sturdy Playtex 18-Hour Comfort Strap Bra. She doesn't believe the rumors she's heard about this waste of humanity, *refuses* to believe them, but then . . .

He smiled at her. *Grinned* at her.

Now she walks down to Room 217 while sooth-ing music wafts from the speakers overhead. She's wearing her spare uniform, the pink one she keeps in her locker and doesn't like much. She looks both ways to make sure no one is paying any attention to her, pretends to study Brady's chart just in case there's a set of prying eyes she's missed, and slips inside. Brady sits in his chair by the window, where he always sits. He's dressed in one of his four plaid shirts and a pair of jeans. His hair has been combed and his cheeks are baby-smooth. A button on his breast pocket pro-claims I WAS SHAVED BY NURSE BARBARA!

He's living like Donald Trump, Ruth Scapelli thinks. He killed eight people and wounded God knows how many more, he tried to kill thousands of teenage girls at a rock-and-roll concert, and here he sits with his meals brought to him by his own personal staff, his clothes laundered, his face shaved. He gets a *massage* three times a week. He visits the *spa* four times a week, and spends time in the *hot tub*.

Living like Donald Trump? Huh. More like a desert chieftain in one of those oil-rich Mideast countries.

And if she told Babineau that he gave her the finger?

Oh no, he'd say. Oh no, Nurse Scapelli. What you saw was nothing but an involuntary muscle twitch. He's still incapable of the thought processes that would lead to such a gesture. Even if that were not the case, why would he make such a gesture to you?

'Because you don't like me,' she says, bending

70

forward with her hands on her pink-skirted knees. 'Do you, Mr Hartsfield? And that makes us even, because I don't like you.'

He doesn't look at her, or give any sign that he's heard her. He only looks out the window at the parking garage across the way. But he *does* hear her, she's sure he does, and his failure to acknowledge her in any way infuriates her more. When she talks, people are supposed to *listen*.

'Am I to believe you popped the buttons on my uniform this morning by some kind of mind control?'

Nothing.

'I know better. I'd been meaning to replace that one. The bodice was a bit too tight. You may fool some of the more credulous staff members, but you don't fool me, Mr Hartsfield. All you can do is sit there. And make a mess in your bed every time you get the chance.'

Nothing.

She glances around at the door to make sure it's shut, then removes her left hand from her knee and reaches out with it. 'All those people you hurt, some of them still suffering. Does that make you happy? It does, doesn't it? How would *you* like it? Shall we find out?'

She first touches the soft ridge of a nipple beneath his shirt, then grasps it between her thumb and index finger. Her nails are short, but she digs in with what she has. She twists first one way, then the other.

'That's pain, Mr Hartsfield. Do you like it?'

His face remains as bland as ever, which makes her angrier still. She bends closer, until

71

their noses are almost touching. Her face more like a fist than ever. Her blue eyes bulge behind her glasses. There are tiny spit-buds at the corners of her lips.

'I could do this to your testicles,' she whispers. 'Perhaps I will.'

Yes. She just might. It's not as if he can tell Babineau, after all. He has four dozen words at most, and few people can understand what he does manage to say. *I want more corn* comes out *Uh-wan-mo-ko*, which sounds like fake Indian talk in an old Western movie. The only thing he says that's perfectly clear is *I want my mother*, and on several occasions Scapelli has taken great pleasure in re-informing him that his mother is dead.

She twists his nipple back and forth. Clockwise, then counter-clockwise. Pinching as hard as she can, and her hands are nurse's hands, which means they are strong.

'You think Dr Babineau is your pet, but you've got that backwards. You're *his* pet. His pet guinea pig. He thinks I don't know about the experimental drugs he's been giving you, but I do. Vitamins, he says. Vitamins, my fanny. I know *everything* that goes on around here. He thinks he's going to bring you all the way back, but that will never happen. You're too far gone. And what if it did? You'd stand trial and go to jail for the rest of your life. And they don't have hot tubs in Waynesville State Prison.'

She's pinching his nipple so hard the tendons on her wrist stand out, and he still shows no sign that he feels anything — just looks out at the parking garage, his face a blank. If she keeps on,

72

one of the nurses is apt to see bruising, swelling, and it will go on his chart.

She lets go and steps back, breathing hard, and the venetian blind at the top of his window gives an abrupt, bonelike rattle. The sound makes her jump and look around. When she turns back to him, Hartsfield is no longer looking at the parking garage. He's looking at *her*. His eyes are clear and aware. Scapelli feels a bright spark of fear and takes a step back.

'I could report Babineau,' she says, 'but doctors have a way of wiggling out of things, especially when it's their word against a nurse's, even a head nurse's. And why would I? Let him experiment on you all he wants. Even Waynesville is too good for you, Mr Hartsfield. Maybe he'll give you something that will kill you. That's what you deserve.'

A food trolley rumbles by in the corridor; someone is getting a late lunch. Ruth Scapelli jerks like a woman awaking from a dream and backs toward the door, looking from Hartsfield to the now silent venetian blind and then back to Hartsfield again.

'I'll leave you to your thoughts, but I want to tell you one more thing before I go. If you ever show me your middle finger again, it *will* be your testicles.'

Brady's hand rises from his lap to his chest. It trembles, but that's a motor control issue; thanks to ten sessions a week downstairs in Physical Therapy, he's gotten at least some muscle tone back.

Scapelli stares, unbelieving, as the middle

finger rises and tilts toward her.

With it comes that obscene grin.

'You're a freak,' she says in a low voice. 'An aberration.'

But she doesn't approach him again. She's suddenly, irrationally afraid of what might happen if she did.

11

Tom Saubers is more than willing to do the favor Hodges has asked of him, even though it means rescheduling a couple of afternoon appointments. He owes Bill Hodges a lot more than a tour through an empty house up in Ridgedale; after all, the ex-cop — with the help of his friends Holly and Jerome — saved the lives of his son and daughter. Possibly his wife's, as well.

He punches off the alarm in the foyer, reading the numbers from a slip of paper clipped to the folder he carries. As he leads Hodges through the downstairs rooms, their footfalls echoing, Tom can't help going into his spiel. Yes, it's quite a long way out from the city center, can't argue the point, but what that means is you get all the city services — water, plowing, garbage removal, school buses, municipal buses — without all the city noise. 'The place is cable-ready, and *way* above code,' he says.

'Great, but I don't want to buy it.'

Tom looks at him curiously. 'What *do* you want?'

Hodges sees no reason not to tell him. 'To know if anyone has been using it to keep an eye on that house across the street. There was a murder-suicide there this past weekend.'

'In 1601? Jesus, Bill, that's *awful*.'

It is, Hodges thinks, and I believe you're already wondering who you should talk to about becoming the selling agent on that one.

Not that he holds that against the man, who went through his own hell as a result of the City Center Massacre.

'See you've left the cane behind,' Hodges comments as they climb to the second floor.

'I sometimes use it at night, especially if the weather is rainy,' Tom says. 'The scientists claim that stuff about your joints hurting more in wet weather is bullshit, but I'm here to tell you that's one old wives' tale you can take to the bank. Now, this is the master bedroom, and you can see how it's set up to catch the morning light. The bathroom is nice and big — the shower has pulsing jets — and just down the hall here . . . '

Yes, it's a fine house, Hodges would expect nothing else here in Ridgedale, but there's no sign anyone has been in it lately.

'Seen enough?' Tom asks.

'I think so, yes. Did you notice anything out of place?'

'Not a thing. And the alarm is a good one. If someone *had* broken in — '

'Yeah,' Hodges says. 'Sorry to get you out on such a cold day.'

'Nonsense. I had to be out and about anyway. And it's good to see you.' They step out the kitchen door, which Tom relocks. 'Although you're looking awfully thin.'

'Well, you know what they say — you can't be too thin or too rich.'

Tom, who in the wake of his City Center injuries was too thin and too poor, gives this oldie an obligatory smile and starts around to the front of the house. Hodges follows a few steps, then stops.

'Could we look in the garage?'

'Sure, but there's nothing in there.'

'Just a peek.'

'Cross every *t* and dot every *i*, huh? Roger that, just let me get the right key.'

Only he doesn't need the key, because the garage door is standing two inches ajar. The two men look at the splinters around the lock silently. At last Tom says, 'Well. How about that.'

'The alarm system doesn't cover the garage, I take it.'

'You take it right. There's nothing to protect.'

Hodges steps into a rectangle with bare wood walls and a poured concrete floor. There are boot prints visible on the concrete. Hodges can see his breath, and he can see something else, as well. In front of the left overhead door is a chair. Someone sat here, looking out.

Hodges has been feeling a growing discomfort on the left side of his midsection, one that's putting out tentacles that curl around to his lower back, but this sort of pain is almost an old friend by now, and it's temporarily overshadowed by excitement.

Someone sat here looking out at 1601, he thinks. I'd bet the farm on it, if I had a farm.

He walks to the front of the garage and sits

where the watcher sat. There are three windows running horizontally across the middle of the door, and the one on the far right has been wiped clean of dust. The view is a straight shot to the big living room window of 1601.

'Hey, Bill,' Tom says. 'Something under the chair.'

Hodges bends to look, although doing so turns up the heat in his gut. What he sees is a black disc, maybe three inches across. He picks it up by the edges. Embossed on it in gold is a single word: STEINER.

'Is it from a camera?' Tom asks.

'From a pair of binoculars. Police departments with fat budgets use Steiner binocs.'

With a good pair of Steiners — and as far as Hodges knows, there's no such thing as a bad pair — the watcher could have put himself right into the Ellerton-Stover living room, assuming the blinds were up . . . and they had been when he and Holly were in that room this morning. Hell, if the women had been watching CNN, the watcher could have read the news crawl at the bottom of the screen.

Hodges doesn't have an evidence Baggie, but there's a travel-sized pack of Kleenex in his coat pocket. He takes out two, carefully wraps the lens cap, and slips it into the inside pocket of his coat. He rises from the chair (provoking another twinge; the pain is bad this afternoon), then spies something else. Someone has carved a single letter into the wood upright between the two overhead doors, perhaps using a pocketknife.

It's the letter Z.

They are almost back to the driveway when Hodges is visited by something new: a searing bolt of agony behind his left knee. It feels as if he's been stabbed. He cries out as much in surprise as from the pain and bends over, kneading at the throbbing knot, trying to make it let go. To loosen up a little, at least.

Tom bends down next to him, and thus neither of them sees the elderly Chevrolet cruising slowly along Hilltop Court. Its fading blue paint is dappled with spots of red primer. The old gent behind the wheel slows down even more, so he can stare at the two men. Then the Chevrolet speeds up, sending a puff of blue exhaust from its tailpipe, and passes the Ellerton-Stover house, headed for the button-hook turnaround at the end of the street.

'What is it?' Tom asks. 'What happened?'

'Cramp,' Hodges says through gritted teeth.

'Rub it.'

Hodges gives him a look of pained humor through his tumbled hair. 'What do you think I'm doing?'

'Let me.'

Tom Saubers, a physical therapy veteran thanks to his attendance at a certain job fair six years ago, pushes Hodges's hand aside. He removes one of his gloves and digs in with his fingers. Hard.

'Ow! Jesus! That fucking hurts!'

'I know,' Tom says. 'Can't be helped. Move as much of your weight to your good leg as you can.'

Hodges does so. The Malibu with its patches of dull red primer paint cruises slowly by once more, this time headed back down the hill. The driver helps himself to another long look, then speeds up again.

'It's letting go,' Hodges says. 'Thank God for small favors.' It is, but his stomach is on fire and his lower back feels like he wrenched it.

Tom is looking at him with concern. 'You sure you're all right?'

'Yeah. Just a charley horse.'

'Or maybe a deep vein thrombosis. You're no kid anymore, Bill. You ought to get that checked out. If anything happened to you while you were with me, Pete would never forgive me. His sister, either. We owe you a lot.'

'All taken care of, got a doctor's appointment tomorrow,' Hodges says. 'Come on, let's get out of here. It's freezing.'

He limps the first two or three steps, but then the pain behind his knee lets go entirely and he's able to walk normally. More normally than Tom. Thanks to his encounter with Brady Hartsfield in April of 2009, Tom Saubers will limp for the rest of his life.

13

When Hodges gets home, his stomach is better but he's dog tired. He tires easily these days and tells himself it's because his appetite has gotten so lousy, but he wonders if that's really it. He's heard the pane of breaking glass and the boys giving their home run cheer twice on his way back from Ridgedale, but he never looks at his phone while driving, partly because it's dangerous (not to mention illegal in this state), mostly because he refuses to become a slave to it.

Besides, he doesn't need to be a mind reader to know from whom at least one of those texts came. He waits until he's hung his coat in the front hall closet, briefly touching the inside pocket to make sure the lens cap is still safe and sound.

The first text is from Holly. We should talk to Pete and Isabelle, but call me first. I have a Q.

The other isn't hers. It reads: Dr Stamos needs to talk to you urgently. You are scheduled tomorrow at 9 AM. Please keep this appointment!

Hodges checks his watch and sees that, although this day seems to have lasted at least a month already, it's only quarter past four. He calls Stamos's office and gets Marlee. He can tell it's her by the chirpy cheerleader's voice, which turns grave when he introduces himself. He doesn't know what those tests showed, but it can't be good. As Bob Dylan once said, you don't need a weatherman to know which way the wind blows.

He bargains for nine thirty instead of nine, because he wants a sit-down with Holly, Pete, and Isabelle first. He won't allow himself to believe that his visit to Dr Stamos's office may be followed by a hospital admission, but he is a realist, and that sudden bolt of pain in his leg scared the shit out of him.

Marlee puts him on hold. Hodges listens to

the Young Rascals for awhile (They must be mighty old Rascals by now, he thinks), and then she comes back. 'We can get you in at nine thirty, Mr Hodges, but Dr Stamos wants me to emphasize that it's imperative that you keep this appointment.'

'How bad is it?' He asks before he can stop himself.

'I don't have any information on your case,' Marlee tells him, 'but I'd say that you should get going on what's wrong as soon as possible. Don't you think so?'

'I do,' Hodges says heavily. 'I'll keep the appointment for sure. And thank you.'

He breaks the connection and stares at his phone. On the screen is a picture of his daughter at seven, bright and smiling, riding high on the backyard swing he put up when they lived on Freeborn Avenue. When they were still a family. Now Allie's thirty-six, divorced, in therapy, and getting over a painful relationship with a man who told her a story as old as Genesis: *I'm going to leave her soon, but this is a bad time.*

Hodges puts the phone down and lifts his shirt. The pain on the left side of his abdomen has subsided to a low mutter again, and that's good, but he doesn't like the swelling he sees below his sternum. It's as if he just put away a huge meal, when in fact he could only eat half of his lunch and breakfast was a bagel.

'What's going on with you?' he asks his swollen stomach. 'I wouldn't mind a clue before I keep that appointment tomorrow.'

He supposes he could get all the clues he

wants by firing up his computer and going to Web MD, but he's come to believe that Internet-assisted self-diagnosis is a game for idiots. He calls Holly, instead. She wants to know if he found anything interesting at 1588.

'*Very* interesting, as that guy on *Laugh-In* used to say, but before I go into that, ask your question.'

'Do you think Pete can find out if Martine Stover was buying a computer? Check her credit cards, or something? Because her mother's was *ancient*. If so, it means she was serious about taking an online course. And if she was serious, then — '

'Then the chances she was working up to a suicide pact with her mother drop drastically.'

'Yes.'

'But it wouldn't rule out the mother deciding to do it on her own. She could have dumped the pills and vodka down Stover's feeding tube while she was asleep, then got into the tub to finish the job.'

'But Nancy Alderson said — '

'They were happy, yeah, I know. I'm only pointing it out. I don't really believe it.'

'You sound tired.'

'Just my usual end-of-the-day slump. I'll perk up after I get some chow.' Never in his life has he felt less like eating.

'Eat a lot. You're too thin. But first tell me what you found in that empty house.'

'Not in the house. In the garage.'

He tells her. She doesn't interrupt. Nor does she say anything when he's done. Holly

82

sometimes forgets she's on the phone, so he gives her a prompt.

'What do you think?'

'I don't know. I mean, I really don't. It's just . . . weird all over. Don't you think so? Or not? Because I could be overreacting. Sometimes I do that.'

Tell me about it, Hodges thinks, but this time he doesn't think she is, and says so.

Holly says, 'You told me you didn't think Janice Ellerton would take anything from a man in a mended parka and workman's clothes.'

'Indeed I did.'

'So that means . . . '

Now he's the one who stays silent, letting her work it out.

'It means two men were up to something. *Two*. One gave Janice Ellerton the Zappit and the bogus questionnaire while she was shopping, and the other watched her house from across the street. And with binoculars! *Expensive* binoculars! I guess those two men might not have been working together, but . . . '

He waits. Smiling a little. When Holly turns her thinking processes up to ten, he can almost hear the cogs spinning behind her forehead.

'Bill, are you still there?'

'Yeah. Just waiting for you to spit it out.'

'Well, it seems like they must have been. To me, anyway. And like they might have had something to do with those two women being dead. There, are you happy?'

'Yes, Holly. I am. I've got a doctor's appointment tomorrow at nine thirty — '

83

'Your test results came back?'

'Yeah. I want to set up a meeting beforehand with Pete and Isabelle. Does eight thirty work for you?'

'Of course.'

'We'll lay out everything, tell them about Alderson and the game console you found and the house at 1588. See what they think. Sound okay?'

'Yes, but *she* won't think anything.'

'You could be wrong.'

'Yes. And the sky could turn green with red polka dots tomorrow. Now go make yourself something to eat.'

Hodges assures her he will, and heats up a can of chicken noodle soup while watching the early news. He eats most of it, spacing out each spoonful, cheering himself on: You can do it, you can do it.

While he's rinsing the bowl, the pain on the left side of his abdomen returns, along with those tentacles curling around to his lower back. It seems to plunge up and down with every heartbeat. His stomach clenches. He thinks of running to the bathroom, but it's too late. He leans over the sink instead, vomiting with his eyes closed. He keeps them that way as he fumbles for the faucet and turns it on full to rinse away the mess. He doesn't want to see what just came out of him, because he can taste a slime of blood in his mouth and throat.

Oy, he thinks, I am in trouble here.

I am in such trouble.

14

Eight P.M.

When her doorbell rings, Ruth Scapelli is watching some stupid reality program which is just an excuse to show young men and women running around in their small clothes. Instead of going directly to the door, she slipper-scuffs into the kitchen and turns on the monitor for the security cam mounted on the porch. She lives in a safe neighborhood, but it doesn't pay to take chances; one of her late mother's favorite sayings was *scum travels*.

She is surprised and uneasy when she recognizes the man at her door. He's wearing a tweed overcoat, obviously expensive, and a trilby with a feather in the band. Beneath the hat, his perfectly barbered silver hair flows dramatically along his temples. In one hand is a slim briefcase. It's Dr Felix Babineau, chief of the Neurology Department and head honcho at the Lakes Region Traumatic Brain Injury Clinic.

The doorbell chimes again and she hurries to let him in, thinking He can't know about what I did this afternoon because the door was shut and no one saw me go in. Relax. It's something else. Perhaps a union matter.

But he has never discussed union matters with her before, although she's been an officer of Nurses United for the last five years. Dr Babineau might not even know her if he passed her on the street unless she was wearing her nurse's uniform. That makes her remember what she's wearing now, an old housecoat and even older slippers (with bunny faces on them!), but it's too late to do anything about that. At least her hair isn't up in rollers.

He should have called, she thinks, but the thought that follows is disquieting: Maybe he wanted to catch me by surprise.

'Good evening, Dr Babineau. Come in out of the cold. I'm sorry to be greeting you in my housecoat, but I wasn't expecting company.'

He comes in and just stands there in the hall. She has to step around him to close the door. Seen up close instead of on the monitor, she thinks that perhaps they're even in the department of sartorial disarray. She's in her housecoat and slippers, true, but his cheeks are speckled with gray stubble. Dr Babineau (no one would dream of calling him Dr Felix) may be quite the fashion plate — witness the cashmere scarf fluffed up around his throat — but tonight he needs a shave, and quite badly. Also, there are purple pouches under his eyes.

'Let me take your coat,' she says.

He puts his briefcase between his shoes, unbuttons the overcoat, and hands it to her, along with the luxy scarf. He still hasn't said a single word. The lasagna she ate for supper, quite delicious at the time, seems to be sinking, and pulling the pit of her stomach down with it.

'Would you like — '

'Come into the living room,' he says, and walks past her as if he owns the place. Ruth Scapelli scurries after.

Babineau takes the remote control from the arm of her easy chair, points it at the television,

86

and hits mute. The young men and women continue to run around, but they do so unaccompanied by the mindless patter of the announcer. Scapelli is no longer just uneasy; now she's afraid. For her job, yes, the position she has worked so hard to attain, but also for herself. There's a look in his eyes that is really no look at all, only a kind of vacancy.

'Could I get you something? A soft drink or a cup of — '

'Listen to me, Nurse Scapelli. And very closely, if you want to keep your position.'

'I . . . I . . . '

'Nor would it end with losing your job.' Babineau puts his briefcase on the seat of her easy chair and undoes the cunning gold clasps. They make little thudding sounds as they fly up. 'You committed an act of assault on a mentally deficient patient today, what might be construed a *sexual* assault, and followed it with what the law calls criminal threatening.'

'I . . . I never . . . '

She can barely hear herself. She thinks she might faint if she doesn't sit down, but his briefcase is in her favorite chair. She makes her way across the living room to the sofa, barking her shin on the coffee table en route, almost hard enough to tip it over. She feels a thin trickle of blood sliding down to her ankle, but doesn't look at it. If she does that, she *will* faint.

'You twisted Mr Hartsfield's nipple. Then you threatened to do the same to his testes.'

'He made an obscene gesture to me!' Scapelli bursts out. 'Showed me his middle finger!'

87

'I will see that you never work in the nursing profession again,' he says, looking into the depths of his briefcase as she half-swoons onto the sofa. His initials are monogrammed on the side of the case. In gold, of course. He drives a new BMW, and that haircut probably cost fifty dollars. Maybe more. He's an overbearing, domineering boss, and now he's threatening to ruin her life over one small mistake. One small error in judgment.

She wouldn't mind if the floor opened up and swallowed her, but her vision is perversely clear. She seems to see every filament on the feather poking out of his hatband, every scarlet thread in his bloodshot eyes, every ugly gray speck of stubble on his cheeks and chin. His hair would be that same rat fur color, she thinks, if he didn't dye it.

'I . . . ' Tears begin to come — hot tears running down her cold cheeks. 'I . . . please, Dr Babineau.' She doesn't know how he knows, and it doesn't matter. The fact is, he does. 'I'll never do it again. Please. *Please*.'

Dr Babineau doesn't bother to answer.

15

Selma Valdez, one of four nurses who work the three-to-eleven shift in the Bucket, gives a perfunctory rap on the door of 217 — perfunctory because the resident never answers — and steps in. Brady is sitting in his chair by the window, looking out into the dark. His bedside

88

lamp is on, showing the golden highlights in his hair. He is still wearing his button reading I WAS SHAVED BY NURSE BARBARA!

She starts to ask if he's ready for a little help in getting ready for bed (he can't unbutton his shirt or pants, but he is capable of shuffling out of them once that's accomplished), but then rethinks the idea. Dr Babineau has added a note to Hartsfield's chart, one written in imperative red ink: 'Patient is not to be disturbed when in a semiconscious state. During these periods, his brain may actually be 'rebooting' itself in small but appreciable increments. Come back and check at half-hour intervals. Do not ignore this directive.'

Selma doesn't think Hartsfield is rebooting jack shit, he's just off in gorkland, but like all the nurses who work in the Bucket, she's a bit afraid of Babineau, and knows he has a habit of showing up at any time, even in the small hours of the morning, and right now it's just gone eight P.M.

At some point since she last checked him, Hartsfield has managed to get up and take the three steps to his bedside table where his game gadget is kept. He doesn't have the manual dexterity needed to play any of the pre-loaded games, but he can turn it on. He enjoys holding it in his lap and looking at the demo screens. Sometimes he'll do it for an hour or more, bent over like a man studying for an important exam. His favorite is the Fishin' Hole demo, and he's looking at it now. A little tune that she remembers from her childhood is playing: *By the sea, by the sea, by the beautiful sea . . .*

She approaches, thinks of saying You really like that one, don't you, but remembers *Do not ignore this directive*, underlined, and looks down at the small five-inches-by-three screen instead. She gets why he likes it; there's something beautiful and fascinating in the way the exotic fish appear, pause, and then zip away with a single flip of their tails. Some are red . . . some are blue . . . some are yellow . . . oh, and there's a pretty pink one —

'Stop looking.'

Brady's voice grates like the hinges on a seldom-opened door, and while there is an appreciable space between the words, they are perfectly clear. Nothing at all like his usual mushy mumble. Selma jumps as if he goosed her instead of just speaking to her. On the Zappit screen there's a momentary flash of blue light that obliterates the fish, but then they're back. Selma glances down at the watch pinned upside-down to her smock and sees it's now eight twenty. Jesus, has she really been standing here for almost twenty minutes?

'Go.'

Brady is still looking down at the screen where the fish swim back and forth, back and forth. Selma drags her eyes away, but it's an effort.

'Come back later.' Pause. 'When I'm done.' Pause. 'Looking.'

Selma does as she's told, and once she's back in the hall, she feels like herself again. He spoke to her, big whoop. And if he enjoys watching the Fishin' Hole demo the way some guys enjoy watching girls in bikinis play volleyball? Again, big whoop. The real question is why they let *kids* have those consoles. They can't be good for their immature brains, can they? On the other hand, kids play computer games all the time, so maybe they're immune. In the meantime, she has plenty to do. Let Hartsfield sit in his chair and look at his gizmo.

After all, he's not hurting anybody.

16

Felix Babineau bends stiffly forward from the waist, like an android in an old sci-fi movie. He reaches into his briefcase and brings out a flat pink gadget that looks like an e-reader. The screen is gray and blank.

'There's a number in here I want you to find,' he says. 'A nine-digit number. If you can find that number, Nurse Scapelli, today's incident will remain between us.'

The first thing that comes to mind is *You must be crazy*, but she can't say that, not when he holds her whole life in his hands. 'How can I? I don't know anything about those electronic gadgets! I can barely work my phone!'

'Nonsense. As a surgical nurse, you were in great demand. Because of your dexterity.'

True enough, but it's been ten years since she worked in the Kiner surgical suites, handing out scissors and retractors and sponges. She was offered a six-week course in microsurgery — the hospital would have paid seventy percent — but she had no interest. Or so she claimed; in truth, she was afraid of failing the course. He's right, though, in her prime she had been fast.

Babineau pushes a button on top of the gadget. She cranes her neck to see. It lights up, and the words WELCOME TO ZAPPIT! appear. This is followed by a screen showing all sorts of icons. Games, she supposes. He swipes the screen once, twice, then tells her to stand next to him. When she hesitates, he smiles. Perhaps it's meant to be pleasant and inviting, but it terrifies her, instead. Because there's nothing in his eyes, no human expression at all.

'Come, Nurse. I won't *bite* you.'

Of course not. Only what if he does?

Nevertheless, she steps closer so she can see the screen, where exotic fish are swimming back and forth. When they flick their tails, bubbles stream up. A vaguely familiar little tune plays.

'Do you see this one? It's called Fishin' Hole.'

'Y-Yes.' Thinking, He really is crazy. He's had some sort of mental breakdown from overwork.

'If you were to tap the bottom of the screen, the game would come up and the music would change, but I don't want you to do that. The demo is all you need. Look for the pink fish. They don't come often, and they're fast, so you have to watch carefully. You can't take your eyes off the screen.'

'Dr Babineau, are you all right?'

It's her voice, but it seems to be coming from far away. He makes no reply, just keeps looking at the screen. Scapelli is looking, too. Those fish are interesting. And the little tune, that's sort of hypnotic. There's a flash of blue light from the screen. She blinks, and then the fish are back. Swimming to and fro. Flicking their flippy tails and sending up burbles of bubbles.

'Each time you see a pink fish, tap it and a number will come up. Nine pink fish, nine numbers. Then you will be done and all this will be behind us. Do you understand?'

She thinks of asking him if she's supposed to write the numbers down or just remember them, but that seems too hard, so she just says yes.

'Good.' He hands her the gadget. 'Nine fish, nine numbers. But just the pink ones, mind.'

Scapelli stares at the screen where the fish swim: red and green, green and blue, blue and yellow. They swim off the left side of the little rectangular screen, then back on at the right. They swim off the right side of the screen, then back on at the left.

Left, right.

Right, left.

Some high, some low.

But where are the pink ones? She needs to tap the pink ones and when she's tapped nine of them, all of this will be behind her.

From the corner of one eye she sees Babineau refastening the clasps on his briefcase. He picks it up and leaves the room. He's going. It doesn't matter. She has to tap the pink fish, and then all of this will be behind her. A flash of blue light from the screen, and then the fish are back. They swim left to right and right to left. The tune plays: *By the sea, by the sea, by the beautiful sea, you and me, you and me, oh how happy we'll be.*

A pink one! She taps it! The number 11 appears! Eight more to go!

She taps a second pink fish as the front door quietly closes, and a third as Dr Babineau's car starts outside. She stands in the middle of her living room, lips parted as if for a kiss, staring down at the screen. Colors shift and move on her cheeks and forehead. Her eyes are wide and unblinking. A fourth pink fish swims into view, this one moving slowly, as if inviting the tap of her finger, but she only stands there.

'Hello, Nurse Scapelli.'

She looks up to see Brady Hartsfield sitting in her easy chair. He's shimmering a bit at the edges, ghostly, but it's him, all right. He's wearing what he was wearing when she visited him in his room that afternoon: jeans and a checked shirt. On the shirt is that button reading I WAS SHAVED BY NURSE BARBARA! But the vacant gaze everyone in the Bucket has grown used to is gone. He's looking at her with lively interest. She remembers her brother looking at his ant farm that way when they were children back in Hershey, Pennsylvania.

He must be a ghost, because fish are swimming in his eyes.

'He'll tell,' Hartsfield says. 'And it won't just be his word against yours, don't get that idea. He had a nanny-cam planted in my room so he can watch me. Study me. It's got a wide-angle lens so he can see the whole room. That kind of lens is called a fish-eye.'

He smiles to show he's made a pun. A red fish swims across his right eye, disappears, and then appears in his left one. Scapelli thinks, His brain is full of fish. I'm seeing his thoughts.

'The camera is hooked up to a recorder. He'll show the board of directors the footage of you torturing me. It didn't actually hurt that much, I don't feel pain the way I used to, but torture is what he'll call it. It won't end there, either. He'll put it on YouTube. And Facebook. And Bad Medicine dot-com. It will go viral. You'll be famous. The Torturing Nurse. And who will come to your defense? Who will stand up for you? No one. Because nobody likes you. They think you're awful. And what do *you* think? Do you think you're awful?'

Now that the idea has been brought fully to her attention, she supposes she is. Anyone who would threaten to twist the testicles of a brain-damaged man *must* be awful. What was she thinking?

'Say it.' He leans forward, smiling.

The fish swim. The blue light flashes. The tune plays.

'Say it, you worthless bitch.'

'I'm awful,' Ruth Scapelli says in her living room, which is empty except for her. She stares down at the screen of the Zappit Commander.

'Now say it like you mean it.'

'I'm awful. I'm an awful worthless bitch.'

'And what is Dr Babineau going to do?'

'Put it on YouTube. Put it on Facebook. Put it on Bad Medicine dot-com. Tell everyone.'

'You'll be arrested.'

'I'll be arrested.'

'They'll put your picture in the paper.'

95

'Of course they will.'
'You'll go to jail.'
'I'll go to jail.'
'Who will stand up for you?'
'No one.'

17

Sitting in Room 217 of the Bucket, Brady stares down at the Fishin' Hole demo. His face is fully awake and aware. It's the face he hides from everyone except Felix Babineau, and Dr Babineau no longer matters. Dr Babineau hardly exists. These days he's mostly Dr Z.

'Nurse Scapelli,' Brady says. 'Let's go into the kitchen.'

She resists, but not for long.

18

Hodges tries to swim below the pain and stay asleep, but it pulls him up steadily until he breaks the surface and opens his eyes. He fumbles for the bedside clock and sees it's two A.M. A bad time to be awake, maybe the worst time. When he suffered insomnia after his retirement, he thought of two A.M. as the suicide hour and now he thinks, That's probably when Mrs Ellerton did it. Two in the morning. The hour when it seems daylight will never come.

He gets out of bed, walks slowly to the bathroom, and takes the giant economy size bottle of

Gelusil out of the medicine cabinet, careful not to look at himself in the mirror. He chugalugs four big swallows, then leans over, waiting to see if his stomach will accept it or hit the ejector button, as it did with the chicken soup.

It stays down and the pain actually begins to recede. Sometimes Gelusil does that. Not always.

He thinks about going back to bed, but he's afraid that dull throb will return as soon as he's horizontal. He shuffles into his office instead and turns on his computer. He knows this is the very worst time to start checking out the possible causes for his symptoms, but he can no longer resist. His desktop wallpaper comes up (another picture of Allie as a kid). He mouses down to the bottom of the screen, meaning to open Firefox, then freezes. There's something new in the dock. Between the balloon icon for text messaging and the camera icon for Face Time, there's a blue umbrella with a red *1* sitting above it.

'A message on Debbie's Blue Umbrella,' he says. 'I'll be damned.'

A much younger Jerome Robinson downloaded the Blue Umbrella app to his computer almost six years ago. Brady Hartsfield, aka Mr Mercedes, wanted to converse with the cop who had failed to catch him, and, although retired, Hodges was very willing to talk. Because once you got dirtbags like Mr Mercedes talking (there weren't very many like him, and thank God for that), they were only a step or two from being caught. This was especially true of the arrogant ones, and Hartsfield had been arrogance personified.

They both had their reasons for communicating on a secure, supposedly untraceable chat site with servers located someplace in deepest, darkest Eastern Europe. Hodges wanted to goad the perpetrator of the City Center Massacre into making a mistake that would help identify him. Mr Mercedes wanted to goad Hodges into killing himself. He had succeeded with Olivia Trelawney, after all.

What kind of life do you have? he had written in his first communication to Hodges — the one that had arrived by snail-mail. What kind, now that the 'thrill of the hunt' is behind you? And then: Want to get in touch with me? Try Under Debbie's Blue Umbrella. I even got you a username: 'kermitfrog19.'

With plenty of help from Jerome Robinson and Holly Gibney, Hodges tracked Brady down, and Holly clobbered him. Jerome and Holly got free city services for ten years; Hodges got a pace-maker. There were sorrows and loss Hodges doesn't want to think about — not even now, all these years later — but you'd have to say that for the city, and especially for those who had been attending the concert at the Mingo that night, all ended well.

At some point between 2010 and now, the blue umbrella icon disappeared from the dock at the bottom of his screen. If Hodges ever wondered what happened to it (he can't remember that he ever did), he probably assumed either Jerome or Holly dumped it in the trash on one of their visits to fix whatever current outrage he had perpetrated on his defenseless Macintosh. Instead, one of them must have tucked it into the apps folder, where the blue umbrella has remained, just out of sight, all these years. Hell, maybe he even did the dragging himself and has forgotten. Memory has a way of slipping a few gears after sixty-five, when people round the third turn start down the home stretch.

He mouses to the blue umbrella, hesitates, then clicks. His desktop screen is replaced by a young couple on a magic carpet floating over an endless sea. Silver rain is falling, but the couple is safe and dry beneath a protective blue umbrella.

Ah, such memories this brings back.

He enters **kermitfrog19** as both his username and his password — isn't that how he did it before, as per Hartsfield's instructions? He can't remember for sure, but there's one way to find out. He bangs the return key.

The machine thinks for a second or two (it seems longer), and then, presto, he's in. He frowns at what he sees. Brady Hartsfield used **merckill** as his handle, short for Mercedes Killer — Hodges has no trouble remembering that — but this is someone else. Which shouldn't surprise him, since Holly turned Hartsfield's fucked-up brain to oatmeal, but somehow it still does.

Z-Boy wants to chat with you!
Do you want to chat with Z-Boy?
Y N

Hodges hits **Y**, and a moment later a message appears. Just a single sentence, half a dozen words, but Hodges reads them over and over again, feeling not fear but excitement. He is onto something here. He doesn't know what it is, but it feels big.

Z-Boy: He's not done with you yet.

Hodges stares at it, frowning. At last he sits forward in his chair and types:

kermitfrog19: Who's not done with me? Who is this?

There's no answer.

19

Hodges and Holly get together with Pete and Isabelle at Dave's Diner, a greasy spoon a block down from the morning madhouse known as Starbucks. With the early breakfast rush over, they have their pick of tables and settle at one in the back. In the kitchen a Badfinger song is playing on the radio and waitresses are laughing.

'All I've got is half an hour,' Hodges says. 'Then I have to run to the doctor's.'

Pete leans forward, looking concerned. 'Nothing serious, I hope.'

'Nope. I feel fine.' This morning he actually does — like forty-five again. That message on his computer, cryptic and sinister though it was, seems to have been better medicine than the Gelusil. 'Let's get to what we've found. Holly, they'll want Exhibit A and Exhibit B. Hand em over.'

Holly has brought her small tartan briefcase to the meeting. From it (and not without reluctance) she brings the Zappit Commander and the lens cap from the garage at 1588. Both are in plastic bags, although the lens cap is still wrapped in tissues.

'What have you two been up to?' Pete asks. He's striving for humorous, but Hodges can hear a touch of accusation there, as well.

'Investigating,' Holly says, and although she isn't ordinarily one for eye contact, she shoots a brief look at Izzy Jaynes, as if to say Get the point?

'Explain,' Izzy says.

Hodges does so while Holly sits beside him with her eyes cast down, her decaf — all she drinks — untouched. Her jaws are moving, though, and Hodges knows she's back on the Nicorette.

'Unbelievable,' Izzy says when Hodges has finished. She pokes at the bag with the Zappit inside. 'You just *took* this. Wrapped it up in newspaper like a piece of salmon from the fish market and carried it out of the house.'

Holly appears to shrink in her chair. Her hands are so tightly clasped in her lap that the knuckles are white.

Hodges usually likes Isabelle well enough, even though she once nearly tripped him up in an interrogation room (this during the Mr Mercedes thing, when he had been hip-deep in an unauthorized investigation), but he doesn't like her much now. He can't like anyone who makes Holly shrink like that.

'Be reasonable, Iz. Think it through. If Holly

101

hadn't found that thing — and purely by accident — it would still be there. You guys weren't going to search the house.'

'You probably weren't going to call the housekeeper, either,' Holly says, and although she still won't look up, there's metal in her voice. Hodges is glad to hear it.

'We would have gotten to the Alderson woman in time,' Izzy says, but those misty gray eyes of hers flick up and to the left as she says it. It's a classic liar's tell, and Hodges knows when he sees it that she and Pete haven't even discussed the housekeeper yet, although they probably *would* have gotten around to her eventually. Pete Huntley may be a bit of a plodder, but plodders are usually thorough, you had to give them that.

'If there were any fingerprints on that gadget,' Izzy says, 'they're gone now. Kiss them goodbye.'

Holly mutters something under her breath, making Hodges remember that when he first met her (and completely underestimated her), he thought of her as Holly the Mumbler.

Izzy leans forward, her gray eyes suddenly not misty at all. '*What* did you say?'

'She said that's silly,' Hodges says, knowing perfectly well that the word was actually *stupid*. 'She's right. It was shoved down between the arm of Ellerton's chair and the cushion. Any fingerprints on it would be blurred, and you know it. Also, *were* you going to search the whole house?'

'We might have,' Isabelle says, sounding sulky. 'Depending on what we get back from forensics.'

Other than in Martine Stover's bedroom and bathroom, there *were* no forensics. They all know this, Izzy included, and there's no need for Hodges to belabor the point.

'Take it easy,' Pete says to Isabelle. 'I invited Kermit and Holly out there, and you agreed.'

'That was before I knew they were going to walk out with . . . '

She trails off. Hodges waits with interest to see how she will finish. Is she going to say *with a piece of the evidence?* Evidence of what? An addiction to computer solitaire, Angry Birds, and Frogger?

'With a piece of Mrs Ellerton's property,' she finishes lamely.

'Well, you've got it now,' Hodges says. 'Can we move on? Perhaps discuss the man who gave it to her in the supermarket, claiming the company was eager for user input on a gadget that's no longer made?'

'And the man who was watching them,' Holly says, still without looking up. 'The man who was watching them from across the street with binoculars.'

Hodges's old partner pokes the bag with the wrapped lens cap inside. 'I'll have this dusted for fingerprints, but I'm not real hopeful, Kerm. You know how people take these caps on and off.'

'Yeah,' Hodges says. 'By the rim. And it was cold in that garage. Cold enough so I could see my breath. The guy was probably wearing gloves, anyway.'

'The guy in the supermarket was most likely working some kind of short con,' Izzy says. 'It's got that smell. Maybe he called a week later, trying to convince her that by taking the obsolete

103

games gadget, she was obligated to buy a more expensive current one, and she told him to go peddle his papers. Or he might have used the info from the questionnaire to hack into her computer.'

'Not *that* computer,' Holly says. 'It was older than dirt.'

'Had a good look around, didn't you?' Izzy says. 'Did you check the medicine cabinets while you were investigating?'

This is too much for Hodges. 'She was doing what you should have done, Isabelle. And you know it.'

Color is rising in Izzy's cheeks. 'We called you in as a courtesy, that's all, and I wish we'd never done it. You two are always trouble.'

'Stop it,' Pete says.

But Izzy is leaning forward, her eyes flicking between Hodges's face and the top of Holly's lowered head. 'These two mystery men — if they existed at all — have nothing to do with what happened in that house. One was probably running a con, the other was a simple peeper.'

Hodges knows he should stay friendly here — increase the peace, and all that — but he just can't do it. 'Some pervo salivating at the thought of watching an eighty-year-old woman undress, or seeing a quadriplegic get a sponge bath? Yeah, that makes sense.'

'Read my lips,' Izzy says. 'Mom killed daughter, then self. Even left a suicide note of sorts — Z, the end. Couldn't be any clearer.'

Z-Boy, Hodges thinks. Whoever's under Debbie's Blue Umbrella this time signs himself Z-Boy.

Holly lifts her head. 'There was also a Z in the garage. Carved into the wood between the doors. Bill saw it. Zappit also begins with Z, you know.'

'Yes,' Izzy says. 'And Kennedy and Lincoln have the same number of letters, proving they were both killed by the same man.'

Hodges sneaks a peek at his watch and sees he'll have to leave soon, and that's okay. Other than upsetting Holly and pissing off Izzy, this meeting has accomplished nothing. Nor can it, because he has no intention of telling Pete and Isabelle what he discovered on his own computer early this morning. That information might shift the investigation into a higher gear, but he's going to keep it on the down-low until he does a little more investigation himself. He doesn't want to think that Pete would fumble it, but —

But he might. Because being thorough is a poor substitute for being thoughtful. And Izzy? She doesn't want to open a can of worms filled with a lot of pulp-novel stuff about cryptic letters and mystery men. Not when the deaths at the Ellerton house are already on the front page of today's paper, along with a complete recap of how Martine Stover came to be paralyzed. Not when Izzy's expecting to take the next step up the police department ladder just as soon as her current partner retires.

'Bottom line,' Pete says, 'this is going down as a murder-suicide, and we're gonna move on. We *have* to move on, Kermit. I'm retiring. Iz will be left with a huge caseload and no new partner for awhile, thanks to the damn budget cuts. This stuff' — He indicates the two plastic bags — 'is sort of interesting, but it doesn't change the clarity of what happened. Unless you think some master criminal set it up? One who drives an old car and mends his coat with masking tape?'

'No, I don't think that.' Hodges is remembering something Holly said about Brady Hartsfield yesterday. She used the word *architect*. 'I think you've got it right. Murder-suicide.'

Holly gives him a brief look of wounded surprise before lowering her eyes again.

'But will you do something for me?'

'If I can,' Pete says.

'I tried the game console, but the screen stayed blank. Probably a dead battery. I didn't want to open the battery compartment, because that little slide panel *would* be a place to check for fingerprints.'

'I'll see that it's dusted, but I doubt — '

'Yeah, I do, too. What I really want is for one of your cyber-wonks to boot it up and check the various game applications. See if there's anything out of the ordinary.'

'Okay,' Pete says, and shifts slightly in his seat when Izzy rolls her eyes. Hodges can't be sure, but he thinks Pete just kicked her ankle under the table.

'I have to go,' Hodges says, and grabs for his wallet. 'Missed my appointment yesterday. Can't miss another one.'

'We'll pick up the check,' Izzy says. 'After you brought us all this valuable evidence, it's the least we can do.'

Holly mutters something else under her breath. This time Hodges can't be sure, even

106

with his trained Holly-ear, but he thinks it might
have been *bitch*.

20

On the sidewalk, Holly jams an unfashionable
but somehow charming plaid hunting cap down
to her ears and then thrusts her hands into her
coat pockets. She won't look at him, only starts
walking toward the office a block away. Hodges's
car is parked outside Dave's, but he hurries after
her.

'Holly.'

'You see how she is.' Walking faster. Still not
looking at him.

The pain in his gut is creeping back, and he's
losing his breath. 'Holly, wait. I can't keep up.'

She turns to him, and he's alarmed to see her
eyes are swimming with tears.

'There's more to it! More more more! But
they're just going to sweep it under the rug and
they didn't even say the real reason which is so
Pete can have a nice retirement party without
this hanging over his head the way you had to
retire with the Mercedes Killer hanging over
yours and so the papers don't make a big deal of
it and you know there's more to it I know you do
and I know you have to get your test results I
want you to get them because I'm so *worried*,
but those poor women . . . I just don't think
. . . they don't deserve to . . . to just be *shoveled
under*!'

She halts at last, trembling. The tears are

already freezing on her cheeks. He tilts her face to look at him, knowing she would shrink away if anyone else tried to touch her that way — yes, even Jerome Robinson, and she loves Jerome, probably has since the day the two of them discovered the ghost-program Brady left in Olivia Trelawney's computer, the one that finally pushed her over the edge and caused her to take her own overdose.

'Holly, we're not done with this. In fact I think we might just be getting started.'

She looks him squarely in the face, another thing she will do with no one else. 'What do you mean?'

'Something new has come up, something I didn't want to tell Pete and Izzy. I don't know what the hell to make of it. There's no time to tell you now, but when I get back from the doctor's, I'll tell you everything.'

'All right, that's fine. Go on, now. And although I don't believe in God, I'll say a prayer for your test results. Because a little prayer can't hurt, can it?'

'No.'

He gives her a quick hug — long hugs don't work with Holly — and starts back to his car, once more thinking of that thing she said yesterday, about Brady Hartsfield being an architect of suicide. A pretty turn of phrase from a woman who writes poetry in her spare time (not that Hodges has ever seen any, or is likely to), but Brady would probably sneer at it, consider it a mile short of the mark. Brady would consider himself a *prince* of suicide.

Hodges climbs into the Prius Holly nagged him into buying and heads for Dr Stamos's office. He's doing a little praying himself: Let it be an ulcer. Even the bleeding kind that needs surgery to sew it up.

Just an ulcer.

Please nothing worse than that.

21

He doesn't have to spend time cooling his heels in the waiting room today. Although he's five minutes early and the room is as full as it was on Monday, Marlee the cheerleader receptionist sends him in before he even has a chance to sit down.

Belinda Jensen, Stamos's nurse, usually greets him at his yearly physicals with smiling good cheer, but she's not smiling this morning, and as Hodges steps on the scale, he remembers his yearly physical is a bit overdue. By four months. Actually closer to five.

The armature on the old-fashioned scale balances at 165. When he retired from the cops in '09, he weighed 230 at the mandatory exit physical. Belinda takes his blood pressure, pokes something in his ear to get his current temperature, then leads him past the exam rooms and directly to Dr Stamos's office at the end of the corridor. She knocks a knuckle on the door, and when Stamos says 'Please come in,' she leaves Hodges at once. Usually voluble, full of tales about her fractious children and bumptious husband, she has today spoken hardly a word.

Can't be good, Hodges thinks, but maybe it's not too bad. Please God, not too bad. Another ten years wouldn't be a lot to ask for, would it? Or if You can't do that, how about five?

Wendell Stamos is a fiftysomething with a fast-receding hairline and the broad-shouldered, trim-waisted build of a pro jock who's stayed in shape after retirement. He looks at Hodges gravely and invites him to sit down. Hodges does so.

'How bad?'

'Bad,' Dr Stamos says, then hastens to add, 'but not hopeless.'

'Don't skate around it, just tell me.'

'It's pancreatic cancer, and I'm afraid we caught it . . . well . . . rather late in the game. Your liver is involved.'

Hodges finds himself fighting a strong and dismaying urge to laugh. No, more than laugh, to just throw back his head and yodel like Heidi's fucking grandfather. He thinks it was Stamos saying *bad but not hopeless*. It makes him remember an old joke. Doctor tells his patient there's good news and bad news; which does the patient want first? Hit me with the bad news, says the patient. Well, says the doctor, you have an inoperable brain tumor. The patient starts to blubber and asks what the good news can possibly be after learning a thing like that. The doctor leans forward, smiling confidentially, and says, I'm fucking my receptionist, and she's *gorgeous*.

110

'I'll want you to see a gastroenterologist immediately. I'm talking today. The best one in this part of the country is Henry Yip, at Kiner. He'll refer you to a good oncologist. I'm thinking that guy will want to start you on chemo and radiation. These can be difficult for the patient, debilitating, but are far less arduous than even five years ago — '

'Stop,' Hodges says. The urge to laugh has thankfully passed.

Stamos stops, looking at him in a brilliant shaft of January sun. Hodges thinks, Barring a miracle, this is the last January I'm ever going to see. Wow.

'What are the chances? Don't sugarcoat it. There's something hanging fire in my life right now, might be something big, so I need to know.'

Stamos sighs. 'Very slim, I'm afraid. Pancreatic cancer is just so goddamned *stealthy*.'

'How long?'

'With treatment? Possibly a year. Even two. And a remission is not entirely out of the ques — '

'I need to think about this,' Hodges says.

'I've heard that many times after I've had the unpleasant task of giving this kind of diagnosis, and I always tell my patients what I'm now going to tell you, Bill. If you were standing on top of a burning building and a helicopter appeared and dropped a rope ladder, would you say you needed to think about it before climbing up?'

Hodges mulls that over, and the urge to laugh returns. He's able to restrain it, but not a smile. It's broad and charming. 'I might,' he says, 'if the helicopter in question only had two gallons of gas left in the tank.'

22

When Ruth Scapelli was twenty-three, before she began to grow the hard shell that encased her in later years, she had a short and bumpy affair with a not-exactly-honest man who owned a bowling alley. She became pregnant and gave birth to a daughter she named Cynthia. This was in Davenport, Iowa, her hometown, where she was working toward her RN at Kaplan University. She was amazed to find herself a mother, more amazed still to realize that Cynthia's father was a slack-bellied forty-year-old with a tattoo reading LOVE TO LIVE AND LIVE TO LOVE on one hairy arm. If he had offered to marry her (he didn't), she would have declined with an inward shudder. Her aunt Wanda helped her raise the child.

Cynthia Scapelli Robinson now lives in San Francisco, where she has a fine husband (no tattoos) and two children, the older of whom is an honor roll student in high school. Her household is a warm one. Cynthia works hard to keep it that way, because the atmosphere in her aunt's home, where she did most of her growing up (and where her mother began to develop that formidable shell) was always chilly, full of recriminations and scoldings that usually began *You forgot to.* The emotional atmosphere was mostly above freezing, but rarely went higher than forty-five degrees. By the time Cynthia was in high school, she was calling her mother by her first name. Ruth Scapelli never objected to this; in fact, she found it a bit of a relief. She missed her daughter's nuptials due to work commitments, but sent a wedding present. It was a clock-radio. These days Cynthia and her mother talk on the phone once or twice a month, and occasionally exchange emails. *Josh doing fine in school, made the soccer team* is followed by a terse reply: *Good for him.* Cynthia has never actually missed her mother, because there was never all that much to miss.

This morning she rises at seven, fixes breakfast for her husband and the two boys, sees Hank off to work, sees the boys off to school, then rinses the dishes and gets the dishwasher going. That is followed by a trip to the laundry room, where she loads the washer and gets *that* going. She does these morning chores without once thinking *You must not forget to*, except someplace down deep she *is* thinking it, and always will. The seeds sown in childhood put down deep roots.

At nine thirty she makes herself a second cup of coffee, turns on the TV (she rarely looks at it, but it's company), and powers up her laptop to see if she has any emails other than the usual come-ons from Amazon and Urban Outfitters. This morning there's one from her mother, sent last night at 10:44 P.M. which translates to 8:44, West Coast time. She frowns at the subject line, which is a single word: Sorry.

She opens it. Her heartbeat speeds up as she reads.

I'm awful. I'm an awful worthless bitch. No one will stand up for me. This is what I have to do. I love you.

I love you. When is the last time her mother said that to her? Cynthia — who says it to her boys at least four times a day — honestly can't remember. She grabs her phone off the counter where it's been charging, and calls first her mother's cell, then the landline. She gets Ruth Scapelli's short, no-nonsense message on both: 'Leave a message. I'll call you back if that seems appropriate.' Cynthia tells her mother to call her right away, but she's terribly afraid her mother may not be able to do that. Not now, perhaps not later, perhaps not at all.

She paces the circumference of her sunny kitchen twice, chewing at her lips, then picks up her cell again and gets the number for Kiner Memorial Hospital. She resumes pacing as she waits to be transferred to the Brain Injury Clinic. She's finally connected to a nurse who identifies himself as Steve Halpern. No, Halpern tells her, Nurse Scapelli hasn't come in, which is surprising. Her shift starts at eight, and in the Midwest it's now twenty to one.

'Try her at home,' he advises. 'She's probably taking a sick day, although it's unlike her not to call in.'

You don't know the half of it, Cynthia thinks. Unless, that is, Halpern grew up in a house where the mantra was *You forgot to.*

She thanks him (can't forget that, no matter how worried she may be) and gets the number of a police department two thousand miles away.

114

She identifies herself and states the problem as calmly as possible.

'My mother lives at 298 Tannenbaum Street. Her name is Ruth Scapelli. She's the head nurse at the Kiner Hospital Brain Injury Clinic. I got an email from her this morning that makes me think . . . '

That she's badly depressed? No. It might not be enough to get the cops out there. Besides, it's not what she really thinks. She takes a deep breath.

'That makes me think she might be considering suicide.'

23

CPC 54 pulls into the driveway at 298 Tannenbaum Street. Officers Amarilis Rosario and Jason Laverty — known as Toody and Muldoon because their car number was featured in an old cop sitcom — get out and approach the door. Rosario rings the doorbell. There's no answer, so Laverty knocks, good and hard. There's still no answer. He tries the door on the off chance, and it opens. They look at each other. This is a good neighborhood, but it's still the city, and in the city most people lock their doors.

Rosario pokes her head in. 'Mrs Scapelli? This is Police Officer Rosario. Want to give us a shout?'

There is no shout.

Her partner chimes in. 'Officer Laverty, ma'am. Your daughter is worried about you. Are you okay?'

Nothing. Laverty shrugs and gestures to the

115

open door. 'Ladies first.'

Rosario steps in, unsnapping the strap on her service weapon without even thinking about it. Laverty follows. The living room is empty but the TV is on, the sound muted.

'Toody, Toody, I don't like this,' Rosario says. 'Can you smell it?'

Laverty can. It's the smell of blood. They find the source in the kitchen, where Ruth Scapelli lies on the floor next to an over-turned chair. Her arms are splayed out as if she tried to break her fall. They can see the deep cuts she's made, long ones up the forearms almost to the elbows, short ones across the wrists. Blood is splattered on the easy-clean tiles, and a great deal more is on the table, where she sat to do the deed. A butcher knife from the wooden block beside the toaster lies on the lazy Susan, placed with grotesque neatness between the salt and pepper shakers and the ceramic napkin holder. The blood is dark, coagulating. Laverty guesses she's been dead for twelve hours, at least.

'Maybe there was nothing good on TV,' he says.

Rosario gives him a dark look and takes a knee close to the body, but not close enough to get blood on her uni, which just came back from the cleaners the day before. 'She drew something before she lost consciousness,' she says. 'See it there on the tile by her right hand? Drew it in her own blood. What do you make it? Is it a 2?'

Laverty leans down for a close look, hands on his knees. 'Hard to tell,' he says. 'Either a 2 or a Z.'

BRADY

'My boy is a genius,' Deborah Hartsfield used to tell her friends. To which she would add, with a winning smile: 'It's not bragging if it's the truth.'

This was before she started drinking heavily, when she still had friends. Once she'd had another son, Frankie, but Frankie was no genius. Frankie was brain-damaged. One evening when he was four years old, he fell down the cellar stairs and died of a broken neck. That was the story Deborah and Brady told, anyway. The truth was a little different. A little more complex.

Brady loved to invent things, and one day he'd invent something that would make the two of them rich, would put them on that famous street called Easy. Deborah was sure of it, and told him so often. Brady believed it.

He managed just Bs and Cs in most of his courses, but in Computer Science I and II he was a straight-A star. By the time he graduated from North Side High, the Hartsfield house was equipped with all sorts of gadgets, some of them — like the blue boxes by which Brady stole cable TV from Midwest Vision — highly illegal. He had a workroom in the basement where Deborah rarely ventured, and it was there that he did his inventing.

Little by little, doubt crept in. And resentment, doubt's fraternal twin. No matter how inspired his creations were, none were moneymakers. There were guys in California — Steve Jobs, for instance — who made incredible fortunes and changed the world just tinkering in their garages, but the things Brady came up with never quite made the grade.

His design for the Rolla, for instance. It was to be a computer-powered vacuum cleaner that would run by itself, turning on gimbals and starting in a new direction each time it met an obstacle. That looked like a sure winner until Brady spotted a Roomba vacuum cleaner in a fancy-shmancy appliance store on Lacemaker Lane. Someone had beaten him to the punch. The phrase *a day late and a dollar short* occurred to him. He pushed it away, but sometimes at night when he couldn't sleep, or when he was coming down with one of his migraines, it recurred.

Yet two of his inventions — and minor ones at that — made the slaughter at City Center possible. They were modified TV remotes he called Thing One and Thing Two. Thing One could change traffic signals from red to green, or vice-versa. Thing Two was more sophisticated. It could capture and store signals sent from automobile key fobs, allowing Brady to unlock those vehicles after their clueless owners had departed. At first he used Thing Two as a burglary tool, opening cars and tossing them for cash or other valuables. Then, as the idea of driving a big car into a crowd of people took vague shape in his mind (along with fantasies of assassinating the President or maybe a hot shit movie star), he used Thing Two on Mrs Olivia

Trelawney's Mercedes, and discovered she kept a spare key in her glove compartment.

That car he left alone, filing the existence of the spare key away for later use. Not long after, like a message from the dark powers that ran the universe, he read in the newspaper that a job fair was to be held at City Center on the tenth of April.

Thousands were expected to show up.

★   ★   ★

After he started working the Cyber Patrol at Discount Electronix and could buy crunchers on the cheap, Brady wired together seven off-brand laptops in his basement workroom. He rarely used more than one of them, but he liked the way they made the room look: like something out of a science fiction movie or a *Star Trek* episode. He wired in a voice-activated system, too, and this was years before Apple made a voice-ac program named Siri a star.

Once again, *a day late and a dollar short.*

Or, in this case, a few billion.

Being in a situation like that, who wouldn't want to kill a bunch of people?

He only got eight at City Center (not counting the wounded, some of them maimed really good), but could have gotten *thousands* at that rock concert. He'd have been remembered forever. But before he could push the button that would have sent ball bearings flying in a jet-propelled, ever-widening deathfan, mutilating and decapitating hundreds of screaming prepubescent girls

119

(not to mention their overweight and overindulgent mommies), someone had turned out all his lights.

That part of his memory was blacked out permanently, it seemed, but he didn't *have* to remember. There was only one person it could have been: Kermit William Hodges. Hodges was supposed to commit suicide like Mrs Trelawney, that was the plan, but he'd somehow avoided both that and the explosives Brady had stashed in Hodges's car. The old retired detective showed up at the concert and thwarted him mere seconds before Brady could achieve his immortality.

Boom, boom, out go the lights.

Angel, angel, down we go.

★　★　★

Coincidence is a tricksy bitch, and it so happened that Brady was transported to Kiner Memorial by Unit 23 out of Firehouse 3. Rob Martin wasn't on the scene — he was at that time touring Afghanistan, all expenses paid by the United States government — but Jason Rapsis was the paramedic onboard, trying to keep Brady alive as 23 raced toward the hospital. If offered a bet on his chances, Rapsis would have bet against. The young man was seizing violently. His heart rate was 175, his blood pressure alternately spiking and falling. Yet he was still in the land of the living when 23 reached Kiner.

There he was examined by Dr Emory

120

Winston, an old hand in the patch-em-up, fix-em-up wing of the hospital some vets called the Saturday Night Knife and Gun Club. Winston collared a med student who happened to be hanging around the ER and chatting up nurses. Winston invited him to do a quick-and-dirty evaluation of the new patient. The student reported depressed reflexes, a dilated and fixed left pupil, and a positive right Babinski.

'Meaning?' Winston asked.

'Meaning this guy is suffering an irreparable brain injury,' said the student. 'He's a gork.'

'Very good, we may make a doctor of you yet. Prognosis?'

'Dead by morning,' said the student.

'You're probably right,' Winston said. 'I hope so, because he's never coming back from this. We'll give him a CAT scan, though.'

'Why?'

'Because it's protocol, son. And because I'm curious to see how much damage there actually is while he's still alive.'

He was still alive seven hours later, when Dr Annu Singh, ably assisted by Dr Felix Babineau, performed a craniotomy to evacuate the massive blood clot that was pressing on Brady's brain and increasing the damage minute by minute, strangling divinely specialized cells in their millions. When the operation was finished, Babineau turned to Singh and offered him a hand that was still encased in a blood-stippled glove.

'That,' he said, 'was amazing.'

Singh shook Babineau's hand, but he did so

121

with a deprecating smile. 'That was *routine*,' he said. 'Done a thousand of them. Well . . . a couple of hundred. What's amazing is this patient's constitution. I can't believe he lived through the operation. The damage to his poor old chump . . . ' Singh shook his head. 'Iy-yi-yi.'

'You know what he was trying to do, I take it?'

'Yes, I was informed. Terrorism on a grand scale. He may live for awhile, but he will never be tried for his crime, and he will be no great loss to the world when he goes.'

It was with this thought in mind that Dr Babineau began slipping Brady — not quite brain-dead, but almost — an experimental drug which he called Cerebellin (although only in his mind; technically, it was just a six-digit number), this in addition to the established protocols of increased oxygenation, diuretics, antiseizure dugs, and steroids. Experimental drug 649558 had shown promising results when tested on animals, but thanks to a tangle of regulatory bureaucracies, human trials were years away. It had been developed in a Bolivian neuro lab, which added to the hassle. By the time human testing commenced (if it ever did), Babineau would be living in a Florida gated community, if his wife had her way. And bored to tears.

This was an opportunity to see results while he was still actively involved in neurological research. If he got some, it was not impossible to imagine a Nobel Prize for Medicine somewhere down the line. And there was no downside as long as he kept the results to himself until human trials were okayed. The man was a murderous degenerate who was never going to wake up, anyway. If by some miracle he did, his consciousness would at best be of the shadowy sort experienced by patients with advanced Alzheimer's disease. Yet even that would be an amazing result.

You may be helping someone farther down the line, Mr Hartsfield, he told his comatose patient. Doing a spoonful of good instead of a shovelful of evil. And if you should suffer an adverse reaction? Perhaps go entirely flatline (not that you have far to go), or even die, rather than showing a bit of increased brain function?

No great loss. Not to you, and certainly not to your family, because you have none.

Nor to the world; the world would be delighted to see you go. He opened a file on his computer titled HARTSFIELD CEREBELLIN TRIALS. There were nine of these trials in all, spread over a fourteen-month period in 2010 and 2011. Babineau saw no change. He might as well have been giving his human guinea pig distilled water.

He gave up.

★   ★   ★

The human guinea pig in question spent fifteen months in the dark, an inchoate spirit who at some point in the sixteenth month remembered his name. He was Brady Wilson Hartsfield. There was nothing else at first. No past, no present, no *him* beyond the six syllables of his name. Then, not long before he would have given up and just floated away, another word came. The word was *control*. It had once meant something important, but he could not think what.

In his hospital room, lying in bed, his glycerin-moistened lips moved and he spoke the word aloud. He was alone; this was still three weeks before a nurse would observe Brady open his eyes and ask for his mother.

'Con . . . trol.'

And the lights came on. Just as they did in his *Star Trek*-style computer workroom when he voice-activated them from the top of the stairs leading down from the kitchen.

That's where he was: in his Elm Street basement, looking just as it had on the day he'd left it for the last time. There was another word that woke up another function, and now that he was here, he remembered that, as well. Because it was a good word.

'Chaos!'

In his mind, he boomed it out like Moses on Mount Sinai. In his hospital bed, it was a whispered croak. But it did the job, because his row of laptop computers came to life. On each screen was the number 20 . . . then 19 . . . then 18 . . .

What is this? What, in the name of God?

For a panicky moment he couldn't remember. All he knew was that if the countdown he saw marching across the seven screens reached zero, the computers would freeze. He would lose them, this room, and the little sliver of consciousness he had somehow managed. He

124

would be buried alive in the darkness of his own hea —

And that was the word! The very one!

'Darkness!'

He screamed it at the top of his lungs — at least inside. Outside it was that same whispered croak from long unused vocal cords. His pulse, respiration, and blood pressure had all begun to rise. Soon Head Nurse Becky Helmington would notice and come to check him, hurrying but not quite running.

In Brady's basement workroom, the count-down on the computers stopped at 14, and on each screen a picture appeared. Once upon a time, those computers (now stored in a cavernous police evidence room and labeled exhibits A through G) had booted up showing stills from a movie called *The Wild Bunch*. Now, however, they showed photographs from Brady's life.

On screen 1 was his brother Frankie, who choked on an apple, suffered his own brain damage, and later fell down the cellar stairs (helped along by his big brother's foot).

On screen 2 was Deborah herself. She was dressed in a clingy white robe that Brady remembered instantly. She called me her honeyboy, he thought, and when she kissed me her lips were always a little damp and I got a hard-on. When I was little, she called that a stiffy. Sometimes when I was in the tub she'd rub it with a warm wet washcloth and ask me if it felt good.

On screen 3 were Thing One and Thing Two,

inventions that had actually worked.

On screen 4 was Mrs Trelawney's gray Mercedes sedan, the hood dented and the grille dripping with blood.

On screen 5 was a wheelchair. For a moment the relevance wouldn't come, but then it clicked in. It was how he had gotten into the Mingo Auditorium on the night of the 'Round Here concert. Nobody worried about a poor old cripple in a wheelchair.

On screen 6 was a handsome, smiling young man. Brady couldn't recall his name, at least not yet, but he knew who the young man was: the old Det-Ret's nigger lawnboy.

And on screen 7 was Hodges himself, wearing a fedora cocked rakishly over one eye and smiling. Gotcha, Brady, that smile said. Whapped you with my whapper and there you lie, in a hospital bed, and when will you rise from it and walk? I'm betting never.

Fucking Hodges, who spoiled everything.

★ ★ ★

Those seven images were the armature around which Brady began to rebuild his identity. As he did so, the walls of his basement room — always his hideaway, his redoubt against a stupid and uncaring world — began to thin. He heard other voices coming through the walls and realized that some were nurses, some were doctors, and some — perhaps — were law enforcement types, checking up on him to make sure he wasn't faking. He both was and wasn't. The truth, like

126

that concerning Frankie's death, was complex.

At first he opened his eyes only when he was sure he was alone, and didn't open them often. There wasn't a lot in his room to look at. Sooner or later he would have to come awake all the way, but even when he did they must not know that he could think much, when in fact he was thinking more clearly every day. If they knew that, they would put him on trial.

Brady didn't want to be put on trial.

Not when he still might have things to do.

* * *

A week before Brady spoke to Nurse Norma Wilmer, he opened his eyes in the middle of the night and looked at the bottle of saline suspended from the IV stand beside his bed. Bored, he lifted his hand to push it, perhaps even knock it to the floor. He did not succeed in doing that, but it was swinging back and forth from its hook before he realized both of his hands were still lying on the counterpane, the fingers turned in slightly due to the muscle atrophy physical therapy could slow but not stop — not, at least, when the patient was sleeping the long sleep of low brainwaves.

Did I do that?

He reached out again, and his hands still did not move much (although the left, his dominant hand, trembled a bit), but he felt his palm touch the saline bottle and put it back in motion.

He thought, That's interesting, and fell asleep. It was the first honest sleep he'd had since

Hodges (or perhaps it had been his nigger lawnboy) put him in this goddam hospital bed.

★ ★ ★

On the following nights — late nights, when he could be sure no one might come in and see — Brady experimented with his phantom hand. Often as he did so he thought of a high school classmate named Henry 'Hook' Crosby, who had lost his right hand in a car accident. He had a prosthetic — obviously fake, so he wore it with a glove — but sometimes he wore a stainless steel hook to school, instead. Henry claimed it was easier to pick things up with the hook, and as a bonus, it grossed out girls when he snuck up behind them and caressed a calf or bare arm with it. He once told Brady that, although he'd lost the hand seven years ago, he sometimes felt it itching, or prickling, as if it had gone numb and was just waking up. He showed Brady his stump, smooth and pink. 'When it gets prickly like that, I'd swear I could scratch my head with it,' he said.

Brady now knew exactly how Hook Crosby felt . . . except he, Brady, *could* scratch his head with his phantom hand. He had tried it. He had also discovered that he could rattle the slats in the venetian blinds the nurses dropped over his window at night. That window was much too far away from his bed to reach, but with the phantom hand he could reach it, anyway. Someone had put a vase of fake flowers on the table next to his bed (he later discovered it was

128

Head Nurse Becky Helmington, the only one on staff to treat him with a degree of kindness), and he could slide it back and forth, easy as pie.

After a struggle — his memory was full of holes — he recalled the name for this sort of phenomenon: telekinesis. The ability to move objects by concentrating on them. Only any real concentration made his head ache fiercely, and his mind didn't seem to have much to do with it. It was his *hand*, his dominant left hand, even though the one lying splay-fingered on the bedspread never moved.

Pretty amazing. He was sure that Babineau, the doctor who came to see him most frequently (or had; lately he seemed to be losing interest), would be over the moon with excitement, but this was one talent Brady intended to keep to himself.

It might come in handy at some point, but he doubted it. Wiggling one's ears was also a talent, but not one that had any useful value. Yes, he could move the bottles on the IV stand, and rattle the blinds, and knock over a picture; he could send ripples through his blankets, as though a big fish were swimming beneath. Sometimes he did one of those things when a nurse was in the room, because their startled reactions were amusing. That, however, seemed to be the extent of this new ability. He had tried and failed to turn on the television suspended over his bed, had tried and failed to close the door to the en suite bathroom. He could grasp the chrome handle — he felt its cold hardness as his fingers closed around it — but the door was too heavy and his phantom hand was too weak. At least, so far. He had an idea that if he continued to exercise it, the hand might grow stronger.

I need to wake up, he thought, if only so I can get some aspirin for this endless fucking headache and actually eat some real food. Even a dish of hospital custard would be a treat. I'll do it soon. Maybe even tomorrow.

But he didn't. Because on the following day, he discovered that telekinesis wasn't the only new ability he'd brought back from wherever he'd been.

★ ★ ★

The nurse who came in most afternoons to check his vitals and most evenings to get him ready for the night (you couldn't say ready for bed when he was always *in* bed) was a young woman named Sadie MacDonald. She was dark-haired and pretty in a washed-out, no-makeup sort of way. Brady had observed her through half-closed eyes, as he observed all visitors to his room in the days since he had come through the wall from his basement workroom where he had first regained consciousness.

She seemed frightened of him, but he came to realize that didn't exactly make him special, because Nurse MacDonald was frightened of everyone. She was the kind of woman who scuttles rather than walks. If someone came into 217 while she was about her duties — Head

130

Nurse Becky Helmington, for instance — Sadie had a tendency to shrink into the background. And she was terrified of Dr Babineau. When she had to be in the room with him, Brady could almost taste her fear.

He came to realize that might not have been an exaggeration.

* * *

On the day after Brady fell asleep thinking of custard, Sadie MacDonald came into Room 217 at quarter past three, checked the monitor above the head of his bed, and wrote some numbers on the clipboard that hung at the foot. Next she'd check the bottles on the IV stand and go to the closet for fresh pillows. She would lift him with one hand — she was small, but her arms were strong — and replace his old pillows with the new ones. That might actually have been an orderly's job, but Brady had an idea that MacDonald was at the bottom of the hospital pecking order. Low nurse on the totem pole, so to speak.

He had decided he would open his eyes and speak to her just as she finished changing the pillows, when their faces were closest. It would scare her, and Brady liked to scare people. Much in his life had changed, but not that. Maybe she would even scream, as one nurse had when he made his coverlet do its rippling thing.

Only MacDonald diverted to the window on her way to the closet. There was nothing out there to see but the parking garage, yet she stood

131

there for a minute . . . then two . . . then three. Why? What was so fascinating about a brick fucking wall?

Only it wasn't *all* brick, Brady realized as he looked out with her. There were long open spaces on each level, and as the cars went up the ramp, the sun flashed briefly on their windshields.

Flash. And flash. And flash.

Jesus Christ, Brady thought. *I'm* the one who's supposed to be in a coma, aren't I? It's like she's having some kind of seiz —

But wait. Wait just a goddam minute.

Looking out *with* her? How can I be looking out with her when I'm lying here in bed?

There went a rusty pickup truck. Behind it came a Jaguar sedan, probably some rich doctor's car, and Brady realized he wasn't looking out *with* her, he was looking out *from* her. It was like watching the scenery from the passenger side while someone else drove the car.

And yes, Sadie MacDonald *was* having a seizure, one so mild she probably didn't even know it was happening. The lights had caused it. The lights on the windshields of the passing cars. As soon as there was a lull in the traffic on that ramp, or as soon as the angle of the sunlight changed a bit, she would come out of it and go about her duties. She would come out of it without even knowing she'd been in it.

Brady knew this.

He knew because he was inside her.

He went a little deeper and realized he could see her thoughts. It was amazing. He could

132

actually watch them flashing back and forth, hither and thither, high and low, sometimes crossing paths in a dark green medium that was — perhaps, he'd have to think about this, and very carefully to be sure — her core consciousness. Her basic Sadie-ness. He tried to go deeper, to identify some of the thoughtfish, although Christ, they went by so fast! Still . . .

Something about the muffins she had at home in her apartment.

Something about a cat she had seen in a pet shop window: black with a cunning white bib.

Something about . . . rocks? Was it rocks?

Something about her father, and that fish was red, the color of anger. Or shame. Or both.

As she turned from the window and headed for the closet, Brady felt a moment of tumbling vertigo. It passed, and he was back inside himself, looking out through his own eyes. She had ejected him without even knowing he was there.

When she lifted him to put two foam pillows with freshly laundered cases behind his head, Brady let his eyes remain in their fixed and half-lidded stare. He did not speak, after all.

He really did need to think about this.

★   ★   ★

During the next four days, Brady tried several times to get inside the heads of those who visited his room. He had a degree of success only once, with a young orderly who came in to mop the floor. The kid wasn't a Mongolian idiot (his

133

mother's term for those with Down syndrome), but he wasn't a Mensa candidate, either. He was looking down at the wet stripes his mop left on the linoleum, watching the brightness of each one fade, and that opened him up just enough. Brady's visit was brief and uninteresting. The kid was wondering if they would have tacos in the caff that evening — big deal.

Then the vertigo, the sense of tumbling. The kid had spit him out like a watermelon seed, never once slowing the pendulum swings of his mop.

With the others who poked into his room from time to time, he had no success at all, and this failure was a lot more frustrating than being unable to scratch his face when it itched. Brady had taken an inventory of himself, and what he had found was dismaying. His constantly aching head sat on top of a skeletal body. He could move, he wasn't paralyzed, but his muscles had atrophied and even sliding a leg two or three inches one way or another took a herculean effort. Being inside Nurse MacDonald, on the other hand, had been like riding on a magic carpet.

But he'd only gotten in because MacDonald had some form of epilepsy. Not much, just enough to briefly open a door. Others seemed to have natural defenses. He hadn't even managed to stay inside the orderly for more than a few seconds, and if *that* ass-munch had been a dwarf, he would have been named Dopey.

Which made him remember a joke. Stranger in New York City asks a beatnik, 'How do you get to Carnegie Hall?' Beatnik replies, 'Practice, man, practice.'

That's what I need to do, Brady thought. Practice and get stronger. Because Kermit William Hodges is out there someplace, and the old Det-Ret thinks he won. I can't allow that. I *won't* allow that.

And so on that rain-soaked evening in mid-November of 2011, Brady opened his eyes, said his head hurt, and asked for his mother. There was no scream. It was Sadie MacDonald's night off, and Norma Wilmer, the nurse on duty, was made of tougher stuff. Nevertheless, she gave a little cry of surprise, and ran to see if Dr Babineau was still in the doctors' lounge.

Brady thought, Now the rest of my life begins.

Brady thought, Practice, man, practice.

BLACKISH

1

Although Hodges has officially made Holly a full partner in Finders Keepers, and there's a spare office (small, but with a street view), she has elected to remain based in the reception area. She's seated there, peering at the screen of her computer, when Hodges comes in at quarter to eleven. And although she's quick to sweep something into the wide drawer above the kneehole of her desk, Hodges's olfactories are still in good working order (unlike some of his malfunctioning equipment further south), and he catches an unmistakable whiff of half-eaten Twinkie.

'What's the story, Hollyberry?'

'You picked that up from Jerome, and you know I hate it. Call me Hollyberry again and I'll go see my mother for a week. She keeps asking me to visit.'

As if, Hodges thinks. You can't stand her, and besides, you're on the scent, my dear. As hooked as a heroin addict.

'Sorry, sorry.' He looks over her shoulder and sees an article from *Bloomberg Business* dated April of 2014. The headline reads ZAPPIT ZAPPED. 'Yeah, the company screwed the pooch and stepped out the door. Thought I told you that yesterday.'

'You did. What's interesting, to me at least, is the inventory.'

'What do you mean?'

'Thousands of unsold Zappits, maybe tens of thousands. I wanted to know what happened to them.'

'And did you find out?'

'Not yet.'

'Maybe they got shipped to the poor children in China, along with all the vegetables I refused to eat as a child.'

'Starving children are not funny,' she says, looking severe.

'No, of course not.'

Hodges straightens up. He filled a prescription for painkillers on his way back from Stamos's office — heavy-duty, but not as heavy as the stuff he may be taking soon — and he feels almost okay. There's even a faint stirring of hunger in his belly, which is a welcome change. 'They were probably destroyed. That's what they do with unsold paperback books, I think.'

'That's a lot of inventory to destroy,' she says, 'considering the gadgets are loaded with games and still work. The top of the line, the Commanders, even came equipped with WiFi. Now tell me about your tests.'

Hodges manufactures a smile he hopes will look both modest and happy. 'Good news, actually. It's an ulcer, but just a little one. I'll have to take a bunch of pills and be careful about my diet. Dr Stamos says if I do that, it should heal on its own.'

She gives him a radiant smile that makes

Hodges feel good about this outrageous lie. Of course, it also makes him feel like dogshit on an old shoe.

'Thank God! You'll do what he says, won't you?'

'You bet.' More dogshit; all the bland food in the world won't cure what ails him. Hodges is not a giver-upper, and under other circumstances he would be in the office of gastroenterologist Henry Yip right now, no matter how bad the odds of beating pancreatic cancer. The message he received on the Blue Umbrella site has changed things, however.

'Well, that's fine. Because I don't know what I'd do without you, Bill. I just don't.'

'Holly — '

'Actually, I do. I'd go back home. And that would be bad for me.'

No shit, Hodges thinks. The first time I met you, in town for your aunt Elizabeth's funeral, your mom was practically leading you around like a mutt on a leash. Do this, Holly, do that, Holly, and for Christ's sake don't do anything embarrassing.

'Now tell me,' she says. 'Tell me the something new. Tell me tell me tell me!'

'Give me fifteen minutes, then I'll spill everything. In the meantime, see if you can find out what happened to all those Commander consoles. It's probably not important, but it might be.'

'Okay. Wonderful news about your tests, Bill.'

'Yeah.'

He goes into his office. Holly swivels her chair

to look after him for a moment, because he rarely closes the door when he's in there. Still, it's not unheard of. She returns to her computer.

2

'He's not done with you yet.'

Holly repeats it in a soft voice. She puts her half-eaten veggie burger down on its paper plate. Hodges has already demolished his, talking between bites. He doesn't mention waking with pain; in this version he discovered the message because he got up to net-surf when he couldn't sleep.

'That's what it said, all right.'

'From Z-Boy.'

'Yeah. Sounds like some superhero's sidekick, doesn't it? 'Follow the adventures of Z-Man and Z-Boy, as they keep the streets of Gotham City safe from crime!''

'That's Batman and Robin. They're the ones who patrol Gotham City.'

'I know that, I was reading Batman comics before you were born. I was just saying.'

She picks up her veggie burger, extracts a shred of lettuce, puts it down again. 'When is the last time you visited Brady Hartsfield?'

Right to the heart of the matter, Hodges thinks admiringly. That's my Holly.

'I went to see him just after the business with the Saubers family, and once more later on. Midsummer, that would have been. Then you and Jerome cornered me and said I had to stop. So I did.'

142

'We did it for your own good.'

'I know that, Holly. Now eat your sandwich.'

She takes a bite, dabs mayo from the corner of her mouth, and asks him how Hartsfield seemed on his last visit.

'The same . . . mostly. Just sitting there, looking out at the parking garage. I talk, I ask him questions, he says nothing. He gives Academy Award brain damage, no doubt about that. But there have been stories about him. That he has some kind of mind-power. That he can turn the water on and off in his bathroom, and does it sometimes to scare the staff. I'd call it bullshit, but when Becky Helmington was the head nurse, she said she'd actually seen stuff on a couple of occasions — rattling blinds, the TV going on by itself, the bottles on his IV stand swinging back and forth. And she's what I'd call a credible witness. I know it's hard to believe — '

'Not so hard. Telekinesis, sometimes called psychokinesis, is a documented phenomenon. You never saw anything like that yourself during any of your visits?'

'Well . . . ' He pauses, remembering. 'Something did happen on my second-to-last visit. There was a picture on the table beside his bed — him and his mother with their arms around each other and their cheeks pressed together. On vacation somewhere. There was a bigger version in the house on Elm Street. You probably remember it.'

'Of course I do. I remember everything we saw in that house, including some of the cheesecake photos of her he had on his computer.' She crosses her arms over her small bosom and makes a moue of distaste. 'That was a *very* unnatural relationship.'

'Tell me about it. I don't know if he ever actually had sex with her — '

'Oough!'

' — but I think he probably wanted to, and at the very least she enabled his fantasies. Anyway, I grabbed the picture and talked some smack about her, trying to get a rise out of him, trying to get him to respond. Because he's *in* there, Holly, and I mean all present and accounted for. I was sure of it then and I'm sure of it now. He just sits there, but inside he's the same human wasp that killed those people at City Center and tried to kill a whole lot more at Mingo Auditorium.'

'And he used Debbie's Blue Umbrella to talk with you, don't forget that.'

'After last night I'm not likely to.'

'Tell me the rest of what happened that time.'

'For just a second he stopped looking out his window at the parking garage across the way. His eyes . . . they rolled in their sockets, and he looked at me. Every hair on the nape of my neck stood up at attention, and the air felt . . . I don't know . . . *electric*.' He forces himself to say the rest. It's like pushing a big rock up a steep hill. 'I arrested some bad doers when I was on the cops, some *very* bad doers — one was a mother who killed her three-year-old for insurance that didn't amount to a hill of beans — but I never felt the presence of evil in any of them once they were caught. It's like evil's some kind of vulture that

144

flies away once these mokes are locked up. But I felt it that day, Holly. I really did. I felt it in Brady Hartsfield.'

'I believe you,' she says in a voice so small it's barely a whisper.

'And he had a Zappit. That's the connection I was trying to make. If it is a connection, and not just a coincidence. There was a guy, I don't know his last name, everyone just called him Library Al, who used to hand Zappits out along with Kindles and paperbacks when he made his rounds. I don't know if Al was an orderly or a volunteer. Hell, he might even have been one of the janitors, doing a little good deed on the side. I think the only reason I didn't pick up on that right away was the Zappit you found at the Ellerton house was pink. The one in Brady's room was blue.'

'How could what happened to Janice Ellerton and her daughter have anything to do with Brady Hartsfield? Unless . . . has anyone reported any telekinetic activity outside of his room? Have there been rumors of that?'

'Nope, but right around the time the Saubers business finished up, a nurse committed suicide in the Brain Injury Clinic. Sliced her wrists in a bathroom right down the hall from Hartsfield's room. Her name was Sadie MacDonald.'

'Are you thinking . . . '

She's picking at her sandwich again, shredding the lettuce and dropping it into her plate. Waiting for him.

'Go on, Holly. I'm not going to say it for you.'

'You're thinking Brady talked her into it

145

somehow? I don't see how that could be possible.'

'I don't, either, but we know Brady has a fascination with suicide.'

'This Sadie MacDonald . . . did she happen to have one of those Zappit things?'

'God knows.'

'How . . . how did . . . '

This time he does help. 'With a scalpel she filched from one of the surgical suites. I got that from the ME's assistant. Slipped her a gift card to DeMasio's, the Italian joint.'

Holly shreds more lettuce. Her plate is starting to look like confetti at a leprechaun birthday party. It's driving Hodges a little nuts, but he doesn't stop her. She's working her way up to saying it. And finally does. 'You're going to see Hartsfield.'

'Yeah, I am.'

'Do you really think you'll get anything out of him? You never have before.'

'I know a little more now.' But what, really, *does* he know? He's not even sure what he suspects. But maybe Hartsfield isn't a human wasp, after all. Maybe he's a spider, and Room 217 at the Bucket is the center of his web, where he sits spinning.

Or maybe it's all coincidence. Maybe the cancer is already eating into my brain, sparking a lot of paranoid ideas.

That's what Pete would think, and his partner — hard to stop thinking of her as Miss Pretty Gray Eyes, now that it's in his head — would say it right out loud.

146

He stands up. 'No time like the present.'

She drops her sandwich onto the pile of mangled lettuce so she can grasp his arm. 'Be careful.'

'I will.'

'Guard your thoughts. I know how crazy that sounds, but I *am* crazy, at least some of the time, so I can say it. If you should have any ideas about . . . well, harming yourself . . . call me. Call me *right away*.'

'Okay.'

She crosses her arms and grasps her shoulders — that old fretful gesture he sees less often now. 'I wish Jerome was here.' Jerome Robinson is in Arizona, taking a semester off from college, building houses as part of a Habitat for Humanity crew. Once, when Hodges used the phrase *garnishing his résumé* in relation to this activity, Holly scolded him, telling him Jerome was doing it because he was a good person. With that, Hodges has to agree — Jerome really is a good person.

'I'm going to be fine. And this is probably nothing. We're like kids worrying that the empty house on the corner is haunted. If we said anything about it to Pete, he'd have us both committed.'

Holly, who actually has been committed (twice), believes some empty houses really might be haunted. She removes one small and ringless hand from one shoulder long enough to grasp his arm again, this time by the sleeve of his overcoat. 'Call me when you get there, and call me again when you leave. Don't forget, because

147

I'll be worrying and I can't call you because — '

'No cell phones allowed in the Bucket, yeah, I know. I'll do it, Holly. In the meantime, I've got a couple of things for you.' He sees her hand dart toward a notepad and shakes his head. 'No, you don't need to write this down. It's simple. First, go on eBay or wherever you go to buy stuff that's no longer available retail and order one of those Zappit Commanders. Can you do that?'

'Easy. What's the other thing?'

'Sunrise Solutions bought out Zappit, then went bankrupt. Someone will be serving as the trustee in bankruptcy. The trustee hires lawyers, accountants, and liquidators to help squeeze every cent out of the company. Get a name and I'll make a call later today or tomorrow. I want to know what happened to all those unsold Zappit consoles, because somebody gave one to Janice Ellerton a long time after both companies were out of business.'

She lights up. 'That's fracking brilliant!'

Not brilliant, just police work, he thinks. I may have terminal cancer, but I still remember how the job is done, and that's something.

That's something good.

3

As he exits the Turner Building and heads for the bus stop (the Number 5 is a quicker and easier way to get across town than retrieving his Prius and driving himself), Hodges is a deeply pre occupied man. He is thinking about how he should approach Brady — how he can open him up. He was an ace in the interrogation room when he was on the job, so there has to be a way. Previously he has only gone to Brady to goad him and confirm his gut belief that Brady is faking his semi-catatonic state. Now he has some real questions, and there must be *some* way he can get Brady to answer them.

I have to poke the spider, he thinks.

Interfering with his efforts to plan the forthcoming confrontation are thoughts of the diagnosis he's just received, and the inevitable fears that go with it. For his life, yes. But there are also questions of how much he may suffer a bit further down the line, and how he will inform those who need to know. Corinne and Allie will be shaken up by the news but basically okay. The same goes for the Robinson family, although he knows Jerome and Barbara, his kid sister (not such a kid now; she'll turn sixteen in a few months) will take it hard. Mostly, though, it's Holly he worries about. She isn't crazy, despite what she said in the office, but she's fragile. Very. She's had two breakdowns in her past, one in high school and one in her early twenties. She's stronger now, but her main sources of support over these last few years have been him and the little company they run together. If they go, she'll be at risk. He can't afford to kid himself about that.

I won't let her break, Hodges thinks. He walks with his head down and his hands stuffed in his pockets, blowing out white vapor. I can't let that happen.

Deep in these thoughts, he misses the primer-spotted Chevy Malibu for the third time in two days. It's parked up the street, opposite the building where Holly is now hunting down the Sunrise Solutions bankruptcy trustee. Standing on the sidewalk next to it is an elderly man in an old Army surplus parka that has been mended with masking tape. He watches Hodges get on the bus, then takes a cell phone from his coat pocket and makes a call.

4

Holly watches her boss — who happens to be the person she loves most in the world — walk to the bus stop on the corner. He looks so *slight* now, almost a shadow of the burly man she first met six years ago. And he has his hand pressed to his side as he walks. He does that a lot lately, and she doesn't think he's even aware of it.

Nothing but a small ulcer, he said. She'd like to believe that — would like to believe *him* — but she's not sure she does.

The bus comes and Bill gets on. Holly stands by the window watching it go, gnawing at her fingernails, wishing for a cigarette. She has Nicorette gum, plenty of it, but sometimes only a cigarette will do.

Quit wasting time, she tells herself. If you really mean to be a rotten dirty sneak, there's no time like the present.

So she goes into his office.

His computer is dark, but he never turns it off

150

until he goes home at night; all she has to do is refresh the screen. Before she can, her eye is caught by the yellow legal pad beside the keyboard. He always has one handy, usually covered with notes and doodles. It's how he thinks.

Written at the top of this one is a line she knows well, one that has resonated with her ever since she first heard the song on the radio: *All the lonely people*. He has underlined it. Beneath are names she knows.

Olivia Trelawney (Widowed)
Martine Stover (Unmarried, housekeeper
    called her 'spinster')
Janice Ellerton (Widowed)
Nancy Alderson (Widowed)

And others. Her own, of course; she is also a spinster. Pete Huntley, who's divorced. And Hodges himself, also divorced.

Single people are twice as likely to commit suicide. Divorced people, four times as likely.

'Brady Hartsfield enjoyed suicide,' she murmurs. 'It was his hobby.'

Below the names, circled, is a jotted note she doesn't understand: *Visitors list? What visitors?*

She hits a random key and Bill's computer lights up, showing his desktop screen with all his files scattered helter-skelter across it. She has scolded him about this time and again, has told him it's like leaving the door of your house unlocked and your valuables all laid out on the dining room table with a sign on them saying

151

PLEASE STEAL ME, and he always says he will do better, and he never does. Not that it would have changed things in Holly's case, because she also has his password. He gave it to her himself. In case something ever happened to him, he said. Now she's afraid something has.

One look at the screen is enough to tell her the something is no ulcer. There's a new file folder there, one with a scary title. Holly clicks on it. The terrible gothic letters at the top are enough to confirm that the document is indeed the last will and testament of one Kermit William Hodges. She closes it at once. She has absolutely no desire to paw through his bequests. Knowing that such a document exists and that he has been reviewing it this very day is enough. Too much, actually.

She stands there clutching at her shoulders and nibbling her lips. The next step would be worse than snooping. It would be prying. It would be burglary.

You've come this far, so go ahead.

'Yes, I have to,' Holly whispers, and clicks on the postage stamp icon that opens his email, telling herself there will probably be nothing. Only there is. The most recent message likely came in while they were talking about what he found early this morning under Debbie's Blue Umbrella. It's from the doctor he went to see. Stamos, his name is. She opens the email and reads: *Here is a copy of your most recent test results, for your files.*

Holly uses the password in the email to open the attachment, sits in Bill's chair, and leans forward, her hands clenched tightly in her lap. By the time she scrolls down to the second of the eight pages, she is crying.

5

Hodges has no more than settled in his seat at the back of the Number 5 when glass breaks in his coat pocket and the boys cheer the home run that just broke Mrs O'Leary's living room window. A man in a business suit lowers his *Wall Street Journal* and looks disapprovingly at Hodges over the top of it.

'Sorry, sorry,' Hodges says. 'Keep meaning to change it.'

'You should make it a priority,' the business-man says, and raises his paper again.

The text is from his old partner. Again. Feeling a strong sense of *déjà vu*, Hodges calls him.

'Pete,' he says, 'what's with all the texts? It isn't as if you don't have my number on speed dial.'

'Figured Holly probably programmed your phone for you and put on some crazy ringtone,' Pete says. 'That'd be her idea of a real knee-slapper. Also figured you'd have it turned up to max volume, you deaf sonofabitch.'

'The text alert's the one on max,' Hodges says. 'When I get a call, the phone just has a mini-orgasm against my leg.'

'Change the alert, then.'

Hours ago he found out he has only months to

live. Now he's discussing the volume of his cell phone.

'I'll absolutely do that. Now tell me why you called.'

'Got a guy in computer forensics who landed on that game gadget like a fly on shit. He loved it, called it retro. Can you believe that? Gadget was probably manufactured all of five years ago and now it's retro.'

'The world is speeding up.'

'It's sure doing something. Anyway, the Zappit is zapped. When our guy plugged in fresh batteries, it popped half a dozen bright blue flashes, then died.'

'What's wrong with it?'

'Some kind of virus is technically possible, the thing supposedly has WiFi and that's mostly how those bugs get downloaded, but he says it's more likely a bad chip or a fried circuit. The point is, it means nothing. Ellerton couldn't have used it.'

'Then why did she keep the charger cord for it plugged in right there in her daughter's bathroom?'

That silences Pete for a moment. Then he says, 'Okay, so maybe it worked for awhile and then the chip died. Or whatever they do.'

It worked, all right, Hodges thinks. She played solitaire on it at the kitchen table. Lots of different kinds, like Klondike and Pyramid and Picture. Which you would know, Peter my dear, if you'd talked to Nancy Alderson. That must still be on your bucket list.

'All right,' Hodges says. 'Thanks for the update.'

'It's your *final* update, Kermit. I have a partner I've worked with quite successfully since you pulled the pin, and I'd like her to be at my retirement party instead of sitting at her desk and sulking over how I preferred you to her right to the bitter end.'

Hodges could pursue this, but the hospital is only two stops away now. Also, he discovers, he wants to separate himself from Pete and Izzy and go his own way on this thing. Pete plods, and Izzy actually drags her feet. Hodges wants to run with it, bad pancreas and all.

'I hear you,' he says. 'Again, thanks.'

'Case closed?'

'Finito.'

His eyes flick up and to the left.

6

Nineteen blocks from where Hodges is returning his iPhone to his overcoat pocket, there is another world. Not a very nice one. Jerome Robinson's sister is there, and she is in trouble.

Pretty and demure in her Chapel Ridge school uniform (gray wool coat, gray skirt, white kneesocks, red scarf wrapped around her neck), Barbara walks down Martin Luther King Avenue with a yellow Zappit Commander in her gloved hands. On it the Fishin' Hole fish dart and swim, although they are almost invisible in the cold bright light of midday.

MLK is one of two main thoroughfares in the part of the city known as Lowtown, and although the population is predominantly black and Barbara is herself black (make that café au lait), she has never been here before, and that single fact makes her feel stupid and worthless. These are her people, their collective ancestors might have toted barges and lifted bales on the same plantation back in the day, for all she knows, and yet she has never been here *one single time*. She has been warned away not only by her parents but by her brother.

'Lowtown's where they drink the beer and then eat the bottle it came in,' he told her once. 'No place for a girl like you.'

A girl like me, she thinks. A nice upper-middle-class girl like me, who goes to a nice private school and has nice white girlfriends and plenty of nice preppy clothes and an allowance. Why, I even have a bank card! I can withdraw sixty dollars from an ATM any time I want! Amazeballs!

She walks like a girl in a dream, and it's a little *like* a dream because it's all so strange and it's less than two miles from home, which happens to be a cozy Cape Cod with an attached two-car garage, mortgage all paid off. She walks past check cashing joints and pawnshops filled with guitars and radios and gleaming pearl-handled straight razors. She walks past bars that smell of beer even with the doors closed against the January cold. She walks past hole-in-the-wall restaurants that smell of grease. Some sell pizza by the slice, some sell Chinese. In the window of one is a propped sign reading HUSH PUPPYS AND COLLARD GREENS LIKE YOUR

MOMMA USED TO MAKE.

Not *my* momma, Barbara thinks. I don't even know what a collard green is. Spinach? Cabbage?

On the corners — *every* corner, it seems — boys in long shorts and loose jeans are hanging out, sometimes standing close to rusty fire barrels to keep warm, sometimes playing hacky sack, sometimes just jiving in their gigantic sneakers, their jackets hung open in spite of the cold. They shout Yo to their homies and hail passing cars and when one stops they hand small glassine envelopes through the open window. She walks block after block of MLK (nine, ten, maybe a dozen, she's lost count) and each corner is like a drive-thru for drugs instead of for hamburgers or tacos.

She passes shivering women dressed in hot-pants, short fake fur jackets, and shiny boots; on their heads they wear amazing wigs of many colors. She passes empty buildings with boarded-up windows. She passes a car that has been stripped to the axles and covered with gang tags. She passes a woman with a dirty bandage over one eye. The woman is dragging a screeching toddler by the arm. She passes a man sitting on a blanket who drinks from a bottle of wine and wiggles his gray tongue at her. It's poor and it's desperate and it's been *right here all along* and she never did anything about it. Never *did* anything? Never even *thought* about it. What she did was her homework. What she did was talk on the phone and text with her BFFs at night. What she did was update her Facebook status and worry about her complexion. She is your basic teen parasite, dining in nice restaurants with her mother and father while her brothers and sisters, *right here all along, less than two miles from her nice suburban home*, drink wine and take drugs to blot out their terrible lives. She is ashamed of her hair, hanging smoothly to her shoulders. She is ashamed of her clean white kneesocks. She is ashamed of her skin color because it's the same as theirs.

'Hey, blackish!' It's a yell from the other side of the street. 'What you doin down here? You got no bi'ness down here!'

Blackish.

It's the name of a TV show, they watch it at home and laugh, but it's also what she is. Not black but blackish. Living a white life in a white neighborhood. She can do that because her parents make lots of money and own a home on a block where people are so screamingly non-prejudiced that they cringe if they hear one of their kids call another one dumbhead. She can live that wonderful white life because she is a threat to no one, she no rock-a da boat. She just goes her way, chattering with her friends about boys and music and boys and clothes and boys and the TV programs they all like and which girl they saw walking with which boy at the Birch Hill Mall.

She is blackish, a word that means the same as useless, and she doesn't deserve to live.

'Maybe you should just end it. Let that be your statement.'

The idea is a voice, and it comes to her with a kind of revelatory logic. Emily Dickinson said her poem was her letter to the world that never wrote to her, they read that in school, but Barbara herself has never written a letter at all. Plenty of stupid essays and book reports and emails, but nothing that really matters.

'Maybe it's time that you did.'

Not her voice, but the voice of a friend.

She stops outside a shop where fortunes are read and the Tarot is told. In its dirty window she thinks she sees the reflection of someone standing beside her, a white man with a smiling, boyish face and a tumble of blond hair on his forehead. She glances around, but there's no one there. It was just her imagination. She looks back down at the screen of the game console. In the shade of the fortune-telling shop's awning, the swimming fish are bright and clear again. Back and forth they go, every now and then obliterated by a bright blue flash. Barbara looks back the way she came and sees a gleaming black truck rolling toward her along the boulevard, moving fast and weaving from lane to lane. It's the kind with oversized tires, the kind the boys at school call a Bigfoot or a Gangsta Large.

'If you're going to do it, you better get to it.'

It's as if someone really is standing beside her. Someone who understands. And the voice is right. Barbara has never considered suicide before, but at this moment the idea seems perfectly rational.

'You don't even need to leave a note,' her friend says. She can see his reflection in the window again. Ghostly. 'The fact that you did it down here will be your letter to the world.'

159

True.

'You know too much about yourself now to go on living,' her friend points out as she returns her gaze to the swimming fish. 'You know too much, and all of it is bad.' Then it hastens to add, 'Which isn't to say you're a horrible person.' She thinks, No, not horrible, just useless.

Blackish.

The truck is coming. The Gangsta Large. As Jerome Robinson's sister steps toward the curb, ready to meet it, her face lights in an eager smile.

7

Dr Felix Babineau is wearing a thousand-dollar suit beneath the white coat that goes flying out behind him as he strides down the hallway of the Bucket, but he now needs a shave worse than ever and his usually elegant white hair is in disarray. He ignores a cluster of nurses who are standing by the duty desk and talking in low, agitated tones.

Nurse Wilmer approaches him. 'Dr Babineau, have you heard — '

He doesn't even look at her, and Norma has to sidestep quickly to keep from being bowled over. She looks after him in surprise.

Babineau takes the red DO NOT DISTURB card he always keeps in the pocket of his exam coat, hangs it on the doorknob of Room 217, and goes in. Brady Hartsfield does not look up. All of his attention is fixed on the game console in his lap, where the fish swim back and forth. There is no music; he has muted the sound.

Often when he enters this room, Felix Babineau disappears and Dr Z takes his place. Not today. Dr Z is just another version of Brady, after all — a projection — and today Brady is too busy to project.

His memories of trying to blow up the Mingo Auditorium during the 'Round Here concert are still jumbled, but one thing has been clear since he woke up: the face of the last person he saw before the lights went out. It was Barbara Robinson, the sister of Hodges's nigger lawnboy. She was sitting almost directly across the aisle from Brady. Now she's here, swimming with the fish they share on their two screens. Brady got Scapelli, the sadistic cunt who twisted his nipple. Now he will take care of the Robinson bitch. Her death will hurt her big brother, but that's not the most important thing. It will put a dagger in the old detective's heart. That's the most important thing.

The most delicious thing.

He comforts her, tells her she's not a horrible person. It helps to get her moving. Something is coming down MLK, he can't be sure what it is because a down-deep part of her is still fighting him, but it's big. Big enough to do the job.

'Brady, listen to me. Z-Boy called.' Z-Boy's actual name is Brooks, but Brady refuses to call him that anymore. 'He's been watching, as you instructed. That cop . . . ex-cop, whatever he is — '

'Shut up.' Not raising his head, his hair

161

tumbled across his brow. In the strong sunlight he looks closer to twenty than thirty.

Babineau, who is used to being heard and who still has not entirely grasped his new subordinate status, pays no attention. 'Hodges was on Hilltop Court yesterday, first at the Ellerton house and then snooping around the one across the street where — '

'*I said shut up!*'

'Brooks saw him get on a Number 5 bus, which means he's probably coming here! And if he's coming here, he *knows*!'

Brady looks at him for just a moment, his eyes blazing, then returns his attention to the screen. If he slips now, allows this educated idiot to divert his concentration —

But he won't allow it. He wants to hurt Hodges, he wants to hurt the nigger lawnboy, he owes them, and this is the way to do it. Nor is it just a matter of revenge. She's the first test subject who was at the concert, and she's not like the others, who were easier to control. But he *is* controlling her, all he needs is ten more seconds, and now he sees what's coming for her. It's a truck. A big black one.

Hey, honey, Brady Hartsfield thinks. Your ride is here.

8

Barbara stands on the curb, watching the truck approach, timing it, but just as she flexes her knees, hands grab her from behind.

162

'Hey, girl, what's up?'

She struggles, but the grip on her shoulders is strong and the truck passes by in a blare of Ghostface Killah. She whirls around, pulling free, and faces a skinny boy about her own age, wearing a Todhunter High letter jacket. He's tall, maybe six and a half feet, so she has to look up. He has a tight cap of brown curls and a goatee. Around his neck is a thin gold chain. He's smiling. His eyes are green and full of fun.

'You good-lookin, that's a fact as well as a compliment, but not from around here, correct? Not dressed like that, and hey, didn't your mom ever tell you not to jaywalk the block?'

'Leave me alone!' She's not scared; she's furious.

He laughs. 'And tough! I like a tough girl. Want a slice and a Coke?'

'I don't want anything from you!'

Her friend has left, probably disgusted with her. It's not my fault, she thinks. It's this boy's fault. This *lout*.

Lout! A blackish word if ever there was one. She feels her face heat up and drops her gaze to the fish on the Zappit screen. They will comfort her, they always do. To think she almost threw the game console away after that man gave it to her! Before she found the fish! The fish always take her away, and sometimes they bring her friend. But she only gets a momentary look before the console vanishes. Poof! Gone! The lout has got it in his long-fingered hands and is staring down at the screen, fascinated.

'Whoa, this is old-school!'

'It's mine!' Barbara shouts. 'Give it back!'

Across the street a woman laughs and yells in a whiskey voice, 'Tell im, sister! Bring down that high neck!'

Barbara grabs for the Zappit. Tall Boy holds it over his head, smiling at her.

'Give it back, I said! Stop being a prick!'

More people are watching now, and Tall Boy plays to the audience. He jinks left, then stutter-steps to the right, probably a move he uses all the time on the basketball court, never losing that indulgent smile. His green eyes sparkle and dance. Every girl at Todhunter is probably in love with those eyes, and Barbara is no longer thinking about suicide, or being blackish, or what a socially unconscious bag of waste she is. Right now she's only mad, and him being cute makes her madder. She plays varsity soccer at Chapel Ridge and now she hoicks her best penalty kick into Tall Boy's shin.

He yells in pain (but it's somehow *amused* pain, which infuriates her even more, because that was a really hard kick), and bends over to grab his ouchy. It brings him down to her level, and Barbara snatches the precious rectangle of yellow plastic. She wheels, skirt flaring, and runs into the street.

'*Honey look out!*' the whiskey-voiced woman screams.

Barbara hears a shriek of brakes and smells hot rubber. She looks to her left and sees a panel truck bearing down on her, the front end heeling to the left as the driver stamps on the brake. Behind the dirty windshield, his face is all dismayed eyes and open mouth. She throws up her hands, dropping the Zappit. All at once the last thing in the world Barbara Robinson wants is to die, but here she is, in the street after all, and it's too late.

She thinks, My ride is here.

9

Brady shuts down the Zappit and looks up at Babineau with a wide smile. 'Got her,' he says. His words are clear, not the slightest bit mushy. 'Let's see how Hodges and the Harvard jungle bunny like that.'

Babineau has a good idea who *she* is, and he supposes he should care, but he doesn't. What he cares about is his own skin. How did he ever allow Brady to pull him into this? When did he stop having a choice?

'It's Hodges I'm here about. I'm quite sure he's on his way right now. To see you.'

'Hodges has been here many times,' Brady says, although it's true the old Det-Ret hasn't been around for awhile. 'He never gets past the catatonic act.'

'He's started putting things together. He's not stupid, you said as much yourself. Did he know Z-Boy when he was just Brooks? He must have seen him around here when he came to visit you.'

'No idea.' Brady is wrung out, sated. What he really wants now is to savor the death of the Robinson girl, then take a nap. There is a lot to

165

be done, great things are afoot, but at the moment he needs rest.

'He can't see you like this,' Babineau says. 'Your skin is flushed and you're covered with sweat. You look like someone who just ran the City Marathon.'

'Then keep him out. You can do that. You're the doctor and he's just another half-bald buzzard on Social Security. These days he doesn't even have the legal authority to ticket a car at an expired parking meter.' Brady's wondering how the nigger lawnboy will take the news. *Jerome*. Will he cry? Will he sink to his knees? Will he rend his garments and beat his breast?

Will he blame Hodges? Unlikely, but that would be best. That would be wonderful.

'All right,' Babineau says. 'Yes, you're right, I can do that.' He's talking to himself as much as to the man who was supposed to be his guinea pig. That turned out to be quite the joke, didn't it? 'For now, at least. But he must still have friends on the police, you know. Probably lots of them.'

'I'm not afraid of them, and I'm not afraid of him. I just don't want to see him. At least, not now.' Brady smiles. 'After he finds out about the girl. *Then* I'll want to see him. Now get out of here.'

Babineau, who is at last beginning to understand who is the boss, leaves Brady's room. As always, it's a relief to do that as himself. Because every time he comes back to Babineau after being Dr Z, there's a little less Babineau to come back to.

10

Tanya Robinson calls her daughter's cell for the fourth time in the last twenty minutes and for the fourth time gets nothing but Barbara's chirpy voicemail.

'Disregard my other messages,' Tanya says after the beep. 'I'm still mad, but mostly what I am right now is worried sick. Call me. I need to know you're okay.'

She drops her phone on her desk and begins pacing the small confines of her office. She debates calling her husband and decides not to. Not yet. He's apt to go nuclear at the thought of Barbara skipping school, and he'll assume that's what she's doing. Tanya at first made that assumption herself when Mrs Rossi, the Chapel Ridge attendance officer, called to ask if Barbara was home sick. Barbara has never played hooky before, but there's always a first time for bad behavior, especially with teenagers. Only she never would have skipped alone, and after further consultation with Mrs Rossi, Tanya has confirmed that all of Barb's close friends are in school today.

Since then her mind has turned to darker thoughts, and one image keeps haunting her: the sign over the Crosstown Expressway the police use for Amber Alerts. She keeps seeing BARBARA ROBINSON on that sign, flashing on and off like some hellish movie marquee.

Her phone chimes the first few notes of 'Ode to Joy' and she races to it, thinking Thank God, oh thank God, I'll ground her for the rest of the win —

Only it's not her daughter's smiling face in the window. It's an ID: CITY POLICE DEPT. MAIN BRANCH. Terror rolls through her stomach and her bowels loosen. For a moment she can't even take the call, because her thumb won't move. At last she manages to press the green ACCEPT button and silence the music. Everything in her office, especially the family photo on her desk, is too bright. The phone seems to float up to her ear.

'Hello?'

She listens.

'Yes, this is she.'

She listens, her free hand rising to cover her mouth and stifle whatever sound wants to come out. She hears herself ask, 'Are you sure it's my daughter? Barbara Rosellen Robinson?'

The policeman who has called to notify her says yes. He's sure. They found her ID in the street. What he doesn't tell her is that they had to wipe off the blood to see the name.

11

Hodges knows something's amiss as soon as he steps out of the skyway that connects Kiner Memorial proper to the Lakes Region Traumatic Brain Injury Clinic, where the walls are painted a soothing pink and soft music plays day and night. The usual patterns have been disrupted, and very little work seems to be getting done. Lunch carts stand marooned, filled with congealing plates of noodly stuff that might once have been the cafeteria's idea of Chinese. Nurses cluster, murmuring in low tones. One appears to be crying. Two interns have their heads together by the water fountain. An orderly is talking on his cell phone, which is technically cause for suspension, but Hodges thinks he's safe enough; no one is paying him any mind.

At least Ruth Scapelli is nowhere in sight, which might improve his chances of getting in to see Hartsfield. It's Norma Wilmer at the duty desk, and along with Becky Helmington, Norma was his source for all things Brady before Hodges quit visiting Room 217. The bad news is that Hartsfield's doctor is also at the duty desk. Hodges has never been able to establish a rapport with him, although God knows he's tried.

He ambles down to the water fountain, hoping Babineau hasn't spotted him and will soon be off to look at PET scans or something, leaving Wilmer alone and approachable. He gets a drink (wincing and placing a hand to his side as he straightens up), then speaks to the interns. 'Is something going on here? The place seems a little riled up.'

They hesitate and glance at each other.

'Can't talk about it,' says Intern One. He still has the remains of his adolescent acne, and looks about seventeen. Hodges shudders at the thought of him assisting in a surgery job more difficult than removing a thumb splinter.

'Something with a patient? Hartsfield, maybe? I only ask because I used to be a cop, and I'm sort of responsible for putting him here.'

169

'Hodges,' says Intern Two. 'Is that your name?'

'Yeah, that's me.'

'You caught him, right?'

Hodges agrees instantly, although if it had been left up to him, Brady would have bagged a lot more in Mingo Auditorium than he managed to get at City Center. No, it was Holly and Jerome Robinson who stopped Brady before he could detonate his devil's load of homemade plastic explosive.

The interns exchange another glance and then One says, 'Hartsfield's the same as ever, just gorking along. It's Nurse Ratched.'

Intern Two gives him an elbow. 'Speak no ill of the dead, asshole. Especially when the guy listening might have loose lips.'

Hodges immediately runs a thumbnail across his mouth, as if sealing his dangerous lips shut.

Intern One looks flustered. 'Head Nurse Scapelli, I mean. She committed suicide last night.'

All the lights in Hodges's head come on, and for the first time since yesterday he forgets that he's probably going to die. 'Are you sure?'

'Sliced her arms and wrists and bled out,' says Two. 'That's what I'm hearing, anyway.'

'Did she leave a note?'

They have no idea.

Hodges heads for the duty desk. Babineau is still there, going over files with Wilmer (who looks flustered at her apparent battlefield promotion), but he can't wait. This is Hartsfield's dirt. He doesn't know how that can be, but it has Brady written all over it. The fucking suicide prince.

He almost calls Nurse Wilmer by her first

170

name, but instinct makes him shy from that at the last moment. 'Nurse Wilmer, I'm Bill Hodges.' A thing she knows very well. 'I worked both the City Center case and the Mingo Auditorium thing. I need to see Mr Hartsfield.'

She opens her mouth, but Babineau is there ahead of her. 'Out of the question. Even if Mr Hartsfield were allowed visitors, which he is not by order of the District Attorney's office, he wouldn't be allowed to see you. He needs peace and calm. Each of your previous unauthorized visits has shattered that.'

'News to me,' Hodges says mildly. 'Every time I've been to see him, he just sits there. Bland as a bowl of oatmeal.'

Norma Wilmer's head goes back and forth. She's like a woman watching a tennis match.

'You don't see what we see after you've left.' Color is rising in Babineau's stubble-flecked cheeks. And there are dark circles under his eyes. Hodges remembers a cartoon from his Sunday school *Living with Jesus* workbook, back in the prehistoric era when cars had fins and girls wore bobby sox. Brady's doc has the same look as the guy in the cartoon, but Hodges doubts if he's a chronic masturbator. On the other hand, he remembers Becky telling him that the neuro doctors are often crazier than the patients.

'And what would that be?' Hodges asks. 'Little psychic tantrums? Do things have a way of falling over after I'm gone? The toilet in his bathroom flushes by itself, maybe?'

'Ridiculous. What you leave is psychic *wreck-age*, Mr Hodges. He's not so brain damaged that

171

he doesn't know you're obsessed with him. Malevolently so. I want you to leave. We've had a tragedy, and many of the patients are upset.'

Hodges sees Wilmer's eyes widen slightly at this, and knows that the patients capable of cognition — many here in the Bucket are not — have no idea that the Head Nurse has offed herself.

'I only have a few questions for him, and then I'll be out of your hair.'

Babineau leans forward. The eyes behind his gold-rimmed glasses are threaded with snaps of red. 'Listen closely, Mr Hodges. One, Mr Hartsfield is not capable of answering your questions. If he could answer questions, he would have been brought to trial for his crimes by now. Two, you have no official standing. Three, if you don't leave now, I will call security and have you escorted from the premises.'

Hodges says, 'Pardon me for asking, but are you all right?'

Babineau draws back as if Hodges has brandished a fist in his face. '*Get out!*'

The little clusters of medical personnel stop talking and look around.

'Gotcha,' Hodges says. 'Going. All good.'

There's a snack alcove near the entrance to the skyway. Intern Two is leaning there, hands in pockets. 'Ooh, baby,' he says. 'You been schooled.'

'So it would seem.' Hodges studies the wares in the Nibble-A-Bit machine. He sees nothing in there that won't set his guts on fire, but that's okay; he's not hungry.

'Young man,' he says, without turning around, 'if you would like to make fifty dollars for doing

172

a simple errand that will cause you no trouble, then get with me.'

Intern Two, a fellow who looks like he might actually attain adulthood at some point in the not-too-distant future, joins him at the Nibble-A-Bit. 'What's the errand?'

Hodges keeps his pad in his back pocket, just as he did when he was a Detective First Class. He scribbles two words — *Call me* — and adds his cell number. 'Give this to Norma Wilmer once Smaug spreads his wings and flies away.'

Intern Two takes the note and folds it into the breast pocket of his scrubs. Then he looks expectant. Hodges takes out his wallet. Fifty is a lot for delivering a note, but he has discovered at least one good thing about terminal cancer: you can toss your budget out the window.

12

Jerome Robinson is balancing boards on his shoulder under the hot Arizona sun when his cell phone rings. The houses they are building — the first two already framed — are in a low-income but respectable neighborhood on the southern outskirts of Phoenix. He puts the boards across the top of a handy wheelbarrow and plucks his phone from his belt, thinking it will be Hector Alonzo, the job foreman. This morning one of the workmen (a workwoman, actually) tripped and fell into a stack of rebar. She broke her collarbone and suffered an ugly facial laceration. Alonzo took her to the St Luke's ER, appointing

173

Jerome temporary foreman in his absence.

It's not Alonzo's name he sees in the little window, but Holly Gibney's face. It's a photo he took himself, catching her in one of her rare smiles.

'Hey, Holly, how are you? I'll have to call you back in a few, it's been a crazy morning here, but — '

'I need you to come home,' Holly says. She sounds calm, but Jerome knows her of old, and in just those six words he can sense strong emotions held in check. Fear chief among them. Holly is still a very fearful person. Jerome's mother, who loves her dearly, once called fear Holly's default setting.

'Home? Why? What's wrong?' His own fear suddenly grips him. 'Is it my dad? Mom? Is it Barbie?'

'It's Bill,' she says. 'He has cancer. A very bad cancer. Pancreatic. If he doesn't get treatment he'll die, he'll probably die *anyway*, but he could have time and he told me it was just a little ulcer because . . . because . . . ' She takes a great ragged breath that makes Jerome wince. '*Because of Brady Fracking Hartsfield!*'

Jerome has no idea what connection Brady Hartsfield can have to Bill's terrible diagnosis, but he knows what he's seeing right now: trouble. On the far side of the building site, two hard-hatted young men — Habitat for Humanity college volunteers like Jerome himself — are giving a beeping, backing cement truck conflicting directions. Disaster looms.

'Holly, give me five minutes and I'll call you back.'

'But you'll come, won't you? Say you'll come. Because I don't think I can talk to him about this on my own and *he has to get into treatment right away!*'

'Five minutes,' he says, and kills the call. His thoughts are spinning so fast that he's afraid the friction will catch his brains on fire, and the blaring sun isn't helping. Bill? With cancer? On one hand it doesn't seem possible, but on the other it seems *completely* possible. He was in top form during the Pete Saubers business, where Jerome and Holly partnered with him, but he'll be seventy soon, and the last time Jerome saw him, before leaving for Arizona in October, Bill didn't look all that well. Too thin. Too pale. But Jerome can't go anywhere until Hector gets back, it would be like leaving the inmates to run the asylum. And knowing the Phoenix hospitals, where the ERs are overrun twenty-four hours a day, he may be stuck here until quitting time.

He sprints for the cement truck, bawling '*Hold up! Hold UP, for Jesus' sake!*' at the top of his lungs.

He gets the clueless volunteers to halt the cement truck they've been misdirecting less than three feet from a freshly dug drainage ditch, and he's bending over to catch his breath when his phone rings again.

Holly, I love you, Jerome thinks, pulling it from his belt once more, but sometimes you drive me absolutely bugfuck.

Only this time it's not Holly's picture he sees. It's his mother's.

Tanya is crying. 'You have to come home,' she

175

says, and Jerome has just long enough to think of something his grandfather used to say: *bad luck keeps bad company*.

It's Barbie after all.

13

Hodges is in the lobby and headed for the door when his phone vibrates. It's Norma Wilmer.

'Is he gone?' Hodges asks.

Norma doesn't have to ask who he's talking about. 'Yes. Now that he's seen his prize patient, he can relax and do the rest of his rounds.'

'I was sorry to hear about Nurse Scapelli.' It's true. He didn't care for her, but it's still true.

'I was, too. She ran the nursing staff like Captain Bligh ran the *Bounty*, but I hate to think of anyone doing . . . that. You get the news and your first reaction is oh no, not her, never. It's the shock of it. Your second reaction is oh yes, that makes perfect sense. Never married, no close friends — not that I knew of, anyway — nothing but the job. Where everybody sort of loathed her.'

'All the lonely people,' Hodges says, stepping out into the cold and turning toward the bus stop. He buttons his coat one-handed and then begins to massage his side.

'Yes. There are a lot of them. What can I do for you, Mr Hodges?'

'I have a few questions. Could you meet me for a drink?'

There's a long pause. Hodges thinks she's

going to tell him no. Then she says, 'I don't suppose your questions could lead to trouble for Dr Babineau?'

'Anything is possible, Norma.'

'That would be nice, but I guess I owe you one, regardless. For not letting on to him that we know each other from back in the Becky Helmington days. There's a watering hole on Revere Avenue. Got a clever name, Bar Bar Black Sheep, and most of the staff drinks closer to the hospital. Can you find it?'

'Yeah.'

'I'm off at five. Meet me there at five thirty. I like a nice cold vodka martini.'

'It'll be waiting.'

'Just don't expect me to get you in to see Hartsfield. It would mean my job. Babineau was always intense, but these days he's downright weird. I tried to tell him about Ruth, and he blew right past me. Not that he's apt to care when he finds out.'

'Got a lot of love for him, don't you?'

She laughs. 'For that you owe me two drinks.'

'Two it is.'

He's slipping his phone back into his coat pocket when it buzzes again. He sees the call is from Tanya Robinson and his thoughts immediately flash to Jerome, building houses out there in Arizona. A lot of things can go wrong on building sites.

He takes the call. Tanya is crying, at first too hard for him to understand what she's saying, only that Jim is in Pittsburgh and she doesn't want to call him until she knows more. Hodges

177

stands at the curb, one palm plastered against his non-phone ear to muffle the sound of traffic.

'Slow down. Tanya, slow down. Is it Jerome? Did something happen to Jerome?'

'No, Jerome's fine. Him I *did* call. It's *Barbara*. She was in Lowtown — '

'What in God's name was she doing in Lowtown, and on a school day?'

'I don't know! All I know is that some boy pushed her into the street and a truck hit her! They're taking her to Kiner Memorial. I'm on my way there now!'

'Are you driving?'

'Yes, what does that have to do with — '

'Get off the phone, Tanya. And slow down. I'm at Kiner now. I'll meet you in the ER.'

He hangs up and heads back to the hospital, breaking into a clumsy trot. He thinks, This goddam place is like the Mafia. Every time I think I'm out, it pulls me back in.

14

An ambulance with its lights flashing is just backing into one of the ER bays. Hodges goes to meet it, pulling out the police ID he still keeps in his wallet. When the paramedic and the EMT pull the stretcher out of the back, he flashes the ID with his thumb placed over the red RETIRED stamp. Technically speaking this is a felony crime — impersonating an officer — and consequently it's a fiddle he uses sparingly, but this time it seems absolutely appropriate.

178

Barbara is medicated but conscious. When she sees Hodges, she grasps his hand tightly. 'Bill? How did you get here so fast? Did Mom call you?'

'Yeah. How are you?'

'I'm okay. They gave me something for the pain. I have . . . they say I have a broken leg. I'm going to miss the basketball season and I guess it doesn't matter because Mom will ground me until I'm, like, twenty-five.' Tears begin to leak from her eyes.

He doesn't have long with her, so questions about what she was doing on MLK Ave, where there are sometimes as many as four drive-by shootings a week, will have to wait. There's something more important.

'Barb, do you know the name of the boy who pushed you in front of the truck?'

Her eyes widen.

'Or get a good look at him? Could you describe him?'

'Pushed . . . ? Oh, no, Bill! No, that's wrong!'

'Officer, we gotta go,' the paramedic says. 'You can question her later.'

'Wait!' Barbara shouts, and tries to sit up. The EMT pushes her gently back down, and she's grimacing with pain, but Hodges is heartened by that shout. It was good and strong.

'What is it, Barb?'

'He only pushed me *after* I ran into the street! He pushed me out of the way! I think he might have saved my life, and I'm glad.' She's crying hard now, but Hodges doesn't believe for a minute it's because of her broken leg. 'I don't

179

want to die, after all. I don't know what was *wrong* with me!'

'We really have to get her in an exam room, Chief,' the paramedic says. 'She needs an X-ray.'

'Don't let them do anything to that boy!' Barbara calls as the ambo guys roll her through the double doors. 'He's tall! He's got green eyes and a goatee! He goes to Todhunter — '

She's gone, the doors clapping back and forth behind her. Hodges walks outside, where he can use his cell phone without being scolded, and calls Tanya back. 'I don't know where you are, but slow down and don't run any red lights getting here. They just took her in, and she's wide awake. She has a broken leg.'

'That's all? Thank God! What about internal injuries?'

'That's for the doctors to say, but she was pretty lively. I think maybe the truck just grazed her.'

'I need to call Jerome. I'm sure I scared the hell out of him. And Jim needs to know.'

'Call them when you get here. For now, get off your phone.'

'*You* can call them, Bill.'

'No, Tanya, I can't. I have to call someone else.'

He stands there, breathing out plumes of white vapor, the tips of his ears going numb. He doesn't want the someone else to be Pete, because Pete is a tad pissed at him right now, and that goes double for Izzy Jaynes. He thinks about his other choices, but there's only one: Cassandra Sheen. He partnered up with her

180

several times when Pete was on vacation, and on one occasion when Pete took six weeks of unexplained personal time. That was shortly after Pete's divorce, and Hodges surmised he was in a spin-dry center, but never asked and Pete never volunteered the information.

He doesn't have Cassie's cell number, so he calls Detective Division and asks to be connected, hoping she's not in the field. He's in luck. After less than ten seconds of McGruff the Crime Dog, she's in his ear.

'Is this Cassie Sheen, the Botox Queen?'

'Billy Hodges, you old whore! I thought you were dead!'

Soon enough, Cassie, he thinks.

'I'd love to bullshit with you, hon, but I need a favor. They haven't closed the Strike Avenue station yet, have they?'

'Nope. It's on the docket for next year, though. Which makes perfect sense. Crime in Lowtown? What crime, right?'

'Yeah, safest part of the city. They may have a kid in for booking, and if my information is right, he deserves a medal instead.'

'Got a name?'

'No, but I know what he looks like. Tall, green eyes, goatee.' He replays what Barbara said and adds, 'He could be wearing a Todhunter High jacket. The arresting officers probably have him for pushing a girl in front of a truck. He actually pushed her out of the way, so she only got clipped instead of mashed.'

'You know this for a fact?'

'Yeah.' This isn't quite the truth, but he

181

believes Barbara. 'Find out his name and ask the cops to hold him, okay? I want to talk to him.'

'I think I can do that.'

'Thanks, Cassie. I owe you one.'

He ends the call and looks at his watch. If he means to talk to the Todhunter kid and still keep his appointment with Norma, time is too tight to be messing around with the city bus service.

One thing Barbara said keeps replaying in his mind: *I don't want to die, after all. I don't know what was wrong with me.*

He calls Holly.

15

She's standing outside the 7-Eleven near the office, holding a pack of Winstons in one hand and plucking at the cellophane with the other. She hasn't had a cigarette in almost five months, a new record, and she doesn't want to start again now, but what she saw on Bill's computer has torn a hole in the middle of a life she has spent the last five years mending. Bill Hodges is her touchstone, the way she measures her ability to interact with the world. Which is only another way of saying that he is the way she measures her sanity. Trying to imagine her life with him gone is like standing on top of a skyscraper and looking at the sidewalk sixty stories below.

Just as she begins to pull the strip on the cellophane, her phone rings. She drops the Winstons into her purse and fishes it out. It's him.

Holly doesn't say hello. She told Jerome she didn't think she could talk to him on her own about what she's discovered, but now — standing on this windy city sidewalk and shivering inside her good winter coat — she has no choice. It just spills out. 'I looked on your computer and I know that snooping's a lousy thing to do but I'm not sorry. I had to because I thought you were lying about it just being an ulcer and you can fire me if you want, I don't care, just as long as you let them fix what's wrong with you.'

Silence at the other end. She wants to ask if he's still there, but her mouth feels frozen and her heart is beating so hard she can feel it all over her body.

At last he says, 'Hols, I don't think it *can* be fixed.'

'At least let them *try*!'

'I love you,' he says. She hears the heaviness in his voice. The resignation. 'You know that, right?'

'Don't be stupid, of course I know.' She starts to cry.

'I'll try the treatments, sure. But I need a couple of days before I check into the hospital. And right now I need *you*. Can you come and pick me up?'

'Okay.' Crying harder than ever, because she knows he's telling the truth about needing her. And being needed is a great thing. Maybe *the* great thing. 'Where are you?'

He tells her, then says, 'Something else.'

'What?'

'I can't fire you, Holly. You're not an employee, you're my partner. Try to remember that.'

183

'Bill?'

'Yeah?'

'I'm not smoking.'

'That's good, Holly. Now come on over here. I'll be waiting in the lobby. It's freezing outside.'

'I'll come as fast as I can while still obeying the speed limit.' She hurries to the corner lot where she parks her car. On the way, she drops the unopened pack of cigarettes into a litter basket.

16

Hodges sketches in his visit to the Bucket for Holly on the ride to the Strike Avenue police station, beginning with the news of Ruth Scapelli's suicide and ending with the odd thing Barbara said before they wheeled her away.

'I know what you're thinking,' Holly says, 'because I'm thinking it, too. That it all leads back to Brady Hartsfield.'

'The suicide prince.' Hodges has helped himself to another couple of painkillers while waiting for Holly, and he feels pretty much okay. 'That's what I'm calling him. Got a ring to it, don't you think?'

'I guess so. But you told me something once.' She's sitting bolt upright behind the wheel of her Prius, eyes darting everywhere as they drive deeper into Lowtown. She swerves to avoid a shopping cart someone has abandoned in the middle of the street. 'You said coincidence doesn't equal conspiracy. Do you remember saying that?'

'Yeah.' It's one of his faves. He has quite a few.

'You said you can investigate a conspiracy forever and come up with nothing if it's actually just a bunch of coincidences all strung together. If you can't find something concrete in the next two days — if *we* can't — you need to give up and start those treatments. Promise me you will.'

'It might take a little longer to — '

She cuts him off. 'Jerome will be back, and he'll help. It will be like the old days.'

Hodges flashes on the title of an old mystery novel, *Trent's Last Case*, and smiles a little. She catches it from the corner of her eye, takes it for acquiescence, and smiles back, relieved.

'Four days,' he says.

'Three. No more. Because every day you don't do something about what's going on inside you, the odds get longer. And they're long already. So don't start your poopy bargaining stuff, Bill. You're too good at it.'

'Okay,' he says. 'Three days. If Jerome will help.'

Holly says, 'He will. And let's try to make it two.'

17

The Strike Avenue cop shop looks like a medieval castle in a country where the king has fallen and anarchy rules. The windows are heavily barred; the motor pool is protected by chainlink fencing and concrete barriers. Cameras bristle in every direction, covering all angles of approach, and still the gray stone building has been gang-tagged, and one of the globes hanging over the main doors has been shattered.

Hodges and Holly empty the contents of their pockets and Holly's purse into plastic baskets and go through a metal detector that beeps reproachfully at Hodges's metal watchband. Holly sits on a bench in the main lobby (which is also being scanned by multiple cameras) and opens her iPad. Hodges goes to the desk, states his business, and after a few moments is met by a slim, gray-haired detective who looks a little like Lester Freamon on *The Wire* — the only cop show Hodges can watch without wanting to throw up.

'Jack Higgins,' the detective says, offering his hand. 'Like the book-writer, only not white.'

Hodges shakes with him and introduces Holly, who gives a little wave and her usual muttered hello before returning her attention to her iPad.

'I think I remember you,' Hodges says. 'You used to be at Marlborough Street station, didn't you? When you were in uniform?'

'A long time ago, when I was young and randy. I remember you, too. You caught the guy who killed those two women in McCarron Park.'

'That was a group effort, Detective Higgins.'

'Make it Jack. Cassie Sheen called. We've got your guy in an interview room. His name is Dereece Neville.' Higgins spells the first name. 'We were going to turn him loose, anyway. Several people who saw the incident corroborate his story — he was jiving around with the girl, she took offense and ran into the street. Neville saw the truck coming, ran after her, tried to push

186

her out of the way, mostly succeeded. Plus, practically everyone down here knows this kid. He's a star on the Todhunter basketball team, probably going to get an athletic scholarship to a Division I school. Great grades, honor student.'

'What was Mr Great Grades doing on the street in the middle of a schoolday?'

'Ah, they were all out. Heating system at the high school shit the bed again. Third time this winter, and it's only January. The mayor says everything's cool down here in the Low, lots of jobs, lots of prosperity, shiny happy people. We'll see him when he runs for reelection. Riding in that armored SUV of his.'

'Was the Neville kid hurt?'

'Scraped palms and nothing else. According to a lady across the street — she was closest to the scene — he pushed the girl and then, I quote, 'Went flyin over the top of her like a bigass bird.''

'Does he understand he's free to go?'

'He does, and agreed to stay. Wants to know if the girl's okay. Come on. Have your little chat with him, and then we'll send him on his way. Unless you see some reason not to.'

Hodges smiles. 'I'm just following up for Miss Robinson. Let me ask him a couple of questions, and we're both out of your hair.'

18

The interview room is small and stifling hot, the overhead heating pipes clanking away. Still, it's probably the nicest one they've got, because there's a little sofa and no perp table with a cuff-bolt sticking out of it like a steel knuckle. The sofa has been mended with tape in a couple of places, and that makes Hodges think of the man Nancy Alderson says she saw on Hilltop Court, the one with the mended coat.

Dereece Neville is sitting on the sofa. In his chino pants and white button-up shirt, he looks neat and squared away. His goatee and gold neck chain are the only real dashes of style. His school jacket is folded over one arm of the sofa. He stands when Hodges and Higgins come in, and offers a long-fingered hand that looks designed expressly for working with a basketball. The pad of the palm has been painted with orange antiseptic.

Hodges shakes with him carefully, mindful of the scrapes, and introduces himself. 'You're in absolutely no trouble here, Mr Neville. In fact, Barbara Robinson sent me to say thanks and make sure you were okay. She and her family are longtime friends of mine.'

'Is *she* okay?'

'Broken leg,' Hodges says, pulling over a chair. His hand creeps to his side and presses there. 'It could have been a lot worse. I'm betting she'll be back on the soccer field next year. Sit down, sit down.'

When the Neville boy sits, his knees seem to come almost up to his jawline. 'It was my fault, in a way. I shouldn't have been goofing with her, but she was just so pretty and all. Still . . . I ain't blind.' He pauses, corrects himself. 'Not blind. What was she on? Do you know?'

Hodges frowns. The idea that Barbara might

188

have been high hasn't crossed his mind, although it should have; she's a teenager, after all, and those years are the Age of Experimentation. But he has dinner with the Robinsons three or four times a month, and he's never seen anything in her that registered as drug use. Maybe he's just too close. Or too old.

'What makes you think she was on something?'

'Just her being down here, for one thing. Those were Chapel Ridge duds she was wearing. I know, because we play em twice every year. Blow em out, too. And she was like in a daze. Standing there on the curb near Mamma Stars, that fortune-telling place, looking like she was gonna walk right out into traffic.' He shrugs. 'So I chatted her up, teased her about jaywalking. She got mad, went all Kitty Pryde on my ass. I thought that was cute, so then . . . ' He looks at Higgins, then back at Hodges. 'This is the fault part, and I'm being straight with you about it, okay?'

'Okay,' Hodges says.

'Well, look — I grabbed her game. Just for a joke, you know. Held it up over my head. I never meant to keep it. So then she kicked me — good hard kick for a girl — and grabbed it back. She sure didn't look stoned then.'

'How *did* she look, Dereece?' The switch to the boy's first name is automatic.

'Oh, man, *mad*! But also scared. Like she just figured out where she was, on a street where girls like her — ones in private school uniforms — don't go, especially by themselves. MLK Ave? Come on, I mean bitch, please.' He leans forward, long-fingered hands clasped between

189

his knees, face earnest. 'She didn't know I was just playing, you see what I mean? She was like in a panic, get me?'

'I do,' Hodges says, and although he sounds engaged (at least he hopes so), he's on autopilot for the moment, stuck on what Neville has just said: *I grabbed her game.* Part of him thinks it can't be connected to Ellerton and Stover. Most of him thinks it must be, it's a perfect fit. 'That must have made you feel bad.'

Neville raises his scratched palms toward the ceiling in a philosophical gesture that says *What can you do?* 'It's this place, man. It's the Low. She stopped being on cloud nine and realized where she was, is all. Me, I'm getting out as soon as I can. *While* I can. Gonna play Div I, keep my grades up so I can get a good job afterward if I ain't — aren't — good enough to go pro. Then I'm getting my family out. It's just me and my mom and my two brothers. My mom's the only reason I've got as far as I have. She ain't never let none of us play in the dirt.' He replays what he just said and laughs. 'She heard me say ain't never, she be in my face.'

Hodges thinks, Kid's too good to be true. Except he is. Hodges is sure of it, and doesn't like to think what might have happened to Jerome's kid sister if Dereece Neville had been in school today.

Higgins says, 'You were wrong to be teasing that girl, but I have to say you made it right. Will you think about what almost happened if you get an urge to do something like that again?'

'Yes, sir, I sure will.'

Higgins holds a hand up. Rather than slap it,

190

Neville taps it gently, with a slightly sarcastic smile. He's a good kid, but this is still Lowtown, and Higgins is still po-po.

Higgins stands. 'Are we good to go, Detective Hodges?'

Hodges nods his appreciation at the use of his old title, but he isn't quite finished. 'Almost. What kind of game was it, Dereece?'

'Old-school.' No hesitation. 'Like a Game Boy, but my little brother had one of those — Mom got it in a rumble sale, or whatever they call those things — and the one the girl had wasn't the same. It was bright yellow, I know that. Not the kind of color you'd expect a girl to like. Not the ones I know, at least.'

'Did you happen to see the screen?'

'Just a glance. It was a bunch of fish swimming around.'

'Thanks, Dereece. How sure are you that she was high? On a scale of one to ten, ten being absolutely positive.'

'Well, say five. I would've said ten when I walked up to her, because she acted like she was going to walk right out into the street, and there was a bigass truck coming, a lot bigger than the panel job that come along behind and whumped her. I was thinking not coke or meth or molly, more something mellow, like ecstasy or pot.'

'But when you started goofing with her? When you took her game?'

Dereece Neville rolls his eyes. 'Man, she woke up *fast*.'

'Okay,' Hodges says. 'All set. And thank you.'

Higgins adds his thanks, then he and Hodges

start toward the door.

'Detective Hodges?' Neville is on his feet again, and Hodges practically has to crane his neck to look at him. 'You think if I wrote down my number, you could give it to her?'

Hodges thinks it over, then takes his pen from his breast pocket and hands it to the tall boy who probably saved Barbara Robinson's life.

19

Holly drives them back to Lower Marlborough Street. He tells her about his conversation with Dereece Neville on the way.

'In a movie, they'd fall in love,' Holly says when he finishes. She sounds wistful.

'Life is not a movie, Hol . . . Holly.' He stops himself from saying *Hollyberry* at the last second. This is not a day for levity.

'I know,' she says. 'That's why I go to them.'

'I don't suppose you know if Zappit consoles came in yellow, do you?'

As is often the case, Holly has the facts at her fingertips. 'They came in ten different colors, and yes, yellow was one of them.'

'Are you thinking what I'm thinking? That there's a connection between what happened to Barbara and what happened to those women on Hilltop Court?'

'I don't know *what* I'm thinking. I wish we could sit down with Jerome the way we did when Pete Saubers got into trouble. Just sit down and talk it all out.'

'If Jerome gets here tonight, and if Barbara's really okay, maybe we can do that tomorrow.'

'Tomorrow's your second day,' she says as she pulls to the curb outside the parking lot they use. 'The second of three.'

'Holly — '

'No!' she says fiercely. 'Don't even start! You promised!' She shoves the gearshift into park and turns to face him. 'You believe Hartsfield has been faking, isn't that right?'

'Yeah. Maybe not from the first time he opened his eyes and asked for his dear old mommy, but I think he's come a long way back since then. Maybe all the way. He's faking the semi-catatonic thing to keep from going to trial. Although you'd think Babineau would know. They must have tests, brain scans and things — '

'Never mind that. If he can think, and if he were to find out that you delayed treatment and died because of him, how do you think he'd feel?'

Hodges makes no answer, so Holly answers for him.

'He'd be happy happy happy! He'd be *fracking delighted*!'

'Okay,' Hodges says. 'I hear you. The rest of today and two more. But forget about my situation for a minute. If he can somehow reach out beyond that hospital room . . . that's scary.'

'I know. And nobody would believe us. That's scary, too. But nothing scares me as much as the thought of you dying.'

He wants to hug her for that, but she's currently wearing one of her many hug-repelling expressions, so he looks at his watch instead. 'I

193

have an appointment, and I don't want to keep the lady waiting.'

'I'm going to the hospital. Even if they won't let me see Barbara, Tanya will be there, and she'd probably like to see a friendly face.'

'Good idea. But before you go, I'd like you to take a shot at tracking down the Sunrise Solutions bankruptcy trustee.'

'His name is Todd Schneider. He's part of a law firm six names long. Their offices are in New York. I found him while you were talking to Mr Neville.'

'You did that on your iPad?'

'Yes.'

'You're a genius, Holly.'

'No, it's just computer research. You were the smart one, to think of it in the first place. I'll call him, if you want.' Her face shows how much she dreads the prospect.

'You don't have to do that. Just call his office and see if you can make an appointment for me to talk to him. As early tomorrow as possible.'

She smiles. 'All right.' Then her smile fades. She points to his midsection. 'Does it hurt?'

'Only a little.' For now that's true. 'The heart attack was worse.' That is true, too, but may not be for long. 'If you get in to see Barbara, say hi for me.'

'I will.'

Holly watches him cross to his car, noting the way his left hand goes to his side after he turns up his collar. Seeing that makes her want to cry. Or maybe howl with outrage. Life can be very unfair. She's known that ever since high school,

194

when she was the butt of everyone's joke, but it still surprises her. It shouldn't, but it does.

20

Hodges drives back across town, fiddling with the radio, looking for some good hard rock and roll. He finds The Knack on BAM-100, singing 'My Sharona,' and cranks the volume. When the song ends, the deejay comes on, talking about a big storm moving east out of the Rockies.

Hodges pays no attention. He's thinking about Brady, and about the first time he saw one of those Zappit game consoles. Library Al handed them out. What was Al's last name? He can't remember. If he ever knew it at all, that is.

When he arrives at the watering hole with the amusing name, he finds Norma Wilmer seated at a table in back, far from the madding crowd of businessmen at the bar, who are bellowing and backslapping as they jockey for drinks. Norma has ditched her nurse's uniform in favor of a dark green pantsuit and low heels. There's already a drink in front of her.

'I was supposed to buy that,' Hodges says, sitting down across from her.

'Don't worry,' she says. 'I'm running a tab, which you will pay.'

'Indeed I will.'

'Babineau couldn't get me fired or even transferred if someone saw me talking to you here and reported back to him, but he could make my life difficult. Of course, I could make his a bit difficult, too.'

'Really?'

'Really. I think he's been experimenting on your old friend Brady Hartsfield. Feeding him pills that contain God knows what. Giving him shots, as well. Vitamins, he says.'

Hodges stares at her in surprise. 'How long has this been going on?'

'Years. It's one of the reasons Becky Helmington transferred. She didn't want to be the whitecap on ground zero if Babineau gave him the wrong vitamin and killed him.'

The waitress comes. Hodges orders a Coke with a cherry in it.

Norma snorts. 'A Coke? Really? Put on your big boy pants, why don't you?'

'When it comes to booze, I spilled more than you'll ever drink, honeypie,' Hodges says. 'What the hell is Babineau up to?'

She shrugs. 'No idea. But he wouldn't be the first doc to experiment on someone the world doesn't give Shit One about. Ever hear of the Tuskegee Syphilis Experiment? The US government used four hundred black men like lab rats. It went on for forty years, and so far as I know, not a single one of *them* ran a car into a bunch of defenseless people.' She gives Hodges a crooked smile. 'Investigate Babineau. Get him in trouble. I dare you.'

'It's Hartsfield I'm interested in, but based on what you're saying, I wouldn't be surprised if Babineau turned — out to be collateral damage.'

'Then hooray for collateral damage.' It comes out *clatteral dammish*, and Hodges deduces

196

she's not on her first drink. He is, after all, a trained investigator.

When the waitress brings his Coke, Norma drains her glass and holds it up. 'I'll have another, and since the gentleman's paying, you might as well make it a double.' The waitress takes her glass and leaves. Norma turns her attention back to Hodges. 'You said you have questions. Go ahead and ask while I can still answer. My mouth is a trifle numb, and will soon be number.'

'Who is on Brady Hartsfield's visitors list?'

Norma frowns at him. '*Visitors* list? Are you kidding? Who told you he had a visitors list?'

'The late Ruth Scapelli. This was just after she replaced Becky as head nurse. I offered her fifty bucks for any rumors she heard about him — which was the going rate with Becky — and she acted like I'd just pissed on her shoes. Then she said, 'You're not even on his visitors list.''

'Huh.'

'Then, just today, Babineau said — '

'Some bullshit about the DA's office. I heard it, Bill, I was there.'

The waitress sets Norma's new drink in front of her, and Hodges knows he'd better finish up fast, before Norma starts to bend his ear about everything from being underappreciated at work to her sad and loveless love life. When nurses drink, they have a tendency to go all in. They're like cops that way.

'You've been working the Bucket for as long as I've been coming there — '

'A lot longer. Twelve years.' *Yearsh*. She raises her glass in a toast and swallows half of her

197

drink. 'And now I have been promoted to head nurse, at least temporarily. Twice the responsibility at the same old salary, no doubt.'

'Seen anybody from the DA's office lately?'

'Nope. There was a whole briefcase brigade at first, along with pet doctors just itching to declare the son of a bitch competent, but they went away discouraged once they saw him drooling and trying to pick up a spoon. Came back a few times just to double-check, fewer briefcase boys every time, but nothing lately. 'S'far's they're concerned, he's a total gork. Badda-boop, badda-bang, over and out.'

'So they don't care.' And why would they? Except for the occasional retrospective on slow news days, interest in Brady Hartsfield has died down. There's always fresh roadkill to pick over.

'You know they don't.' A lock of hair has fallen in her eyes. She blows it back. 'Did anyone try to stop you, all the times you were in to visit him?'

No, Hodges thinks, but it's been a year and a half since I dropped by. 'If there *is* a visitors list — '

'It'd be Babineau's, not the DA's. When it comes to the Mercedes Killer, DA is like honey-badger, Bill. He don't give a shit.'

'Huh?'

'Never mind.'

'Could you check and see if there is such a list? Now that you've been promoted to head nurse?'

She considers, then says, 'It wouldn't be on the computer, that would be too easy to check, but Scapelli kept a couple of file folders in a locked drawer at the duty desk. She was a great

198

one for keeping track of who's naughty and who's nice. If I found something, would it be worth twenty to you?'

'Fifty, if you could call me tomorrow.' Hodges isn't sure she'll even remember this conversation tomorrow. 'Time is of the essence.'

'If such a list exists, it's probably just power-tripping bullshit, you know. Babineau likes to keep Hartsfield to his little old self.'

'But you'll check?'

'Yeah, why not? I know where she hides the key to her locked drawer. Shit, most of the nurses on the floor know. Hard to get used to the idea old Nurse Ratched's dead.'

Hodges nods.

'He can move things, you know. Without touching them.' Norma's not looking at him; she's making rings on the table with the bottom of her glass. It looks like she's trying to replicate the Olympic logo.

'Hartsfield?'

'Who are we talking about? Yeah. He does it to freak out the nurses.' She raises her head. 'I'm drunk, so I'll tell you something I'd never say sober. I wish Babineau *would* kill him. Just give him a hot shot of something really toxic and boot him out the door. Because he scares me.' She pauses, then adds, 'He scares all of us.'

21

Holly reaches Todd Schneider's personal assistant just as he's getting ready to shut up shop and leave for the day. The PA says Mr Schneider should be available between eight thirty and nine tomorrow. After that he has meetings all day.

Holly hangs up, washes her face in the tiny lavatory, reapplies deodorant, locks the office, and gets rolling toward Kiner Memorial just in time to catch the worst of the evening rush hour. It's six o'clock and full dark by the time she arrives. The woman at the information desk checks her computer and tells her that Barbara Robinson is in Room 528 of Wing B.

'Is that Intensive Care?' Holly asks.

'No, ma'am.'

'Good,' Holly says, and sets sail, sensible low heels clacking.

The elevator doors open on the fifth floor and there, waiting to get on, are Barbara's parents. Tanya has her cell phone in her hand, and looks at Holly as if at an apparition. Jim Robinson says he'll be damned.

Holly shrinks a little. 'What? Why are you looking at me that way? What's wrong?'

'Nothing,' Tanya says. 'It's just that I was going to call you — '

The elevator doors start to close. Jim sticks out an arm and they bounce back. Holly gets out.

' — as soon as we got down to the lobby,' Tanya resumes, and points to a sign on the wall. It shows a cell phone with a red line drawn through it.

'Me? Why? I thought it was just a broken leg. I mean, I know a broken leg is serious, of course it is, but — '

'She's awake and she's fine,' Jim says, but he and Tanya exchange a glance which suggests that isn't precisely true. 'It's a pretty clean break, actually, but they found a nasty bump on the back of her head and decided to keep her overnight just to be on the safe side. The doc who fixed her leg said he's ninety-nine percent sure she'll be good to go in the morning.'

'They did a tox screen,' Tanya said. 'No drugs in her system. I wasn't surprised, but it was still a relief.'

'Then what's wrong?'

'Everything,' Tanya says simply. She looks ten years older than when Holly saw her last. 'Hilda Carver's mom drove Barb and Hilda to school, it's her week, and she said Barbara was fine in the car — a little quieter than usual, but otherwise fine. Barbara told Hilda she had to go to the bathroom, and that was the last Hilda saw of her. She said Barb must have left by one of the side doors in the gym. The kids actually call those the skip doors.'

'What does Barbara say?'

'She won't tell us *anything.*' Her voice shakes, and Jim puts an arm around her. 'But she says she'll tell you. That's why I was going to call you. She says you're the only one who might understand.'

22

Holly walks slowly down the corridor to Room 528, which is all the way at the end. Her head is down, and she's thinking hard, so she almost bumps into the man wheeling the cart of well-thumbed paperback books and Kindles with PROPERTY OF KINER HOSP taped below the screens.

'Sorry,' Holly tells him. 'I wasn't looking where I was going.'

'That's all right,' Library Al says, and goes on his way. She doesn't see him pause and look back at her; she is summoning all her courage for the conversation to come. It's apt to be emotional, and emotional scenes have always terrified her. It helps that she loves Barbara.

Also, she's curious.

She taps on the door, which is ajar, and peeps around it when there's no answer. 'Barbara? It's Holly. Can I come in?'

Barbara offers a wan smile and puts down the battered copy of *Mockingjay* she's been reading. Probably got it from the man with the cart, Holly thinks. She's cranked up in the bed, wearing pink pajamas instead of a hospital johnny. Holly guesses her mother must have packed the PJs, along with the ThinkPad she sees on Barb's night table. The pink top lends Barbara a bit of vivacity, but she still looks dazed. There's no bandage on her head, so the bump mustn't have been all *that* bad. Holly wonders if they are keeping Barbara overnight for some other reason. She can only think of one, and she'd like to believe it's ridiculous, but she can't quite get there.

'Holly! How did you get here so fast?'

'I was coming to see you.' Holly enters and

closes the door behind her. 'When somebody's in the hospital, you go to see them if it's a friend, and we're friends. I met your parents at the elevator. They said you wanted to talk to me.'

'Yes.'

'How can I help, Barbara?'

'Well . . . can I ask you something? It's pretty personal.'

'Okay.' Holly sits down in the chair next to the bed. Gingerly, as if the seat might be wired for electricity.

'I know you had some bad times. You know, when you were younger. Before you worked for Bill.'

'Yes,' Holly says. The overhead light isn't on, just the lamp on the night table. Its glow encloses them and gives them their own little place to be. 'Some very bad ones.'

'Did you ever try to kill yourself?' Barbara gives a small, nervous laugh. 'I told you it was personal.'

'Twice.' Holly says it without hesitation. She feels surprisingly calm. 'The first time, I was just about your age. Because kids at school were mean to me, and called me mean names. I couldn't cope. But I didn't try very hard. I just took a handful of aspirin and decongestant tablets.'

'Did you try harder the second time?'

It's a tough question, and Holly thinks it over carefully. 'Yes and no. It was after I had some trouble with my boss, what they call sexual harassment now. Back then they didn't call it much of anything. I was in my twenties. I took

203

stronger pills, but still not enough to do the job and part of me knew that. I was very unstable back then, but I wasn't stupid, and the part that wasn't stupid wanted to live. Partly because I knew Martin Scorsese would make some more movies, and I wanted to see them. Martin Scorsese is the best director alive. He makes long movies like novels. Most movies are only like short stories.'

'Did your boss, like, *attack* you?'

'I don't want to talk about it, and it doesn't matter.' Holly doesn't want to look up, either, but reminds herself that this is Barbara and forces herself to. Because Barbara has been her friend in spite of all of Holly's ticks and tocks, all of Holly's bells and whistles. And is now in trouble herself. 'The reasons never matter, because suicide goes against every human instinct, and that makes it insane.'

Except maybe in certain cases, she thinks. Certain *terminal* cases. But Bill isn't terminal.

I won't let him be terminal.

'I know what you mean,' Barbara says. She turns her head from side to side on her pillow. In the lamplight, tear-tracks gleam on her cheeks. 'I know.'

'Is that why you were in Lowtown? To kill yourself?'

Barbara closes her eyes, but tears squeeze through the lashes. 'I don't think so. At least not at first. I went there because the voice told me to. My friend.' She pauses, thinks. 'But he wasn't my friend, after all. A friend wouldn't want me to kill myself, would he?'

Holly takes Barbara's hand. Touching is ordinarily hard for her, but not tonight. Maybe it's because she feels they are enclosed in their own secret place. Maybe it's because this is Barbara. Maybe both. 'What friend is this?'

Barbara says, 'The one with the fish. The one inside the game.'

23

It's Al Brooks who wheels the library cart through the hospital's main lobby (passing Mr and Mrs Robinson, who are waiting for Holly), and it's Al who takes another elevator up to the skyway that connects the main hospital to the Traumatic Brain Injury Clinic. It's Al who says hello to Nurse Rainier at the duty desk, a long-timer who hellos him back without looking up from her computer screen. It's still Al rolling his cart down the corridor, but when he leaves it in the hall and steps into Room 217, Al Brooks disappears and Z-Boy takes his place.

Brady is in his chair with his Zappit in his lap. He doesn't look up from the screen. Z-Boy takes his own Zappit from the left pocket of his loose gray tunic and turns it on. He taps the Fishin' Hole icon and on the starter screen the fish begin to swim: red ones, yellow ones, gold ones, every now and then a fast-moving pink one. The tune tinkles. And every now and then the console gives off a bright flash that paints his cheeks and turns his eyes into blue blanks.

They remain that way for almost five minutes,

one sitting and one standing, both staring at the swimming fish and listening to the tinkling melody. The blinds over Brady's window rattle restlessly. The coverlet on his bed snaps down, then back up again. Once or twice Z-Boy nods his understanding. Then Brady's hands loosen and let go of the game console. It slides down his wasted legs, then between them, and clatters to the floor. His mouth falls open. His eyelids drop to half-mast. The rise and fall of his chest inside his checked shirt becomes imperceptible.

Z-Boy's shoulders straighten. He gives himself a little shake, clicks off his Zappit, and drops it back into the pocket from which it came. From his right pocket he takes an iPhone. A person with considerable computer skills has modified it with several state-of-the-art security devices, and the built-in GPS has been turned off. There are no names in the Contacts folder, only a few initials. Z-Boy taps *FL*.

The phone rings twice and FL answers in a fake Russian accent. 'Ziss iss Agent Zippity-Doo-Dah, comrade. I avait your commands.'

'You haven't been paid to make bad jokes.'

Silence. Then: 'All right. No jokes.'

'We're moving ahead.'

'We'll move ahead when I get the rest of my money.'

'You'll have it tonight, and you'll go to work immediately.'

'Roger-dodger,' FL says. 'Give me something hard next time.'

There's not going to be a next time, Z-Boy thinks.

'Don't screw this up.'

'I won't. But I don't work until I see the green.'

'You'll see it.'

Z-Boy breaks the connection, drops the phone into his pocket, and leaves Brady's room. He heads back past the duty desk and Nurse Rainier, who is still absorbed in her computer. He leaves the cart in the snack alcove and crosses the skyway. He walks with a spring in his step, like a much younger man.

In an hour or two, Rainier or one of the other nurses will find Brady Hartsfield either slumped in his chair or sprawled on the floor on top of his Zappit. There won't be much concern; he has slipped into total unconsciousness many times before, and always comes out of it.

Dr Babineau says it's part of the rebooting process, that each time Hartsfield returns, he's slightly improved. Our boy is getting well, Babineau says. You might not believe it to look at him, but our boy is really getting well.

You don't know the half of it, thinks the mind now occupying Library Al's body. You don't know the fucking half of it. But you're starting to, Dr B. Aren't you?

Better late than never.

24

'That man who yelled at me on the street was wrong,' Barbara says. 'I believed him because the voice told me to believe him, but he was wrong.'

Holly wants to know about the voice from the game, but Barbara may not be ready to talk about that yet. So she asks who the man was, and what he yelled.

'He called me blackish, like on that TV show. The show is funny, but on the street it's a put-down. It's — '

'I know the show, and I know how some people use it.'

'But I'm *not* blackish. Nobody with a dark skin is, not really. Not even if they live in a nice house on a nice street like Teaberry Lane. We're all black, all the time. Don't you think I know how I get looked at and talked about at school?'

'Of course you do,' says Holly, who has been looked at and talked about plenty in her own time; her high school nickname was Jibba-Jibba.

'The teachers talk about gender equality, and racial equality. They have a zero tolerance policy, and they mean it — at least most of them do, I guess — but anyone can walk through the halls when the classes are changing and pick out the black kids and the Chinese transfer students and the Muslim girl, because there's only two dozen of us and we're like a few grains of pepper that somehow got into the salt shaker.'

She's picking up steam now, her voice outraged and indignant but also weary.

'I get invited to parties, but there are a lot of parties I don't get invited to, and I've only been asked out on dates twice. One of the boys who asked me was white, and everyone looked at us when we went into the movies, and someone threw popcorn at the back of our heads. I guess at the AMC 12, racial equality stops when the lights go down. And one time when I was playing soccer? Here I go, dribbling the ball up the sideline, got a clear shot, and this white dad in a golf shirt tells his daughter, 'Guard that jig!' I pretended I didn't hear it. The girl kind of smirked. I wanted to knock her over, right there where he could see it, but I didn't. I swallowed it. And once, when I was a freshman, I left my English book on the bleachers at lunch, and when I went back to get it, someone had put a note in it that said BUCKWHEAT'S GIRL-FRIEND. I swallowed that, too. For days it can be good, weeks, even, and then there's something to swallow. It's the same with Mom and Dad, I know it is. Maybe it's different for Jerome at Harvard, but I bet sometimes even he has to swallow it.'

Holly squeezes her hand, but says nothing.

'I'm not *blackish*, but the voice said I was, just because I didn't grow up in a tenement with an abusive dad and a drug addict mom. Because I never ate a collard green, or even knew exactly what it was. Because I say *pork chop* instead of *poke chop*. Because they're poor down there in the Low and we're doing just fine on Teaberry Lane. I have my cash card, and my nice school, and Jere goes to Harvard, but . . . but, don't you see . . . Holly, don't you *see* that I never — '

'You never had a choice about those things,' Holly says. 'You were born where you were and what you were, the same as me. The same as all of us, really. And at sixteen, you've never been asked to change anything but your clothes.'

'Yes! And I know I shouldn't be ashamed, but the voice *made* me ashamed, it made me feel like a useless parasite, *and it's still not all gone*. It's like it left a trail of slime inside my head. Because I never *had* been in Lowtown before, and it's *horrible* down there, and compared to them I really *am* blackish, and I'm afraid that voice may never go away and my life will be *spoiled*.'

'You have to strangle it.' Holly speaks with dry, detached certainty.

Barbara looks at her in surprise.

Holly nods. 'Yes. You have to choke that voice until it's dead. It's the first job. If you don't take care of yourself, you can't get better. And if you can't get better, you can't make anything else better.'

Barbara says, 'I can't just go back to school and pretend Lowtown doesn't exist. If I'm going to live, I have to do something. Young or not, I have to do something.'

'Are you thinking about some kind of volunteer work?'

'I don't know *what* I'm thinking about. I don't know what there is for a kid like me. But I'm going to find out. If it means going back down there, my parents won't like it. You have to help me with them, Holly. I know it's hard for you, but *please*. You have to tell them that I need to shut that voice up. Even if I can't choke it to death right away, maybe I can at least quiet it down.'

'All right,' Holly says, although she dreads it. 'I will.' An idea occurs to her and she brightens. 'You should talk to the boy who pushed you out of the way of the truck.'

'I don't know how to find him.'

'Bill will help you,' Holly says. 'Now tell me about the game.'

'It broke. The truck ran over it, I saw the pieces, and I'm glad. Every time I close my eyes I can see those fish, especially the pink number-fish, and hear the little song.' She hums it, but it rings no bells with Holly.

A nurse comes in wheeling a meds cart. She asks Barbara what her pain level is. Holly is ashamed she didn't think to ask herself, and first thing. In some ways she is a very bad and thoughtless person.

'I don't know,' Barbara says. 'A five, maybe?'

The nurse opens a plastic pill tray and hands Barbara a little paper cup. There are two white pills in it. 'These are custom-tailored Five pills. You'll sleep like a baby. At least until I come in to check your pupils.'

Barbara swallows the pills with a sip of water. The nurse tells Holly she should leave soon and let 'our girl' get some rest.

'Very soon,' Holly says, and when the nurse is gone, she leans forward, face intent, eyes bright. 'The game. How did you get it, Barb?'

'A man gave it to me. I was at the Birch Street Mall with Hilda Carver.'

'When was this?'

'Before Christmas, but not much before. I remember, because I still hadn't found anything for Jerome, and I was starting to get worried. I saw a nice sport coat in Banana Republic, but it was *way* expensive, and besides, he's going to be building houses until May. You don't have much reason to wear a sport coat when you're doing that, do you?'

'I guess not.'

'Anyway, this man came up to us while Hilda and I were having lunch. We're not supposed to talk to strangers, but it's not like we're little kids anymore, and besides, it was in the food court with people all around. Also, he looked nice.'

The worst ones usually do, Holly thinks.

'He was wearing a terrific suit that must have cost mucho megabucks and carrying a briefcase. He said his name was Myron Zakim and he worked for a company called Sunrise Solutions. He gave us his card. He showed us a couple of Zappits — his briefcase was full of them — and said we could each have one free if we'd fill out a questionnaire and send it back. The address was on the questionnaire. It was on the card, too.'

'Do you happen to remember the address?'

'No, and I threw his card away. Besides, it was only a box number.'

'In New York?'

Barbara thinks it over. 'No. Here in the city.'

'So you took the Zappits.'

'Yes. I didn't tell Mom, because she would have given me a big lecture about talking to that guy. I filled out the questionnaire, too, and sent it in. Hilda didn't, because her Zappit didn't work. It just gave out a single blue flash and went dead. So she threw it away. I remember her saying that's all you could expect when someone said something was free.' Barbara giggles. 'She sounded just like her mother.'

'But yours did work.'

'Yes. It was old-fashioned but kind of . . . you know, kind of fun, in a silly way. At first. I wish mine had been broken, then I wouldn't have the *voice*.' Her eyes slip closed, then slowly reopen. She smiles. 'Whoa! Feel like I might be floating away.'

'Don't float away yet. Can you describe the man?'

'A white guy with white hair. He was old.'

'Old-old, or just a little bit old?'

Barbara's eyes are growing glassy. 'Older than Dad, not as old as Grampa.'

'Sixty-fiveish?'

'Yeah, I guess. Bill's age, more or less.' Her eyes suddenly spring wide open. 'Oh, guess what? I remember something. I thought it was a little weird, and so did Hilda.'

'What was that?'

'He said his name was Myron Zakim, and his card said Myron Zakim, but there were initials on his briefcase that were different.'

'Can you remember what they were?'

'No . . . sorry . . . ' She's floating away, all right.

'Will you think about that first thing when you wake up, Barb? Your mind will be fresh then, and it might be important.'

'Okay . . . '

'I wish Hilda hadn't thrown hers away,' Holly says. She gets no reply, nor expects one; she often talks to herself. Barbara's breathing has grown deep and slow. Holly begins buttoning her coat.

'Dinah has one,' Barbara says in a faraway dreaming voice. '*Hers* works. She plays Crossy Road on it . . . and Plants Vs. Zombies . . . also, she downloaded the whole *Divergent* trilogy, but she said it came in all jumbled up.'

Holly stops buttoning. She knows Dinah Scott, has seen her at the Robinson house many times, playing board games or watching TV, often staying for supper. And drooling over Jerome, as all of Barbara's friends do.

'Did the same man give it to her?'

Barbara doesn't answer. Biting her lip, not wanting to press her but needing to, Holly shakes Barbara by the shoulder and asks again.

'No,' Barbara says in the same faraway voice. 'She got it from the website.'

'What website was that, Barbara?'

Her only answer is a snore. Barbara is gone.

25

Holly knows that the Robinsons will be waiting for her in the lobby, so she hurries into the gift shop, lurks behind a display of teddy bears (Holly is an accomplished lurker), and calls Bill. She asks if he knows Barbara's friend Dinah Scott.

'Sure,' he says. 'I know most of her friends. The ones that come to the house, anyway. So do you.'

'I think you should go to see her.'

'You mean tonight?'

'I mean right away. She's got a Zappit.' Holly takes a deep breath. 'They're dangerous.' She

214

can't quite bring herself to say what she is coming to believe: that they are suicide machines.

26

In Room 217, orderlies Norm Richard and Kelly Pelham lift Brady back into bed while Mavis Rainier supervises. Norm picks up the Zappit console from the floor and stares at the swimming fish on the screen.

'Why doesn't he just catch pneumonia and die, like the rest of the gorks?' Kelly asks.

'This one's too ornery to die,' Mavis says, then notices Norm staring down at the swimming fish. His eyes are wide and his mouth is hung ajar.

'Wake up, splendor in the grass,' she says, and snatches the gadget away. She pushes the power button and tosses it into the top drawer of Brady's nightstand. 'We've got miles to go before we sleep.'

'Huh?' Norm looks down at his hands, as if expecting to see the Zappit still in them.

Kelly asks Nurse Rainier if maybe she wants to take Hartsfield's blood pressure. 'O_2 looks a little low,' he says.

Mavis considers this, then says, 'Fuck him.' They leave.

27

In Sugar Heights, the city's poshest neighborhood, an old Chevy Malibu spotted with primer paint creeps up to a closed gate on Lilac Drive. Artfully scrolled into the wrought iron are the initials Barbara Robinson failed to remember: *FB*. Z-Boy gets out from behind the wheel, his old parka (a rip in the back and another in the left sleeve thriftily mended with masking tape) flapping around him. He taps the correct code into the keypad, and the gates begin to swing open. He gets back into the car, reaches under the seat, and brings out two items. One is a plastic soda bottle with the neck cut off. The interior has been packed with steel wool. The other is a .32-caliber revolver. Z-Boy slips the muzzle of the .32 into this homemade silencer — another Brady Hartsfield invention — and holds it on his lap. With his free hand he pilots the Malibu up the smooth, curving driveway.

Ahead, the porch-mounted motion lights come on.

Behind, the wrought iron gates swing silently shut.

LIBRARY AL

It didn't take Brady long to realize he was pretty much finished as a physical being. He was born stupid but didn't stay that way, as the saying goes.

Yes, there was physical therapy — Dr Babineau decreed it, and Brady was hardly in a position to protest — but there was only so much therapy could accomplish. He was eventually able to shamble thirty feet or so along the corridor some patients called the Torture Highway, but only with the help of Rehab Care Coordinator Ursula Haber, the bull dyke Nazi who ran the place.

'One more step, Mr Hartsfield,' Haber would exhort, and when he managed one more step the bitch would ask for one more and one more after that. When Brady was finally allowed to collapse into his wheelchair, trembling and soaked with sweat, he liked to imagine stuffing oil-soaked rags up Haber's snatch and setting them on fire.

'Good job!' she'd cry. '*Good* job, Mr Hartsfield!'

And if he managed to gargle something that bore a passing resemblance to *thank you*, she would look around at whoever happened to be near, smiling proudly. Look! My pet monkey can talk!

He *could* talk (more and better than they knew), and he could shamble ten yards up the Torture Highway. On his best days he could eat custard without spilling too much down his front. But he couldn't dress himself, couldn't tie his shoes, couldn't wipe himself after taking a shit, couldn't even use the remote control (so reminiscent of Thing One and Thing Two back in the good old days) to watch television. He could grasp it, but his motor control wasn't even close to good enough for him to manipulate the small buttons. If he did manage to hit the power button, he usually ended up staring at nothing but a blank screen and the SEARCHING FOR SIGNAL message. This infuriated him — in the early days of 2012, *everything* infuriated him — but he was careful not to show it. Angry people were angry for a reason, and gorks weren't supposed to have reasons for anything.

Sometimes lawyers from the District Attorney's office dropped by. Babineau protested these visits, telling the lawyers they were setting him back and therefore working against their own long-term interests, but it did no good.

Sometimes cops came with the lawyers from the DA's office, and once a cop came on his own. He was a fat cocksucker with a crewcut and a cheerful demeanor. Brady was in his chair, so the fat cocksucker sat on Brady's bed. The fat cocksucker told Brady that his niece had been at the 'Round Here concert. 'Just thirteen years old and crazy about that band,' he said, chuckling. Still chuckling, he leaned forward over his big stomach and punched Brady in the balls.

'A little something from my niece,' the fat cocksucker said. 'Did you feel it? Man, I hope so.'

Brady did feel it, but not as much as the fat cocksucker probably hoped, because everything had gone kind of vague between his waist and knees. Some circuit in his brain that was supposed to be controlling that area had burned out, he supposed. That would ordinarily be bad news, but it was good news when you had to cope with a right hook to the family jewels. He sat there, his face blank. A little drool on his chin. But he filed away the fat cocksucker's name. Moretti. It went on his list.

Brady had a long list.

★　★　★

He retained a thin hold over Sadie MacDonald by virtue of that first, wholly accidental safari into her brain. (He retained an even greater hold over the idiot orderly's brain, but visiting there was like taking a vacation in Lowtown.) On several occasions Brady was able to nudge her toward the window, the site of her first seizure. Usually she only glanced out and then went about her work, which was frustrating, but one day in June of 2012, she had another of those mini-seizures. Brady found himself looking out through her eyes once more, but this time he was not content to stay on the passenger side, just watching the scenery. This time he wanted to drive.

Sadie reached up and caressed her breasts. Squeezed them. Brady felt a low tingle begin between Sadie's legs. He was getting her a little hot. Interesting, but hardly useful.

He thought of turning her around and walking her out of the room. Going down the corridor. Getting a drink of water from the fountain. His very own organic wheelchair. Only what if someone talked to him? What would he say? Or what if Sadie took over again once she was away from the sunflashes, and started screaming that Hartsfield was inside of her? They'd think she was crazy. They might put her on leave. If they did that, Brady would lose his access to her.

He burrowed deeper into her mind instead, watching the thought-fish go flashing back and forth. They were clearer now, but mostly uninteresting.

One, though . . . the red one . . .

It came into view as soon as he thought about it, because he was making *her* think of it.

Big red fish.

A fatherfish.

Brady snatched at it and caught it. It was easy. His body was next to useless, but inside Sadie's mind he was as agile as a ballet dancer. The fatherfish had molested her regularly between the ages of six and eleven. Finally he had gone all the way and fucked her. Sadie told a teacher at school, and her father was arrested. He had killed himself while out on bail.

Mostly to amuse himself, Brady began to release his own fish into the aquarium of Sadie MacDonald's mind: tiny poisonous blowfish that were little more than exaggerations of thoughts she herself harbored in the twilight area that exists between the conscious mind and the subconscious.

That she had led him on.

That she had actually *enjoyed* his attentions.

That she was responsible for his death.

That when you looked at it that way, it hadn't been suicide at all. When you looked at it that way, she had murdered him.

Sadie jerked violently, hands flying up to the sides of her head, and turned away from the window. Brady felt that moment of nauseating, tumbling vertigo as he was ejected from her mind. She looked at him, her face pale and dismayed.

'I think I passed out for a second or two,' she said, then laughed shakily. 'But you won't tell, will you, Brady?'

Of course not, and after that he found it easier and easier to get into her head. She no longer had to look at the sunlight on the windshields across the way; all she had to do was come into the room. She was losing weight. Her vague prettiness was disappearing. Sometimes her uniform was dirty and sometimes her stockings were torn. Brady continued to plant his depth charges: you led him on, you enjoyed it, you were responsible, you don't deserve to live.

Hell, it was something to do.

★ ★ ★

Sometimes the hospital got freebies, and in September of 2012 it received a dozen Zappit game consoles, either from the company that made them or from some charity organization. Admin shipped them to the tiny library next to

221

the hospital's nondenominational chapel. There an orderly unpacked them, looked them over, decided they were stupid and outdated, and stuck them on a back shelf. It was there that Library Al Brooks found them in November, and took one for himself.

Al enjoyed a few of the games, like the one where you had to get Pitfall Harry safely past the crevasses and poisonous snakes, but what he enjoyed most was Fishin' Hole. Not the game itself, which was stupid, but the demo screen. He supposed people would laugh, but it was no joke to Al. When he was upset about something (his brother yelling at him about not putting out the garbage for Thursday morning pickup, or a crabby call from his daughter in Oklahoma City), those slowly gliding fish and the little tune always mellowed him out. Sometimes he lost all track of time. It was amazing.

On an evening not long before 2012 became 2013, Al had an inspiration. Hartsfield in 217 was incapable of reading, and had shown no interest in books or music on CD. If someone put earphones on his head, he clawed at them until he got them off, as if he found them confining. He would also be incapable of manipulating the small buttons below the Zappit's screen, but he could look at the Fishin' Hole demo. Maybe he'd like it, or some of the other demo screens. If he did, maybe some of the other patients (to his credit, Al never thought of them as gorks) would, too, and that would be a good thing, because a few of the brain-damaged patients in the Bucket were occasionally violent.

If the demo screens calmed them down, the docs, nurses, and orderlies — even the janitors — would have an easier time.

He might even get a bonus. It probably wouldn't happen, but a man could dream.

★   ★   ★

He entered Room 217 one afternoon in early December of 2012, shortly after Hartsfield's only regular visitor had left. This was an ex-detective named Hodges, who had been instrumental in Hartsfield's capture, although he hadn't been the one who had actually smacked his head and damaged his brain.

Hodges's visits upset Hartsfield. After he was gone, things fell over in 217, the water turned on and off in the shower, and sometimes the bathroom door flew open or slammed shut. The nurses had seen these things, and were sure Hartsfield was causing them, but Dr Babineau pooh-poohed that idea. He claimed it was exactly the kind of hysterical notion that got a hold on certain women (even though several of the Bucket nurses were men). Al knew the stories were true, because he had seen manifestations himself on several occasions, and he did not think of himself as a hysterical person. Quite the opposite.

On one memorable occasion he had heard something in Hartsfield's room as he was passing, opened the door, and saw the window-blinds doing a kind of maniacal boogaloo. This was shortly after one of Hodges's visits. It had gone on for nearly thirty seconds before the blinds stilled again.

Although he tried to be friendly — he tried to be friendly with everyone — Al did not approve of Bill Hodges. The man seemed to be gloating over Hartsfield's condition. Reveling in it. Al knew Hartsfield was a bad guy who had murdered innocent people, but what the hell did that matter when the man who had done those things no longer existed? What remained was little more than a husk. So what if he could rattle the blinds, or turn the water on and off? Such things hurt no one.

★ ★ ★

'Hello, Mr Hartsfield,' Al said on that night in December. 'I brought you something. Hope you'll take a look.'

He turned the Zappit on and poked the screen to bring up the Fishin' Hole demo. The fish began to swim and the tune began to play. As always, Al was soothed, and took a moment to enjoy the sensation. Before he could turn the console so Hartsfield could see, he found himself pushing his library cart in Wing A, on the other side of the hospital.

The Zappit was gone.

This should have upset him, but it didn't. It seemed perfectly okay. He was a little tired, and seemed to be having trouble gathering his scattered thoughts, but otherwise he was fine. Happy. He looked down at his left hand and saw he had drawn a large Z on the back with the pen he always kept in the pocket of his tunic.

Z for Z-Boy, he thought, and laughed.

★ ★ ★

Brady did not make a decision to leap into Library Al; seconds after the old geezer looked down at the console in his hand, Brady was in. There was no sense of being an interloper in the library guy's head, either. For now it was Brady's body, as much as a Hertz sedan would have been his car for as long as he chose to drive it.

The library guy's core consciousness was still there — someplace — but it was just a soothing hum, like the sound of a furnace in the cellar on a cold day. Yet he had access to all of Alvin Brooks's memories and all of his stored knowledge. There was a fair amount of this latter, because before retiring from his full-time job at the age of fifty-eight, the man had been an electrician, then known as Sparky Brooks instead of Library Al. If Brady had wanted to rewire a circuit, he could have done so easily, although he understood he might no longer have this ability once he returned to his own body.

Thinking of his body alarmed him, and he bent over the man slumped in the chair. The eyes were half-closed, showing only the whites. The tongue lolled from one corner of the mouth. Brady put a gnarled hand on Brady's chest and felt a slow rise and fall. So *that* was all right, but God, he looked *horrible*. A skin-wrapped skeleton. This was what Hodges had done to him.

225

He left the room and toured the hospital, feeling a species of mad exhilaration. He smiled at everyone. He couldn't help it. With Sadie MacDonald he had been afraid of fucking up. He still was, but not so much. This was better. He was wearing Library Al like a tight glove. When he passed Anna Corey, the A Wing head housekeeper, he asked how her husband was bearing up with those radiation treatments. She told him Ellis was doing pretty well, all things considered, and thanked him for asking.

In the lobby, he parked his cart outside the men's bathroom, went in, sat on the toilet, and examined the Zappit. As soon as he saw the swimming fish, he understood what must have happened. The idiots who had created this particular game had also created, certainly by accident, a hypnotic effect. Not everyone would be susceptible, but Brady thought plenty of people would be, and not just those prone to mild seizures, like Sadie MacDonald.

He knew from reading he'd done in his basement control room that several electronic console and arcade games were capable of initiating seizures or light hypnotic states in perfectly normal people, causing the makers to print a warning (in extremely fine print) on many of the instruction sheets: do not play for prolonged periods, do not sit closer than three feet to the screen, do not play if you have a history of epilepsy.

The effect wasn't restricted to video games, either. At least one episode of the Pokémon cartoon series had been banned outright when thousands of kids complained of headaches, blurred vision, nausea, and seizures. The culprit was believed to be a sequence in the episode where a series of missiles were set off, causing a strobe effect. Some combination of the swimming fish and the little tune worked the same way. Brady was surprised the company that made the Zappit consoles hadn't been deluged with complaints. He found out later that there *had* been complaints, but not many. He came to believe that there were two reasons for that. First, the dumbshit Fishin' Hole game itself did not have the same effect. Second, hardly anybody bought the Zappit game consoles to begin with. In the jargon of computer commerce, it was a brick.

Still pushing his cart, the man wearing Library Al's body returned to Room 217 and placed the Zappit on the table by the bed — it merited further study and thought. Then (and not without regret) Brady left Library Al Brooks. There was that moment of vertigo, and then he was looking up instead of down. He was curious to see what would happen next.

At first Library Al just stood there, a piece of furniture that looked like a human being. Brady reached out to him with his invisible left hand and patted his cheek. Then he reached for Al's mind with his own, expecting to find it shut to him, as Nurse MacDonald's had been once she came out of her fugue state.

But the door was wide open.

Al's core consciousness had returned, but there was a bit less now. Brady suspected that some of it had been smothered by his presence. So what? People killed off brain cells when they drank too much, but they had plenty of spares. The same was true of Al. At least for now.

Brady saw the Z he had drawn on the back of Al's hand — for no reason, just because he could — and spoke without opening his mouth.

'Hey there, Z-Boy. Go on now. Get out. Head over to A Wing. But you won't talk about this, will you?'

'Talk about what?' Al asked, looking puzzled.

Brady nodded as well as he could nod, and smiled as well as he could smile. He was already wishing to be in Al again. Al's body was old, but at least it *worked*.

'That's right,' he told Z-Boy. 'Talk about what.'

★   ★   ★

2012 became 2013. Brady lost interest in trying to strengthen his telekinetic muscles. There was really no point, now that he had Al. Each time he got inside, his grip was stronger, his control better. Running Al was like running one of those drones the military used to keep an eye on the ragheads in Afghanistan . . . and then to bomb the living shit out of their bosses.

Lovely, really.

Once he had Z-Boy show the old Det-Ret one of the Zappits, hoping Hodges would become fascinated by the Fishin' Hole demo. Being inside Hodges would be wonderful. Brady would make it his first priority to pick up a pencil and poke out the old Det-Ret's eyes. But Hodges only glanced at the screen and handed it back to Library Al.

Brady tried again a few days later, this time with Denise Woods, the PT associate who came into his room twice a week to exercise his arms and legs. She took the console when Z-Boy handed it to her, and looked at the swimming fish quite a bit longer than Hodges had. *Something* happened, but it wasn't quite enough. Trying to enter her was like pushing against a firm rubber diaphragm: it gave a little, enough for him to glimpse her feeding her young son scrambled eggs in his high chair, but then it pushed him back out.

She handed the Zappit back to Z-Boy and said, 'You're right, they're pretty fish. Now why don't you go hand out some books, Al, and let Brady and me work on those pesky knees of his?'

So there it was. He didn't have the same instantaneous access to others that he'd had to Al, and a little thought was all it took for Brady to understand why. Al had been preconditioned to the Fishin' Hole demo, had watched it dozens of times before bringing his Zappit to Brady. That was a crucial difference, and a crushing disappointment. Brady had imagined having dozens of drones among whom he could pick and choose, but that wasn't going to happen unless there was a way to re-rig the Zappit and enhance the hypnotic effect. Might there be such a way?

As someone who had modified all sorts of gadgets in his time — Thing One and Thing

229

Two, for instance — Brady believed there was. The Zappit was WiFi equipped, after all, and WiFi was the hacker's best friend. Suppose, for instance, he were to program in a flashing light? A kind of strobe, like the one that had buzzed the brains of those kids exposed to the missile-firing sequence in the Pokémon episode?

The strobe could serve another purpose, as well. While taking a community college course called Computing the Future (this was just before he dropped out of school for good), Brady's class had been assigned a long CIA report, published in 1995 and declassified shortly after 9/11. It was called 'The Operational Potential of Subliminal Perception,' and explained how computers could be programmed to transmit messages so rapidly that the brain recognized them not as messages per se, but as original thoughts. Suppose he were able to embed such a message inside the strobe flash? SLEEP NOW ALL OKAY, for instance, or maybe just RELAX. Brady thought those things, combined with the demo screen's existing hypnotics, would be pretty effective. Of course he might be wrong, but he would have given his mostly useless right hand to find out.

He doubted if he ever would, because there were two seemingly insurmountable problems. One was getting people to look at the demo screen long enough for the hypnotic effect to take hold. The other was even more basic: how in God's name was he supposed to modify *anything*? He had no computer access, and even if he had, what good would it be? He couldn't even tie his fucking shoes! He considered using Z-Boy, and rejected the idea almost immediately. Al Brooks lived with his brother and his brother's family, and if Al all of a sudden started demonstrating advanced computer knowledge and capability, there would be questions. Especially when they already had questions about Al, who had grown absentminded and rather peculiar. Brady supposed they thought he was suffering the onset of senility, which wasn't all that far from the truth.

It seemed that Z-Boy was running out of spare brain cells after all.

★   ★   ★

Brady grew depressed. He had reached the all too familiar point where his bright ideas collided head-on with gray reality. It had happened with the Rolla vacuum cleaner; it had happened with his computer-assisted vehicle backing device; it had happened with his motorized, programmable TV monitor, which was supposed to revolutionize home security. His wonderful inspirations always came to nothing.

Still, he had one human drone to hand, and after a particularly infuriating visit from Hodges, Brady decided he might cheer up if he put his drone to work. Accordingly, Z-Boy visited an Internet café a block or two down from the hospital, and after five minutes on a computer (Brady was exhilarated to be sitting in front of a screen again), he discovered where Anthony Moretti, aka the fat testicle-punching cocksucker, lived. After leaving the Internet café, Brady walked Z-Boy into an Army surplus store

231

and bought a hunting knife.

The next day when he left the house, Moretti found a dead dog stretched out on the welcome mat. Its throat had been cut. Written in dogblood on the windshield of his car was YOUR WIFE & KIDS ARE NEXT.

★ ★ ★

Doing this — being *able* to do this — cheered Brady up. Payback is a bitch, he thought, and I am that bitch.

He sometimes fantasized about sending Z-Boy after Hodges and shooting him in the belly. How good it would be to stand over the Det-Ret, watching him shudder and moan as his life ran through his fingers!

It would be great, but Brady would lose his drone, and once in custody, Al might point the police at *him*. There was something else, as well, something even bigger: *it wouldn't be enough*. He owed Hodges more than a bullet in the belly followed by ten or fifteen minutes of suffering. Much more. Hodges needed to live, breathing toxic air inside a bag of guilt from which there was no escape. Until he could no longer stand it, and killed himself.

Which had been the original plan, back in the good old days.

No way, though, Brady thought. No way to do any of it. I've got Z-Boy — who'll be in an assisted living home if he keeps on the way he's going — and I can rattle the blinds with my phantom hand. That's it. That's the whole deal.

But then, in the summer of 2013, the dark funk he'd been living in was pierced by a shaft of light. He had a visitor. A real one, not Hodges or a suit from the District Attorney's office, checking to see if he had magically improved enough to stand trial for a dozen different felony crimes, the list headed by eight counts of willful murder at City Center.

There was a perfunctory knock at the door, and Becky Helmington poked her head in. 'Brady? There's a young woman here to see you. Says she used to work with you, and she's brought you something. Do you want to see her?'

Brady could think of only one young woman that might be. He considered saying no, but his curiosity had come back along with his malice (perhaps they were even the same thing). He gave one of his floppy nods, and made an effort to brush his hair out of his eyes.

His visitor entered timidly, as if there might be hidden mines under the floor. She was wearing a dress. Brady had never seen her in a dress, would have guessed she didn't even own one. But her hair was still cropped close to her skull in a half-assed crewcut, as it had been when they had worked together on the Discount Electronix Cyber Patrol, and she was still as flat as a board in front. He remembered some comedian's joke: If no tits count for shit, Cameron Diaz is gonna be around for a long time. But she had put on a little powder to cover her pitted skin (amazing) and even a dash of lipstick (more amazing still). In one hand she held a wrapped package.

'Hey, man,' Freddi Linklatter said with unaccustomed shyness. 'How're you doing?'

This opened all sorts of possibilities.

Brady did his best to smile.

BADCONCERT.COM

Cora Babineau wipes the back of her neck with a monogrammed towel and frowns at the monitor in the basement exercise room. She has done only four of her six miles on the treadmill, she hates to be interrupted, and the weirdo is back.

Cling-clong goes the doorbell and she listens for her husband's footsteps above her, but there's nothing. On the monitor, the old man in the ratty parka — he looks like one of those bums you see standing at intersections, holding up signs that say things like HUNGRY, NO JOB, ARMY VETERAN, PLEASE HELP — just stands there.

'Dammit,' she mutters, and pauses the treadmill. She climbs the stairs, opens the door to the back hallway, and shouts, '*Felix! It's your weirdo friend! That Al!*'

No response. He's in his study again, possibly looking at the game-thing he seems to have fallen in love with. The first few times she mentioned Felix's strange new obsession to her friends at the country club, it was a joke. It doesn't seem so funny now. He's sixty-three, too old for kids' computer games and too young to have gotten so forgetful, and she's begun to wonder if he might not be suffering early-onset Alzheimer's. It has also crossed her mind that

Felix's weirdo friend is some kind of drug pusher, but isn't the guy awfully old for that? And if her husband wants drugs, he can certainly supply himself; according to him, half the doctors at Kiner are high at least half the time.

Cling-clong, goes the doorbell.

'Jesus on a pony,' she says, and goes to the door herself, growing more irritated with each long stride. She's a tall, gaunt woman whose female shape has been exercised nearly to oblivion. Her golf tan remains even in the depths of winter, only turning a pale shade of yellow that makes her look as if she's suffering chronic liver disease.

She opens the door. The January night rushes in, chilling her sweaty face and arms. 'I think I would like to know who you are,' she says, 'and what you and my husband are up to together. Would that be too much to ask?'

'Not at all, Mrs Babineau,' he says. 'Sometimes I'm Al. Sometimes I'm Z-Boy. Tonight I'm Brady, and boy oh boy, it's nice to be out, even on such a cold night.'

She looks down at his hand. 'What's in that jar?'

'The end of all your troubles,' says the man in the mended parka, and there's a muffled bang. The bottom of the soda bottle blows out in shards, along with scorched threads from the steel wool. They float in the air like milkweed fluff.

Cora feels something hit her just below her shrunken left breast and thinks, This weirdo son of a bitch just punched me. She tries to take a breath and at first can't. Her chest feels strangely dead; warmth is pooling above the elastic top of

238

her tracksuit pants. She looks down, still trying to take that all-important breath, and sees a stain spreading on the blue nylon.

She raises her eyes to stare at the geezer in the doorway. He's holding out the remains of the bottle as if it's a present, a little gift to make up for showing up unannounced at eight in the evening. What's left of the steel wool pokes out of the bottom like a charred boutonniere. She finally manages a breath, but it's mostly liquid. She coughs, and sprays blood.

The man in the parka steps into her house and sweeps the door shut behind him. He drops the bottle. Then he pushes her. She staggers back, knocking a decorative vase from the end table by the coathooks, and goes down. The vase shatters on the hardwood floor like a bomb. She drags in another of those liquid breaths — I'm drowning, she thinks, drowning right here in my front hall — and coughs out another spray of red.

'Cora?' Babineau calls from somewhere deep in the house. He sounds as if he's just woken up. 'Cora, are you okay?'

Brady raises Library Al's foot and carefully brings Library Al's heavy black workshoe down on the straining tendons of Cora Babineau's scrawny throat. More blood bursts from her mouth; her sun-cured cheeks are now stippled with it. He steps down hard. There's a crackling sound as stuff breaks inside her. Her eyes bulge . . . bulge . . . and then they glaze over.

'You were a tough one,' Brady remarks, almost affectionately.

A door opens. Slippered feet come running,

and then Babineau is there. He's wearing a dressing gown over ridiculous Hugh Hefner-style silk pajamas. His silver hair, usually his pride, is in wild disarray. The stubble on his cheeks has become an incipient beard. In his hand is a green Zappit console from which the little Fishin' Hole tune tinkles: *By the sea, by the sea, by the beautiful sea*. He stares at his wife lying on the hall floor.

'No more workouts for her,' Brady says in that same affectionate tone.

'*What did you DO?*' Babineau screams, as if it isn't obvious. He runs to Cora and tries to fall to his knees beside her, but Brady hooks him under the armpit and hauls him back up. Library Al is by no means Charles Atlas, but he is ever so much stronger than the wasted body in Room 217.

'No time for that,' Brady says. 'The Robinson girl is alive, which necessitates a change of plan.'

Babineau stares at him, trying to gather his thoughts, but they elude him. His mind, once so sharp, has been blunted. And it's this man's fault.

'Look at the fish,' Brady says. 'You look at yours and I'll look at mine. We'll both feel better.'

'No,' Babineau says. He wants to look at the fish, he always wants to look at them now, but he's afraid to. Brady wants to pour his mind into Babineau's head like some strange water, and each time that happens, less of his essential self remains afterward.

'Yes,' Brady says. 'Tonight you need to be Dr Z.'

'I refuse!'

'You're in no position to refuse. This is coming unraveled. Soon the police will be at your door. Or Hodges, and that would be even worse. He won't read you your rights, he'll just hit you with that homemade sap of his. Because he's a mean motherfucker. And because you were right. He *knows*.'

'I won't . . . I can't . . . ' Babineau looks down at his wife. Ah God, her eyes. Her bulging eyes. 'The police would never believe . . . I'm a respected doctor! We've been married for thirty-five years!'

'Hodges will. And when Hodges gets the bit in his teeth, he turns into Wyatt fucking Earp. He'll show the Robinson girl your picture. She'll look at it and say oh wow, yes, that's the man who gave me the Zappit at the mall. And if you gave her a Zappit, you probably gave one to Janice Ellerton. Oops! And there's Scapelli.'

Babineau stares, trying to comprehend this disaster.

'Then there's the drugs you fed me. Hodges may know about them already, because he's a fast man with a bribe and most of the nurses in the Bucket know. It's an open secret, because you never tried to hide it.' Brady gives Library Al's head a sad shake. 'Your arrogance.'

'Vitamins!' It's all Babineau can manage.

'Even the cops won't believe that if they subpoena your files and search your computers.' Brady glances down at Cora Babineau's sprawled body. 'And there's your wife, of course. How are you going to explain her?'

'I wish you'd died before they brought you in,' Babineau says. His voice is rising, becoming a whine. 'Or on the operating table. You're a *Frankenstein*!'

'Don't confuse the monster with the creator,' Brady says, although he doesn't actually give Babineau much credit in the creation department. Dr B.'s experimental drug may have something to do with his new abilities, but it had little or nothing to do with his recovery. He's positive that was his own doing. An act of sheer willpower. 'Meanwhile, we have a visit to make, and we don't want to be late.'

'To the man-woman.' There's a word for that, Babineau used to know it, but now it's gone. Like the name that goes with it. Or what he ate for dinner. Each time Brady comes into his head, he takes a little more when he leaves. Babineau's memory. His knowledge. His *self*.

'That's right, the man-woman. Or, to give her sexual preference its scientific name, *Ruggus munchus*.'

'No.' The whine has become a whisper. 'I'm going to stay right here.'

Brady raises the gun, the barrel now visible within the blown-out remains of the makeshift silencer. 'If you think I really need you, you're making the worst mistake of your life. And the last one.'

Babineau says nothing. This is a nightmare, and soon he will wake up.

'Do it, or tomorrow the housekeeper will find you lying dead next to your wife, unfortunate victims of a home invasion. I would rather finish my business as Dr Z — your body is ten years younger than Brooks's, and not in bad shape — but I'll do what I have to. Besides, leaving you to face Kermit Hodges would be mean of me. He's a nasty man, Felix. You have no idea.'

Babineau looks at the elderly fellow in the mended parka and sees Hartsfield looking out of Library Al's watery blue eyes. Babineau's lips are trembling and wet with spittle. His eyes are rimmed with tears. Brady thinks that with his white hair standing up around his head as it is now, the Babster looks like Albert Einstein in that photo where the famous physicist is sticking his tongue out.

'How did I get into this?' he moans.

'The way everybody gets into everything,' Brady says gently. 'One step at a time.'

'Why did you have to go after the girl?' Babineau bursts out.

'It was a mistake,' Brady says. Easier to admit that than the whole truth: he couldn't wait. He wanted the nigger lawnboy's sister to go before anyone else blotted out her importance. 'Now stop fucking around and look at the fishies. You know you want to.'

And he does. That's the worst part. In spite of everything Babineau now knows, he does.

He looks at the fish.

He listens to the tune.

After awhile he goes into the bedroom to dress and get money out of the safe. He makes one more stop before leaving. The bathroom medicine cabinet is well stocked, on both her side and his.

243

He takes Babineau's BMW, leaving the old Malibu where it is for the time being. He also leaves Library Al, who has gone to sleep on the sofa.

2

Around the time Cora Babineau is opening her front door for the last time, Hodges is sitting down in the living room of the Scott family's home on Allgood Place, just one block over from Teaberry Lane, where the Robinsons live. He swallowed a couple of painkillers before getting out of the car, and isn't feeling bad, all things considered.

Dinah Scott is on the sofa, flanked by her parents. She looks quite a bit older than fifteen tonight, because she's recently back from a rehearsal at North Side High School, where the Drama Club will soon be putting on *The Fantasticks*. She has the role of Luisa, Angie Scott has told Hodges, a real plum. (This causes Dinah to roll her eyes.) Hodges is across from them in a La-Z-Boy very much like the one in his own living room. From the deep divot in the seat, he deduces it is Carl Scott's normal evening roost.

On the coffee table in front of the sofa is a bright green Zappit. Dinah brought it down from her room right away, which allows Hodges to further deduce that it wasn't buried under sports gear in her closet, or left under the bed with the dust bunnies. It wasn't sitting forgotten in her locker at school. No, it was where she could lay her hands on it at once. Which means she's been using it, old-school or not.

'I'm here at the request of Barbara Robinson,' he tells them. 'She was struck by a truck today — '

'Omigod,' Dinah says, a hand going to her mouth.

'She's okay,' Hodges says. 'Broken leg is all. They're keeping her overnight for observation, but she'll be home tomorrow and probably back in school next week. You can sign her cast, if kids still do that.'

Angie puts an arm around her daughter's shoulders. 'What does that have to do with Dinah's game?'

'Well, Barbara had one, and it gave her a shock.' Based on what Holly told Hodges while he was driving over here, that's no lie. 'She was crossing a street at the time, lost her bearings for a minute, and bammo. A boy pushed her clear, or it would have been much worse.'

'Jesus,' Carl says.

Hodges leans forward, looking at Dinah. 'I don't know how many of these gadgets are defective, but it's clear from what happened to Barb, and a couple of other incidents we know of, that at least some of them are.'

'Let this be a lesson to you,' Carl says to his daughter. 'The next time someone tells you a thing's free, be on your guard.'

This prompts another eye-roll of the perfect teenage variety.

'The thing I'm curious about,' Hodges says, 'is

how you came by yours in the first place. It's kind of a mystery, because the Zappit company didn't sell many. They were bought out by another company when it flopped, and that company went bankrupt in April two years ago. You'd think the Zappit consoles would have been held for resale, to help pay the bills — '

'Or destroyed,' Carl says. 'That's what they do with unsold paperbacks, you know.'

'I'm actually aware of that,' Hodges says. 'So tell me, Dinah, how *did* you get it?'

'I went on the website,' she says. 'I'm not in trouble, am I? I mean, I didn't know, but Daddy always says ignorance of the law is no excuse.'

'You're in zero trouble,' Hodges assures her. 'What website was this?'

'It was called badconcert.com. I looked for it on my phone when Mom called me at rehearsal and said you were coming over, but it's gone. I guess they gave away all the ones they had.'

'Or found out the things were dangerous, and folded their tents without warning anyone,' Angie Scott says, looking grim.

'How bad could the shock be, though?' Carl asks. 'I opened up the back when Dee brought it down from her room. There's nothing in there but four rechargeable double As.'

'I don't know about that stuff,' Hodges says. His stomach is starting to hurt again in spite of the dope. Not that his stomach is actually the problem; it's an adjacent organ only six inches long. He took a moment after his meeting with Norma Wilmer to check the survival rate of patients with pancreatic cancer. Only six percent of them manage to live five years. Not what you'd call cheery news. 'So far I haven't even managed to re-program my iPhone's text message alert so it doesn't scare innocent bystanders.'

'I can do that for you,' Dinah says. 'Easy-peasy. I have Crazy Frog on mine.'

'Tell me about the website first.'

'There was a tweet, okay? Someone at school told me about it. It got picked up on lots of social media sites. Facebook . . . Pinterest . . . Google Plus . . . you know the ones I'm talking about.'

Hodges doesn't, but nods.

'I can't remember the tweet exactly, but pretty close. Because they can only be a hundred and forty characters long. You know that, right?'

'Sure,' Hodges says, although he barely grasps what a tweet is. His left hand is trying to sneak its way to the pain in his side. He makes it stay put.

'This one said something like . . . ' Dinah closes her eyes. It's rather theatrical, but of course she just *did* come from a Drama Club rehearsal. ' ''Bad news, some nut got the 'Round Here concert canceled. Want some good news? Maybe even a free gift? Go to badconcert.com.'' ' She opens her eyes. 'That's probably not exact, but you get the idea.'

'I do, yeah.' He jots the website name in his notebook. 'So you went there . . . '

'Sure. Lots of kids went there. It was kind of funny, too. There was a Vine of 'Round Here singing their big song from a few of years ago,

247

'Kisses on the Midway,' it was called, and after about twenty seconds there's an explosion sound and this quacky voice saying, 'Oh damn, show canceled.''

'I don't think that's so funny,' Angie says. 'You all could have been killed.'

'There must have been more to it than that,' Hodges says.

'Sure. It said that there were like two thousand kids there, a lot of them at their first concert, and, they got screwed out of the experience of a lifetime. Although, um, *screwed* wasn't the word they used.'

'I think we can fill in that blank, dear one,' Carl says.

'And then it said that 'Round Here's corporate sponsor had received a whole bunch of Zappit game consoles, and they wanted to give them away. To, you know, kind of make up for the concert.'

'Even though that was almost six years ago?' Angie looks incredulous.

'Yeah. Kind of weird, when you think of it.'

'But you didn't,' Carl said. 'Think of it.'

Dinah shrugs, looking petulant. 'I did, but it seemed okay.'

'Famous last words,' her father says.

'So you just . . . what?' Hodges asks. 'Emailed in your name and address and got that' — he points to the Zappit — 'in the mail?'

'There was a little more to it than that,' Dinah says. 'You had to, like, be able to prove you were actually there. So I went to see Barb's mom. You know, Tanya.'

'Why?'

'For the pictures. I think I have mine somewhere, but I couldn't find them.'

'Her room,' Angie says, and this time she's the one with the eye-roll.

Hodges's side has picked up a slow, steady throb. 'What pictures, Dinah?'

'Okay, it was Tanya — she doesn't mind if we call her that — who took us to the concert, see? There was Barb, me, Hilda Carver, and Betsy.'

'Betsy would be . . . ?'

'Betsy DeWitt,' Angie says. 'The deal was, the moms drew straws to see who would take the girls. Tanya lost. She took Ginny Carver's van, because it was the biggest.'

Hodges nods his understanding.

'So anyway, when we got there,' Dinah says, 'Tanya took pictures of us. We *had* to have pictures. Sounds stupid, I guess, but we were just little kids. I'm into Mendoza Line and Raveonettes now, but back then 'Round Here was a really big deal to us. Especially Cam, the lead singer. Tanya used our phones. Or maybe she used her own, I can't exactly remember. But she made sure we all had copies, only I couldn't find mine.'

'You had to send a picture to the website as proof of attendance.'

'Right, by email. I was afraid the pics would only show us standing in front of Mrs Carver's van and that wouldn't be enough, but there were two that showed the Mingo Auditorium in the background, with all the people lined up. I thought even that might not be good enough,

249

because it didn't show the sign with the band's name on it, but it was, and I got the Zappit in the mail just a week later. It came in a big padded envelope.'

'Was there a return address?'

'Uh-huh. I can't remember the box number, but the name was Sunrise Solutions. I guess they were the tour sponsors.'

It's possible that they were, Hodges thinks, the company wouldn't have been bankrupt back then, but he doubts it. 'Was it mailed from here in the city?'

'I don't remember.'

'I'm pretty sure it was,' Angie says. 'I picked the envelope up off the floor and tossed it in the trash. I'm the French maid around here, you know.' She shoots her daughter a look.

'Soh-ree,' Dinah says.

In his notebook, Hodges writes *Sunrise Solutions based NYC, but pkg mailed front here.*

'When did all this go down, Dinah?'

'I heard about the tweet and went to the website last year. I can't remember exactly, but I know it was before the Thanksgiving break. And like I said, it came lickety-split. I was really surprised.'

'So you've had it for two months, give or take.'

'Yes.'

'And no shocks?'

'No, nothing like that.'

'Have you ever had any experiences where you were playing with it — let's say with the Fishin' Hole game — and you kind of lost track of your surroundings?'

250

Mr and Mrs Scott look alarmed at this, but Dinah gives him an indulgent smile. 'You mean like being hypnotized? Eenie-meenie, chili-beanie?'

'I don't know *what* I mean, exactly, but okay, say that.'

'Nope,' Dinah says cheerily. 'Besides, Fishin' Hole is really dumb. It's for little kids. You use the joystick thingie beside the keypad to operate Fisherman Joe's net, see? And you get points for the fish you catch. But it's too easy. Only reason I check back on that one is to see if the pink fish are showing numbers yet.'

'Numbers?'

'Yes. The letter that came with the game explained about them. I tacked it on my bulletin board, because I'd really like to win that moped. Want to see it?'

'I sure would.'

When she bounces upstairs to get it, Hodges asks if he can use the bathroom. Once in there, he unbuttons his shirt and looks at his throbbing left side. It seems a little swollen and feels a little hot to the touch, but he supposes both of those things could be his imagination. He flushes the toilet and takes two more of the white pills. Okay? he asks his throbbing side. Can you just shut up awhile and let me finish here?

Dinah has scrubbed off most of her stage makeup, and now it's easy for Hodges to imagine her and the other three girls at nine or ten, going to their first concert and as excited as Mexican jumping beans in a microwave. She hands him the letter that came with the game.

At the top of the sheet is a rising sun, with the

251

words SUNRISE SOLUTIONS bent over it in an arc, pretty much what you'd expect, only it doesn't look like any corporate logo Hodges has ever seen. It's strangely amateurish, as if the original was drawn by hand. It's a form letter with the girl's name plugged in to give it a more personal feel. Not that anybody's apt to be fooled by that in this day and age, Hodges thinks, when even mass mailings from insurance companies and ambulance chasing lawyers come personalized.

Dear Dinah Scott!
Congratulations! We hope you will enjoy your Zappit game console, which comes pre-loaded with 65 fun and challenging games. It is also WiFi equipped so you can visit your favorite Internet sites and download books as a member of the Sunrise Readers Circle! You are receiving this FREE GIFT to make up for the concert you missed, but of course we hope you will tell all your friends about your wonderful Zappit experience. And there's more! Keep checking the Fishin' Hole demo screen, and keep tapping those pink fish, because someday — you won't know when until it happens! — you will tap them and they will turn into numbers! If the fish you tap add up to one of the numbers below, you will win a GREAT PRIZE! But the numbers will only be visible for a short time, so KEEP CHECKING! Add to the fun by staying in touch with others in 'The Zappit Club' by going to zeetheend.com, where you can also claim your prize if

you are one of the lucky ones! Thanks from all of us at Sunrise Solutions, and the whole Zappit team!

There was an unreadable signature, hardly more than a scribble. Below that:

Lucky numbers for Dinah Scott:

1034=$25 gift certificate at Deb
1781=$40 gift card at Atom Arcade
1946=$50 gift certificate at Carmike Cinemas

7459=Wave 50cc moped-scooter (Grand Prize)

'You actually believed this bullshit?' Carl Scott asks.

Although the question is delivered with a smile, Dinah tears up. 'All right, I'm stupid, so shoot me.'

Carl hugs her, kisses her temple. 'Know what? I would have swallowed it at your age, too.'

'Have you been checking the pink fish, Dinah?' Hodges asks.

'Yes, once or twice a day. That's actually harder than the game, because the pink ones are fast. You have to concentrate.'

Of course you do, Hodges thinks. He likes this less and less. 'But no numbers, huh?'

'Not so far.'

'Can I take that?' he asks, pointing to the Zappit. He thinks about telling her he'll give it back later, but doesn't. He doubts if he will. 'And the letter?'

'On one condition,' she says.

Hodges, pain now subsiding, is able to smile. 'Name it, kiddo.'

'Keep checking the pink fish, and if one of my numbers comes up, *I* get the prize.'

'It's a deal,' Hodges says, thinking, Someone wants to give you a prize, Dinah, but I doubt very much if it's a moped or a cinema gift certificate. He takes the Zappit and the letter, and stands up. 'I want to thank you all very much for your time.'

'Welcome,' Carl says. 'And when you figure out just what the hell this is all about, will you tell us?'

'You got it,' Hodges says. 'One more question, Dinah, and if I sound stupid, remember that I'm pushing seventy.'

She smiles. 'At school, Mr Morton says the only stupid question — '

'Is the one you don't ask, yeah. I've always felt that way myself, so here it comes. Everybody at North Side High knows about this, right? The free consoles, the number-fish, and the prizes?'

'Not just our school, all the other ones, too. Twitter, Facebook, Pinterest, Yik Yak . . . that's how they *work*.'

'And if you were at the concert and you could prove it, you were eligible to get one of these.'

'Uh-huh.'

'What about Betsy DeWitt? Did she get one?'

Dinah frowns. 'No, and that's kind of funny, because she still had her pictures from that night, and she sent one to the website. But she didn't do it as soon as I did, she's an awful procrastinator, so maybe they were all out. If you snooze, you lose type of thing.'

Hodges thanks the Scotts again for their time, wishes Dinah good luck with the play, and goes back down the walk to his car. When he slides behind the wheel, it's cold enough inside to see his breath. The pain surfaces again: four hard pulses. He waits them out, teeth clamped, trying to tell himself these new, sharper pains are psychosomatic, because he now knows what's wrong with him, but the idea won't quite wash. Two more days suddenly seems like a long time to wait for treatment, but he will wait. Has to, because an awful idea is rising in his mind. Pete Huntley wouldn't believe it, and Izzy Jaynes would probably think he needed a quick ambulance ride to the nearest funny farm. Hodges doesn't quite believe it himself, but the pieces are coming together, and although the picture that's being revealed is a crazy one, it also has a certain nasty logic.

He starts his Prius and points it toward home, where he will call Holly and ask her to try and find out if Sunrise Solutions ever sponsored a 'Round Here tour. After that he will watch TV. When he can no longer pretend that what's on interests him, he'll go to bed and lie awake and wait for morning.

Only he's curious about the green Zappit.

Too curious, it turns out, to wait. Halfway between Allgood Place and Harper Road, he pulls into a strip mall, parks in front of a dry cleaning shop that's closed for the night, and powers the gadget up. It flashes bright white, and

255

then a red **Z** appears, growing closer and bigger until the slant of the Z colors the whole screen red. A moment later it flashes white again, and a message appears: WELCOME TO **ZAPPIT!** WE LOVE TO PLAY! HIT ANY KEY TO BEGIN, OR JUST SWIPE THE SCREEN!

Hodges swipes, and game icons appear in neat rows. Some are console versions of ones he watched Allie play at the mall when she was a little girl: Space Invaders, Donkey Kong, Pac-Man, and that little yellow devil's main squeeze, Ms Pac-Man. There are also the various solitaire games Janice Ellerton had been hooked on, and plenty of other stuff Hodges has never heard of. He swipes again, and there it is, between SpellTower and Barbie's Fashion Walk: Fishin' Hole. He takes a deep breath and taps the icon.

THINKING ABOUT **FISHIN' HOLE**, the screen advises. A little worry-circle goes around for ten seconds or so (it seems longer), and then the demo screen appears. Fish swim back and forth, or do loop-the-loops, or shoot up and down on diagonals. Bubbles rise from their mouths and flipping tails. The water is greenish at the top, shading to blue farther down. A little tune plays, not one Hodges recognizes. He watches and waits to feel something — sleepy seems the most likely.

The fish are red, green, blue, gold, yellow. They're probably supposed to be tropical fish, but they have none of the hyper-reality Hodges has seen in Xbox and PlayStation commercials on TV. These fish are basically cartoons, and primitive ones, at that. No wonder the Zappit flopped, he thinks, but yeah, okay, there's something mildly hypnotic about the way the fish move, sometimes alone, sometimes in pairs, every now and then in a rainbow school of half a dozen.

And jackpot, here comes a pink one. He taps at it, but it's moving just a mite too fast, and he misses. Hodges mutters 'Shit!' under his breath. He looks up at the darkened dry cleaning store's window for a moment, because he really is feeling a trifle dozy. He lightly smacks first his left cheek and then his right with the hand not holding the game, and looks back down. There are more fish now, weaving back and forth in complicated patterns.

Here comes another pink one, and this time he succeeds in tapping it before it whisks off the left side of the screen. It blinks (almost as if to say Okay, Bill, you got me that time) but no number appears. He waits, watches, and when another pink one appears, he taps again. Still no number, just a pink fish that has no counterpart in the real world.

The tune seems louder now, and at the same time slower. Hodges thinks, It really is having some kind of effect. It's mild, and probably completely accidental, but it's there, all right.

He pushes the power button. The screen flashes THANKS FOR PLAYING SEE YOU SOON and goes dark. He looks at the dashboard clock and is astonished to see he has been sitting here looking at the Zappit for over ten minutes. It felt more like two or three. Five, at the very most. Dinah didn't talk about losing time while looking at the Fishin' Hole demo screen, but he hadn't asked about that, had he? On the other hand, he's on two fairly heavy-duty painkillers, and that probably played a part in what just happened. If anything actually did, that is.

No numbers, though.

The pink fish had just been pink fish.

Hodges slips the Zappit into his coat pocket along with his phone and drives home.

3

Freddi Linklatter — once a computer-repair colleague of Brady's before the world discovered Brady Hartsfield was a monster — sits at her kitchen table, spinning a silver flask with one finger as she waits for the man with the fancy briefcase.

Dr Z is what he calls himself, but Freddi is no fool. She knows the name that goes with the briefcase initials: Felix Babineau, head of neurology at Kiner Memorial.

Does he know that *she* knows? She's guessing he does, and doesn't care. But it's weird. *Very*. He's in his sixties, an authentic golden oldie, but he reminds her of somebody much younger. Someone who is, in fact, this Dr Babineau's most famous (infamous, really) patient.

Around and around goes the flask. Etched on the side is *GH & FL, 4Ever*. Well, 4Ever lasted just about two years, and Gloria Hollis has been gone for quite awhile now. Babineau — or Dr Z, as he styles himself, like the villain in a comic book — was part of the reason why.

'He's creepy,' Gloria said. 'The older guy is, too. And the money's creepy. It's too much. I don't know what they got you into, Fred, but sooner or later it's going to blow up in your face, and I don't want to be part of the collateral damage.'

Of course Gloria had also met someone else — someone quite a bit better-looking than Freddi, with her angular body and lantern jaw and pitted cheeks — but she didn't want to talk about that part of it, oh no.

Around and around goes the flask.

It all seemed so simple at first, and how could she refuse the money? She never saved much when she worked on the Discount Electronix Cyber Patrol, and the work she'd been able to find as an independent IT when the store closed had barely been enough to keep her off the street. It might have been different if she'd had what Anthony Frobisher, her old boss, liked to call 'people skills,' but those had never been her forte. When the old geezer who called himself Z-Boy made his offer (and dear God, that was *really* a comic book handle), it had been like a gift from God. She had been living in a shitty apartment on the South Side, in the part of town commonly referred to as Hillbilly Heaven, and a month behind on the rent in spite of the cash the guy had already given her. What was she supposed to do? Refuse five thousand dollars? Get real.

Around and around goes the flask.

The guy is late, maybe he's not coming at all,

and that might be for the best.

She remembers the geezer casting his eyes around the two-room apartment, most of her possessions in paper bags with handles (all too easy to see those bags gathered around her as she tried to sleep beneath a Crosstown Expressway underpass). 'You'll need a bigger place,' he said.

'Yeah, and the farmers in California need rain.' She remembers peering into the envelope he handed her. Remembers riffling the fifties, and what a comfy sound they made. 'This is nice, but by the time I get square with all the people I owe, there won't be much left.' She could stiff most of those people, but the geezer didn't need to know that.

'There'll be more, and my boss will take care of getting you an apartment where you may be asked to accept certain shipments.'

That started alarm bells ringing. 'If you're thinking about drugs, let's just forget the whole thing.' She held out the cash-stuffed envelope to him, much as it hurt to do that.

He pushed it back with a little grimace of contempt. 'No drugs. You'll not be asked to sign for anything even slightly illegal.'

So here she is, in a condo close to the lakeshore. Not that there's much of a lake view from only six stories up, and not that the place is a palace. Far from it, especially in the winter. You can only catch a wink of the water between the newer, nicer highrises, but the wind finds its way through just fine, thanks, and in January, that wind is *cold*. She has the joke thermostat cranked to eighty, and is still wearing three shirts and longjohns under her carpenter jeans. Hill-billy Heaven is in the rearview mirror, though, that's something, but the question remains: is it enough?

Around and around goes the silver flask. *GH & FL, 4Ever.* Only nothing is 4Ever.

The lobby buzzer goes, making her jump. She picks up the flask — her one souvenir of the glorious Gloria days — and heads to the inter-com. She quashes an urge to do her Russian spy accent again. Whether he calls himself Dr Babineau or Dr Z, the guy is a little scary. Not Hillbilly-Heaven, crystal-meth-dope-dealer scary, but in a different way. Better to play this straight, get it over with, and hope to Christ she doesn't find herself in too much trouble if the deal blows up in her face.

'Is this the famous Dr Z?'

'Of course it is.'

'You're late.'

'Am I keeping you from something important, Freddi?'

No, nothing important. Nothing she does is particularly important these days.

'You brought the money?'

'Of course.' Sounding impatient. The old geezer with whom she had commenced this nutty busi-ness had the same impatient way of speaking. He and Dr Z looked nothing alike, but they *sounded* alike, enough to make her wonder if they weren't brothers. Only they also sounded like that some-one else, the old colleague she used to work with. The one who turned out to be Mr Mercedes.

Freddi doesn't want to think about that any

more than she wants to think about the various hacks she's done on Dr Z's behalf. She hits the buzzer beside the intercom.

She goes to her door to wait for him, taking a nip of Scotch to fortify herself. She tucks the flask into the breast pocket of her middle shirt, then reaches into the pocket of the one beneath, where she keeps her breath mints. She doesn't believe Dr Z would give Shit One if he smelled booze on her breath, but she always used to pop a mint after a nip when she was working at Discount Electronix, and old habits are strong habits. She takes her Marlboros from the pocket of her top shirt and lights one. It will further mask the smell of the booze, and calm her a little more, and if he doesn't like her secondhand smoke, tough titty.

'This guy has set you up in a pretty nice apartment and paid you almost thirty thousand dollars over the last eighteen months or so,' Gloria had said. 'Tall tickets for something any hacker worth her salt could do in her sleep, at least according to you. So *why* you? And why so much?'

More stuff Freddi doesn't want to think about.

It all started with the picture of Brady and his mom. She found it in the junk room at Discount Electronix, shortly after the staff had been told the Birch Hill Mall store was closing. Their boss, Anthony 'Tones' Frobisher, must have taken it out of Brady's work cubby and tossed it back there after the world found out that Brady was the infamous Mercedes Killer. Freddi had no great love for Brady (although they *did* have a few meaningful conversations about gender identity, back in the day). Wrapping the picture and taking it to the hospital was pure impulse. And the few times she'd visited him afterwards had been pure curiosity, plus a little pride at the way Brady had reacted to her. He *smiled*.

'He responds to you,' the new head nurse — Scapelli — said after one of Freddi's visits. 'That's very unusual.'

By the time Scapelli replaced Becky Helmington, Freddi knew that the mysterious Dr Z who took over supplying her with cash was in reality Dr Felix Babineau. She didn't think about that, either. Or about the cartons that eventually began arriving from Terre Haute via UPS. Or the hacks. She became an expert in not thinking, because once you started doing that, certain connections became obvious. And all because of that damn picture. Freddi wishes now she'd resisted the impulse, but her mother had a saying: Too late always comes too early.

She hears his footsteps coming down the hall. She opens the door before he can ring the bell, and the question is out of her mouth before she knows she is going to ask it.

'Tell me the truth, Dr Z — are you Brady?'

4

Hodges is barely inside his front door and still taking off his coat when his cell rings. 'Hey, Holly.'

'Are you all right?'

He can see a lot of calls from her starting with

this exact same greeting. Well, it's better than Drop dead, motherfucker. 'Yeah, I'm good.'

'One more day, and then you start treatments. And once you start, you don't stop. Whatever the doctors say, you do.'

'Stop worrying. A deal is a deal.'

'I'll stop worrying when you're cancer free.'

Don't, Holly, he thinks, and closes his eyes against the unexpected sting of tears. Don't, don't, don't.

'Jerome is coming tonight. He called from his plane to ask about Barbara, and I told him everything she told me. He'll be in at eleven o'clock. A good thing he left when he did, because a storm is coming. It's supposed to be a bad one. I offered to rent him a car the way I do for you when you go out of town, it's very easy now that we have the corporate account — '

'That you lobbied for until I gave in. Believe me, I know.'

'But he doesn't need a car. His father is picking him up. They'll go in to see Barbara at eight tomorrow, and bring her home if the doctor says she can go. Jerome said he can be at our office by ten, if that's okay.'

'Sounds fine,' Hodges says, wiping his eyes. He doesn't know how much Jerome can help, but he knows it will be very good to see him. 'Anything more he can find out from her about that damn gadget — '

'I asked him to do that. Did you get Dinah's?'

'Yeah. And tried it. There's something up with the Fishin' Hole demo screen, all right. It makes you sleepy if you look at it too long. Purely accidental, I think, and I don't see how most kids would be affected, because they'd want to go right to the game.'

He fills her in on the rest of what he learned from Dinah.

Holly says, 'So Dinah didn't get her Zappit the same way as Barbara and the Ellerton woman.'

'No.'

'And don't forget Hilda Carver. The man calling himself Myron Zakim gave her one, too. Only hers didn't work. Barb said it just gave a single blue flash and died. Did you see any blue flashes?'

'Nope.' Hodges is peering at the scant contents of his refrigerator for something his stomach might accept, and settles on a carton of banana-flavored yogurt. 'And there were pink fish, but when I succeeded in tapping a couple — which ain't easy — no numbers appeared.'

'I bet they did on Mrs Ellerton's.'

Hodges thinks so, too. It's early to generalize, but he's starting to think the number-fish only show up on the Zappits that were handed out by the man with the briefcase, Myron Zakim. Hodges also thinks someone is playing games with the letter Z, and along with a morbid interest in suicide, games were part of Brady Hartsfield's modus operandi. Except Brady is stuck in his room at Kiner Memorial, goddammit. Hodges keeps coming up against that irrefutable fact. If Brady Hartsfield has stooges to do his dirt, and it's starting to seem that he does, how is he running them? And why would they run for him, anyway?

265

'Holly, I need you to heat up your computer and check something out. Not a biggie, just a *t* that needs to be crossed.'

'Tell me.'

'I want to know if Sunrise Solutions sponsored the 'Round Here tour in 2010, when Hartsfield tried to blow up the Mingo Auditorium. Or *any* 'Round Here tour.'

'I can do that. Did you have supper?'

'Taking care of that right now.'

'Good. What are you having?'

'Steak, shoestring potatoes, and a salad,' Hodges says, looking at the carton of yogurt with a mixture of distaste and resignation. 'Got a leftover apple tart for dessert.'

'Heat it up in the microwave and put a scoop of vanilla ice cream on top. Yummy!'

'I'll take that under consideration.'

He shouldn't be amazed when she calls back five minutes later with the information he requested, it's just Holly being Holly, but he still is. 'Jesus, Holly, already?'

With no idea that she is echoing Freddi Linklatter almost word for word, Holly says, 'Ask for something hard next time. You might like to know that 'Round Here broke up in 2013. Those boy bands don't seem to last very long.'

'No,' Hodges says, 'once they start having to shave, the little girls lose interest.'

'I wouldn't know,' Holly says. 'I was always a Billy Joel fan. Also Michael Bolton.'

Oh, Holly, Hodges mourns. And not for the first time.

'Between 2007 and 2012, the group did six

nationwide tours. The first four were sponsored by Sharp Cereals, which gave out free samples at their concerts. The last two, including the one at the Mingo, were sponsored by PepsiCo.'

'No Sunrise Solutions.'

'No.'

'Thanks, Holly. I'll see you tomorrow.'

'Yes. Are you eating your dinner?'

'Sitting down to it now.'

'All right. And try to see Barbara before you start your treatments. She needs friendly faces, because whatever was wrong with her hasn't worn off yet. She said it was like it left a trail of slime inside her head.'

'I'll make sure of it,' Hodges says, but that is a promise he's not able to keep.

5

Are you Brady?

Felix Babineau, who sometimes calls himself Myron Zakim and sometimes Dr Z, smiles at the question. It wrinkles his unshaven cheeks in a decidedly creepy way. Tonight he's wearing a furry ushanka instead of his trilby, and his white hair kind of squishes out around the bottom. Freddi wishes she hadn't asked the question, wishes she didn't have to let him in, wishes she'd never heard of him. If he *is* Brady, he's a walking haunted house.

'Ask me no questions and I'll tell you no lies,' he says.

She wants to let it go and can't. 'Because you

sound like him. And that hack the other one brought me after the boxes came . . . that was a Brady hack if I ever saw one. Good as a signature.'

'Brady Hartsfield is a semi-catatonic who can barely walk, let alone write a hack to be used on a bunch of obsolete game consoles. Some of which have proved to be defective as well as obsolete. I did not get my money's worth from those Sunrise Solutions motherfuckers, which pisses me off to the max.'

Pisses me off to the max. A phrase Brady used all the time back in their Cyber Patrol days, usually about their boss or some idiot customer who managed to spill a mocha latte into his CPU.

'You've been very well paid, Freddi, and you're almost done. Why don't we leave it at that?'

He brushes past her without waiting for a reply, puts his briefcase on the table, and snaps it open. He takes out an envelope with her initials, FL, printed on it. The letters slant backward. During her years on the Discount Electronix Cyber Patrol, she saw similar backslanted printing on hundreds of work orders. Those were the ones Brady filled out.

'Ten thousand,' Dr Z says. 'Final payment. Now go to work.'

Freddi reaches for the envelope. 'You don't need to hang around if you don't want to. The rest is basically automatic. It's like setting an alarm clock.'

And if you're really Brady, she thinks, you could do it yourself. I'm good at this stuff, but you were better.

He lets her fingers touch the envelope, then pulls it back. 'I'll stay. Not that I don't trust you.'

Right, Freddi thinks. As if.

His cheeks once more wrinkle in that unsettling smile. 'And who knows? We might get lucky and see the first hit.'

'I'll bet most of the people who got those Zappits have already thrown them away. It's a fucking *toy*, and some of them don't even work. Like you said.'

'Let me worry about that,' says Dr Z. Once again his cheeks wrinkle and pull back. His eyes are red, as if he's been smoking the rock. She thinks of asking him what, exactly, they are doing, and what he hopes to accomplish . . . but she already has an idea, and does she want to be sure? Besides, if this *is* Brady, what harm can it do? He had hundreds of ideas, all of them crackpot.

Well.

Most of them.

She leads the way into what was meant to be a spare bedroom and has now become her work-station, the sort of electronic refuge she always dreamed of and could never afford — a hidey-hole that Gloria, with her good looks, infectious laugh, and 'people skills,' could never understand. In here the baseboard heaters hardly work at all, and it's five degrees colder than the rest of the apartment. The computers don't mind. They like it.

'Go on,' he says. 'Do it.'

She sits down at the top-of-the-line desktop Mac with its twenty-seven-inch screen, refreshes it, and types in her password — a random collection of numbers. There's a file simply marked Z, which she opens with another password. The subfiles are marked Z-1 and Z-2. She uses a third password to open Z-2, then begins to rapidly click away at her keyboard. Dr Z stands by her left shoulder. He's a disturbing negative presence at first, but then she gets lost in what she's doing, as she always does.

Not that it takes long; Dr Z has given her the program, and executing it is child's play. To the right of her computer, sitting on a high shelf, is a Motorola signal repeater. When she finishes by simultaneously hitting COMMAND and the Z key, the repeater comes to life. A single word appears in yellow dots: SEARCHING. It blinks like a traffic light at a deserted intersection.

They wait, and Freddi becomes aware that she's holding her breath. She lets it go in a whoosh, momentarily puffing out her thin cheeks. She starts to get up, and Dr Z puts a hand on her shoulder. 'Let's give it a little longer.'

They give it five minutes, the only sound the soft hum of her equipment and the keening of the wind off the frozen lake. SEARCHING blinks on and on.

'All right,' he says at last. 'I knew it was too much to hope for. All things in good time, Freddi. Let's go back into the other room. I'll give you your final payment and then be on my wa — '

SEARCHING in yellow suddenly turns to FOUND in green.

'*There!*' he shouts, making her jump. '*There, Freddi! There's the first one!*'

Her final doubts are swept away and she

270

knows for sure. All it takes is that shout of triumph. It's Brady, all right. He's become a living Russian nesting doll, which goes perfectly with his furry Russian hat. Look inside Babineau and there's Dr Z. Look inside Dr Z, and there, pulling all the levers, is Brady Hartsfield. God knows how it can be, but it is.

FOUND in green is replaced with LOADING in red. After mere seconds, LOADING is replaced with TASK COMPLETE. After that, the repeater begins to search again.

'All right,' he says, 'I'm satisfied. Time for me to go. It's been a busy night, and I'm not done yet.'

She follows him into the main room, shutting the door to her electronic hideaway behind her. She has come to a decision that's probably long overdue. As soon as he's gone, she's going to kill the repeater and delete the final program. Once that's done, she'll pack a suitcase and go to a motel. Tomorrow she's getting the fuck out of this city and heading south to Florida. She's had it with Dr Z, and his Z-Boy sidekick, and winter in the Midwest.

Dr Z puts on his coat, but drifts to the window instead of going to the door. 'Not much of a view. Too many highrises in the way.'

'Yeah, it sucks the big one.'

'Still, it's better than mine,' he says, not turning. 'All I've had to look at for the last five and a half years is a parking garage.'

Suddenly she's at her limit. If he's still in the same room with her sixty seconds from now, she'll go into hysterics. 'Give me my money. Give

271

it to me and then get the fuck out. We're done.'

He turns. In his hand is the short-barreled pistol he used on Babineau's wife. 'You're right, Freddi. We are.'

She reacts instantly, knocking the pistol from his hand, kicking him in the groin, karate-chopping him like Lucy Liu when he doubles over, and running out the door while screaming her head off. This mental film-clip plays out in full color and Dolby sound as she stands rooted to the spot. The gun goes bang. She staggers back two steps, collides with the easy chair where she sits to watch TV, collapses across it, and rolls to the floor, coming down headfirst. The world begins to darken and draw away. Her last sensation is warmth above as she begins to bleed and below as her bladder lets loose.

'Final payment, as promised.' The words come from a great distance.

Blackness swallows the world. Freddi falls into it and is gone.

6

Brady stands perfectly still, watching the blood seep from beneath her. He's listening for someone to pound on her door, wanting to know if everything is all right. He doesn't expect that will happen, but better safe than sorry.

After ninety seconds or so, he puts the gun back in his overcoat pocket, next to his Zappit. He can't resist one more look into the computer room before leaving. The signal repeater continues its endless, automated search. He has, against all odds, completed an amazing journey. What the final results will be is impossible to predict, but that there will be *some* result he is certain. And it will eat into the old Det-Ret like acid. Revenge really is best when eaten cold.

He has the elevator to himself going down. The lobby is similarly empty. He walks around the corner, turning up the collar of Babineau's expensive overcoat against the wind, and tweets the locks of Babineau's Beemer. He gets in and starts it up, but only for the heater. Something needs doing before he moves on to his next destination. He doesn't really *want* to do it, because, whatever his failings as a human being, Babineau has a gorgeously intelligent mind, and a great deal of it is still intact. Destroying that mind is too much like those dumb and superstitious ISIS fucks hammering irreplaceable treasures of art and culture to rubble. Yet it must be done. No risks can be allowed, because the body is also a treasure. Yes, Babineau has slightly high blood pressure and his hearing has gone downhill in the last few years, but tennis and twice-weekly trips to the hospital gym have kept his muscles in fairly good shape. His heart ticks along at seventy beats a minute, with no misses. He's not suffering from sciatica, gout, cataracts, or any of the other outrages that affect many men at his age.

Besides, the good doctor is what he's got, at least for now.

With that in mind, Brady turns inward and finds what remains of Felix Babineau's core

273

consciousness — the brain within the brain. It has been scarred and ravaged and diminished by Brady's repeated occupancies, but it is still there, still Babineau, still capable (theoretically at least) of taking back control. It is, however, defenseless, like some armored creature stripped of its shell. It's not exactly flesh; Babineau's core self is more like densely packed wires made of light.

Not without regret, Brady seizes them with his phantom hand and tears them apart.

7

Hodges spends the evening slowly eating his yogurt and watching the Weather Channel. The winter storm, ridiculously dubbed Eugenie by the Weather Channel wonks, is still coming and is expected to hit the city sometime late tomorrow.

'Hard to be more exact as of now,' the balding, bespectacled wonk says to the knockout blond wonk in the red dress. 'This one gives new meaning to the term stop-and-go traffic.'

The knockout wonk laughs as if her partner in meteorology has said something outrageously witty, and Hodges uses the remote to turn them off.

The zapper, he thinks, looking at it. That's what everyone calls these things. Quite the invention, when you stop to think of it. You can access hundreds of different channels by remote control. Never even have to get up. As if you're inside the television instead of in your chair. Or

274

in both places at the same time. Sort of a miracle, really.

As he goes into the bathroom to brush his teeth, his cell phone buzzes. He looks at the screen and has to laugh, even though it hurts to do it. Now that he's in the privacy of his own home, with nobody to be bothered by the home run text alert, his old partner calls instead.

'Hey, Pete, nice to know you still remember my number.'

Pete has no time for banter. 'I'm going to tell you something, Kermit, and if you decide to run with it, I'm like Sergeant Schultz on *Hogan's Heroes*. Remember him?'

'Sure.' What Hodges feels in his gut right now isn't a pain-cramp, but one of excitement. Weird how similar they are. 'I know nothing.'

'Right. It has to be that way, because as far as this department is concerned, the murder of Martine Stover and the suicide of her mother is officially a closed case. We are certainly not going to reopen it because of a coincidence, and that's right from the top. Are we clear on that?'

'As glass,' Hodges says. 'What's the coincidence?'

'The head nurse in the Kiner Brain Injury Clinic committed suicide last night. Ruth Scapelli.'

'I heard,' Hodges says.

'While on one of your pilgrimages to visit the delightful Mr Hartsfield, I presume.'

'Yeah.' No need to tell Pete that he never got in to see the delightful Mr Hartsfield.

'Scapelli had one of those game gadgets. A

Zappit. She apparently threw it in the trash before she bled out. One of the forensics guys found it.'

'Huh.' Hodges goes back into the living room and sits down, wincing when his body folds in the middle. 'And that's your idea of a coincidence?'

'Not necessarily mine,' Pete says heavily.

'But?'

'But I just want to retire in peace, goddammit! If there's a ball to carry on this one, Izzy can carry it.'

'But Izzy don't want to carry no steenkin ball.'

'No. Neither does the captain, or the commish.'

Hearing this, Hodges is forced to slightly revise his opinion of his old partner as a burnt-out case. 'You actually spoke to them? Tried to keep this thing alive?'

'To the captain. Over Izzy Jaynes's objections, may I add. Her *strident* objections. The captain talked to the commish. Late this evening I got the word to drop it, and you know why.'

'Yeah. Because it connects to Brady two ways. Martine Stover was one of his City Center victims. Ruth Scapelli was his nurse. It would take a moderately bright reporter about six minutes to put those things together and stir up a nice fat scare story. That's what you got from Captain Pedersen?'

'That's what I got. No one in police administration wants the spotlight back on Hartsfield, not when he's still judged incompetent to assist in his own defense and thus unable to stand trial. Hell, no one in city government wants it.'

276

Hodges is silent, thinking hard — maybe as hard as ever in his life. He learned the phrase *to cross the Rubicon* way back in high school, and grasped its meaning without Mrs Bradley's explanation: to make an irrevocable decision. What he learned later, sometimes to his sorrow, is that one comes upon most Rubicons unprepared. If he tells Pete that Barbara Robinson also had a Zappit and may also have had suicide on her mind when she left school and went to Lowtown, Pete will almost have to go back to Pedersen. Two Zappit-related suicides can be written off as coincidence, but three? And okay, Barbara didn't actually succeed, thank God, but she's another person with a connection to Brady. She was at the 'Round Here concert, after all. Along with Hilda Carver and Dinah Scott, who *also* received Zappits. But are the police capable of believing what he's starting to believe? It's an important question, because Hodges loves Barbara Robinson and does not want to see her privacy violated without some concrete result to show for it.

'Kermit? Are you there?'

'Yeah. Just thinking. Did the Scapelli woman have any visitors last night?'

'Can't tell you, because the neighbors haven't been interviewed. It was a suicide, not a murder.'

'Olivia Trelawney also committed suicide,' Hodges says. 'Remember?'

It's Pete's turn to be silent. Of course he remembers, and he also remembers it was an *assisted* suicide. Hartsfield planted a nasty malware worm in her computer, made her think she was being haunted by the ghost of a young mother killed at City Center. It helped that most people in the city had come to believe Olivia Trelawney's carelessness with her ignition key was partially responsible for the massacre.

'Brady always enjoyed — '

'I know what he always enjoyed,' Pete says. 'No need to belabor the point. I've got one other scrap for you, if you want it.'

'Hit me.'

'I spoke to Nancy Alderson around five this afternoon.'

Good for you, Pete, Hodges thinks. Doing a little more than punching the clock in your last few weeks.

'She said that Mrs Ellerton already bought her daughter a new computer. For her online class. Said it's under the basement stairs, still in the carton. Ellerton was going to give it to Martine for her birthday next month.'

'Planning for the future, in other words. Not the act of a suicidal woman, is it?'

'No, I wouldn't say so. I have to go, Kerm. The ball is in your court. Play it or let it lie. Up to you.'

'Thanks, Pete. I appreciate the heads-up.'

'I wish it was like the old days,' Pete says. 'We would have gone after this thing and let the chips fall.'

'But it's not.' Hodges is rubbing his side again.

'No. It's not. You take care of yourself. Put on some goddam weight.'

'I'll give it my best shot,' Hodges says, but he's talking to no one. Pete is gone.

He brushes his teeth, takes a painkiller, and climbs slowly into his pajamas. Then he goes to bed and stares up into the darkness, waiting for sleep or morning, whichever comes first.

8

Brady was careful to take Babineau's ID badge from the top of his bureau after donning Babineau's clothes, because the magnetic strip on the back turns it into an all-access pass. At ten-thirty that night, around the time Hodges is finally getting a bellyful of the Weather Channel, he uses it for the first time, to enter the gated employees' parking lot behind the main hospital building. The lot is loaded in the daytime, but at this hour he has his pick of spaces. He chooses one as far from the pervasive glare of the arc-sodiums as he can get. He tilts back the seat of Dr B.'s luxury ride and kills the engine.

He drifts into sleep and finds himself cruising through a light fog of disconnected memories, all that remains of Felix Babineau. He tastes the peppermint lipstick of the first girl he ever kissed, Marjorie Patterson at East Junior High, in Joplin, Missouri. He sees a basketball with the word VOIT printed on it in fading black letters. He feels warmth in his training pants as he pees himself while coloring behind his gammer's sofa, a huge dinosaur covered in faded green velour.

Childhood memories are apparently the last things to go.

Shortly after two A.M. he flinches from a

brilliant recollection of his father slapping him for playing with matches in the attic of their house and starts awake with a gasp in the Beemer's bucket seat. For a moment the clearest detail of that memory lingers: a vein pulsing in his father's flushed neck, just above the collar of his blue Izod golf shirt.

Then he's Brady again, wearing a Babineau skin-suit.

9

While mostly confined to Room 217, and to a body that no longer works, Brady has had months to plan, to revise those plans, and revise the revisions. He has made mistakes along the way (he wishes he'd never used Z-Boy to send Hodges a message using the Blue Umbrella site, for instance, and he should have waited before going after Barbara Robinson), yet he has persevered, and here he is, on the verge of success.

He has mentally rehearsed this part of the operation dozens of times, and now moves ahead confidently. A swipe of Babineau's card gets him in the door marked MAINTENANCE A. On the floors above, the machines that run the hospital are heard as a muted hum, if they are heard at all. Down here they're a steady thunder, and the tile hallway is stiflingly hot. But it's deserted, as he expected. A city hospital never falls into a deep sleep, but in the early hours of the morning it shuts its eyes and dozes.

The maintenance crew's break room is also deserted, as is the shower and changing area beyond it. Padlocks secure some of the lockers, but the majority of them are open. He tries one after the other, checking sizes, until he finds a gray shirt and a pair of work-pants that are Babineau's approximate size. He takes off Babineau's clothes and puts on the maintenance worker's stuff, not neglecting to transfer the bottle of pills he took from Babineau's bathroom. It's a potent his 'n hers mixture. On one of the hooks by the showers he sees the final touch: a red-and-blue Groundhogs baseball cap. He takes it, adjusts the plastic band in back, and pulls it low over his forehead, making sure to get all of Babineau's silver hair covered up.

He walks the length of Maintenance A and turns right into the hospital laundry, which is humid as well as hot. Two housekeepers are sitting in plastic contour chairs between two rows of gigantic Foshan dryers. Both are fast asleep, one with an overturned box of animal crackers spilling into the lap of her green nylon skirt. Further down, past the washing machines, two laundry carts are parked against the cinderblock wall. One is filled with hospital johnnies, the other piled high with fresh bedlinens. Brady takes a handful of johnnies, puts them on top of the neatly folded sheets, and rolls the cart on down the hall.

It takes a change of elevators and a walk across the skyway to reach the Bucket, and he sees exactly four people on the journey. Two are nurses whispering together outside a med supply

281

closet; two are interns in the doctors' lounge, laughing quietly over something on a laptop computer. None of them notice the graveyard-shift maintenance man, head down as he pushes an overloaded cart of laundry.

The point where he's most apt to be noticed — and perhaps recognized — is the nurses' station in the middle of the Bucket. But one of the nurses is playing solitaire on her computer, and the other is writing notes, propping her head up with her free hand. That one catches movement out of the corner of her eye and without raising her head asks how he's doing.

'Yeah, good,' Brady says. 'Cold night, though.'

'Uh-huh, and I heard there's snow coming.' She yawns and goes back to her notes.

Brady rolls his basket down the hall, stopping just short of 217. One of the Bucket's little secrets is that here the patient rooms have two doors, one marked and one unmarked. The unmarked ones open into the closets, making it possible to restock linens and other necessaries at night without disturbing the patients' rest . . . or their disturbed minds. Brady grabs a few of the johnnies, takes a quick look around to make sure he is still unobserved, and slips through this unmarked door. A moment later he's looking down at himself. For years he has fooled everyone into believing that Brady Hartsfield is what the staff calls (only among themselves) a gork, a ding, or a LOBNH: lights are on but nobody's home. Now he really is one.

He bends and strokes one lightly stubbled cheek. Runs the pad of his thumb over one closed lid, feeling the raised curve of eyeball beneath. Lifts one hand, turns it over, and lays it gently palm-up on the coverlet. From the pocket of the borrowed gray trousers he takes the bottle of pills and spills half a dozen in the upturned palm. Take, eat, he thinks. This is my body, broken for you.

He enters that broken body one final time. He doesn't need to use the Zappit to do this now, nor does he have to worry that Babineau will seize control and run away like the Gingerbread Man. With Brady's mind gone, Babineau is the gork. Nothing left in there but a memory of his father's golf shirt.

Brady looks around the inside of his head like a man giving a hotel room one last check after a long-term stay. Anything hanging forgotten in the closet? A tube of toothpaste left in the bathroom? Maybe a cufflink under the bed?

No. Everything is packed and the room is empty. He closes his hand, hating the draggy way the fingers move, as if the joints are filled with sludge. He opens his mouth, lifts the pills, and drops them in. He chews. The taste is bitter. Babineau, meanwhile, has collapsed bonelessly to the floor. Brady swallows once. And again. There. It's done. He closes his eyes, and when he opens them again, he's staring beneath the bed at a pair of slippers Brady Hartsfield will never wear again.

He gets to Babineau's feet, brushes himself off, and takes one more look at the body that carried him around for almost thirty years. The one that stopped being of any use to him the

283

second time he was smashed in the head at Mingo Auditorium, just before he could trigger the plastic explosive strapped to the underside of his wheelchair. Once he might have worried that this drastic step would backfire on him, that his consciousness and all his grand plans would die along with his body. No more. The umbilical cord has been severed. He has crossed the Rubicon.

So long, Brady, he thinks, it was good to know you.

This time when he pushes the laundry cart past the nurses' station, the one who was playing solitaire is gone, probably to the bathroom. The other is asleep on her notes.

10

But it's quarter to four now, and there's so much more to do.

After changing back into Babineau's clothes, Brady leaves the hospital the same way he entered and drives toward Sugar Heights. Because Z-Boy's homemade silencer is kaput and an unmuffled gunshot is likely to be reported in the town's ritziest neighborhood (where rent-a-cops from Vigilant Guard Service are never more than a block or two away), he stops at Valley Plaza, which is on the way. He checks the empty lot for cop cars, sees none, and drives around to the loading area of Discount Home Furnishings.

God, it's so good to be out! Fucking *wonderful*!

284

Walking to the front of the Beemer, he breathes deeply of the cold winter air, wrapping the sleeve of Babineau's expensive topcoat around the .32's short barrel as he goes. It won't be as good as Z-Boy's silencer, and he knows it's a risk, but not a big one. Just the one shot. He looks up first, wanting to see the stars, but clouds have blanked out the sky. Oh, well, there will be other nights. Many of them. Possibly thousands. He is not limited to Babineau's body, after all.

He aims and fires. A small round hole appears in the Beemer's windshield. Now comes another risk, driving the last mile to Sugar Heights with a bullet hole in the glass just above the steering wheel, but this is the time of night when the suburban streets are at their emptiest and the cops also doze, especially in the better neighborhoods.

Twice headlights approach him and he holds his breath, but both times they pass by without slowing. January air comes in through the bullet hole, making a thin wheezing sound. He makes it back to Babineau's McMansion without incident. No need to tap the code this time; he just hits the gate opener clipped to the visor. When he reaches the top of the drive, he veers onto the snow-covered lawn, bounces over a hard crust of plowed snow, clips a bush, and stops.

Home again, home again, jiggety-jog.

Only problem is, he neglected to bring a knife. He could get one in the house, he has another piece of business in there, but he doesn't want to make two trips. He has miles to go before he sleeps, and he's anxious to start rolling them. He opens the center console and paws through it. Surely a dandy like Babineau will keep spare grooming implements, even a fingernail clipper will do . . . but there's nothing. He tries the glove compartment, and in the folder containing the Beemer's documents (leather, of course) he finds an Allstate insurance card laminated in plastic. It will serve. They are, after all, the Good Hands people.

Brady pushes back the sleeve of Babineau's cashmere overcoat and the shirt beneath, then drags a corner of the laminated card over his forearm. It produces nothing but a thin red line. He goes again, bearing down much harder, lips pulled back in a grimace. This time the skin splits and blood flows. He gets out of the car holding his arm up, then leans back in. He tips a spatter of droplets first onto the seat and then onto the bottom arc of the steering wheel. There's not much, but it won't take much. Not when combined with the bullet hole in the windshield.

He bounds up the porch steps, each springy leap a small orgasm. Cora is lying beneath the hall coathooks, just as dead as ever. Library Al is still asleep on the couch. Brady shakes him, and when he only gets a few muffled grunts, he grabs Al with both hands and rolls him onto the floor. Al's eyes creak open.

'Huh? Wha?'

The stare is dazed but not completely blank. There's probably no Al Brooks left inside that plundered head, but there's still a bit of the alter ego Brady has created. Enough.

'Hey there, Z-Boy,' Brady says, squatting down.

'Hey,' Z-Boy croaks, struggling to sit up. 'Hey there, Dr Z. I'm watching that house, just like you told me. The woman — the one who can still walk — she uses that Zappit all the time. I watch her from the g'rage across the street.'

'You don't have to do that anymore.'

'No? Say, where are we?'

'My house,' Brady says. 'You killed my wife.'

Z-Boy stares at the white-haired man in the overcoat, his mouth hung open. His breath is awful, but Brady doesn't draw away. Slowly, Z-Boy's face begins to crumple. It's like watching a car crash in slow motion. 'Kill? . . . did not!'

'Yes.'

'No! Never would!'

'You did, though. But only because I told you to.'

'Are you sure? I don't remember.'

Brady takes him by the shoulder. 'It wasn't your fault. You were hypnotized.'

Z-Boy's face brightens. 'By Fishin' Hole!'

'Yes, by Fishin' Hole. And while you were, I told you to kill Mrs Babineau.'

Z-Boy looks at him with doubt and woe. 'If I did, it wasn't my fault. I was hypnotized and can't even remember.'

'Take this.'

Brady hands Z-Boy the gun. Z-Boy holds it up, frowning as if at some exotic artifact.

'Put it in your pocket, and give me your car keys.'

287

Z-Boy stuffs the .32 absently into his pants pocket and Brady winces, expecting the gun to go off and put a bullet in the poor sap's leg. At last Z-Boy holds out his keyring. Brady pockets it, stands up, and crosses the living room.

'Where are you going, Dr Z?'

'I won't be long. Why don't you sit on the couch until I get back?'

'I'll sit on the couch until you get back,' Z-Boy says.

'Good idea.'

Brady goes into Dr Babineau's study. There's an ego wall crammed with framed photos, including one of a younger Felix Babineau shaking hands with the second President Bush, both of them grinning like idiots. Brady ignores the pictures; he's seen them many times before, during the months when he was learning how to be in another person's body, what he now thinks of as his student driver days. Nor is he interested in the desktop computer. What he wants is the MacBook Air sitting on the credenza. He opens it, powers it up, and types in Babineau's password, which happens to be CEREBELLIN.

'Your drug didn't do shit,' Brady says as the main screen comes up. He's actually not sure of this, but it's what he chooses to believe.

His fingers rattle the keyboard with a practiced speed of which Babineau would have been incapable, and a hidden program, one Brady installed himself on a previous visit to the good doctor's head, pops up. It's labeled FISHIN' HOLE. He types again, and the program reaches out to the repeater in Freddi Linklatter's

288

computer hideaway.

WORKING, the laptop's screen says, and below this: 3 FOUND.

Three found! Three already!

Brady is delighted but not really surprised, even though it's the graveyard of the morning. There are a few insomniacs in every crowd, and that includes the crowd that has received free Zappits from badconcert.com. What better way to while away the sleepless hours before dawn than with a handy game console? And before playing solitaire or Angry Birds, why not check those pink fish on the Fishin' Hole demo screen, and see if they've finally been programmed to turn into numbers when tapped? A combination of the right ones will win prizes, but at four in the morning, that may not be the prime motivator. Four in the morning is usually an unhappy time to be awake. It's when unpleasant thoughts and pessimistic ideas come to the fore, and the demo screen is soothing. It's also addictive. Al Brooks knew that before he became Z-Boy; Brady knew from the moment he saw it. Just a lucky coincidence, but what Brady has done since — what he has *prepared* — is no coincidence. It's the result of long and careful planning in the prison of his hospital room and his wasted body.

He shuts down the laptop, tucks it under his arm, and starts to leave the study. At the doorway he has an idea and goes back to Babineau's desk. He opens the center drawer and finds exactly what he wants — he doesn't even have to rummage. When your luck is running, it's running.

Brady returns to the living room. Z-Boy is sitting on the sofa, head lowered, shoulders slumped, hands dangling between his thighs. He looks unutterably weary.

'I have to go now,' Brady says.

'Where?'

'Not your business.'

'Not my business.'

'Exactly right. You should go back to sleep.'

'Here on the couch?'

'Or in one of the bedrooms upstairs. But you need to do something first.' He hands Z-Boy the felt-tip pen he found in Babineau's desk. 'Make your mark, Z-Boy, just like when you were in Mrs Ellerton's house.'

'They were alive when I was watching from the g'rage, I know that much, but they might be dead now.'

'They probably are, yes.'

'I didn't kill them, too, did I? Because it seems like I was in the bathroom, at least. And drawed a Z there.'

'No, no, nothing like th — '

'I looked for the Zappit like you asked me to, I'm sure of that. I looked hard, but I didn't find it anywhere. I think maybe she throwed it away.'

'That doesn't matter anymore. Just make your mark here, okay? Make it in at least ten places.' A thought occurs. 'Can you still count to ten?'

'One . . . two . . . three . . . '

Brady glances at Babineau's Rolex. Quarter past four. Morning rounds in the Bucket begin at five. Time is fleeting on winged feet. 'That's

290

great. Make your mark in at least ten places. Then you can go back to sleep.'

'Okay. I'll make my mark in at least ten places, then I'll sleep, then I'll drive over to that house you want me to watch. Or should I stop doing that now that they're dead?'

'I think you can stop now. Let's review, okay? Who killed my wife?'

'I did, but it wasn't my fault. I was hypnotized, and I can't even remember.' Z-Boy begins to cry. 'Will you come back, Dr Z?'

Brady smiles, exposing Babineau's expensive dental work. 'Sure.' His eyes move up and to the left as he says it.

He watches the old guy shuffle to the huge God-I'm-rich television mounted on the wall and draw a large Z on the screen. Zs all over the murder scene aren't absolutely necessary, but Brady thinks it will be a nice touch, especially when the police ask the former Library Al for his name and he tells them it's Z-Boy. Just a bit of extra filigree on a finely crafted piece of jewelry.

Brady goes to the front door, stepping over Cora again on the way. He bops down the porch steps and does a dance move at the bottom, snapping Babineau's fingers. That hurts a little, just a touch of incipient arthritis, but so what? Brady knows what real pain is, and a few twinges in the old phalanges ain't it.

He jogs to Al's Malibu. Not much of a ride compared to the late Dr Babineau's BMW, but it will get him where he needs to go. He starts it and frowns when classical shit comes pouring out of the dashboard speaker. He switches to

BAM-100 and finds some Black Sabbath from back when Ozzy was still cool. He takes a final look at the Beemer parked askew on the lawn, then gets rolling.

Miles to go before he sleeps, and then the final touch, the cherry on top of the sundae. He won't need Freddi Linklatter for that, only Dr B.'s MacBook. He's running without a leash now.

He's free.

11

Around the time Z-Boy is proving that he can still count to ten, Freddi Linklatter's blood-caked lashes come unstuck from her blood-caked cheeks. She finds herself looking into a gaping brown eye. It takes her several long moments to decide it isn't really an eye, only a swirl of woodgrain that *looks* like an eye. She is lying on the floor and suffering the worst hangover of her life, even worse than after that cataclysmic party to celebrate her twenty-first, when she mixed crystal meth with Ronrico. She thought later that she was lucky to have survived that little experiment. Now she almost wishes she hadn't, because this is worse. It's not only her head; her chest feels like Marshawn Lynch has been using her for a tackling dummy.

She tells her hands to move and they reluctantly answer the call. She places them in push-up position and shoves. She comes up, but her top shirt stays down, stuck to the floor in a pool of what looks like blood and smells suspiciously like Scotch. So that's what she was drinking, and fell over her own stupid feet. Smacked her head. But dear God, how much did she put away?

It wasn't like that, she thinks. Someone came, and you know who it was.

It's a simple process of deduction. Lately she's only had two visitors here, the Z-Dudes, and the one who wears the ratty parka hasn't been around for awhile.

She tries to get to her feet, and can't make it at first. Nor can she take more than shallow breaths. Deeper ones hurt her above her left breast. It feels like something is sticking in there.

My flask?

I was spinning it while I waited for him to show up. To give me the final payment and get out of my life.

'Shot me,' she croaks. 'Fucking Dr Z shot me.'

She staggers into the bathroom and is hardly able to believe the train wreck she sees in the mirror. The left side of her face is covered with blood, and there's a purple knob rising from a gash above her left temple, but that's not the worst. Her blue chambray shirt is also matted with blood — mostly from the head wound, she hopes, head wounds bleed like crazy — and there's a round black hole in the left breast pocket. He shot her, all right. Now she remembers the bang and the smell of gunsmoke just before she passed out.

She tweezes her shaking fingers into the breast pocket, still taking those shallow breaths, and pulls out her pack of Marlboro Lights. There's the bullet hole right through the middle of the M. She drops the cigarettes into the basin, works at the buttons of the shirt, and lets it fall to the floor. The smell of Scotch is stronger now. The shirt beneath is khaki, with big flap pockets. When she tries to pull the flask from the one on the left, she utters a low mewl of agony — all she can manage without taking a deeper breath — but when she gets it free, the pain in her chest lessens a little. The bullet also went through the flask, and the prongs on the side closest to her skin are bright with blood. She drops the ruined flask on top of the Marlboros, and goes to work on the khaki shirt's buttons. This takes longer, but eventually it also falls to the floor. Beneath it is an American Giant tee, the kind that also has a pocket. She reaches into it and takes out a tin of Altoids. There's a hole in this, too. The tee has no buttons, so she works her pinky finger into the bullet hole in the pocket and pulls. The shirt tears, and at last she's looking at her own skin, freckled with blood.

There's a hole just where the scant swell of her breast begins, and in it she can see a black thing. It looks like a dead bug. She tears the rip in the shirt wider, using three fingers now, then reaches in and grasps the bug. She wiggles it like a loose tooth.

'Oooo . . . ooooh . . . ooooh, FUCK . . . '

It comes free, not a bug but a slug. She looks at it, then drops it into the sink with the other stuff. In spite of her aching head and the throbbing in her chest, Freddi realizes how absurdly fortunate she has been. It was just a little gun, but at such close range, even a little gun should have done the job. It would have, too, if not for a one-in-a-thousand lucky break. First through the cigarettes, then through the flask — which had been the real stopper — then through the Altoids tin, then into her. How close to her heart? An inch? Less?

Her stomach clenches, wanting to puke. She won't let it, can't let it. The hole in her chest will start bleeding again, but that's not the main thing. Her head will explode. *That's* the main thing.

Her breathing is a little easier now that she's removed the flask with its nasty (but lifesaving) prongs of metal. She plods back into her living room and stares at the puddle of blood and Scotch on the floor. If he had bent over and put the muzzle of the gun to the back of her neck . . . just to make sure . . .

Freddi closes her eyes and fights to retain consciousness as waves of faintness and nausea float through her. When it's a little better, she goes to her chair and sits down very slowly. Like an old lady with a bad back, she thinks. She stares at the ceiling. What now?

Her first thought is to call 911, get an ambulance over here and go to the hospital, but what will she tell them? That a man claiming to be a Mormon or a Jehovah's Witness knocked on her door, and when she opened it, he shot her? Shot her why? For what? And why would she, a woman living alone, open her door to a stranger at ten thirty in the evening?

That isn't all. The police will come. In her

bedroom is an ounce of pot and an eightball of coke. She could get rid of that shit, but what about the shit in her computer room? She's got half a dozen illegal hacks going on, plus a ton of expensive equipment that she didn't exactly buy. The cops will want to know if just perchance, Ms Linklatter, the man who shot you had something to do with said electronic gear. Maybe you owed him money for it? Maybe you were working with him, stealing credit card numbers and other personal info? And they can hardly miss the repeater, blinking away like a Las Vegas slot machine as it sends out its endless signal via WiFi, delivering a customized malware worm every time it finds a live Zappit.

What's *this*, Ms Linklatter? What exactly does it do?

And what will she tell them?

She looks around, hoping to see the envelope of cash lying on the floor or the couch, but of course he took it with him. If there was ever cash in there at all, and not just cut-up strips of newspaper. She's here, she's shot, she's had a concussion (please God not a fracture) and she's low on dough. What to do?

Turn off the repeater, that's the first thing. Dr Z has got BradyHartsfield inside him, and Brady is a bad motorcycle. Whatever the repeater's doing is nasty shit. She was going to turn it off anyway, wasn't she? It's all a little vague, but wasn't that the plan? To turn it off and exit stage left? She doesn't have that final payment to help finance her flight, but despite her loose habits with cash, there's still a few thousand in the bank, and Corn Trust opens at nine. Plus, there's her ATM card. So turn off the repeater, nip that creepy zeetheend site in the bud, wash the gore off her face, and get the fuck out of Dodge. Not by plane, these days airport security areas are like baited traps, but by any bus or train headed into the golden west. Isn't that the best idea?

She's up and shuffling toward the door of the computer room when the obvious reason why it is *not* the best idea hits her. Brady is gone, but he wouldn't leave if he couldn't monitor his projects from a distance, especially the repeater, and doing that is the easiest thing in the world. He's smart about computers — brilliant, actually, although it pisses her off to admit it — and he's almost certainly left himself a back door into her setup. If so, he can check in any time he wants; all it will take is a laptop. If she shuts his shit down, he'll know, and he'll know she's still alive.

He'll come back.

'So what do I do?' Freddi whispers. She trudges to her window, shivering — it's so fucking cold in this apartment once winter comes — and looks out into the dark. 'What do I do now?'

12

Hodges is dreaming of Bowser, the feisty little mongrel he had when he was a kid. His father hauled Bowser to the vet and had him put down, over Hodges's weeping protests, after ole Bowse

297

bit the newspaper boy badly enough to require stitches. In this dream Bowser is biting *him*, biting him in the side. He won't let go even when young Billy Hodges offers him the best treat in the treat bag, and the pain is excruciating. The doorbell is ringing and he thinks, That's the paperboy, go bite *him*, you're supposed to bite *him*.

Only as he swims up from this dream and back into the real world, he realizes it isn't the doorbell, it's the phone by his bed. The landline. He gropes for it, drops it, picks it up off the duvet, and manages a furry approximation of hello.

'Figured you'd have your cell on do not disturb,' Pete Huntley says. He sounds wide awake and weirdly jovial. Hodges squints at the bedside clock but can't read it. His bottle of painkillers, already half empty, is blocking the digital readout. Jesus, how many did he take yesterday?

'I don't know how to do that, either.' Hodges struggles to a sitting position. He can't believe the pain has gotten so bad so fast. It's as if it was just waiting to be identified before pouncing with all its claws out.

'You need to get a life, Kerm.'

A little late for that, he thinks, swinging his legs out of bed.

'Why are you calling at . . . ' He moves the bottle of pills. 'At twenty to seven in the morning?'

'Couldn't wait to give you the good news,' Pete says. 'Brady Hartsfield is dead. A nurse discovered him on morning rounds.'

Hodges shoots to his feet, producing a stab of pain he hardly feels. 'What? *How?*'

'There'll be an autopsy later today, but the doctor who examined him is leaning toward suicide. There's a residue of *something* on his tongue and gums. The doc on call took a sample, and a guy from the ME's office is taking another as we speak. They're going to rush the analysis, Hartsfield being such a rock star and all.'

'Suicide,' Hodges says, running a hand through his already crazed hair. The news is simple enough, but he still can't seem to take it in. '*Suicide?*'

'He was always a fan,' Pete says. 'I believe you might have said that yourself, and more than once.'

'Yeah, but . . . '

But what? Pete's right, Brady *was* a fan of suicide, and not just the other guy's. He had been ready to die at the City Center Job Fair in 2009, if things worked out that way, and a year later he rolled a wheelchair into Mingo Auditorium with three pounds of plastic explosive strapped to the seat. Which put his ass at ground zero. Only that was then, and things have changed. Haven't they?

'But what?'

'I don't know,' Hodges says.

'I do. He finally found a way to do it. Simple as that. In any case, if you thought Hartsfield was somehow involved in the deaths of Ellerton, Stover, and Scapelli — and I have to tell you I had my own thoughts along that line — you can

299

stop worrying. He's a gone goose, a toasty turkey, a baked buzzard, and we all say hooray.'

'Pete, I need to process this a little.'

'No doubt,' Pete says. 'You had quite the history with him. Meanwhile, I have to call Izzy. Get her day started on the good foot.'

'Will you call me when you get back the analysis of whatever he swallowed?'

'Indeed I will. Meanwhile, *sayonara* Mr Mercedes, right?'

'Right, right.'

Hodges hangs up the phone, walks into the kitchen, and puts on a pot of coffee. He should have tea, coffee will burn the shit out of his poor struggling innards, but right now he doesn't care. And he won't take any pills, not for awhile. He needs to be as clearheaded about this as he possibly can.

He snatches his mobile off the charger and calls Holly. She answers at once, and he wonders briefly what time she gets up. Five? Even earlier? Maybe some questions are best left unanswered. He tells her what Pete just told him, and for once in her life, Holly Gibney does not gild her profanity.

'You've got to be fucking kidding me!'

'Not unless Pete was kidding, and I don't think he was. He doesn't try joking until mid-afternoon, and he's not very good at it then.'

Silence for a moment, and then Holly asks, 'Do you believe it?'

'That he's dead, yes. It could hardly be a case of mistaken identity. That he committed suicide? To me that seems . . . ' He fishes for the right phrase, can't find it, and repeats what he said to his old partner not five minutes before. 'I don't know.'

'Is it over?'

'Maybe not.'

'That's what I think, too. We have to find out what happened to the Zappits that were left over after the company went broke. I don't understand how Brady Hartsfield could have had anything to do with them, but so many of the connections go back to him. And to the concert he tried to blow up.'

'I know.' Hodges is again picturing a web with a big old spider at the center of it, one full of poison. Only the spider is dead.

And we all say hooray, he thinks.

'Holly, can you be at the hospital when the Robinsons come to pick up Barbara?'

'I can do that.' After a pause she adds, 'I'd like to do that. I'll call Tanya to make sure it's okay, but I'm sure it is. Why?'

'I want you to show Barb a six-pack. Five elderly white guys in suits, plus Dr Felix Babineau.'

'You think Myron Zakim was Hartsfield's *doctor?* That he was the one who gave Barbara and Hilda those Zappits?'

'At this point it's just a hunch.'

But that's modest. It's actually a bit more. Babineau gave Hodges a cock-and-bull story to keep him out of Brady's room, then nearly blew a gasket when Hodges asked if he was all right. And Norma Wilmer claims he's been conducting unauthorized experiments on Brady. *Investigate Babineau*, she said in Bar Bar Black Sheep. *Get*

301

him in trouble. I dare you. As a man who probably has only months to live, that doesn't seem like much of a dare.

'Okay. I respect your hunches, Bill. And I'm sure I can find a society-page picture of Dr Babineau from one of those charity events they're always having for the hospital.'

'Good. Now refresh me on the name of the bankruptcy trustee guy.'

'Todd Schneider. You should call him at eight thirty. If I'm with the Robinsons, I won't be in until later. I'll bring Jerome with me.'

'Yeah, good. Have you got Schneider's number?'

'I emailed it to you. You remember how to access your email, don't you?'

'It's cancer, Holly, not Alzheimer's.'

'Today is your last day. Remember that, too.'

How can he forget? They'll put him in the hospital where Brady died, and that will be that, Hodges's last case left hanging fire. He hates the idea, but there's no way around it. This is going fast.

'Eat some breakfast.'

'I will.'

He ends the call, and looks longingly at the fresh pot of coffee. The smell is wonderful. He turns it down the sink and gets dressed. He does not eat breakfast.

13

Finders Keepers seems very empty without Holly at her desk in the reception area, but at least the seventh floor of the Turner Building is quiet; the noisy crew from the travel agency down the hall won't start to arrive for at least another hour.

Hodges thinks best with a yellow pad in front of him, jotting down ideas as they come, trying to tease out the connections and form a coherent picture. It's the way he worked when he was on the cops, and he was capable of making those connections more often than not. He won a lot of citations over the years, but they're piled helter-skelter on a shelf in his closet instead of hanging on a wall. The citations never mattered to him. The reward was the flash of light that came with the connections. He found himself unable to give it up. Hence Finders Keepers instead of retirement.

This morning there are no notes, only doodles of stick men climbing a hill, and cyclones, and flying saucers. He's pretty sure most of the pieces to this puzzle are now on the table and all he has to do is figure out how to put them together, but Brady Hartsfield's death is like a pileup on his personal information highway, blocking all traffic. Every time he glances at his watch, another five minutes have gone by. Soon enough he'll have to call Schneider. By the time he gets off the phone with him, the noisy travel agency crew will be arriving. After them, Barbara and Jerome. Any chance of quiet thought will be gone.

Think of the connections, Holly said. *They all go back to him. And the concert he tried to blow up.*

Yes; yes they do. Because the only ones eligible to receive free Zappits from that website were people — young girls then, for the most part, teenagers now — who could prove they were at the 'Round Here show, and the website is now defunct. Like Brady, badconcert.com is a gone goose, a toasty turkey, a baked buzzard, and we all say hooray.

At last he prints two words amid the doodles, and circles them. One is *Concert*. The other is *Residue*.

He calls Kiner Memorial, and is transferred to the Bucket. Yes, he's told, Norma Wilmer is in, but she's busy and can't come to the phone. Hodges guesses she's *very* busy this morning, and hopes her hangover isn't too bad. He leaves a message asking that she call him back as soon as she can, and emphasizes that it's urgent.

He continues doodling until eight twenty-five (now it's Zappits he's drawing, possibly because he's got Dinah Scott's in his coat pocket), then calls Todd Schneider, who answers the phone personally.

Hodges identifies himself as a volunteer consumer advocate working with the Better Business Bureau, and says he's been tasked with investigating some Zappit consoles that have shown up in the city. He keeps his tone easy, almost casual. 'This is no big deal, especially since the Zappits were given away, but it seems that some of the recipients are downloading books from something called the Sunrise Readers Circle, and they're coming through garbled.'

'Sunrise Readers Circle?' Schneider sounds bemused. No sign he's getting ready to put up a shield of legalese, and that's the way Hodges wants to keep it. 'As in Sunrise Solutions?'

'Well, yes, that's what prompted the call. According to my information, Sunrise Solutions bought out Zappit, Inc., before going bankrupt.'

'That's true, but I've got a ton of paperwork on Sunrise Solutions, and I don't recall anything about a Sunrise Readers Circle. And it would have stood out like a sore thumb. Sunrise was basically involved in gobbling up small electronics companies, looking for that one big hit. Which they never found, unfortunately.'

'What about the Zappit Club? Ring any bells?'

'Never heard of it.'

'Or a website called zeetheend.com?' As he asks this question, Hodges smacks himself in the forehead. He should have checked that site for himself instead of filling a page with dumb doodles.

'Nope, never heard of that, either.' Now comes a tiny rattle of the legal shield. 'Is this a consumer fraud issue? Because bankruptcy laws are very clear on the subject, and — '

'Nothing like that,' Hodges soothes. 'Only reason we're even involved is because of the jumbled downloads. And at least one of the Zappits was dead on arrival. The recipient wants to send it back, maybe get a new one.'

'Not surprised someone got a dead console if it was from the last batch,' Schneider says. 'There were a lot of defectives, maybe thirty percent of the final run.'

'As a matter of personal curiosity, how many were in that final run?'

'I'd have to look up the number to be sure, but I think around forty thousand units. Zappit sued the manufacturer, even though suing Chinese companies is pretty much a fool's game, but by then they were desperate to stay afloat. I'm only giving you this information because the whole business is done and dusted.'

'Understood.'

'Well, the manufacturing company — Yicheng Electronics — came back with all guns blazing. Probably not because of the money at stake, but because they were worried about their reputation. Can't blame them there, can you?'

'No.' Hodges can't wait any longer for pain relief. He takes out his bottle of pills, shakes out two, then reluctantly puts one back. He puts it under his tongue to melt, hoping it will work faster that way. 'I guess you can't.'

'Yicheng claimed the defective units were damaged in shipping, probably by water. They said if it had been a software problem, *all* the games would have been defective. Makes a degree of sense to me, but I'm no electronics genius. Anyway, Zappit went under, and Sunrise Solutions elected not to proceed with the suit. They had bigger problems by then. Creditors snapping at their heels. Investors jumping ship.'

'What happened to that final shipment?'

'Well, they were an asset, of course, but not a very valuable one, due to the defect issue. I held onto them for awhile, and we advertised in the trades to retail companies that specialize in discounted items. Chains like the Dollar Store and Economy Wizard. Are you familiar with those?'

'Yeah.' Hodges had bought a pair of factory-second loafers at the local Dollar Store. They cost more than a buck, but they weren't bad. Wore well.

'Of course we had to make it clear that as many as three in every ten Zappit Commanders — that's what the last iteration was called — might be defective, which meant each one would have to be checked. That killed any chance for selling the whole shipment. Checking the units one by one would have been too labor intensive.'

'Uh-huh.'

'So, as bankruptcy trustee, I decided to have them destroyed and claim a tax credit, which would have amounted to . . . well, quite a lot. Not by General Motors standards, but mid-six figures. Clear the books, you understand.'

'Right, makes sense.'

'But before I could do that, I got a call from a fellow at a company called Gamez Unlimited, right there in your city. That's games with a Z on the end. Called himself the CEO. Probably CEO of a three-man operation working out of two rooms or a garage.' Schneider chuckles a big business New York chuckle. 'Since the computer. revolution really got rolling, these outfits pop up like weeds, although I never heard of any of them actually *giving* product away. It smells a trifle scammy, don't you think?'

'Yeah,' Hodges says. The dissolving pill is exceedingly bitter, but the relief is sweet. He thinks that's the case with a great many things in life. A *Reader's Digest* insight, but that doesn't make it invalid. 'It does, actually.'

The legal shield has gone bye-bye. Schneider is animated now, wrapped up in his own story. 'The guy offered to buy eight hundred Zappits at eighty dollars apiece, which was roughly a hundred dollars cheaper than the suggested retail. We dickered a bit and settled on a hundred.'

'Per unit.'

'Yes.'

'Comes to eighty thousand dollars,' Hodges says. He's thinking of Brady, who had been hit with God only knew how many civil suits, for sums mounting into the tens of millions of dollars. Brady, who'd had — if Hodges's memory serves him right — about eleven hundred dollars in the bank. 'And you got a check for that amount?'

He's not sure he'll get an answer to the question — many lawyers would close the discussion off at this point — but he does. Probably because the Sunrise Solutions bankruptcy is all tied up in a nice legal bow. For Schneider, this is like a postgame interview. 'Correct. Drawn on the Gamez Unlimited account.'

'Cleared okay?'

Todd Schneider chuckles his big business chuckle. 'If it hadn't, those eight hundred Zappit consoles would have been recycled into new computer goodies along with the rest.'

Hodges scribbles some quick math on his doodle-decorated pad. If thirty percent of the eight hundred units were defective, that leaves five hundred and sixty working consoles. Or maybe not that many. Hilda Carver got one that had presumably been vetted — why else give it to her? — but according to Barbara, it had given a single blue flash and then died.

'So off they went.'

'Yes, via UPS from a warehouse in Terre Haute. A very small recoupment, but something. We do what we can for our clients, Mr Hodges.'

'I'm sure you do.' And we all say hooray, Hodges thinks. 'Do you recall the address those eight hundred Zappits went to?'

'No, but it will be in the files. Give me your email and I'll be happy to send it to you, on condition you call me back and tell me what sort of scam these Gamez people have been working.'

'Happy to do that, Mr Schneider.' It'll be a box number, Hodges thinks, and the box holder will be long gone. Still, it will need to be checked out. Holly can do it while he's in the hospital, getting treatment for something that almost certainly can't be cured. 'You've been very helpful, Mr Schneider. One more question, and I'll let you go. Do you happen to remember the name of the Gamez Unlimited CEO?'

'Oh, yes,' Schneider says. 'I assumed that's why the company was Gamez with a Z instead of an S.'

'I don't follow.'

'The CEO's name was Myron Zakim.'

14

Hodges hangs up and opens Firefox. He types in zeetheend and finds himself looking at a cartoon man swinging a cartoon pickaxe. Clouds of dirt fly up, forming the same message over and over.

SORRY, WE'RE STILL UNDER CONSTRUCTION

BUT KEEP CHECKING BACK!

'We are made to persist, that's how we find out who we are.'

Tobias Wolfe

Another idea worthy of *Reader's Digest*, Hodges thinks, and goes to his window. Morning traffic on Lower Marlborough is moving briskly. He realizes, with wonder and gratitude, that the pain in his side has entirely disappeared for the first time in days. He could almost believe nothing is wrong with him, but the bitter taste in his mouth contradicts that.

The bitter taste, he thinks. The *residue*.

His cell rings. It's Norma Wilmer, her voice pitched so low he has to strain to hear. 'If this is about the so-called visitors list, I haven't had a chance to look for it yet. This place is crawling with police and cheap suits from the district attorney's office. You'd think Hartsfield escaped instead of died.'

'It's not about the list, although I still need that info, and if you can get it to me today, it's worth another fifty dollars. Get it to me before noon, and I'll make it a hundred.'

'Jesus, what's the big deal with this? I asked Georgia Frederick — she's been bouncing back and forth between Ortho and the Bucket for the last ten years — and she says the only person she ever saw visiting Hartsfield besides you was some ratty chick with tattoos and a Marine haircut.'

This rings no bells with Hodges, but there *is* a faint vibration. Which he doesn't trust. He wants to put this thing together too badly, and that means he must step with special care.

'What *do* you want, Bill? I'm in a fucking linen closet, it's hot, and I've got a headache.'

'My old partner called and told me Brady swallowed some shit and killed himself. What that says to me is he must have stockpiled enough dope over time to do it. Is that possible?'

'It is. It's also possible I could land a 767 jumbo jet if the whole flight crew died of food poisoning, but both things are very fucking unlikely. I'll tell you what I told the cops and the two most annoying yappers from the DA's office. Brady got Anaprox-DS on PE days, one pill with food before, one late in the day if he asked, which he rarely did. Anaprox isn't really much more powerful when it comes to controlling pain than Advil, which you can buy OTC. He also had Extra Strength Tylenol on his chart, but only asked for it on a few occasions.'

'How did the DA guys react to that?'

'Right now they're operating under the theory that he swallowed a shitload of Anaprox.'

'But you don't buy it?'

'Of course I don't! Where would he hide that many pills, up his bony bedsored ass? I have to go. I'll get back to you on the visitors list. If there ever was one, that is.'

311

'Thank you, Norma. Try some Anaprox for that headache of yours.'

'Fuck you, Bill.' But she says it with a laugh.

15

The first thought to cross Hodges's mind when Jerome walks in is Holy shit, kiddo, you grew up!

When Jerome Robinson came to work for him — first as the kid who cut his grass, then as an all-around handyman, finally as the tech angel who kept his computer up and running — he was a weedy teenager, going about five-eight and a hundred and forty pounds. The young giant in the doorway is six-two if he's an inch, and at least a hundred and ninety. He was always good-looking, but now he's movie star good-looking and all muscled out.

The subject in question breaks into a grin, strides quickly across the office, and embraces Hodges. He squeezes, but lets go in a hurry when he sees Hodges wince. 'Jesus, sorry.'

'You didn't hurt me, just happy to see you, my man.' His vision is a little blurry and he wipes at his eyes with the heel of his hand. 'You're a sight for sore eyes.'

'You too. How you feeling?'

'Right now, good. I've got pills for pain, but you're better medicine.'

Holly is standing in the doorway, sensible winter coat unzipped, small hands linked at her waist. She's watching them with an unhappy smile. Hodges wouldn't have believed there was such a thing, but apparently there is.

'Come on over, Holly,' he says. 'No group hug, I promise. Have you filled Jerome in on this business?'

'He knows about Barbara's part, but I thought I'd better let you tell the rest.'

Jerome briefly cups the back of Hodges's neck with a big warm hand. 'Holly says you're going into the hospital tomorrow for more tests and a treatment plan, and if you try to argue, I'm supposed to tell you to shut up.'

'Not shut up,' Holly says, looking at Jerome severely. 'I never used that phrase.'

Jerome grins. 'You had be quiet on your lips, but shut up in your eyes.'

'Fool,' she says, but the smile returns. Happy we're together, Hodges thinks, sad because of the reason why. He breaks up this strangely pleasant sibling rivalry by asking how Barbara is.

'Okay. Fractures of the tibia and fibula, mid-shaft. Could have happened on the soccer field or skiing on a bunny slope. Supposed to heal with no problem. She's got a cast and is already complaining about how it itches underneath. Mom went out to get her a scratcher thing.'

'Holly, did you show her the six-pack?'

'I did, and she picked out Dr Babineau. Never even hesitated.'

I have a few questions for you, Doc, Hodges thinks, and I intend to get some answers before my last day is over. If I have to squeeze you to get them, make your eyes pop out a little, that will be just fine.

Jerome settles on one corner of Hodges's desk, his

313

usual perch. 'Run through the whole thing for me, from the beginning. I might see something new.'

Hodges does most of the talking. Holly goes to the window and looks out on Lower Marlborough, arms crossed, hands cupping her shoulders. She adds something from time to time, but mostly she just listens.

When Hodges is done, Jerome asks, 'How sure are you about this mind-over-matter thing?'

Hodges considers. 'Eighty percent. Maybe more. It's wild, but there are too many stories to discount it.'

'If he could do it, it's my fault,' Holly says without turning from the window. 'When I hit him with your Happy Slapper, Bill, it could have rearranged his brains somehow. Given him access to the ninety percent of gray matter we never use.'

'Maybe,' Hodges says, 'but if you hadn't clobbered him, you and Jerome would be dead.'

'Along with a lot of other people,' Jerome says. 'And the hit might not have had anything to do with it. Whatever Babineau was feeding him could have done more than bring him out of his coma. Experimental drugs sometimes have unexpected effects, you know.'

'Or it could have been a combination of the two,' Hodges says. He can't believe they're having this conversation, but not to have it would fly in the face of rule one in the detective biz: you go where the facts lead you.

'He hated you, Bill,' Jerome says. 'Instead of killing yourself, which is what he wanted, you came after him.'

'And turned his own weapon against him,'

Holly adds, still without turning and still hugging herself. 'You used Debbie's Blue Umbrella to force him into the open. It was him who sent you that message two nights ago, I know it was. Brady Hartsfield, calling himself Z-Boy.' Now she turns. 'It's as plain as the nose on your face. You stopped him at the Mingo — '

'No, I was downstairs having a heart attack. You were the one who stopped him, Holly.'

She shakes her head fiercely. 'He doesn't know that, *because he never saw me*. Do you think I could forget what happened that night? I'll never forget it. Barbara was sitting across the aisle a few rows up, and it was her he was looking at, not me. I shouted something at him, and hit him as soon as he started to turn his head. Then I hit him again. Oh God, I hit him so *hard*.'

Jerome starts toward her, but she motions him back. Eye contact is hard for her, but now she's looking straight at Hodges, and her eyes are blazing.

'*You* goaded him out into the open, *you* were the one who figured out his password so we could crack his computer and find out what he was going to do. You were the one he always blamed. I *know* that. And then you kept going to his room, sitting there and talking to him.'

'And you think that's why he did this, whatever *this* is?'

'*No!*' She nearly shrieks it. '*He did it because he was fracking crazy!*' There's a pause, and then in a meek voice she says she's sorry for raising her voice.

'Don't apologize, Hollyberry,' Jerome says.

'You thrill me when you're masterful.'

She makes a face at him. Jerome snorts a laugh and asks Hodges about Dinah Scott's Zappit. 'I'd like a look at it.'

'My coat pocket,' Hodges says, 'but watch out for the Fishin' Hole demo.'

Jerome rummages in Hodges's coat, rejects a roll of Tums and the ever-present detective's notebook, and brings out Dinah's green Zappit. 'Holy joe. I thought these things went out with VCRs and dial-up modems.'

'They pretty much did,' Holly says, 'and the price didn't help. I checked. A hundred and eighty-nine dollars, suggested retail, back in 2012. Ridiculous.'

Jerome tosses the Zappit from hand to hand. His face is grim, and he looks tired. Well, sure, Hodges thinks. He was building houses in Arizona yesterday. Had to rush home because his normally cheerful sister tried to kill herself.

Maybe Jerome sees some of this on Hodges's face. 'Barb's leg will be fine. It's her mind I'm a little worried about. She talks about blue flashes, and a voice she heard. Coming from the game.'

'She says it's still in her head,' Holly adds. 'Like some piece of music that turns into an earworm. It will probably pass in time, now that her game is broken, but what about the others who got the consoles?'

'With the badconcert website down, is there any way of finding out how many others did?'

Holly and Jerome look at each other, then give identical head shakes.

'Shit,' Hodges says. 'I mean I'm not all that

surprised, but still . . . shit.'

'Does this one give out blue flashes?' Jerome still hasn't turned the Zappit on, just keeps playing hot potato with it.

'Nope, and the pink fish don't turn into numbers. Try it for yourself.'

Instead of doing that, Jerome turns it over and opens the battery compartment. 'Plain old double As,' he says. 'The rechargeable kind. No magic there. But the Fishin' Hole demo really makes you sleepy?'

'It did me,' Hodges says. He does not add that he was medicated up the wazoo at the time. 'Right now I'm more interested in Babineau. He's part of this. I don't understand how that partnership came about, but if he's still alive, he's going to tell us. And there's someone else involved, too.'

'The man the housekeeper saw,' Holly says. 'The one who drives an old car with the primer spots. Do you want to know what I think?'

'Hit me.'

'One of them, either Dr Babineau or the man with the old car, paid a visit to the nurse, Ruth Scapelli. Hartsfield must have had something against her.'

'How could he send anyone anywhere?' Jerome asks, sliding the battery cover back into place with a click. 'Mind control? According to you, Bill, the most he could do with his teleki-whatzis was turn on the water in his bathroom, and it's hard for me to accept even that. It could be just so much talk. A hospital legend instead of an urban one.'

'It has to be the games,' Hodges muses. 'He

317

did something to the games. Amped them up, somehow.'

'From his hospital room?' Jerome gives him a look that says be serious.

'I know, it doesn't make sense, not even if you add in the telekinesis. But it has to be the games. *Has* to be.'

'Babineau will know,' Holly says.

'She's a poet and don't know it,' Jerome says moodily. He's still tossing the console back and forth. Hodges has a feeling that he's resisting an impulse to throw it on the floor and stomp on it, and that's sort of reasonable. After all, one just like it almost got his sister killed.

No, Hodges thinks. Not just like it. The Fishin' Hole demo on Dinah's Zappit generates a mild hypnotic effect, but nothing else. And it's probably . . .

He straightens suddenly, provoking a twinge of pain in his side. 'Holly, have you searched for Fishin' Hole info on the Net?'

'No,' she says. 'I never thought of it.'

'Would you do it now? What I want to know — '

'If there's chatter about the demo screen. I should have thought of that myself. I'll do it now.' She hurries into the outer office.

'What I don't understand,' Hodges says, 'is why Brady would kill himself before seeing how it all came out.'

'You mean before seeing how many kids he could get to off themselves,' Jerome says. 'Kids who were at that fucking concert. Because that's what we're talking about, isn't it?'

'Yeah,' Hodges says. 'There are too many

318

blank spots, Jerome. Far too many. I don't even know *how* he killed himself. If he actually did.'

Jerome presses the heels of his hands to his temples as if to keep his brain from swelling. 'Please don't tell me you think he's still alive.'

'No, he's dead, all right. Pete wouldn't make a mistake about that. What I'm saying is maybe somebody murdered him. Based on what we know, Babineau would be the prime suspect.'

'Holy poop!' Holly cries from the other room.

Hodges and Jerome happen to be looking at each other when she says it, and there is a moment of divine harmony as they both struggle against laughter.

'What?' Hodges calls. It's all he can manage without bursting into mad brays of hilarity, which would hurt his side as well as Holly's feelings.

'I found a site called Fishin' Hole Hypnosis! The start-page warns parents not to let their kids look at the demo screen too long! It was first noticed in the arcade game version back in 2005! The Game Boy fixed it, but the Zappit . . . wait a sec . . . they *said* they did, but they didn't! There's a whole big long thread!'

Hodges looks at Jerome.

'She means an online conversation,' Jerome says.

'A kid in Des Moines passed out, hit his head on the edge of his desk, and fractured his skull!' She sounds almost gleeful as she gets up and rushes back to them. Her cheeks are flushed and rosy. 'There would have been lawsuits! I bet that's one of the reasons the Zappit company went out of business! It might even have been one of the reasons why Sunrise Solutions — '

The phone on her desk begins to ring.

'Oh, frack,' she says, turning toward it.

'Tell whoever it is that we're closed today.'

But after saying Hello, you've reached Finders Keepers, Holly just listens. Then she turns, holding out the handset.

'It's Pete Huntley. He says he has to talk to you right away, and he sounds . . . funny. Like he's sad or mad or something.'

Hodges goes into the outer office to find out what's got Pete sounding sad or mad or something.

Behind him, Jerome finally powers up Dinah Scott's Zappit.

In Freddi Linklatter's computer nest (Freddi herself has taken four Excedrin and gone to sleep in her bedroom), 44 FOUND changes to 45 FOUND. The repeater flashes LOADING.

Then it flashes TASK COMPLETE.

16

Pete doesn't say hello. What he says is, 'Take it, Kerm. Take it and beat it until the truth falls out. Bitch is in the house with a couple of SKIDs, and I'm out back in a whatever-it-is. Potting shed, I think, and it's cold as hell.'

Hodges is at first too surprised to answer, and not because a pair of SKIDs — the city cops' acronym for State Criminal Investigation Division detectives — is on some scene Pete is working. He's surprised (in truth almost flabbergasted) because in all their long association he's only heard Pete use the b-word in connection with an actual woman a single time. That was when speaking of his mother-in-law, who urged Pete's wife to leave, and took her in, along with the children, when she finally did. The bitch he's talking about this time can only be his partner, aka Miss Pretty Gray Eyes.

'Kermit? Are you there?'

'I'm here,' Hodges says. 'Where are you?'

'Sugar Heights. Dr Felix Babineau's house on scenic Lilac Drive. Hell, his fucking *estate*. You know who Babineau is, I know you do. No one kept closer tabs on Brady Hartsfield than you. For awhile there he was your fucking hobby.'

'*Who* you're talking about, yes. *What* you're talking about, no.'

'This whole thing is going to blow up, partner, and Izzy doesn't want to get hit with the shrapnel when it does. She's got ambitions, see? Chief of Detectives in ten years, maybe Chief of Police in fifteen. I get it, but that doesn't mean I like it. She called Chief Horgan behind my back, and Horgan called the SKIDs. If it's not officially their case now, it will be by noon. They've got their perp, but the shit's not right. I know it, and Izzy does, too. She just doesn't give a rat's ass.'

'You need to slow down, Pete. Tell me what's going on.'

Holly is hovering anxiously. Hodges shrugs his shoulders and raises a finger: wait.

'Housekeeper gets here at seven thirty, okay? Nora Everly by name. And at the top of the drive she sees Babineau's BMW on the lawn, with a bullet hole in the windshield. She looks inside, sees blood on the steering wheel and the seat, calls 911. There's a cop car five minutes away — in the Heights there's *always* one five minutes away — and when it arrives, Everly's sitting in her car with all the doors locked, shaking like a leaf. The unis tell her to stay put, and go to the door. The place is unlocked. Mrs Babineau — Cora — is lying dead in the hall, and I'm sure the bullet the ME digs out of her will match the one forensics dug out of the Beemer. On her forehead — are you ready for this? — there's the letter Z in black ink. More all around the downstairs, including one on the TV screen. Just like the one at the Ellerton place, and I think it was right about then my partner decided she wanted no part of this particular tarbaby.'

Hodges says, 'Yeah, probably,' just to keep Pete talking. He grabs the pad beside Holly's computer and prints BABINEAU'S WIFE MURDERED in big block letters, like a newspaper headline. Her hand flies to her mouth.

'While one of the cops is calling Division, the other one hears snores coming from upstairs. Like a chainsaw on idle, he said. So they go up, guns drawn, and in one of the three guest bedrooms, count em, *three*, the place is fucking huge, they find an old fart fast asleep. They wake him up and he gives his name as Alvin Brooks.'

'Library Al!' Hodges shouts. 'From the hospital! The first Zappit I ever saw was one he showed me!'

'Yeah, that's the guy. He had a Kiner ID badge in his shirt pocket. And without prompting, he says he killed Mrs Babineau. Claims he did it while he was hypnotized. So they cuff him, take him downstairs, and sit him on the couch. That's where Izzy and me found him when we entered the scene half an hour or so later. I don't know what's wrong with the guy, whether he had a nervous breakdown or what, but he's on Planet Purple. He keeps going off on tangents, spouting all sorts of weird shit.'

Hodges recollects something Al said to him on one of his last visits to Brady's room — right around Labor Day weekend of 2014, that would have been. 'Never so good as what you don't see.'

'Yeah.' Pete sounds surprised. 'Like that. And when Izzy asked who hypnotized him, he said it was the fish. The ones by the beautiful sea.'

To Hodges, this now makes sense.

'On further questioning — I did it, by then Izzy must have been in the kitchen, busy ditching the whole thing without asking for my input — he said Dr Z told him to, I quote, 'make his mark.' Ten times, he said, and sure enough, there are ten Zs, including the one on the deceased's forehead. I asked him if Dr Z was Dr Babineau, and he said no, Dr Z was Brady Hartsfield. Crazy, see?'

'Yeah,' Hodges says.

'I asked him if he shot Dr Babineau, too. He just shook his head and said he wanted to go back to sleep. Right around then Izzy comes tripping back from the kitchen and says Chief Horgan called the SKIDs, on account of Dr B. is a high-profile guy and this is going to be a

323

high-profile case, and besides, a pair of them happened to be right here in the city, waiting to be called to testify in a case, isn't that convenient. She won't meet my eye, she's all flushed, and when I start pointing around at all the Zs, asking her if they don't look familiar, she won't talk about it.'

Hodges has never heard such anger and frustration in his old partner's voice.

'So then my cell rings, and . . . you remember when I reached out to you this morning I said the doc on call took a sample of the residue in Hartsfield's mouth? Before the ME guy even got there?'

'Yeah.'

'Well, the phone call was from that doc. Simonson, his name is. The ME's analysis won't be back for two days at the soonest, but Simonson did one right away. The stuff in Hartsfield's mouth was a combination of Vicodin and Ambien. Hartsfield wasn't prescribed either one, and he could hardly dance his way down to the nearest med locker and score some, could he?'

Hodges, who already knows what Brady was taking for pain, agrees that that would be unlikely.

'Right now Izzy's in the house, probably watching from the background and keeping her mouth shut while the SKIDs question this Brooks guy, who honest-to-God can't remember his own name unless he's prompted. Otherwise he calls himself Z-Boy. Like something out of a Marvel comic book.'

Clutching the pen in his hand almost hard

enough to snap it in two, Hodges prints more headline caps on the pad, with Holly bending over to read as he writes: LIBRARY AL LEFT THE MESSAGE ON DEBBIE'S BLUE UMBRELLA.

Holly stares at him with wide eyes.

'Just before the SKIDs arrived — man, they didn't take long — I asked Brooks if he also killed Brady Hartsfield. Izzy says to him, 'Don't answer that!''

'She said *what*?' Hodges exclaims. He doesn't have much room in his head right now to worry about Pete's deteriorating relationship with his partner, but he's still amazed. Izzy's a police detective, after all, not Library Al's defense attorney.

'You heard me. Then she looks at me and says, 'You haven't given him the words.' So I turn to one of the uniforms and ask, 'Did you guys Mirandize this gentleman?' And of course they say yeah. I look at Izzy and she's redder in the face than ever, but she won't back down. She says, 'If we fuck this up, it won't come back on you, you're done in another couple of weeks, but it'll come back on me, and hard.''

'So the state boys turn up . . . '

'Yeah, and now I'm out here in the late Mrs Babineau's potting shed, or whatever the fuck it is, freezing my ass off. The richest part of the city, Kerm, and I'm in a shack colder than a well-digger's belt buckle. I bet Izzy knows I'm calling you, too. Tattling to my dear old Uncle Kermit.'

Pete is probably right about that. But if Miss Pretty Gray Eyes is as set on climbing the ladder as Pete believes, she's probably thinking of an uglier word: snitching.

'This Brooks guy is out of whatever little mind he's got left, which makes him the perfect donkey to pin the tail on when this hits the media. You know how they're going to lay it out?'

Hodges does, but lets Pete say it.

'Brooks got it in his head that he was some avenger of justice called Z-Boy. He came here, he killed Mrs Babineau when she opened the door, then killed the doc himself when Babineau got in his Beemer and tried to flee. Brooks then drove to the hospital and fed Hartsfield a bunch of pills from the Babineaus' private stash. I don't doubt that part, because they had a fucking pharmacy in their medicine cabinet. And sure, he could have gotten up to the Brain Injury Clinic without any problem, he's got an ID card, and he's been a hospital fixture for the last six or seven years, but *why*? And what did he do with Babineau's body? Because it's not here.'

'Good question.'

Pete plunges on. 'They'll say Brooks loaded it into his own car and ditched it somewhere, probably in a ravine or a culvert, and probably when he was coming back from feeding Hartsfield those pills, but why do that when he left the woman's body lying right there in the hall? And why come back here in the first place?'

'They'll say — '

'Yeah, that he's crazy! Sure they will! Perfect answer for anything that doesn't make sense! And if Ellerton and Stover come up at all — which they probably won't — they'll say he killed them, too!'

If they do, Hodges thinks, Nancy Alderson will

backstop the story, at least to a degree. Because it was undoubtedly Library Al that she saw watching the house on Hilltop Court.

'They'll hang Brooks out to dry, wade through the press coverage, and call it good. But there's more to it, Kerm. Got to be. If you know anything, if you've got even a single thread to pull, pull it. Promise me you will.'

I have more than one, Hodges thinks, but Babineau's the key, and Babineau has disappeared.

'How much blood was in the car, Pete?'

'Not a lot, but forensics has already confirmed it's Babineau's type. That's not conclusive, but . . . shit. I gotta go. Izzy and one of the SKID guys just came out the back door. They're looking for me.'

'All right.'

'Call me. And if you need anything I can access, let me know.'

'I will.'

Hodges ends the call and looks up, wanting to fill Holly in, but Holly is no longer beside him.

'Bill.' Her voice is low. 'Come in here.'

Puzzled, he walks to the door of his office, where he stops dead. Jerome is behind the desk, sitting in Hodges's swivel chair. His long legs are splayed out and he's looking at Dinah Scott's Zappit. His eyes are wide open but empty. His mouth hangs ajar. There are fine drops of spittle on his lower lip. A tune is tinkling from the gadget's tiny speaker, but not the same tune as last night — Hodges is sure of it.

'Jerome?' He takes a step forward, but before

he can take another, Holly grabs him by the belt. Her grip is surprisingly strong.

'No,' she says in the same low voice. 'You shouldn't startle him. Not when he's like that.'

'What, then?'

'I had a year of hypnotherapy when I was in my thirties. I was having problems with . . . well, never mind what I was having problems with. Let me try.'

'Are you sure?'

She looks at him, her face now pale, her eyes fearful. 'No, but we can't leave him like that. Not after what happened to Barbara.'

The Zappit in Jerome's limp hands gives off a bright blue flash. Jerome doesn't react, doesn't blink, only continues staring at the screen while the music tinkles.

Holly takes a step forward, then another. 'Jerome?'

No answer.

'Jerome, can you hear me?'

'Yes,' Jerome says, not looking up from the screen.

'Jerome, where are you?'

And Jerome says, 'At my funeral. Everyone is there. It's beautiful.'

17

Brady became fascinated with suicide at the age of twelve, while reading *Raven*, a true-crime book about the mass suicides in Jonestown, Guyana. There, more than nine hundred people — a third of them children — died after drinking fruit juice laced with cyanide. What interested Brady, aside from the thrillingly high body count, was the lead-up to the final orgy. Long before the day when whole families swallowed the poison together and nurses (*actual nurses*)! used hypodermics to squirt death down the throats of squalling infants, Jim Jones was preparing his followers for their apotheosis with fiery sermons and suicide rehearsals he called White Nights. He first filled them with paranoia, then hypnotized them with the glamour of death.

As a senior, Brady wrote his only A paper, for a half-assed sociology class called American Life. The paper was called 'American Deathways: A Brief Study of Suicide in the US'. In it he cited the statistics for 1999, then the most recent year for which they were available. More than forty thousand people had killed themselves during that year, usually with guns (the most reliable go-to method), but with pills running a close second. They also hung themselves, drowned themselves, bled out, stuck their heads in gas ovens, set themselves on fire, and rammed their cars into bridge abutments. One inventive fellow (this Brady did not put into his report; even then he was careful not to be branded an oddity) stuck a 220-volt line up his rectum and electrocuted himself. In 1999, suicide was the tenth leading cause of death in America, and if you added in the ones that were reported as accidents or 'natural causes,' it would undoubt-edly be right up there with heart disease, cancer, and car crashes. Most likely still behind them, but not *far* behind.

Brady quoted Albert Camus, who said, 'There is but one truly serious philosophical problem, and that is suicide.'

He also quoted a famous psychiatrist named Raymond Katz, who stated flatly, 'Every human being is born with the suicide gene.' Brady did not bother to add the second part of Katz's statement, because he felt it took some of the drama out of it: 'In most of us, it remains dormant.'

In the ten years between his graduation from high school and that disabling moment in the Mingo Auditorium, Brady's fascination with suicide — including his own, always seen as part of some grand and historic gesture — continued.

This seed has now, against all the odds, fully blossomed.

He will be the Jim Jones of the twenty-first century.

18

Forty miles north of the city, he can wait no longer. Brady pulls into a rest area on I–47, kills the laboring engine of Z-Boy's Malibu, and powers up Babineau's laptop. There's no WiFi here, as there is at some rest areas, but thanks to Big Momma Verizon, there's a cell tower not four miles away, standing tall against the thickening clouds. Using Babineau's MacBook Air, he can go anywhere he wants and never have to leave this nearly deserted parking lot. He thinks (and not for the first time) that a touch of telekinesis is nothing compared to the power of the Internet. He's sure thousands of suicides have incubated in the potent soup of its social media sites, where the trolls run free and the bullying goes on endlessly. That's *real* mind over matter.

He's not able to type as fast as he'd like to — the damp air pushing in with the coming storm has worsened the arthritis in Babineau's fingers — but eventually the laptop is mated to the high-powered gear back in Freddi Linklatter's computer room. He won't have to stay mated to it for long. He clicks on a hidden file he placed on the laptop during one of his previous visits inside Babineau's head.

OPEN LINK TO ZEETHEEND? Y N

He centers the cursor on Y, hits the return key, then waits. The worry-circle goes around and around and around. Just as he's begun to wonder if something has gone wrong, the laptop flashes the message he's been waiting for:

ZEETHEEND IS NOW ACTIVE

Good. Zeetheend is just a little icing on the cake. He has been able to disseminate only a limited number of Zappits — and a significant portion of his shipment was defective, for Christ's sake — but teenagers are herd creatures, and herd creatures are in mental and emotional lockstep. It's why fish school and bees swarm. It's why the swallows come back each year to Capistrano. In human behavior, it's why 'the wave' goes around at football and baseball stadiums, and why individuals will lose themselves in a crowd simply because the crowd is there.

Teenage boys have a tendency to wear the same baggy shorts and grow the same scruff on their faces, lest they be excluded from the herd. Teenage girls adopt the same styles of dress and go crazy for the same musical groups. It's We R Your Bruthas this year; not so long ago it was 'Round Here and One Direction. Back in the day it was New Kids on the Block. Fads sweep through teenagers like a measles epidemic, and from time to time, one of those fads is suicide. In southern Wales, dozens of teens hung themselves between 2007 and 2009, with messages on social networking sites stoking the craze. Even the goodbyes they left were couched in Netspeak: Me2 and CU L8er.

Wildfires vast enough to burn millions of acres can be started by a single match thrown into dry brush. The Zappits Brady has distributed through his human drones are hundreds of matches. Not all of them will light, and some of those that do won't stay lit. Brady knows this, but he has zeetheend.com to serve as both backstop and accelerant. Will it work? He's far from sure, but time is too short for extensive tests.

And if it does?

Teen suicides all over the state, maybe all over the Midwest. Hundreds, perhaps thousands. How would you like that, ex-Detective Hodges? Would that improve your retirement, you meddlesome old fuck?

He swaps Babineau's laptop for Z-Boy's game console. It's fitting to use this one. He thinks of it as Zappit Zero, because it's the first one he ever saw, on the day Al Brooks brought it into his room, thinking Brady might like it. Which he did. Oh yes, very much.

The extra program, with the number-fish and the subliminal messages, hasn't been added to this one, because Brady doesn't need it. Those things are strictly for the targets. He watches the fish swim back and forth, using them to settle and focus, then closes his eyes. At first there's only darkness, but after a few moments red lights begin to appear — more than fifty now. They are like dots on a computer map, except they don't remain stationary. They swim back and forth, left to right, up and down, crisscrossing. He settles on one at random, his eyes rolling beneath his closed lids as he follows its progress. It begins to slow, and slow, and slow. It stills, then starts growing bigger. It opens like a flower.

He's in a bedroom. There's a girl, staring fixedly down at the fish on her own Zappit, which she received free from badconcert. com. She's in her bed because she didn't go to school today. Maybe she said she was sick.

'What's your name?' Brady asks.

Sometimes they just hear a voice coming from the game console, but the ones who are most susceptible actually see him, like some kind of avatar in a video game. This girl is one of the latter, an auspicious beginning. But they always respond better to their names, so he'll keep saying it. She looks without surprise at the young man sitting beside her on the bed. Her face is pale. Her eyes are dazed.

'I'm Ellen,' she says. 'I'm looking for the right numbers.'

Of course you are, he thinks, and slips into her. She's forty miles south of him, but once the demo screen has opened them, distance doesn't matter. He could control her, turn her into one of his drones, but he doesn't want to do that any more than he wanted to slip into Mrs Trelawney's house some dark night and cut her throat. Murder isn't control; murder is just murder.

Suicide is control.

'Are you happy, Ellen?'

'I used to be,' she says. 'I could be again, if I find the right numbers.'

Brady gives her a smile that's both sad and charming. 'Yes, but the numbers are like life,' he says. 'Nothing adds up, Ellen. Isn't that true?'

'Uh-huh.'

'Tell me something, Ellen — what are you worried about?' He could find it himself, but it will be better if she tells him. He knows there's something, because everyone worries, and teenagers worry most of all.

'Right now? The SAT.'

Ah-ha, he thinks, the infamous Scholastic Assessment Test, where the Department of Academic Husbandry separates the sheep from the goats.

'I'm so bad at math,' she says. 'I reek.'

'Bad at the numbers,' he says, nodding sympathetically.

'If I don't score at least six-fifty, I won't get into a good school.'

'And you'll be lucky to score four hundred,' he says. 'Isn't that the truth, Ellen?'

'Yes.' Tears well in her eyes and begin to roll down her cheeks.

'And then you'll do badly on the English, too,' Brady says. He's opening her up, and this is the best part. It's like reaching into an animal that's stunned but still alive, and digging its guts out. 'You'll freeze up.'

'I'll probably freeze up,' Ellen says. She's sobbing audibly now. Brady checks her short-term memory and finds that her parents have gone to work and her little brother is at school. So crying is all right. Let the bitch make all the noise she wants.

'Not probably. You *will* freeze up, Ellen. Because you can't handle the pressure.'

She sobs.

'Say it, Ellen.'

'I can't handle the pressure. I'll freeze, and if I don't get into a good school, my dad will be disappointed and my mother will be mad.'

'What if you can't get into *any* school? What if the only job you can get is cleaning houses or folding clothes in a laundromat?'

'My mother will hate me!'

'She hates you already, doesn't she, Ellen?'

'I don't . . . I don't think . . . '

'Yes she does, she hates you. Say it, Ellen. Say 'My mother hates me.''

'My mother hates me. Oh God, I'm so scared and my life is so awful!'

This is the great gift bestowed by a combination of Zappit-induced hypnosis and Brady's own ability to invade minds once they are in that open and suggestible state. Ordinary fears, the ones kids like this live with as a kind of unpleasant background noise, can be turned into ravening monsters. Small balloons of paranoia can be inflated until they are as big as floats in the Macy's Thanksgiving Day Parade.

'You could stop being scared,' Brady says. 'And you could make your mother very, very sorry.'

Ellen smiles through her tears.

'You could leave all this behind.'

'I could. I could leave it behind.'

'You could be at peace.'

'Peace,' she says, and sighs.

How wonderful this is. It took weeks with Martine Stover's mother, who was always leaving the demo screen to play her goddam solitaire, and days with Barbara Robinson. With Ruth Scapelli and this pimple-faced crybaby in her poofy-pink girl's bedroom? Mere minutes. But then, Brady thinks, I always had a steep learning curve.

'Do you have your phone, Ellen?'

'Here.' She reaches under a decorative throw pillow. Her phone is also poofy-pink.

'You should post on Facebook and Twitter. So all your friends can read it.'

'What should I post?'

'Say 'I am at peace now. You can be, too. Go to zeetheend. com.''

She does it, but at an oozingly slow speed.

When they're in this state, it's like they're underwater. Brady reminds himself of how well this is going and tries not to become impatient. When she's done and the messages are sent — more matches flicked into dry tinder — he suggests that she go to the window. 'I think you could use some fresh air. It might clear your head.'

'I could use some fresh air,' she says, throwing back the duvet and swinging her bare feet out of bed.

'Don't forget your Zappit,' he says.

She takes it and walks to the window.

'Before you open the window, go to the main screen, where the icons are. Can you do that, Ellen?'

'Yes . . . ' A long pause. The bitch is slower than cold molasses. 'Okay, I see the icons.'

'Great. Now go to Wipe Words. It's the blackboard-and-eraser icon.'

'I see it.'

'Tap it twice, Ellen.'

She does so, and the Zappit gives an acknowledging blue flash. If anyone tries to use this particular game console again, it will give a final blue flash and drop dead.

'Now you can open the window.'

Cold air rushes in, blowing her hair back. She wavers, seems on the edge of waking, and for a moment Brady feels her slipping away. Control is still hard to maintain at a distance, even when they're in a hypnotic state, but he's sure he'll hone his technique to a nice sharp point. Practice makes perfect.

'Jump,' Brady whispers. 'Jump, and you won't

have to take the SAT. Your mother won't hate you. She'll be sorry. Jump and all the numbers will come right. You'll get the best prize. The prize is sleep.'

'The prize is sleep,' Ellen agrees.

'Do it now,' Brady murmurs as he sits behind the wheel of Al Brooks's old car with his eyes closed.

Forty miles south, Ellen jumps from her bedroom window. It's not a long drop, and there's banked snow against the house. It's old and crusty, but it still cushions her fall to a degree, so instead of dying, she only breaks a collarbone and three ribs. She begins to scream in pain, and Brady is blown out of her head like a pilot strapped to an F-111 ejection seat.

'Shit!' he screams, and pounds the steering wheel. Babineau's arthritis flares all the way up his arm, and that makes him angrier still. 'Shit, shit, *shit*!'

19

In the pleasantly upscale neighborhood of Branson Park, Ellen Murphy struggles to her feet. The last thing she remembers is telling her mother she was too sick to go to school — a lie so she could tap pink fish and hunt for prizes on the pleasantly addictive Fishin' Hole demo. Her Zappit is lying nearby, the screen cracked. It no longer interests her. She leaves it and begins staggering toward the front door on bare feet. Each breath she takes is a stab in the side.

But I'm alive, she thinks. At least I'm alive. What was I thinking? What in God's name was I thinking?

Brady's voice is still with her: the slimy taste of something awful that she swallowed while it was still alive.

20

'Jerome?' Holly asks. 'Can you still hear me?'

'Yes.'

'I want you to turn off the Zappit and put it on Bill's desk.' And then, because she's always been a belt-and-suspenders kind of girl, she adds: 'Facedown.'

A frown creases his broad brow. 'Do I have to?'

'Yes. Right now. And without looking at the damn thing.'

Before Jerome can follow this order, Hodges catches one final glimpse of the fish swimming, and one more bright blue flash. A momentary dizziness — perhaps caused by his pain pills, perhaps not — sweeps through him. Then Jerome pushes the button on top of the console, and the fish disappear.

What Hodges feels isn't relief but disappointment. Maybe that's crazy, but given his current medical problem, maybe it's not. He's seen hypnosis used from time to time to help witnesses achieve better recall, but has never grasped its full power until now. He has an idea, probably blasphemous in this situation, that the

Zappit fish might be better medicine for pain than the stuff Dr Stamos prescribed.

Holly says, 'I'm going to count down from ten to one, Jerome. Each time you hear a number, you'll be a little more awake. Okay?'

For several seconds Jerome says nothing. He sits calmly, peacefully, touring some other reality and perhaps trying to decide if he would like to live there permanently. Holly, on the other hand, is vibrating like a tuning fork, and Hodges can feel his fingernails biting into his palms as he clenches his fists.

At last Jerome says, 'Okay, I guess. Since it's you, Hollyberry.'

'Here we go. Ten . . . nine . . . eight . . . you're coming back . . . seven . . . six . . . five . . . waking up . . . '

Jerome raises his head. His eyes are aimed at Hodges, but Hodges isn't sure the boy is seeing him.

'Four . . . three . . . almost there . . . two . . . one . . . *wake up!*' She claps her hands together.

Jerome gives a hard jerk. One hand brushes Dinah's Zappit and knocks it to the floor. Jerome looks at Holly with an expression of surprise so exaggerated it would be funny under other circumstances.

'What just happened? Did I go to sleep?'

Holly collapses into the chair ordinarily reserved for clients. She takes a deep breath and wipes her cheeks, which are damp with sweat.

In a way,' Hodges says. 'The game hypnotized you. Like it hypnotized your sister.'

'Are you sure?' Jerome asks, then looks at his watch. 'I guess you are. I just lost fifteen minutes.'

'Closer to twenty. What do you remember?'

'Tapping the pink fish and turning them into numbers. It's surprisingly hard to do. You have to watch closely, really concentrate, and the blue flashes don't help.'

Hodges picks the Zappit up off the floor.

'I wouldn't turn that on,' Holly says sharply.

'Not going to. But I did last night, and I can tell you there were no blue flashes, and you could tap pink fish until your finger went numb without getting any numbers. Also, the tune is different now. Not much, but a little.'

Holly sings, pitch perfect: ' '*By the sea, by the sea, by the beautiful sea, you and me, you and me, oh how happy we'll be!*' ' My mother used to sing it to me when I was little.'

Jerome is staring at her with more intensity than she can deal with, and she looks away, flustered. 'What? What is it?'

'There were words,' he says, 'but not those.'

Hodges heard no words, only the tune, but doesn't say so. Holly asks Jerome if he can remember them.

His pitch isn't as good as hers, but it's close enough for them to be sure that yes, it's the tune they heard. ' '*You can sleep, you can sleep, it's a beautiful sleep . . .* ' ' He stops. 'That's all I can remember. If I'm not just making it up, that is.'

Holly says, 'Now we know for sure. Someone amped the Fishin' Hole screen.'

'Shot it full of 'roids,' Jerome adds.

341

'What does that even mean?' Hodges asks.

Jerome nods to Holly and she says, 'Someone loaded a stealth program into the demo, which is mildly hypnotic to begin with. The program was dormant when Dinah had the Zappit, and still dormant when you looked at it last night, Bill — which was lucky for you — but someone turned it on after that.'

'Babineau?'

'Him or someone else, if the police are right and Babineau is dead.'

'It could have been a preset,' Jerome says to Holly. Then, to Hodges: 'You know, like an alarm clock.'

'Let me get this straight,' Hodges says. 'The program was in there all along, and only became active once Dinah's Zappit was turned on today?'

'Yes,' Holly says. 'There's probably a repeater at work, don't you think, Jerome?'

'Yeah. A computer program that pumps out the update constantly, waiting for some schlub — me, in this case — to turn on a Zappit and activate the WiFi.'

'This could happen with *all* of them?'

'If the stealth program is in all of them, sure,' Jerome says. 'Brady set this up.' Hodges begins to pace, hand going to his side as if to contain the pain and hold it in. 'Brady fucking Hartsfield.'

'How?' Holly asks.

'I don't know, but it's the only thing that fits. He tries to blow up the Mingo during that concert. We stop him. The audience, most of

342

them young girls, is saved.'

'By you, Holly,' Jerome says.

'Be quiet, Jerome. Let him tell it.' Her eyes suggest she knows where Hodges is going.

'Six years pass. Those young girls, most of them in elementary or middle school in 2010, are in high school. Maybe in college. 'Round Here is long gone and the girls are young women now, they've moved on to other kinds of music, but then they get an offer they can't refuse. A free game console, and all they have to do is be able to prove they were at the 'Round Here show that night. The console probably looks as out-of-date to them as a black-and-white TV, but what the hell, it's free.'

'Yes!' Holly says. 'Brady was still after them. This is his revenge, but not just on them. It's his revenge on *you*, Bill.'

Which makes me responsible, Hodges thinks bleakly. Except what else could I do? What else could any of us do? He was going to bomb the place.

'Babineau, going under the name of Myron Zakim, bought eight hundred of those consoles. It had to be him, because he's loaded. Brady was broke and I doubt Library Al could have fronted even twenty thousand dollars from his retirement savings. Those consoles are out there now. And if they all get this amped-up program once they're turned on . . .'

'Hold it, go back,' Jerome says. 'Are you really saying that a respected neurosurgeon got involved in this shit?'

'That's what I'm saying, yeah. Your sister ID'd

343

him, and we already know the respected neurosurgeon was using Brady Hartsfield as a lab rat.'

'But now Hartsfield's dead,' Holly says. 'Which leaves Babineau, who may also be dead.'

'Or not,' Hodges says. 'There was blood in his car, but no body. Wouldn't be the first time some doer tried to fake his own death.'

'I've got to check something on my computer,' Holly says. 'If those free Zappits are getting a new program as of today, then maybe . . . ' She hurries out.

Jerome begins, 'I don't understand how any of this can be, but — '

'Babineau will be able to tell us,' Hodges says. 'If he's still alive.'

'Yes, but wait a minute. Barb talked about hearing a voice, telling her all sorts of awful things. I didn't hear any voice, and I sure don't feel like offing myself.'

'Maybe you're immune.'

'I'm not. That screen got me, Bill, I mean I was *gone*. I heard words in the little tune, and I think there were words in the blue flashes, too. Like subliminal messages. But . . . no voice.'

There could be all sorts of reasons for that, Hodges thinks, and just because Jerome didn't hear the suicide voice, it doesn't mean that most of the kids who got those free games won't.

'Let's say this repeater gadget was only turned on during the last fourteen hours,' Hodges says. 'We know it can't have been earlier than when I tried out Dinah's game, or I would have seen the number-fish and the blue flashes. So here's a question: can those demo screens be amped up even if the gadgets are off?'

'No way,' Jerome says. 'They have to be turned on. But once they are . . . '

'*It's active!*' Holly shouts. '*That fracking zeetheend site is active!*'

Jerome rushes to her desk in the outer office. Hodges follows more slowly.

Holly turns up the volume on her computer, and music fills the offices of Finders Keepers. Not 'By the Beautiful Sea' this time, but 'Don't Fear the Reaper.' As it spools out — *forty thousand men and women every day, another forty thousand coming every day* — Hodges sees a candlelit funeral parlor and a coffin buried in flowers. Above it, smiling young men and women come and go, moving side to side, crisscrossing, fading, reappearing. Some of them wave; some flash the peace sign. Below the coffin is a series of messages in letters that swell and contract like a slowly beating heart.

AN END TO PAIN
AN END TO FEAR
NO MORE ANGER
NO MORE DOUBT
NO MORE STRUGGLE
PEACE
PEACE
PEACE

Then a stuttering series of blue flashes. Embedded in them are words. Or call them what they really are, Hodges thinks. Drops of poison.

345

'Turn it off, Holly.' Hodges doesn't like the way she's looking at the screen — that wide-eyed stare, so much like Jerome's a few minutes ago.

She moves too slowly to suit Jerome. He reaches over her shoulder and crashes her computer.

'You shouldn't have done that,' she says reproachfully. 'I could lose data.'

'That's exactly what the fucking website is for,' Jerome says. 'To make you lose data. To make you lose your *shit*. I could read the last one, Bill. In the blue flash. It said *do it now*.'

Holly nods. 'There was another one that said *tell your friends*.'

'Does the Zappit direct them to that . . . that thing?' Hodges asks.

'It doesn't have to,' Jerome says. 'Because the ones who find it — and plenty will, including kids who never got a free Zappit — will spread the word on Facebook and all the rest.'

'He wanted a suicide epidemic,' Holly says. 'He set it in motion somehow, then killed himself.'

'Probably to get there ahead of them,' Jerome says. 'So he can meet them at the door.'

Hodges says, 'Am I supposed to believe a rock song and a picture of a funeral is going to get kids to kill themselves? The Zappits, I can accept that. I've seen how they work. But this?'

Holly and Jerome exchange a glance, one that Hodges can read easily: How do we explain this to him? How do you explain a robin to someone who's never seen a bird? The glance alone is almost enough to convince him.

'Teenagers are vulnerable to stuff like this,' Holly says. 'Not all of them, no, but plenty. I would have been when I was seventeen.'

'And it's catching,' Jerome says. 'Once it starts . . . *if* it starts . . . ' He finishes with a shrug.

'We need to find that repeater gadget and turn it off,' Hodges says. 'Limit the damage.'

'Maybe it's at Babineau's house,' Holly says. 'Call Pete. Find out if there's any computer stuff there. If there is, make him pull all the plugs.'

'If he's with Izzy, he'll let it go to voicemail,' Hodges says, but he makes the call and Pete picks up on the first ring. He tells Hodges that Izzy has gone back to the station with the SKIDs to await the first forensics reports. Library Al Brooks is already gone, taken into custody by the first responding cops, who will get partial credit for the bust.

Pete sounds tired.

'We had a blow-up. Me and Izzy. Big one. I tried to tell her what you told me when we started working together — how the case is the boss, and you go where it leads you. No ducking, no handing it off, just pick it up and follow the red thread all the way home. She stood there listening with her arms folded, nodding her head every now and then. I actually thought I was getting through to her. Then you know what she asked me? If I knew the last time there was a woman in the top echelon of the city police. I said I didn't, and she said that was because the answer was never. She said the first one was going to be her. Man, I thought I knew her.' Pete utters what may be the most humorless laugh

347

Hodges has ever heard. 'I thought she was *police*.'

Hodges will commiserate later, if he gets a chance. Right now there's no time. He asks about the computer gear.

'We found nothing except an iPad with a dead battery,' Pete says. 'Everly, the housekeeper, says he had a laptop in his study, almost brand new, but it's gone.'

'Like Babineau,' Hodges says. 'Maybe it's with him.'

'Maybe. Remember, if I can help, Kermit — '

'I'll call, believe me.'

Right now he'll take all the help he can get.

21

The result with the girl named Ellen is infuriating — like the Robinson bitch all over again — but at last Brady calms down. It worked, that's what he needs to focus on. The shortness of the drop combined with the snowbank was just bad luck. There will be plenty of others. He has a lot of work ahead of him, a lot of matches to light, but once the fire is burning, he can sit back and watch.

It will burn until it burns itself out.

He starts Z-Boy's car and pulls out of the rest area. As he merges with the scant traffic headed north on 1–47, the first flakes spin out of the white sky and hit the Malibu's windshield. Brady drives faster. Z-Boy's piece of crap isn't equipped for a snowstorm, and once he leaves

348

the turnpike, the roads will grow progressively worse. He needs to beat the weather.

Oh, I'll beat it, all right, Brady thinks, and grins as a wonderful idea hits him. Maybe Ellen is paralyzed from the neck down, a head on a stick, like the Stover bitch. It's not likely, but it's possible, a pleasant daydream with which to while away the miles.

He turns on the radio, finds some Judas Priest, and lets it blast. Like Hodges, he enjoys the hard stuff.

THE SUICIDE PRINCE

Brady won many victories in Room 217, but necessarily had to keep them to himself. Coming back from the living death of coma; discovering that he could — because of the drug Babineau had administered, or because of some fundamental alteration in his brainwaves, or perhaps due to a combination of the two — move small objects simply by thinking about them; inhabiting Library Al's brain and creating inside him a secondary personality, Z-Boy. And mustn't forget getting back at the fat cop who hit him in the balls when he couldn't defend himself. Yet the best, the absolute best, was nudging Sadie MacDonald into committing suicide. That was power.

He wanted to do it again.

The question that desire raised was a simple one: who next? It would be easy to make Al Brooks jump from a bridge overpass or swallow drain cleaner, but Z-Boy would go with him, and without Z-Boy, Brady would be stuck in Room 217, which was really nothing more than a prison cell with a parking garage view. No, he needed Brooks just where he was. And *as* he was.

More important was the question of what to do about the bastard responsible for putting him here. Ursula Haber, the Nazi who ran the PT department, said rehab patients needed GTG: goals to grow. Well, he was growing, all right, and

350

revenge against Hodges was a worthy goal, but how to get it? Inducing Hodges to commit suicide wasn't the answer, even if there was a way to try it. He'd played the suicide game already with Hodges. And lost.

When Freddi Linklatter appeared with the picture of him and his mother, Brady was still over a year and a half from realizing how he could finish his business with Hodges, but seeing Freddi gave him a badly needed jump-start. He would need to be careful, though. Very careful.

A step at a time, he told himself as he lay awake in the small hours of the night. Just one step at a time. I have great obstacles, but I also have extraordinary weapons.

Step one was having Al Brooks remove the remaining Zappits from the hospital library. He took them to his brother's house, where he lived in an apartment over the garage. That was easy, because no one wanted them, anyway. Brady thought of them as ammo. Eventually he would find a gun that could use it.

Brooks took the Zappits on his own, although operating under commands — thoughtfish — that Brady implanted in the shallow but useful Z-Boy persona. He had become wary of entering Brooks completely and taking him over, because it burned through the old fellow's brains too fast. He had to ration those times of total immersion, and use them wisely. It was a shame, he enjoyed his vacations outside the hospital, but people were starting to notice that Library Al had become a trifle foggy upstairs. If he became *too* foggy, he would be forced out of his volunteer job. Worse, Hodges might notice. That would not be good. Let the old Det-Ret vacuum up all the rumors about telekinesis he wanted, Brady was fine with that, but he didn't want Hodges to catch even a whiff of what was really going on.

Despite the risk of mental depletion, Brady took complete command of Brooks in the spring of 2013, because he needed the library computer. *Looking* at it could be done without total immersion, but *using* it was another thing. And it was a short visit. All he wanted to do was set up a Google alert, using the keywords *Zappit* and *Fishin' Hole*.

Every two or three days he sent Z-Boy to check the alert and report back. His instructions were to switch to the ESPN site if someone wandered over to see what he was surfing (they rarely did; the library was really not much more than a closet, and the few visitors were usually looking for the chapel next door).

The alerts were interesting and informative. It seemed a great many people had experienced either semi-hypnosis or actual seizure activity after looking at the Fishin' Hole demo screen for too long. That effect was more powerful than Brady would have believed. There was even an article about it in the *New York Times* business section, and the company was in trouble because of it.

Trouble it didn't need, because it was already tottering. You didn't have to be a genius (which Brady believed he was) to know that Zappit, Inc. would soon either go bankrupt or be swallowed up by a larger company. Brady was betting on bankruptcy. What company would be stupid enough to pick up an outfit making game consoles that were hopelessly out of date and ridiculously expensive, especially when one of the games was dangerously defective?

Meanwhile, there was the problem of how to jigger the ones he had (they were stored in the closet of Z-Boy's apartment, but Brady considered them his property) so that people would look at them longer. He was stuck on that when Freddi made her visit. When she was gone, her Christian duty done (not that Frederica Bimmel Linklatter was or ever had been a Christian), Brady thought long and hard.

Then, in late August of 2013, after a particularly aggravating visit from the Det-Ret, he sent Z-Boy to her apartment.

★　★　★

Freddi counted the money, then studied the old fellow in the green Dickies standing slump-shouldered in the middle of what passed for her living room. The money had come from Al Brooks's account at Midwest Federal. The first withdrawal from his meager savings, but far from the last.

'Two hundred bucks for a few questions? Yeah, I can do that. But if what you really came for is a blowjob, you need to go somewhere else, old-timer. I'm a dyke.'

'Just questions,' Z-Boy said. He handed her a Zappit and told her to look at the Fishin' Hole demo screen. 'But you shouldn't look longer than thirty seconds or so. It's, urn, weird.'

'Weird, huh?' She gave him an indulgent smile and turned her attention to the swimming fish. Thirty seconds became forty. That was allowable according to the directives Brady had given him before sending him on this mission (he always called them missions, having discovered that Brooks associated the word with heroism). But after forty-five, he grabbed it back.

Freddi looked up, blinking. 'Whoo. It messes with your brain, doesn't it?'

'Yeah. It kinda does.'

'I read in *Gamer Programming* that the Star Smash arcade game does something like that, but you have to play it for like, half an hour before the effect kicks in. This is a lot faster. Do people know about it?'

Z-Boy ignored the question. 'My boss wants to know how you would fix this so people would look at the demo screen longer, and not go right to the game. Which doesn't have the same effect.'

Freddi adopted her fake Russian accent for the first time. 'Who is fearless leader, Z-Boy? You be good fellow and tell Comrade X, *da*?'

Z-Boy's brow wrinkled. 'Huh?'

Freddi sighed. 'Who's your boss, handsome?'

'Dr Z.' Brady had anticipated the question — he knew Freddi of old — and this was another directive. Brady had plans for Felix Babineau, but as yet they were vague. He was still feeling his way. Flying on instruments.

'Dr Z and his sidekick Z-Boy,' she said, lighting a cigarette. 'On the path to world domination. My, my. Does that make me Z-Girl?'

This wasn't part of his directives, so he stayed silent.

'Never mind, I get it,' she said, chuffing out smoke. 'Your boss wants an eye-trap. The way to do it is to turn the demo screen itself into a game. Gotta be simple, though. Can't get bogged down in a lot of complex programming.' She held up the Zappit, now turned off. 'This thing is pretty brainless.'

'What kind of game?'

'Don't ask me, bro. That's the creative side. Never was my forte. Tell your boss to figure it out. Anyway, once this thing is powered up and getting a good WiFi signal, you need to install a root kit. Want me to write this down?'

'No.' Brady had allocated a bit of Al Brooks's rapidly diminishing memory storage space for this very task. Besides, when the job needed to be done, Freddi would be the one doing it.

'Once the kit's in, source code can be downloaded from another computer.' She adopted the Russian accent again. 'From secret Base Zero under polar ice-kep.'

'Should I tell him that part?'

'No. Just tell him root kit plus source code. Got it?'

'Yes.'

'Anything else?'

'Brady Hartsfield wants you to come visit him again.'

Freddi's eyebrows shot up almost to her crewcut. 'He *talks* to you?'

'Yes. It's hard to understand him at first, but

'after awhile you can.'

Freddi looked around her living room — dim, cluttered, smelling of last night's take-out Chinese — as if it interested her. She was finding this conversation increasingly creepy.

'I don't know, man. I did my good deed, and I was never even a Girl Scout.'

'He'll pay you,' Z-Boy said. 'Not very much, but . . .'

'How much?'

'Fifty dollars a visit?'

'Why?'

Z-Boy didn't know, but in 2013, there was still a fair amount of Al Brooks behind his forehead, and that was the part that understood. 'I think . . . because you were a part of his life. You know, when you and him used to go out to fix people's computers. In the old days.'

★   ★   ★

Brady didn't hate Dr Babineau with the same intensity that he hated K. William Hodges, but that didn't mean Dr B. wasn't on his shit list. Babineau had used him as a guinea pig, which was bad. He had lost interest in Brady when his experimental drug didn't seem to be working, which was worse. Worst of all, the shots had resumed once Brady had regained conscious-ness, and who knew what they were doing? They could kill him, but as a man who had assiduously courted his own death, that wasn't what kept him awake nights. What did was the possibility that the shots might interfere with his new

356

abilities. Babineau pooh-poohed Brady's supposed mind-over-matter powers in public, but he actually believed they might exist, even though Brady had been careful never to exhibit his talent to the doctor, despite Babineau's repeated urgings. He believed any psychokinetic abilities were also a result of what he called Cerebellin.

The CAT scans and MRIs had also resumed. 'You're the Eighth Wonder of the World,' Babineau told him after one of these — in the fall of 2013, this was. He was walking beside Brady as an orderly wheeled him back to Room 217. Babineau was wearing what Brady thought of as his gloaty face. 'The current protocols have done more than halt the destruction of your brain cells; they have stimulated the growth of new ones. More robust ones. Do you have any idea how remarkable that is?'

You bet, asshole, Brady thought. So keep those scans to yourself. If the DA's office found out, I'd be in trouble.

Babineau was patting Brady's shoulder in a proprietary way Brady hated. Like he was patting his pet dog. 'The human brain is made up of approximately one hundred billion nerve cells. Those in the Broca's Area of yours were gravely injured, but they have recovered. In fact, they are creating neurons unlike any I've ever seen. One of these days you're going to be famous not as a person who took lives, but as one responsible for saving them.'

If so, Brady thought, it's a day you won't be around to see.

Count on it, dickweed.

The creative side was never my forte, Freddi told Z-Boy. True enough, but it was *always* Brady's, and as 2013 became 2014, he had plenty of time to think of ways the Fishin' Hole demo screen might be juiced up and turned into what Freddi had called an eye-trap. Yet none of them seemed quite right.

They did not talk about the Zappit effect during her visits; mostly they reminisced (with Freddi necessarily doing most of the talking) about the old days on the Cyber Patrol. All the crazy people they'd met on their outcalls. And Anthony 'Tones' Frobisher, their asshole boss. Freddi went on about him constantly, turning things she should have said into things she had, and *right to his face!* Freddi's visits were monotonous but comforting. They balanced his desperate nights, when he felt he might spend the rest of his life in Room 217, at the mercy of Dr Babineau and his 'vitamin shots.'

I have to stop him, Brady thought. I have to *control* him.

To do that, the amped-up version of the demo screen had to be just right. If he flubbed his first chance to get into Babineau's mind, there might not be another.

★ ★ ★

The TV now played at least four hours a day in Room 217. This was per an edict from Babineau, who told Head Nurse Helmington that he was 'exposing Mr Hartsfield to external stimuli.'

Mr Hartsfield didn't mind *News at Noon* (there was always an exciting explosion or a mass tragedy somewhere in the world), but the rest of the stuff — cooking shows, talk shows, soap operas, bogus medicine men — was drivel. Yet one day, while sitting in his chair by the window and watching *Prize Surprise* (staring in that direction, at least), he had a revelation. The contestant who had survived to the Bonus Round was given a chance to win a trip to Aruba on a private jet. She was shown an oversized computer screen where big colored dots were shuffling around. Her job was to touch five red ones, which would turn into numbers. If the numbers she touched added up to a total within a five-digit range of 100, she'd win.

Brady watched her wide eyes moving from side to side as she studied the screen, and knew he'd found what he was looking for. The pink fish, he thought. They're the ones that move the fastest, and besides, red is an angry color. Pink is . . . what? What was the word? It came, and he smiled. It was the radiant one that made him look nineteen again.

Pink was *soothing*.

★　★　★

Sometimes when Freddi visited, Z-Boy left his library cart in the hall and joined them. On one of these occasions, during the summer of 2014, he handed Freddi an electronic recipe. It had been written on the library computer, and

359

during one of the increasingly rare occasions when Brady did not just give instructions but slid into the driver's seat and took over completely. He had to, because this had to be just right. There was no room for error.

Freddi scanned it, got interested, and read it more closely. 'Say,' she said, 'this is pretty clever. And adding subliminal messaging is cool. Nasty, but cool. Did the mysterious Dr Z think this up?'

'Yeah,' Z-Boy said.

Freddi switched her attention to Brady. 'Do you know who this Dr Z is?'

Brady shook his head slowly back and forth.

'Sure it's not you? Because this looks like your work.'

Brady only stared at her vacantly until she looked away. He had let her see more of him than Hodges or anyone on the nursing or PT staff, but he had no intention of letting her see *into* him. Not at this point, at least. Too much chance she might talk. Besides, he still didn't know exactly what he was doing. They said that the world would beat a path to your door if you built a better mousetrap, but since he did not as yet know if this one would catch mice, it was best to keep quiet. And Dr Z didn't exist yet.

But he would.

★　★　★

On an afternoon not long after Freddi received the electronic recipe explaining just how to jigger the Fishin' Hole demo screen, Z-Boy visited Felix Babineau in his office. The doctor spent an hour there most days he was in the hospital, drinking coffee and reading the newspaper. There was an indoor putting green by the window (no parking garage view for Babineau), where he sometimes practiced his short game. That was where he was when Z-Boy came in without knocking.

Babineau looked at him coldly. 'Can I help you? Are you lost?'

Z-Boy held out Zappit Zero, which Freddi had upgraded (after buying several new computer components paid for out of Al Brooks's rapidly shrinking savings account). 'Look at this,' he said. 'I'll tell you what to do.'

'You need to leave,' Babineau said. 'I don't know what kind of bee you have in your bonnet, but this is my private space and my private time. Or do you want me to call security?'

'Look at it, or you'll be seeing yourself on the evening news. 'Doctor performs experiments with untested South American drug on accused mass murderer Brady Hartsfield.''

Babineau stared at him with his mouth open, at that moment looking very much as he would after Brady began to whittle away his core consciousness. 'I have no idea what you're talking about.'

'I'm talking about Cerebellin. Years away from FDA approval, if ever. I accessed your file, and took two dozen photos with my phone. I also took photos of the brain scans you've been keeping to yourself. You broke lots of laws, Doc. Look at the game and it stays between us. Refuse, and your career is over. I'll give you five seconds to decide.'

Babineau took the game and looked at the swimming fish. The little tune tinkled. Every now and then there was a flash of blue light.

'Start tapping the pink ones, doctor. They'll turn into numbers. Add them up in your head.'

'How long do I have to do this for?'

'You'll know.'

'Are you crazy?'

'You lock your office when you're not here, which is smart, but there are lots of all-access security cards floating around this place. And you left your computer on, which seems kind of crazy to me. Look at the fish. Tap the pink ones. Add up the numbers. That's all you have to do, and I'll leave you alone.'

'This is blackmail.'

'No, blackmail is for money. This is just a trade. Look at the fish. I won't ask you again.'

Babineau looked at the fish. He tapped at a pink one and missed. He tapped again, missed again. Muttered 'Fuck!' under his breath. It was quite a bit harder than it looked, and he began to get interested. The blue flashes should have been annoying, but they weren't. They actually seemed to help him focus. Alarm at what this geezer knew started to fade into the background of his thoughts.

He succeeded in tapping one of the pink fish before it could shoot off the left side of the screen and got a nine. That was good. A good start. He forgot why he was doing this. Catching the pink fish was the important thing.

The tune played.

One floor up, in Room 217, Brady stared at his own Zappit, and felt his breathing slow. He closed his eyes and looked at a single red dot. That was Z-Boy. He waited . . . waited . . . and then, just as he was beginning to think his target might be immune, a second dot appeared. It was faint at first, but gradually grew bright and clear.

Like watching a rose blossom, Brady thought.

The two dots began to swim playfully back and forth. He settled his concentration on the one that was Babineau. It slowed and became stationary.

Gotcha, Brady thought.

But he had to be careful. This was a stealth mission.

The eyes he opened were Babineau's. The doctor was still staring at the fish, but he had ceased to tap them. He had become . . . what was the word they used? A gork. He had become a gork.

Brady did not linger on that first occasion, but it didn't take long to understand the wonders to which he'd gained access. Al Brooks was a piggy bank. Felix Babineau was a vault. Brady had access to his memories, his stored knowledge, his abilities. While in Al, he could have rewired an electrical circuit. In Babineau, he could have performed a craniotomy and rewired a human brain. Further, he had proof of something he had only theorized about and hoped for: he could take possession of others at a distance. All it took was that state of Zappit-induced hypnosis to

363

open them up. The Zappit Freddi had modified made for a very efficient eye-trap, and good God, it worked so *fast*.

He couldn't wait to use it on Hodges.

Before leaving, Brady released a few thought-fish into Babineau's brain, but only a few. He intended to move very carefully with the doctor. Babineau needed to be thoroughly habituated to the screen — which was now what those specializing in hypnosis called an inducement device — before Brady announced himself. One of that day's thoughtfish was the idea that the CAT scans on Brady weren't producing anything of real interest, and ought to cease. The Cerebellin shots should also cease.

Because Brady's not making sufficient progress. Because I'm a dead end. Also, I might be caught.

'Getting caught would be bad,' Babineau murmured.

'Yes,' Z-Boy said. 'Getting caught would be bad for both of us.'

Babineau had dropped his putter. Z-Boy picked it up and put it in his hand.

* * *

As that hot summer morphed into a cold and rainy fall, Brady strengthened his hold on Babineau. He released thoughtfish carefully, like a game warden stocking a pond with trout. Babineau began to feel an urge to get touchy-feely with a few of the younger nurses, risking a sexual harass-ment complaint. Babineau occasionally stole pain medication from the Bucket's Pyxis Med Station,

364

using the ID card of a fictional doctor — a fiddle Brady set up via Freddi Linklatter. Babineau did this even though he was bound to be caught if he kept on, and had other, safer ways of getting pills. He stole a Rolex watch from the Neuro lounge one day (although he had one of his own) and put it in the bottom drawer of his office desk, where he promptly forgot it. Little by little, Brady Hartsfield — who could barely walk — took possession of the doctor who had presumed to take possession of him, and put him in a guilt-trap that had many teeth. If he did something foolish, like trying to tell someone what was going on, the trap would snap shut.

At the same time he began sculpting the Dr Z personality, doing it much more carefully than he had with Library Al. For one thing, he was better at it now. For another, he had finer materials to work with. In October of that year, with hundreds of thoughtfish now swimming in Babineau's brain, he began assuming control of the doctor's body as well as his mind, taking it on longer and longer trips. Once he drove all the way to the Ohio state line in Babineau's BMW, just to see if his hold would weaken with distance. It didn't. It seemed that once you were in, you were in. And it was a fine trip. He stopped at a roadside restaurant and pigged out on onion rings.

Tasty!

* * *

As the 2014 holiday season approached, Brady found himself in a state he hadn't known since

365

earliest childhood. It was so foreign to him that the Christmas decorations had been taken down and Valentine's Day was approaching before he realized what it was.

He felt contented.

Part of him fought this feeling, labeling it a little death, but part of him wanted to accept it. Embrace it, even. And why not? It wasn't as though he were stuck in Room 217, or even in his own body. He could leave whenever he wanted, either as a passenger or as a driver. He had to be careful not to be in the driver's seat too much or stay too long, that was all. Core consciousness, it seemed, was a limited resource. When it was gone, it was gone.

Too bad.

If Hodges had continued to make his visits, Brady would have had another of those goals to grow — getting him to look at the Zappit in his drawer, entering him, and planting suicidal thought-fish. It would have been like using Debbie's Blue Umbrella all over again, only this time with suggestions that were much more powerful. Not really suggestions at all, but commands.

The only problem with the plan was that Hodges had stopped coming. He had appeared just after Labor Day, spouting all his usual bullshit — *I know you're in there, Brady, I hope you're suffering, Brady, can you really move things around without touching them, Brady, if you can let me see you do it* — but not since. Brady surmised that Hodges's disappearance from his life was the real source of this unusual

366

and not entirely welcome contentment. Hodges had been a burr under his saddle, infuriating him and making him gallop. Now the burr was gone, and he was free to graze, if he wanted to.

He sort of did.

* * *

With access to Dr Babineau's bank account and investment portfolio as well as his mind, Brady went on a computer spending spree. The Babster withdrew the money and made the purchases; Z-Boy delivered the equipment to Freddi Linklatter's cheesedog of a crib.

She really deserves an apartment upgrade, Brady thought. I ought to do something about that.

Z-Boy also brought her the rest of the Zappits he'd pilfered from the library, and Freddi amped the Fishin' Hole demos in all of them . . . for a price, of course. And although the price was high, Brady paid it without a qualm. It was the doc's money, after all, the dough of Babineau. As to what he might do with the juiced-up consoles, Brady had no idea. Eventually he might want another drone or two, he supposed, but he saw no reason to trade up right away. He began to understand what contentment actually was: the emotional version of the horse latitudes, where all the winds died away and one simply drifted.

It ensued when one ran out of goals to grow.

* * *

This state of affairs continued until February 13th of 2015, when Brady's attention was caught by an item on *News at Noon*. The anchors, who had been laughing it up over the antics of a couple of baby pandas, put on their Oh Shit This Is So Awful faces when the chyron behind them changed from the pandas to a broken-heart logo.

'It's going to be a sad Valentine's Day in the suburb of Sewickley,' said the female half of the duo.

'That's right, Betty,' said the male half. 'Two survivors of the City Center Massacre, twenty-six-year-old Krista Countryman and twenty-four-year-old Keith Frias, have committed suicide in the Countryman woman's home.'

It was Betty's turn. 'Ken, the shocked parents say the couple washoping to be married in May of this year, but both were badly injured in the attack perpetrated by Brady Hartsfield, and the continuing physical and mental pain was apparently too much for them. Here's Frank Denton, with more.'

Brady was on high alert now, sitting as close to bolt upright in his chair as he could manage, eyes shining. Could he legitimately claim those two? He believed he could, which meant his City Center score had just gone up from eight to ten. Still shy of a dozen, but hey! Not bad.

Correspondent Frank Denton, also wearing his best Oh Shit expression, went blah-de-blah for awhile, and then the picture switched to the Countryman chick's pore ole daddy, who read the suicide note the couple had left. He blubbered through most of it, but Brady caught the gist. They'd had a beautiful vision of the afterlife, where their wounds would be healed, the burden of their pain would be lifted, and they could be married in perfect health by their Lord and Savior, Jesus Christ.

'Boy, that's sad,' the male anchor opined at the end of the story. 'So sad.'

'It sure is, Ken,' Betty said. Then the screen behind them flashed a picture showing a bunch of idiots in wedding clothes standing in a swimming pool, and her sad face clicked off and the happy one came back on. 'But this should cheer you up — twenty couples decided to get married in a swimming pool in Cleveland, where it's only *twenty degrees*!'

'I hope they had a hunka-hunka burning love,' Ken said, showing his perfectly capped teeth in a grin. '*Brrrr!* Here's Patty Newfield with the details.'

How many more could I get? Brady wondered. He was on fire. I've got nine augmented Zappits, plus the two my drones have and the one in my drawer. Who says I have to be done with those job-hunting assholes?

Who says I can't run up the score?

★   ★   ★

Brady continued to keep track of Zappit, Inc. during his fallow period, sending Z-Boy to check the Google alert once or twice weekly. The chatter about the hypnotic effect of the Fishin' Hole screen (and the lesser effect of the Whistling Birds demo) died down and was replaced by speculation about just when the company would go under — it was no longer a matter of if. When Sunrise Solutions bought Zappit out, a blogger who called himself Electric Whirlwind wrote, 'Wow! This is like a couple of cancer patients with six weeks to live deciding to elope.'

Babineau's shadow personality was now well established, and it was Dr Z who began to research the survivors of the City Center Massacre on Brady's behalf, making a list of the ones most badly injured, and thus most vulnerable to suicidal thoughts. A couple of them, like Daniel Starr and Judith Lorna, were still wheelchair-bound. Lorna might get out of hers; Starr, never. Then there was Martine Stover, paralyzed from the neck down and living with her mother over in Ridgedale.

I'd be doing them a favor, Brady thought. *Really I would.*

He decided Stover's mommy would make a good start. His first idea was to have Z-Boy mail her a Zappit ('A Free Gift for You!'), but how could he be sure she wouldn't just throw it away? He only had nine, and didn't want to risk wasting one. Juicing them up had cost him (well, Babineau) quite a lot of money. It might be better to send Babineau on a personal mission. In one of his tailored suits, set off by a sober dark tie, he looked a lot more trustworthy than Z-Boy in his rumpled green Dickies, and he was the sort of older guy that chicks like Stover's mother had a tendency to dig. All Brady had to do was work up a believable story. Something about test marketing, maybe? Possibly a book club? A prize competition?

He was still sifting scenarios — there was no hurry — when his Google alert announced an expected death: Sunrise Solutions had gone bye-bye. This was in early April. A trustee had been appointed to sell off the assets, and a list of so-called 'real goods' would soon appear in the usual sell-sites. For those who couldn't wait, a list of all Sunrise Solutions' unsaleable crapola could be found in the bankruptcy filing. Brady thought this was interesting, but not interesting enough to have Dr Z look up the list of assets. There were probably crates of Zappits among them, but he had nine of his own, and surely that would be enough to play with.

A month later he changed his mind about that.

★   ★   ★

One of *News at Noon's* most popular features was called 'Just A Word From Jack.' Jack O'Malley was a fat old dinosaur who had probably started in the biz when TV was still black-and-white, and he bumbled on for five minutes or so at the end of every newscast about whatever was on what remained of his mind. He wore huge black-rimmed glasses, and his jowls quivered like Jell-O when he talked. Ordinarily Brady found him quite enter-taining, a bit of comic relief, but there was nothing amusing about that day's Word From Jack. It opened whole new vistas.

'The families of Krista Countryman and Keith Frias have been flooded with condolences as a result of a story this station ran not long ago,'

Jack said in his grouchy Andy Rooney voice. 'Their decision to terminate their lives when they could no longer live with unending and unmitigated pain has reignited the debate on the ethics of suicide. It also reminded us — unfortunately — of the coward who caused that unending, unmitigated pain, a monster named Brady Wilson Hartsfield.'

That's me, Brady thought happily. When they even give your middle name, you know you're an authentic boogeyman.

'If there is a life after this one,' Jack said (out-of-control Andy Rooney brows drawing together, jowls flapping), 'Brady Wilson Hartsfield will pay the full price for his crimes when he gets there. In the meantime, let us consider the silver lining in this dark cloud of woe, because there really is one.

'A year after his cowardly killing spree at City Center, Brady Wilson Hartsfield attempted an even more heinous crime. He smuggled a large quantity of plastic explosive into a concert at Mingo Auditorium, with the intent to murder thousands of teens who were there to have a good time. In this he was thwarted by retired detective William Hodges and a brave woman named Holly Gibney, who smashed the homicidal loser's skull before he could detonate . . . '

Here Brady lost the thread. Some woman named Holly Gibney had been the one to smash him in the head and almost kill him? Who the fuck was Holly Gibney? And why had no one ever told him this in the five years since she'd turned his lights out and landed him in this room? How was that possible?

Very easily, he decided. When the coverage was fresh, he'd been in a coma. Later on, he thought, I just assumed it was either Hodges or his nigger lawnboy.

He would look Gibney up on the Web when he got a chance, but she wasn't the important thing. She was part of the past. The future was a splendid idea that had come to him as his best inventions always had: whole and complete, needing only a few modifications along the way to make it perfect.

He powered up his Zappit, found Z-Boy (currently handing out magazines to patients waiting in OB/GYN), and sent him to the library computer. Once he was seated in front of the screen, Brady shoved him out of the driver's seat and took control, hunched over and squinting at the monitor with Al Brooks's nearsighted eyes. On a website called Bankruptcy Assets 2015, he found the list of all the stuff Sunrise Solutions had left behind. There was junk from a dozen different companies, listed alphabetically. Zappit was the last, but as far as Brady was concerned, far from least. Heading the list of their assets was 45,872 (Zappit Commanders, suggested retail price $189.99. They were being sold in lots of four hundred, eight hundred, and one thousand. Below, in red, was the caveat that part of the shipment was defective, 'but most are in perfect working condition.'

Brady's excitement had Library Al's old heart laboring. His hands left the keyboard and curled into fists. Getting more of the City Center survivors to commit suicide paled in comparison to the grand idea that now possessed him: finishing what he had tried to do that night at the Mingo. He could see himself writing to Hodges from beneath the Blue Umbrella: *You think you stopped me? Think again.*

How wonderful that would be!

He was pretty sure Babineau had more than enough money to buy a Zappit console for everyone who had been there that night, but since Brady would have to handle his targets one at a time, it wouldn't do to go overboard.

He had Z-Boy bring Babineau to him. Babineau didn't want to come. He was afraid of Brady now, which Brady found delicious.

'You're going to be buying some goods,' Brady said.

'Buying some goods.' Docile. No longer afraid. Babineau had entered Room 217, but it was now Dr Z standing slump-shouldered in front of Brady's chair.

'Yes. You'll want to put money in a new account. I think we'll call it Gamez Unlimited. That's Gamez with a Z.'

'With a Z. Like me.' The head of the Kiner Neurology Department managed a small, vacuous smile.

'Very good. Let's say a hundred and fifty thousand dollars. You'll also be setting Freddi Linklatter up in a new and bigger apartment. So she can receive the goods you buy, and then work on them. She's going to be a busy girl.'

'I'll be setting her up in a new and bigger apartment so — '

'Just shut up and listen. She'll be needing some more equipment, too.'

Brady leaned forward. He could see a bright future ahead, one where Brady Wilson Hartsfield was crowned the winner years after the Det-Ret thought the game had ended.

'The most important piece of equipment is called a repeater.'

HEADS AND SKINS

1

It's not pain that wakes Freddi, but her bladder. It feels like it's bursting. Getting out of bed is a major operation. Her head is banging, and it feels like she's wearing a plaster cast on her chest. It doesn't hurt too much, mostly it's just stiff and so heavy. Each breath is a clean-and-jerk.

The bathroom looks like something out of a slasher movie, and she closes her eyes as soon as she sits on the john so she won't have to look at all the blood. So lucky to be alive, she thinks as something that feels like ten gallons of pee rushes out of her. Just so goddam lucky. And why am I in the center of this clusterfuck? Because I took him that picture. My mother was right, no good deed goes unpunished.

But if there was ever a time for clear thinking it's now, and she has to admit to herself that taking Brady the picture wasn't what has led her to this place, sitting in her bloody bathroom with a knot on her head and a gunshot wound in her chest. It was going *back* that had done that, and she'd gone back because she was being paid to do so — fifty dollars a visit. Which made her sort of a call girl, she supposed.

You know what all this is about. You could tell yourself you only knew when you peeked at the thumb drive Dr Z brought you, the one that activates the creepy website, but you knew when you were installing updates on all those Zappits, didn't you? A regular assembly line of them, forty or fifty a day, until all the ones that weren't defective were loaded landmines. Over five hundred. You knew it was Brady all along, and Brady Hartsfield is crazy.

She yanks up her pants, flushes, and leaves the bathroom. The light coming in the living room window is muted, but it still hurts her eyes. She squints, sees it's starting to snow, and shuffles to the kitchen, working for every breath. Her fridge is mostly stocked with cartons of leftover Chinese, but there's a couple of cans of Red Bull in the door shelf. She grabs one, chugs half, and feels a bit better. It's probably a psychological effect, but she'll take it.

What am I going to do? What in the name of God? Is there any way out of this mess?

She goes into her computer room, shuffling a little faster now, and refreshes her screen. She googles her way to zeetheend, hoping she'll get the cartoon man swinging his cartoon pickaxe, and her heart sinks when the picture filling the screen shows a candlelit funeral parlor, instead — exactly what she saw when she booted up the thumb drive and looked at the starter screen, instead of just importing the whole thing blind, as instructed. That dopey Blue Oyster Cult song is playing.

She scrolls past the messages below the coffin, each one swelling and fading like slow heartbeats (AN END TO PAIN, AN END TO FEAR) and clicks on POST A COMMENT. Freddi doesn't know how long this electronic poison pill has been active, but long enough for it to have generated hundreds of comments already.

Bedarkened77: This dares to speak the truth!

AliceAlways401: I wish I had the guts, things are so bad at home now.

Verbana The Monkey: Bear the pain, people, suicide is gutless!!!

KittycatGreeneyes: No, suicide is PAINLESS, it brings on many changes.

Verbana the Monkey isn't the only naysayer, but Freddi doesn't have to scroll through all the comments to see that he (or she) is very much in the minority. This is going to spread like the flu, Freddi thinks.

No, more like ebola.

She looks up at the repeater just in time to see 171 FOUND tick up to 172. Word about the number-fish is spreading fast, and by tonight almost all of the rigged Zappits will be active. The demo screen hypnotizes them, makes them receptive. To what? Well, to the idea that they should visit zeetheend, for one thing. Or maybe the Zappit People won't even have to go there. Maybe they'll just highside it. Will people obey a hypnotic command to off themselves? Surely not, right?

Right?

Freddi doesn't dare risk killing the repeater for fear of a return visit from Brady, but the website?

You're going down, motherfucker,' she says,

381

and begins to rattle away at her keyboard.

Less than thirty seconds later, she's staring with disbelief at a message on her screen: THIS FUNCTION IS NOT ALLOWED. She reaches out to try again, then stops. For all she knows, another go at the website may nuke all her stuff — not just her computer equipment, but her credit cards, her bank account, her cell phone, even her fucking driver's license. If anyone knows how to program such evil shit, it's Brady.

Fuck. I have to get out of here.

She'll throw some clothes in a suitcase, call a cab, go to the bank, and draw out everything she's got. There might be as much as four thousand dollars. (In her heart, she knows it's more like three.) From the bank to the bus station. The snow swirling outside her window is supposed to be the beginning of a big storm, and that may preclude a quick getaway, but if she has to wait a few hours at the station, she will. Hell, if she has to *sleep* there, she will. This is all Brady. He's set up an elaborate Jonestown protocol of which the rigged Zappits are only a part, and she helped him do it. Freddi has no idea if it will work, and she doesn't intend to wait around to find out. She's sorry for the people who might be sucked in by the Zappits, or tipped into attempting suicide by that fucking zeetheend website instead of just thinking about it, but she has to take care of *numero uno*. There's no one else to do it.

Freddi makes her way back to the bedroom as rapidly as she can. She gets her old Samsonite from the closet, and then oxygen depletion

382

caused by shallow breathing and too much excitement turns her legs to rubber. She makes it to the bed, sits on it, and lowers her head.

Easy does it, she thinks. Get your breath back. One thing at a time.

Only, thanks to her foolish effort to crash the website, she doesn't know how much time she has, and when 'Boogie Woogie Bugle Boy' begins to play from the top of her dresser, she utters a little scream. Freddi doesn't want to answer her phone, but gets up, anyway. Sometimes it's better to know.

2

The snow remains light until Brady gets off the interstate at Exit 7, but on State Road 79 — he's out in the boondocks now — it starts to come down a little harder. The tar is still bare and wet, but the snow will start to accumulate on it soon enough, and he's still forty miles from where he intends to hole up and get busy.

Lake Charles, he thinks. Where the real fun begins.

That's when Babineau's laptop awakens and chimes three times — an alert Brady programmed into it. Because safe is always better than sorry. He has no time to pull over, not when he's racing this goddam storm, but he can't afford not to. Ahead on the right is a boarded-up building with two metal girls in rusting bikinis on the roof, holding up a sign reading PORNO PALACE and XXX and WE DARE TO BARE.

In the middle of the dirt parking lot — which the snow is now starting to sugarcoat — there's a For Sale sign.

Brady pulls in, shifts to park, and opens the laptop. The message on the screen puts a significant crack right down the middle of his good mood.

11:04 AM: UNAUTHORIZED ATTEMPT
TO MODIFY/CANCEL
ZEETHEEND.COM
DENIED
SITE ACTIVE

He opens the Malibu's glove compartment and there is Al Brooks's battered cell phone, right where he always kept it. A good thing, too, because Brady forgot to bring Babineau's.

So sue me, he thinks. You can't remember everything, and I've been busy.

He doesn't bother going to Contacts, just dials Freddi's number from memory. She hasn't changed it since the old Discount Electronix days.

3

When Hodges excuses himself to use the bathroom, Jerome waits until he's out the door, then goes to Holly, who's standing at the window and watching the snow fall. It's still light here in the city, the flakes dancing in the air and seeming to defy gravity. Holly once more has her arms crossed over her chest so she can grip her shoulders.

'How bad is he?' Jerome asks in a low voice. 'Because he doesn't look good.'

'It's pancreatic cancer, Jerome. How good does anyone look with that?'

'Can he get through the day, do you think? Because he wants to, and I really think he could use some closure on this.'

'Closure on Hartsfield, you mean. Brady fracking Hartsfield. Even though he's fracking *dead*.'

'Yes, that's what I mean.'

'I think it's bad.' She turns to him and forces herself to meet his eyes, a thing that always makes her feel stripped bare. 'Do you see the way he keeps putting his hand against his side?'

Jerome nods.

'He's been doing that for weeks now and calling it indigestion. He only went to the doctor because I nagged him into it. And when he found out what was wrong, he tried to lie.'

'You didn't answer the question. Can he get through the day?'

'I think so. I hope so. Because you're right, he needs this. Only we have to stick with him. Both of us.' She releases one shoulder so she can grip his wrist. 'Promise me, Jerome. No sending the skinny girl home so the boys can play in the treehouse by themselves.'

He pries her hand loose and gives it a squeeze. 'Don't worry, Hollyberry. No one's breaking up the band.'

'Hello? Is that you, Dr Z?'

Brady has no time to play games with her. The snow is thickening every second, and Z-Boy's crappy old Malibu, with no snow tires and over a hundred thousand miles on the clock, will be no match for the storm once it really gets whooping. Under other circumstances, he'd want to know how she's even alive, but since he has no intention of turning back and rectifying that situation, it's a moot question.

'You know who it is, and I know what you tried to do. Try it again and I'll send in the men who are watching the building. You're lucky to be alive, Freddi. I wouldn't tempt fate a second time.'

'I'm sorry.' Almost whispering. This is not the fuck-you-and-fuck-your-mother riot grrrl Brady worked with on the Cyber Patrol. Yet she's not entirely broken, or she wouldn't have tried messing with the computer gear.

'Have you told anyone?'

'No!' She sounds horrified at the thought. Horrified is good.

'Will you?'

'*No!*'

'That's the right answer, because if you do, I'll know. You're under surveillance, Freddi. Remember it.'

He ends the call without waiting for a reply, more furious with her for being alive than for what she tried to do. Will she believe that fictitious men are watching the building, even though he left her for dead? He thinks so. She's had dealings with both Dr Z and Z-Boy; who knows how many other drones he might have at his command?

In any case, there's nothing else he can do about it now. Brady has a long, long history of blaming others for his problems, and now he blames Freddi for not dying when she was supposed to.

He drops the Malibu's gearshift into drive and steps on the gas. The tires spin in the thin carpet of snow covering the defunct Porno Palace's parking lot, but catch once they get on the state road again, where the formerly brown soft shoulders are now turning white. Brady eases Z-Boy's car up to sixty. That will soon be too fast for conditions, but he'll hold the needle there as long as he can.

5

Finders Keepers shares the seventh-floor bathrooms with the travel agency, but right now Hodges has the men's to himself, for which he is grateful. He's bent over one of the sinks, right hand gripping the washbasin's rim, left pressed to his side. His belt is still unbuckled, and his pants are sinking past his hips under the weight of the stuff in his pockets: change, keys, wallet, phone.

He came in here to take a shit, an ordinary excretory function he's been performing all his life, but when he started to strain, the left half of his midsection went nuclear. It makes his previous pain seem like a bunch of warm-up notes before the full concert begins, and if it's this bad now, he dreads to think what may lie ahead.

No, he thinks, dread is the wrong word. Terror is the right one. For the first time in my life, I'm terrified of the future, where I see everything that I am or ever was first submerged, then erased. If the pain itself doesn't do it, the heavier drugs they give me to stifle it will.

Now he understands why pancreatic is called the stealth cancer, and why it's almost always deadly. It lurks, building up its troops and sending out secret emissaries to the lungs, the lymph nodes, the bones and the brain. Then it blitzkriegs, not understanding, in its stupid rapacity, that victory can only bring its own death.

Hodges thinks, Except maybe that's what it wants. Maybe it's self-hating, born with a desire not to murder the host but to kill itself. Which makes cancer the *real* suicide prince.

He brings up a long, resounding burp, and that makes him feel a little better, who knows why. It won't last long, but he'll take any measure of relief he can get. He shakes out three of his pain-killers (already they make him think of shooting a popgun at a charging elephant) and swallows them with water from the tap. Then he splashes more cold water on his face, trying to bring up a little color. When that doesn't work, he slaps himself briskly — two hard ones on each cheek. Holly and Jerome must not know how bad it's gotten. He was promised this day and he means to take every minute of it. All the way to midnight, if necessary.

He's leaving the bathroom, reminding himself to straighten up and stop pressing his side, when his phone buzzes. Pete wanting to resume his bitch-a-thon, he thinks, but it's not. It's Norma Wilmer.

'I found that file,' she says. 'The one the late great Ruth Scapelli — '

'Yeah,' he says. 'The visitors list. Who's on it?'

'There *is* no list.'

He leans against the wall and closes his eyes. 'Ah, sh — '

'But there is a single memo with Babineau's letterhead on it. It says, and I quote, 'Frederica Linklatter to be admitted both during and after visiting hours. She is aiding in B. Hartsfield's recovery.' Does that help?'

Some girl with a Marine haircut, Hodges thinks. A ratty chick with a bunch of tats.

It rang no bells at the time, but there *was* that faint vibration, and now he knows why. He met a skinny girl with buzz-cut hair at Discount Electronix back in 2010, when he, Jerome, and Holly were closing in on Brady. Even six years later he can remember what she said about her co-worker on the Cyber Patrol: *It's something with his mom, betcha anything. He's freaky about her.*

'Are you still there?' Norma sounds irritated.

'Yeah, but I have to go.'

'Didn't you say there'd be some extra money if — '

389

'Yeah. I'll take care of you, Norma.' He ends the call.

The pills are doing their work, and he's able to manage a medium-fast walk back to the office. Holly and Jerome are at the window overlooking Lower Marlborough Street, and he can tell by their expressions when they turn to the sound of the opening door that they've been talking about him, but he has no time to think about that. Or brood on it. What he's thinking about are those rigged Zappits. The question ever since they started to put things together was how Brady could have had anything to do with modifying them when he was stuck in a hospital room and barely able to walk. But he knew somebody who almost certainly had the skills to do it for him, didn't he? Someone he used to work with. Somebody who came to visit him in the Bucket, with Babineau's written approval. A punky chick with a lot of tats and a yard of attitude.

'Brady's visitor — his *only* visitor — was a woman named Frederica Linklatter. She — '

'Cyber Patrol!' Holly nearly screams. 'He worked with her!'

'Right. There was also a third guy — the boss, I think. Do either of you remember his name?'

Holly and Jerome look at each other, then shake their heads.

'That was a long time ago, Bill,' Jerome says. 'And we were concentrating on Hartsfield by then.'

'Yeah. I only remember Linklatter because she was sort of unforgettable.'

'Can I use your computer?' Jerome asks.

'Maybe I can find the guy while Holly looks for the girl's addy.'

'Sure, go for it.'

Holly is at hers already, sitting bolt upright and clicking away. She's also talking out loud as she often does when she's deeply involved in something. 'Frack. Whitepages doesn't have a number or address. Long shot, anyway, a lot of single women don't . . . wait, hold the fracking phone . . . here's her Facebook page . . .'

'I'm not really interested in her summer vacation snaps or how many friends she's got,' Hodges says.

'Are you sure about that? Because she's only got six friends, andone of them is Anthony Frobisher. I'm pretty sure that was the name of the — '

'*Frobisher!*' Jerome yells from Hodges's office. '*Anthony Frobisher was the third Cyber Patrol guy!*'

'Beat you, Jerome,' Holly says. She looks smug. 'Again.'

6

Unlike Frederica Linklatter, Anthony Frobisher is listed, both as himself and as Your Computer Guru. Both numbers are the same — his cell, Hodges assumes. He evicts Jerome from his office chair and settles there himself, doing it slowly and carefully. The explosion of pain he felt while sitting on the toilet is still fresh in his mind.

The phone is answered on the first ring.

'Computer Guru, Tony Frobisher speaking. How can I help you?'

'Mr Frobisher, this is Bill Hodges. You probably don't remember me, but — '

'Oh, I remember you, all right.' Frobisher sounds wary. 'What do you want? If it's about Hartsfield — '

'It's about Frederica Linklatter. Do you have a current address for her?'

'Freddi? Why would I have *any* address for her? I haven't seen her since DE closed.'

'Really? According to her Facebook page, you and she are friends.'

Frobisher laughs incredulously. 'Who else has she got listed? Kim Jong-un? Charles Manson? Listen, Mr Hodges, that smartmouth bitch *has* no friends. The closest thing to one was Hartsfield, and I just got a news push on my phone saying he's dead.'

Hodges has no idea what a news push is, and no desire to learn. He thanks Frobisher and hangs up. He's guessing that none of Freddi Linklatter's half dozen Facebook friends are real friends, that she just added them to keep from feeling like a total outcast. Holly might have done that same thing, once upon a time, but now she actually *has* friends. Lucky for her, and lucky for them. Which begs the question: how does he locate Freddi Linklatter?

The outfit he and Holly runs isn't called Finders Keepers for nothing, but most of their specialized search engines are constructed to locate bad people with bad friends, long police records, and colorful want sheets. He *can* find her, in this computerized age few people are able to drop entirely off the grid, but he needs it to happen fast. Every time some kid turns on one of those free Zappits, it's loading up pink fish, blue flashes, and — based on Jerome's experience — a subliminal message suggesting that a visit to zee-theend would be in order.

You're a detective. One with cancer, granted, but still a detective. So let go of the extraneous shit and detect.

It's hard, though. The thought of all those kids — the ones Brady tried and failed to kill at the 'Round Here concert — keeps getting in the way. Jerome's sister was one of them, and if not for Dereece Neville, Barbara might be dead now instead of just in a leg cast. Maybe hers was a test model. Maybe the Ellerton woman's was, too. That makes a degree of sense. But now there are all those other Zappits, a flood of them, and they must have gone *somewhere*, goddammit.

That finally turns on a lightbulb.

'Holly! I need a phone number!'

7

Todd Schneider is in, and affable. 'I understand you folks are in for quite a storm, Mr Hodges.'

'So they say.'

'Having any luck tracking down those defective consoles?'

'That's actually why I'm calling. Do you happen to have the address that consignment of Zappit Commanders was sent to?'

'Of course. Can I call you back with it?'

'How about if I hang on? It's rather urgent.'

'An urgent consumer advocacy issue?' Schneider sounds bemused. 'That sounds almost un-American. Let me see what I can do.'

A click and Hodges is on hold, complete with soothing strings that fail to soothe. Holly and Jerome are both in the office now, crowding the desk. Hodges makes an effort not to put his hand to his side. The seconds stretch out and form a minute. Then two. Hodges thinks, Either he's on another call and forgotten me, or he can't find it.

The hold music disappears. 'Mr Hodges? Still there?'

'Still here.'

'I have that address. It's Gamez Unlimited — Gamez with a Z, if you remember — at 442 Maritime Drive. Care of Ms Frederica Linklatter. Does that help?'

'It sure does. Thank you, Mr Schneider.' He hangs up and looks at his two associates, one slender and winter-pale, the other bulked up from his house-building stint in Arizona. Along with his daughter Allie, now living on the other side of the country, they are the people he loves most at this end of his life.

He says, 'Let's take a ride, kids.'

8

Brady turns off SR-79 and onto Vale Road at Thurston's Garage, where a number of local plow-for-pay boys are gassing their trucks, loading up with salted sand, or just standing around, drinking coffee and jabbering. It crosses Brady's mind to pull in and see if he can get some studded snow tires on Library Al's Malibu, but given the crowd the storm has brought to the garage, it would probably take all afternoon. He's close to his destination now, and decides to go for it. If he gets snowed in once he's there, who gives a shit? Not him. He's been out to the camp twice already, mostly to scope the place out, but the second time he also laid in some supplies.

There's a good three inches of snow on Vale Road, and the going is greasy. The Malibu slides several times, once almost all the way to the ditch. He's sweating heavily, and Babineau's arthritic fingers are throbbing from Brady's deathgrip on the steering wheel.

At last he sees the tall red posts that are his final landmark. Brady pumps the brakes and makes the turn at walking pace. The last two miles are on an unnamed, one-lane camp road, but thanks to the overarching trees, the driving here is the easiest he's had in the last hour. In some places the road is still bare. That won't last once the main body of the storm arrives, which will happen around eight o'clock tonight, according to the radio.

He comes to a fork where wooden arrows nailed to a huge old-growth fir point in different directions. The one on the right reads BIG BOB'S BEAR CAMP. The one on the left reads HEADS AND SKINS. Ten feet or so above the arrows, already wearing a thin hood of snow, a security camera peers down.

Brady turns left and finally allows his hands to relax. He's almost there.

9

In the city, the snow is still light. The streets are clear and traffic is moving well, but the three of them pile into Jerome's Jeep Wrangler just to be on the safe side. 442 Maritime Drive turns out to be one of the condos that sprang up like mushrooms on the south side of the lake in the go-go eighties. Back then they were a big deal. Now most are half empty. In the foyer, Jerome finds F. LINKLATTER in 6-A. He reaches for the buzzer, but Hodges stops him before he can push it.

'What?' Jerome asks.

Holly says primly, 'Watch and learn, Jerome. This is how we roll.'

Hodges pushes other buttons at random, and gets a male voice in return on the fourth try. 'Yeah?'

'FedEx,' Hodges says.

'Who'd send me something by FedEx?' The voice sounds mystified.

'Couldn't tell you, buddy. I don't make the news, I just report it.'

The door to the lobby gives out an ill-tempered rattle. Hodges pushes through and holds it for the others. There are two elevators, one with an out-of-order sign taped to it. On the one that works someone has posted a note that reads, **Whoever has the barking dog on 4, I will find you.**

'I find that rather ominous,' Jerome says.

The elevator door opens and as they get in, Holly begins to rummage in her purse. She finds her box of Nicorette and pops one. When the elevator opens on the sixth floor, Hodges says, 'If she's there, let me do the talking.'

6-A is directly across from the elevator. Hodges knocks. When there's no answer, he raps. When there's still no answer, he hammers with the side of his fist.

'Go away.' The voice on the other side of the door sounds weak and thin. The voice of a little girl with the flu, Hodges thinks.

He hammers again. 'Open up, Ms Linklatter.'

'Are you the police?'

He could say yes, it wouldn't be the first time since retiring from the force that he impersonated a police officer, but instinct tells him not to do it this time.

'No. My name is Bill Hodges. We met before, briefly, back in 2010. It was when you worked at — '

'Yeah, I remember.'

One lock turns, then another. A chain falls. The door opens, and the tangy smell of pot wafts into the corridor. The woman in the doorway has got a half-smoked fatty tweezed between the thumb and forefinger of her left hand. She's thin almost to the point of emaciation, and pale as milk. She's wearing a strappy tee-shirt with BAD BOY BAIL BONDS, BRADENTON FLA on the front. Below this is the motto IN JAIL? WE BAIL!, but that part is hard to read because of the bloodstain.

'I should have called you,' Freddi says, and although she's looking at Hodges, he has an idea it's really herself she's speaking to. 'I would have, if I'd thought of it. You stopped him before, right?'

'Jesus, lady, what happened?' Jerome asks.

'I probably packed too much.' Freddi gestures at a pair of mismatched suitcases standing behind her in the living room. 'I should have listened to my mother. She said to always travel light.'

'I don't think he's talking about the suitcases,' Hodges says, cocking a thumb at the fresh blood on Freddi's shirt. He steps in, Jerome and Holly right behind him. Holly closes the door.

'I know what he's talking about,' Freddi says. 'Fucker shot me. Bleeding started again when I hauled the suitcases out of the bedroom.'

'Let me see,' Hodges says, but when he steps toward her, Freddi takes a compensatory step back and crosses her arms in front of her, a Holly-esque gesture that touches Hodges's heart.

'No. I'm not wearing a bra. Hurts too much.'

Holly pushes past Hodges. 'Show me where the bathroom is. Let me look.' She sounds okay to Hodges — calm — but she's chewing the shit out of that nicotine gum.

Freddi takes Holly by the wrist and leads her past the suitcases, pausing a moment to hit the joint. She lets the smoke out in a series of smoke signals as she talks. 'The equipment is in the spare room. On your right. Get a good look.'

And then, returning to her original scripture: 'If I hadn't packed so much, I'd be gone now.'

Hodges doubts it. He thinks she would have passed out in the elevator.

10

Heads and Skins isn't as big as the Babineau McMansion in Sugar Heights, but damned near. It's long, low, and rambling. Beyond it, the snow-covered ground slopes down to Lake Charles, which has frozen over since Brady's last visit.

He parks in front and walks carefully around to the west side, Babineau's expensive loafers sliding in the accumulating snow. The hunting camp is in a clearing, so there's a lot more snow to slip around in. His ankles are freezing. He wishes he'd thought to bring some boots, and once more reminds himself that you can't think of everything.

He takes the key to the generator shed from inside the electric meter box, and the keys to the house from inside the shed. The gennie is a top-of-the-line Generac Guardian. It's silent now, but will probably kick on later. Out here in the boonies, the electricity goes down in almost every storm.

Brady returns to the car for Babineau's laptop. The camp is WiFi equipped, and the laptop is all he needs to keep him connected to his current project, and abreast of developments. Plus the Zappit, of course.

Good old Zappit Zero.

The house is dark and chilly, and his first acts upon entering are the prosaic ones any returning homeowner might perform: he turns on the lights and boosts the thermostat. The main room is huge and pine-paneled, lit by a chandelier made of polished caribou bones, from back in the days when there were still caribou in these woods. The fieldstone fireplace is a maw, almost big enough to roast a rhino in. Overhead are thick, crisscrossing beams, darkened by years of woodsmoke from the fireplace. Next to one wall stands a cherrywood buffet as long as the room itself, lined with at least fifty liquor bottles, some nearly empty, some with the seals still intact. The furniture is old, mismatched, and plushy — deep easy chairs, and a gigantic sofa where innumerable bimbos have been banged over the years. Plenty of extra-marital fucking has gone on out here in addition to the hunting and fishing. The skin in front of the fireplace belonged to a bear brought down by Dr Elton Marchant, who has now gone to that great operating room in the sky. The mounted heads and stuffed fish are trophies belonging to nearly a dozen other docs, past and present. There's a particularly fine sixteen-point buck that Babineau himself brought down back when he was really Babineau. Out of season, but what the hell.

Brady puts the laptop on an antique rolltop desk at the far end of the room and fires it up before taking off his coat. First he checks in on the repeater, and is delighted to see it's now reading 243 FOUND.

He thought he understood the power of the

400

eye-trap, and has seen how addictive that demo screen is even *before* it's juiced up, but this is success beyond his wildest expectations. Far beyond. There haven't been any new warning chimes from zeetheend, but he goes there next anyway, just to see how it's doing. Once again his expectations are exceeded. Over seven thousand visitors so far, seven *thousand*, and the number ticks up steadily even as he watches.

He drops his coat and does a nimble little dance on the bearskin rug. It tires him out fast — when he makes his next switch, he'll be sure to choose someone in their twenties or thirties — but it warms him up nicely.

He snags the TV remote from the buffet and clicks on the enormous flatscreen, one of the camp's few nods to life in the twenty-first century. The satellite dish pulls in God knows how many channels and the HD picture is to die for, but Brady is more interested in local programming today. He punches the source button on the remote until he's looking back down the camp road leading to the outside world. He doesn't expect company, but he has two or three busy days ahead of him, the most important and productive days of his life, and if someone tries to interrupt him, he wants to know about it beforehand.

The gun closet is a walk-in job, the knotty-pine walls lined with rifles and hung with pistols on pegs. The pick of the litter, as far as Brady's concerned, is the FN SCAR 17S with the pistol grip. Capable of firing six hundred fifty rounds a minute and illegally converted to full auto by a proctologist who is also a gun nut, it is the Rolls-Royce of grease guns. Brady takes it out, along with a few extra clips and several heavy boxes of Winchester .308s, and props it against the wall beside the fireplace. He thinks about starting a fire — seasoned wood is already stacked in the hearth — but he has one other thing to do first. He goes to the site for city breaking news and scrolls down rapidly, looking for suicides. None yet, but he can remedy that.

'Call it a Zappitizer,' he says, grinning, and powers up the console. He makes himself comfortable in one of the easy chairs and begins following the pink fish. When he closes his eyes, they're still there. At first, anyway. Then they become red dots moving on a field of black.

Brady picks one at random and goes to work.

11

Hodges and Jerome are staring at a digital display reading 244

FOUND when Holly leads Freddi into her computer room.

'She's all right,' Holly says quietly to Hodges. 'She shouldn't be, but she is. She's got a hole in her chest that looks like — '

'Like what I said it is.' Freddi sounds a little stronger now. Her eyes are red, but that's probably from the dope she's been smoking. 'He shot me.'

'She had some mini-pads and I taped one over the wound,' Holly says. 'It was too big for a

Band-Aid.' She wrinkles her nose. 'Oough.'

'Fucker shot me.' It's as if Freddi's still trying to get it straight in her mind.

'Which fucker would that be?' Hodges asks. 'Felix Babineau?'

'Yeah, him. Fucking Dr Z. Only he's really Brady. So is the other one. Z-Boy.'

'Z-Boy?' Jerome asks. 'Who the hell is Z-Boy?'

'Older guy?' Hodges asks. 'Older than Babineau? Frizzy white hair? Drives a beater with primer paint on it? Maybe wears a parka with tape over some of the rips?'

'I don't know about his car, but I know the parka,' Freddi says. 'That's my boy Z-Boy.' She sits in front of her desktop Mac — currently spinning out a fractal screensaver — and takes a final drag on her joint before crushing it out in an ashtray full of Marlboro butts. She's still pale, but some of the fuck-you attitude Hodges remembers from their previous meeting is coming back. 'Dr Z and his faithful sidekick, Z-Boy. Except they're both Brady. Fucking matryoshka dolls is what they are.'

'Ms Linklatter?' Holly says.

'Oh, go ahead and call me Freddi. Any chick who sees the teacups I call tits gets to call me Freddi.'

Holly blushes, but goes ahead. When she's on the scent, she always does. 'Brady Hartsfield is dead. It was an overdose last night or early this morning.'

'Elvis has left the building?' Freddi considers the idea, then shakes her head. 'Wouldn't that be nice. If it was true.'

And wouldn't it be nice I could totally believe she's crazy, Hodges thinks.

Jerome points at the readout above her jumbo monitor. It's now flashing 247 FOUND. 'Is that thing searching or downloading?'

'Both.' Freddi's hand is pressing at the makeshift bandage under her shirt in an automatic gesture that reminds Hodges of himself. 'It's a repeater. I can turn it off — at least I think I can — but you have to promise to protect me from the men who are watching the building. The website, though . . . no good. I've got the IP address and the password, but I still couldn't crash the server.'

Hodges has a thousand questions, but as 247 FOUND clicks up to 248, only two seem of paramount importance. 'What's it searching for? And what's it downloading?'

'You have to promise me protection first. You have to take me somewhere safe. Witness Protection, or whatever.'

'He doesn't have to promise you anything, because I already know,' Holly says. There's nothing mean in her tone; if anything, it's comforting. 'It's searching for Zappits, Bill. Each time somebody turns one on, the repeater finds it and upgrades the Fishin' Hole demo screen.'

'Turns the pink fish into number-fish and adds the blue flashes,' Jerome amplifies. He looks at Freddi. 'That's what it's doing, right?'

Now it's the purple, blood-caked lump on her forehead that her hand goes to. When her fingers touch it, she winces and pulls back. 'Yeah. Of the eight hundred Zappits that were delivered here,

404

two hundred and eighty were defective. They either froze while they were booting up or went ka-bloosh the first time you tried to open one of the games. The others were okay. I had to install a root kit into each and every one of them. It was a lot of work. *Boring* work. Like attaching widgets to wadgets on an assembly line.'

'That means five hundred and twenty were okay,' Hodges says.

'The man can subtract, give him a cigar.' Freddi glances at the readout. 'And almost half of them have updated already.' She laughs, a sound with absolutely no humor in it. 'Brady may be nuts, but he worked this out pretty good, don't you think?'

Hodges says, 'Turn it off.'

'Sure. When you promise to protect me.'

Jerome, who has firsthand experience with how fast the Zappits work and what unpleasant ideas they implant in a person's mind, has no interest in standing by while Freddi tries to dicker with Bill. The Swiss Army Knife he carried on his belt while in Arizona has been retrieved from his luggage and is now back in his pocket. He unfolds the biggest blade, shoves the repeater off its shelf, and slices the cables mating it to Freddi's system. It falls to the floor with a moderate crash, and an alarm begins to bong from the CPU under the desk. Holly bends down, pushes something, and the alarm shuts up.

'There's a switch, moron!' Freddi shouts. 'You didn't have to do that!'

'You know what, I did,' Jerome says. 'One of

those fucking Zappits almost got my sister killed.' He steps toward her, and Freddi cringes back. 'Did you have any idea what you were doing? Any fucking idea at all? I think you must have. You look stoned but not stupid.'

Freddi begins to cry. 'I didn't. I swear I didn't. Because I didn't want to.'

Hodges takes a deep breath, which reawakens the pain. 'Start from the beginning, Freddi, and take us through it.'

'And as quickly as you can,' Holly adds.

12

Jamie Winters was nine when he attended the 'Round Here concert at the Mac with his mother. Only a few subteen boys were there that night; the group was one of those dismissed by most boys his age as girly stuff. Jamie, however, liked girly stuff. At nine he hadn't yet been sure that he was gay (wasn't even sure he knew what that meant). All he knew was that when he saw Cam Knowles, 'Round Here's lead singer, he felt funny in the pit of his stomach.

Now he's pushing sixteen and knows exactly what he is. With certain boys at school, he prefers to leave off the last letter of his first name because with those boys he likes to be Jami. His father knows what he is, as well, and treats him like some kind of freak. Lenny Winters — a man's man if ever there was one — owns a successful building company, but today all four of Winters Construction's current jobs are shut

406

down because of the impending storm. Lenny is in his home office instead, up to his ears in paperwork and stewing over the spreadsheets covering his computer screen.

'Dad!'

'What do you want?' Lenny growls without looking up. 'And why aren't you in school? Was it canceled?'

'*Dad!*'

This time Lenny looks around at the boy he sometimes refers to (when he thinks Jamie isn't in earshot) as 'the family queer.' The first thing he's aware of is that his son is wearing lipstick, rouge, and eye shadow. The second thing is the dress. Lenny recognizes it as one of his wife's. The kid is too tall for it, and it stops halfway down his thighs.

'*What* the *fuck!*'

Jamie is smiling. Jubilant. 'It's how I want to be buried!'

'What are you — ' Lenny gets up so fast his chair tumbles over. That's when he sees the gun the boy is holding. He must have taken it from Lenny's side of the closet in the master bedroom.

'Watch this, Dad!' Still smiling. As if about to demonstrate a really cool magic trick. He raises the gun and places the muzzle against his right temple. His finger is curled around the trigger. The nail has been carefully coated with sparkle polish.

'Put that down, Son! *Put it* — '

Jamie — or Jami, which is how he has signed his brief suicide note — pulls the trigger. The gun is a .357, and the report is deafening. Blood

407

and brains fly in a fan and decorate the doorframe with gaud. The boy in his mother's dress and makeup falls forward, the left side of his face pushed out like a balloon.

Lenny Winters gives voice to a series of high, wavering screams. He screams like a girl.

13

Brady disconnects from Jamie Winters just as the boy puts the gun to his head, afraid — terrified, actually — of what may happen if he's still in there when the bullet enters the head he's been messing with. Would he be spit out like a seed, as he was when he was inside the half-hypnotized dumbo mopping the floor in 217, or would he die along with the kid?

For a moment he thinks he's left it until too late, and the steady chiming he hears is what everyone hears when they exit this life. Then he's back in the main room of Heads and Skins with the Zappit console in his sagging hand and Babineau's laptop in front of him. That's where the chiming is coming from. He looks at the screen and sees two messages. The first reads 248 FOUND. That's the good news. The second is the bad news:

REPEATER NOW OFFLINE

Freddi, he thinks. I didn't believe you had the guts. I really didn't. You bitch.

His left hand gropes along the desk and closes

on a ceramic skull filled with pens and pencils. He brings it up, meaning to smash it into the screen and destroy that infuriating message. What stops him is an idea. A horribly *plausible* idea.

Maybe she *didn't* have the guts. Maybe somebody else killed the repeater. And who could that someone else be? Hodges, of course. The old Det-Ret. His fucking *nemesis*.

Brady knows he isn't exactly right in the head, has known that for years now, and understands this could be nothing but paranoia. Yet it makes a degree of sense. Hodges stopped his gloating visits to Room 217 almost a year and a half ago, but he was sniffing around the hospital just yesterday, according to Babineau.

And he always knew I was faking, Brady thinks. He said so, time and time again: *I know you're in there, Brady.* Some of the suits from the DA's office had said the same thing, but with them it had only been wishful thinking; they wanted to put him on trial and have done with him. Hodges, though . . .

'He said it with conviction,' Brady says.

And maybe this isn't such terrible news, after all. Half of the Zappits Freddi loaded up and Babineau sent out are now active, which means most of those people will be as open to invasion as the little fag he just dealt with. Plus, there's the website. Once the Zappit people start killing themselves — with a little help from Brady Wilson Hartsfield, granted — the website will push others over the edge: monkey see, monkey do. At first it will be just the ones who were closest to doing it anyway, but they will lead by example and there will be many more. They'll march off the edge of life like stampeding buffalo going over a cliff.

But still.

Hodges.

Brady remembers a poster he had in his room when he was a boy: *If life hands you lemons, make lemonade!* Words to live by, especially when you kept in mind that the only way to make them into lemonade was to squeeze the hell out of them.

He grabs Z-Boy's old but serviceable flip phone and once again dials Freddi's number from memory.

14

Freddi gives a small scream when 'Boogie Woogie Bugle Boy' starts tootling away from somewhere in the apartment. Holly puts a gentling hand on her shoulder and looks a question at Hodges. He nods and follows the sound, with Jerome on his heels. Her phone is on top of her dresser, amid a clutter of hand cream, Zig-Zag rolling papers, roach clips, and not one but two good-sized bags of pot.

The screen says Z-BOY, but Z-Boy, once known as Library Al Brooks, is currently in police custody and not likely to be making any calls.

'Hello?' Hodges says. 'Is that you, Dr Babineau?'

Nothing . . . or almost. Hodges can hear breathing.

'Or should I call you Dr Z?'

Nothing.

'How about Brady, will that work?' He still can't quite believe this in spite of everything Freddi has told them, but he *can* believe that Babineau has gone schizo, and actually thinks that's who he is. 'Is it you, asshole?'

The sound of the breathing continues for another two or three seconds, then it's gone. The connection has been broken.

15

'It's possible, you know,' Holly says. She has joined them in Freddi's cluttered bedroom. 'That it really could be Brady, I mean. Personality projection is well documented. In fact, it's the second-most-common cause of so-called demonic possession. The most common being schizophrenia. I saw a documentary about it on — '

'No,' Hodges says. 'Not possible. Not.'

'Don't blind yourself to the idea. Don't be like Miss Pretty Gray Eyes.'

'What's that supposed to mean?' Oh God, now the tendrils of pain are reaching all the way down to his balls.

'That you shouldn't turn away from the evidence just because it points in a direction you don't want to go. You know Brady was different when he regained consciousness. He came back with certain abilities most people don't have. Telekinesis may only have been one of them.'

'I never saw him actually moving shit around.'

411

'But you believe the nurses who did. Don't you?'

Hodges is silent, head lowered, thinking.

'Answer her,' Jerome says. His tone is mild, but Hodges can hear impatience underneath.

'Yeah. I believed at least some of them. The levelheaded ones like Becky Helmington. Their stories matched up too well to be fabrications.'

'Look at me, Bill.'

This request — no, this *command* — coming from Holly Gibney is so unusual that he raises his head.

'Do you really believe *Babineau* reconfigured the Zappits and set up that website?'

'I don't have to believe it. He got Freddi to do those things.'

'Not the website,' a tired voice says.

They look around. Freddi is standing in the doorway.

'If I'd set it up, I could shut it down. I just got a thumb drive with all the website goodies on it from Dr Z. Plugged it in and uploaded it. But once he was gone, I did a little investigating.'

'Started with a DNS lookup, right?' Holly says.

Freddi nods. 'Girl's got some skills.'

To Hodges, Holly says, 'DNS stands for Domain Name Server. It hops from one server to the next, like using stepping-stones to cross a creek, asking 'Do you know this site?' It keeps going and keeps asking until it finds the right server.' Then, to Freddi: 'But once you found the IP address, you still couldn't get in?'

'Nope.'

Holly says, 'I'm sure Babineau knows a lot about human brains, but I doubt very much if he has the computer smarts to lock up a website like that.'

'I was just hired help,' Freddi says. 'It was Z-Boy who brought me the program for retooling the Zappits, written down like a recipe for coffee cake, or something, and I'd bet you a thousand dollars that all he knows about computers is how to turn them on — assuming he can find the button in back — and navigate to his favorite porn sites.'

Hodges believes her about that much. He's not sure the police will when they finally catch hold of this thing, but Hodges does. And . . . *Don't be like Miss Pretty Gray Eyes.*

That stung. It stung like hell.

'Also,' Freddi says, 'there was a double dot after each step in the program directions. Brady used to do that. I think he learned it when he was taking computer classes in high school.'

Holly grabs Hodges's wrists. There's blood on one of her hands, from patching Freddi's wound. Along with her other bells and whistles, Holly is a clean-freak, and that she's neglected to wash the blood off says all that needs to be said about how fiercely she's working this.

'Babineau was giving Hartsfield experimental drugs, which was unethical, but that's *all* he was doing, because bringing Brady back was all he was interested in.'

'You don't know that for sure,' Hodges says.

She's still holding him, more with her eyes than her hands. Because she's ordinarily averse

413

to eye contact, it's easy to forget how burning that gaze can be when she turns it up to eleven and pulls the knobs off.

'There's really just one question,' Holly says. 'Who's the suicide prince in this story? Felix Babineau or Brady Hartsfield?'

Freddi speaks in a dreamy, sing-songy voice. 'Sometimes Dr Z was just Dr Z and sometimes Z-Boy was just Z-Boy, only then it was like both of them were on drugs. When they were wide awake, though, it *wasn't* them. When they were awake, it was Brady inside. Believe what you want, but it was him. It's not just the double dots or the backslanted printing, it's everything. I worked with that skeevy motherfucker. I know.'

She steps into the room.

'And now, if none of you amateur detectives object, I'm going to roll myself another joint.'

16

On Babineau's legs, Brady paces the big living room of Heads and Skins, thinking furiously. He wants to go back into the world of the Zappit, wants to pick a new target and repeat the delicious experience of pushing someone over the edge, but he has to be calm and serene to do that, and he's far from either.

Hodges.

Hodges in Freddi's apartment.

And will Freddi spill her guts? Friends and neighbors, does the sun rise in the east?

There are two questions, as Brady sees it. The

414

first is whether or not Hodges can take down the website. The second is whether or not Hodges can find him out here in the williwags.

Brady thinks the answer to both questions is yes, but the more suicides he causes in the meantime, the more Hodges will suffer. When he looks at it in that light, he thinks that Hodges finding his way out here could be a good thing. It could be making lemonade from lemons. In any case, he has time. He's many miles north of the city, and he's got winter storm Eugenie on his side.

Brady goes back to the laptop and confirms that zeetheend is still up and running. He checks the visitors' count. Over nine thousand now, and most of them (but by no means all) will be teenagers interested in suicide. That interest peaks in January and February, when dark comes early and it seems spring will never arrive. Plus, he's got Zappit Zero, and with that he can work on plenty of kids personally. With Zappit Zero, getting to them is as easy as shooting fish in a barrel.

Pink fish, he thinks, and snickers.

Calmer now that he sees a way of dealing with the old Det-Ret should he try showing up like the cavalry in the last reel of a John Wayne western, Brady picks up the Zappit and turns it on. As he studies the fish, a fragment of some poem read in high school occurs to him, and he speaks it aloud.

'Oh do not ask what is it, let us go and make our visit.'

He closes his eyes. The zipping pink fish become zipping red dots, each one a bygone concertgoer who is at this very moment studying his or her gift Zappit and hoping to win prizes.

Brady picks one, brings it to a halt, and watches it bloom. Like a rose.

17

'Sure, there's a police computer forensics squad,' Hodges says, in answer to Holly's question. 'If you want to call three part-time crunchers a squad, that is. And no, they won't listen to me. I'm just a civilian these days.' Nor is that the worst of it. He's a civilian who used to be a cop, and when retired cops try meddling in police business, they are called uncles. It is not a term of respect.

'Then call Pete and have him do it,' Holly says. 'Because that fracking suicide site has to come down.'

The two of them are back in Freddi Linklatter's version of Mission Control. Jerome is in the living room with Freddi. Hodges doesn't think she's apt to flee — Freddi's terrified of the probably fictional men posted outside her building — but stoner behavior is difficult to predict. Other than how they usually want to get more stoned, that is.

'Call Pete and tell him to have one of the computer geeks call me. Any cruncher with half a brain will be able to doss the site and knock it down that way.'

'Doss it?'

'Big D, little o, big S. Stands for Denial of

416

Services. The guy needs to connect to a BOT network and . . . ' She sees Hodges's mystified expression. 'Never mind. The idea is to flood the suicide site with requests for services — thousands, millions. Choke the fracking thing and crash the server.'

'You can do that?'

'I can't, and Freddi can't, but a police department geek freak will be able to tap enough computing power. If he can't do it from the police computers, he'll get Homeland Security to do it. Because this *is* a security issue, right? Lives are at stake.'

They are, and Hodges makes the call, but Pete's cell goes directly to voicemail. Next he tries his old pal Cassie Sheen, but the desk officer who takes his call tells him Cassie's mother had some sort of diabetic crisis and Cassie took her to the doctor.

Out of other options, he calls Isabelle.

'Izzy, it's Bill Hodges. I tried to get Pete, but — '

'Pete's gone. Done. Kaput.'

For one awful moment Hodges thinks she means he's dead.

'Left a memo on my desk. It said he was going to go home, turn off his cell, pull the plug on the landline, and sleep for the next twenty-four hours. He further shared that today was his last day as working police. He can do it, too, doesn't even have to touch his vacation time, of which he has piles. He's got enough personal days to see him through to retirement. And I think you better scratch that retirement party off your

417

calendar. You and your weirdo partner can hit a movie that night, instead.'

'You're blaming me?'

'You and your Brady Hartsfield fixation. You infected Pete with it.'

'No. He wanted to chase the case. You were the one who wanted to hand it off, then duck down in the nearest foxhole. Gotta say I'm kind of on Pete's side when it comes to that one.'

'See? See? That's exactly the attitude I'm talking about. Wake up, Hodges, this is the real world. I'm telling you for the last time to quit sticking your long beak into what isn't your busi — '

'And I'm telling *you* that if you want to have any fucking chance of promotion, you need to get your head out of your ass and listen to me.'

The words are out before he can think better of them. He's afraid she'll hang up, and if she does, where will he go then? But there's only shocked silence.

'Suicides. Have any been reported since you got back from Sugar Heights?'

'I don't kn — '

'Well, look! Right now!'

He can hear the faint tapping of Izzy's keyboard for five seconds or so. Then: 'One just came over the wire. Kid in Lakewood shot himself. Did it in front of his father, who called it in. Hysterical, as you might expect. What's that got to do with — '

'Tell the cops on the scene to look for a Zappit game console. Just like the one Holly found at the Ellerton house.'

'That again? You're like a broken rec — '

'They'll find one. And you may have more Zappit suicides before the day's over. Possibly a lot more.'

Website! Holly mouths. *Tell her about the website!*

'Also, there's a suicide website called zeetheend. Just went up today. It needs to come down.'

She sighs and speaks as though to a child. 'There are all *kinds* of suicide websites. We got a memo about it from Juvenile Services just last year. They pop up on the Net like mushrooms, usually created by kids who wear black tee-shirts and spend all their free time holed up in their bedrooms. There's a lot of bad poetry and stuff about how to do it painlessly. Along with the usual bitching about how their parents don't understand them, of course.'

'This one is different. It could start an avalanche. It's loaded with subliminal messages. Have someone from computer forensics call Holly Gibney ASAP.'

'That would be outside of protocol,' she says coolly. 'I'll have a look, then go through channels.'

'Have one of your rent-a-geeks call Holly in the next five minutes, or when the suicides start cascading — and I'm pretty sure they will — I'll make it clear to anyone who'll listen that I went to you and you tied me up in red tape. My listeners will include the daily paper and *8 Alive*. The department does not have a lot of friends in either place, especially since those two unis shot an unarmed black kid to death on MLK last summer.'

419

Silence. Then, in a softer voice — a hurt voice, maybe — she says, 'You're supposed to be on *our* side, Billy. Why are you acting this way?'

Because Holly was right about you, he thinks.

Out loud he says, 'Because there isn't much time.'

18

In the living room, Freddi is rolling another joint. She looks at Jerome over the top of it as she licks the paper closed. 'You're a big one, aren't you?'

Jerome makes no reply.

'What do you go? Two-ten? Two-twenty?'

Jerome has nothing to say to this, either.

Undeterred, she sparks the joint, inhales, and holds it out to him. Jerome shakes his head.

'Your loss, big boy. This is pretty good shit. Smells like dog pee, I know, but pretty good shit, just the same.'

Jerome says nothing.

'Cat got your tongue?'

'No. I was thinking about a sociology class I took when I was a high school senior. We did a four-week mod on suicide, and there was one statistic I never forgot. Every teen suicide that makes it onto social media spawns seven attempts, five that are show and two that are go. Maybe you should think about that instead of running the tough-girl act into the ground.'

Freddi's lower lip trembles. 'I didn't know. Not really.'

'Sure you did.'

She drops her eyes to the joint. It's her turn to say nothing.

'My sister heard a voice.'

At that, Freddi looks up. 'What kind of voice?'

'One from the Zappit. It told her all sorts of mean things. About how she was trying to live white. About how she was denying her race. About how she was a bad and worthless person.'

'And that reminds you of someone?'

'Yes.' Jerome is thinking of the accusatory shrieks he and Holly heard coming from Olivia Trelawney's computer long after that unfortunate lady was dead. Shrieks programmed by Brady Hartsfield, and designed to drive Trelawney toward suicide like a cow down a slaughterhouse chute. 'Actually, it does.'

'Brady was fascinated by suicide,' Freddi says. 'He was always reading about it on the Web. He meant to kill himself with the others at that concert, you know.'

Jerome does know. He was there. 'Do you really think he got in touch with my sister telepathically? Using the Zappit as . . . what? A kind of conduit?'

'If he could take over Babineau and the other guy — and he did, whether you believe it or not — then yeah, I think he could do that.'

'And the others with updated Zappits? Those two hundred and forty-something others?'

Freddi only looks at him through her veil of smoke.

'Even if we take down the website . . . what about them? What about when that voice starts

421

telling them they're dogshit on the world's shoe, and the only answer is to take a long walk off a short dock?'

Before she can reply, Hodges does it for her. 'We have to stop the voice. Which means stopping *him*. Come on, Jerome. We're going back to the office.'

'What about me?' Freddi asks plaintively.

'You're coming. And Freddi?'

'What?'

'Pot's good for pain, isn't it?'

'Opinions on that vary, as you might guess, the establishment in this fucked-up country being what it is, so all I can tell you is that for me, it makes that delicate time of the month a lot less delicate.'

'Bring it along,' Hodges says. 'Also the rolling papers.'

19

They go back to Finders Keepers in Jerome's Jeep. The back is full of Jerome's junk, meaning Freddi has to sit on someone's lap, and it's not going to be Hodges's. Not in his current condition. So he drives and Jerome gets Freddi.

'Hey, this is sort of like getting a date with John Shaft,' Freddi says with a smirk. 'The big private dick who's a sex machine to all the chicks.'

'Don't get used to it,' Jerome says.

Holly's cell rings. It's a guy named Trevor Jeppson, from the police department's Computer Forensics Squad. Holly is soon speaking in

422

a jargon Hodges doesn't understand — something about BOTS and the darknet. Whatever she's getting back from the guy seems to please her, because when she breaks the connection, she's smiling.

'He's never dossed a website before. He's like a kid on Christmas morning.'

'How long will it take?'

'With the password and the IP address already in hand? Not long.'

Hodges parks in one of the thirty-minute spaces in front of the Turner Building. They won't be here long — if he gets lucky, that is — and given his recent run of bad luck, he considers the universe owes him a good turn.

He goes into his office, closes the door, then hunts through his ratty old address book for Becky Helmington's number. Holly has offered to program the address book into his phone, but Hodges has kept putting it off. He *likes* his old address book. Probably never get around to making the changeover now, he thinks. Trent's Last Case, and all that.

Becky reminds him she doesn't work in the Bucket any longer. 'Maybe you forgot that?'

'I didn't forget. You know about Babineau?'

Her voice drops. 'God, yes. I heard that Al Brooks — Library Al — killed Babineau's wife and might have killed him. I can hardly believe it.'

I could tell you lots of stuff you'd hardly believe, Hodges thinks.

'Don't count Babineau out yet, Becky. I think he might be on the run. He was giving Brady

423

Hartsfield experimental drugs of some kind, and they may have played a part in Hartsfield's death.'

'Jesus, for real?'

'For real. But he can't be too far, not with this storm coming in. Can you think of anyplace he might have gone? Does Babineau own a summer cottage, anything like that?'

She doesn't even need to think about it. 'Not a cottage, a hunting camp. It isn't just him, though. Four or maybe five docs co-own the place.' Her voice drops to that confidential pitch again. 'I hear they do more than hunt out there. If you know what I mean.'

'Where is out there?'

'Lake Charles. The camp has some cutesy-horrible name. I can't remember it offhand, but I bet Violet Tranh would know. She spent a weekend there once. Said it was the drunkest forty-eight hours of her life, and she came back with chlamydia.'

'Will you call her?'

'Sure. But if he's on the run, he might be on a plane, you know. Maybe to California or even overseas. The flights were still taking off and landing this morning.'

'I don't think he would have dared to try the airport with the police looking for him. Thanks, Becky. Call me back.'

He goes to the safe and punches in the combination. The sock filled with ball bearings — his Happy Slapper — is back home, but both of his handguns are here. One is the Glock .40 he carried on the job. The other is a .38, the Victory

424

model. It was his father's. He takes a canvas sack from the top shelf of the safe, puts the guns and four boxes of ammunition into it, then gives the drawstring a hard yank.

No heart attack to stop me this time, Brady, he thinks. This time it's just cancer, and I can live with that.

The idea surprises him into laughter. It hurts.

From the other room comes the sound of three people applauding. Hodges is pretty sure he knows what it means, and he's not wrong. The message on Holly's computer reads ZEETHEEND IS EXPERIENCING TECHNICAL DIFFICULTIES. Below is this: CALL 1-800-273-TALK.

'It was that guy Jeppson's idea,' Holly says, not looking up from what she's doing. 'It's the National Suicide Prevention Hotline.'

'Good one,' Hodges says. 'And those are good, too. You're a woman with hidden talents.' In front of Holly is a line of joints. The one she adds makes an even dozen.

'She's fast,' Freddi says admiringly. 'And look how neat they are. Like they came out of a machine.'

Holly gives Hodges a defiant look. 'My therapist says an occasional marijuana cigarette is perfectly okay. As long as I don't go overboard, that is. The way some people do.' Her eyes glide to Freddi, then back to Hodges. 'Besides, these aren't for me. They're for you, Bill. If you need them.'

Hodges thanks her, and has a moment to reflect on how far the two of them have come, and how pleasant, by and large, the trip has been. But too short. Far too short. Then his phone rings. It's Becky.

'The name of the place is Heads and Skins. I told you it was cutesy-horrible. Vi doesn't remember how to get there — I'm guessing she had more than a few shots on the ride, just to get her motor running — but she does remember they went north on the turnpike for quite a ways, and stopped for gas at a place called Thurston's Garage after they got off. Does that help?'

'Yeah, a ton. Thanks, Becky.' He ends the call. 'Holly, I need you to find Thurston's Garage, north of the city. Then I want you to call Hertz at the airport and rent the biggest four-wheel drive they've got left. We're going on a road trip.'

'My Jeep — ' Jerome begins.

'Is small, light, and old,' Hodges says . . . although these are not the only reasons he wants a different vehicle built to go in the snow. 'It'll be fine to get us out to the airport, though.'

'What about me?' Freddi asks.

'WITSEC,' Hodges says, 'as promised. It'll be like a dream come true.'

20

Jane Ellsbury was a perfectly normal baby — at six pounds, nine ounces, a little underweight, in fact — but by the time she was seven, she weighed ninety pounds and was familiar with the chant that sometimes haunts her dreams to this day: *Fatty fatty, two by four, can't get through the bathroom door, so she does it on the floor.* In June of 2010, when her mother took her to the 'Round Here concert as a fifteenth birthday present, she weighed two hundred and ten. She could still get through the bathroom door with no problem, but it had become difficult for her to tie her shoes. Now she's twenty, her weight has risen to three hundred and twenty, and when the voice begins to speak to her from the free Zappit she got in the mail, everything it says makes perfect sense to her. The voice is low, calm, and reasonable. It tells her that nobody likes her and everybody laughs at her. It points out that she can't stop eating — even now, with tears running down her face, she's snarfing her way through a bag of chocolate pinwheel cookies, the kind with lots of gooey marshmallow inside. Like a more kindly version of the ghost of Christmas Yet to Come, who pointed out certain home truths to Ebenezer Scrooge, it sketches in a future which boils down to fat, fatter, fattest. The laughter along Carbine Street in Hillbilly. Heaven, where she and her parents live in a walk-up apartment. The looks of disgust. The jibes, like *Here comes the Goodyear Blimp* and *Look out, don't let her fall on you!* The voice explains, logically and reasonably, that she will never have a date, will never be hired for a good job now that political correctness has rendered the circus fat lady extinct, that by the age of forty she will have to sleep sitting up because her enormous breasts will make it impossible for her lungs to do their work, and before she dies of a heart attack at fifty, she'll be using a DustBuster

427

to get the crumbs out of the deepest creases in her rolls of fat. When she tries to suggest to the voice that she could lose some weight — go to one of those clinics, maybe — it doesn't laugh. It only asks her, softly and sympathetically, where the money will come from, when the combined incomes of her mother and father are barely enough to satisfy an appetite that is basically insatiable. When the voice suggests they'd be better off without her, she can only agree.

Jane — known to the denizens of Carbine Street as Fat Jane — lumbers into the bathroom and takes the bottle of OxyContin pills her father has for his bad back. She counts them. There are thirty, which should be more than enough. She takes them five at a time, with milk, eating a chocolate marshmallow cookie after each swallow. She begins to float away. I'm going on a diet, she thinks. I'm going on a long, long diet.

That's right, the voice from the Zappit tells her. And you'll never cheat on this one, Jane — will you?

She takes the last five Oxys. She tries to pick up the Zappit, but her fingers will no longer close on the slim console. And what does it matter? She could never catch the speedy pink fish in this condition, anyway. Better to look out the window, where the snow is burying the world in clean linen.

No more fatty-fatty-two-by-four, she thinks, and when she slips into unconsciousness, she goes with relief.

21

Before going to Hertz, Hodges swings Jerome's Jeep into the turn-around in front of the Airport Hilton.

'This is supposed to be Witness Protection?' Freddi asks. '*This?*'

Hodges says, 'Since I don't happen to have a safe house at my disposal, it will have to do. I'll register you under my name. You go in, you lock the door, you watch TV, you wait until this thing is over.'

'And change the dressing on that wound,' Holly says.

Freddi ignores her. She's focused on Hodges. 'How much trouble am I going to be in? When it's over?'

'I don't know, and I don't have time to discuss it with you now.'

'Can I at least order room service?' There's a faint gleam in Freddi's bloodshot eyes. 'I'm not in so much pain now, and I've got a wicked case of the munchies.'

'Knock yourself out,' Hodges says.

Jerome adds, 'Only check the peephole before you let in the waiter. Make sure it isn't one of Brady Hartsfield's Men in Black.'

'You're kidding,' Freddi says. 'Right?'

The hotel lobby is dead empty on this snowy afternoon. Hodges, who feels as if he woke up to Pete's telephone call approximately three years ago, walks to the desk, does his business there, and comes back to where the others are sitting. Holly is tapping away at something on her iPad, and doesn't look up. Freddi holds out her hand for the key folder, but Hodges gives it to Jerome, instead.

'Room 522. Take her up, will you? I want to talk to Holly.'

Jerome raises his eyebrows, and when Hodges doesn't elaborate, he shrugs and takes Freddi by the arm. 'John Shaft will now escort you to your suite.'

She pushes his hand away. 'Be lucky if it even has a minibar.' But she gets up and walks with him toward the elevators.

'I found Thurston's Garage,' Holly says. 'It's fifty-six miles north on 1–47, the direction the storm's coming from, unfortunately. After that it's State Road 79. The weather really doesn't look g — '

'We'll be okay,' Hodges says. 'Hertz is holding a Ford Expedition for us. It's a nice heavy vehicle. And you can give me the turn-by-turn later. I want to talk to you about something else.' Gently, he takes her iPad and turns it off.

Holly looks at him with her hands clasped in her lap, waiting.

22

Brady comes back from Carbine Street in Hill-billy Heaven refreshed and exhilarated — the Ellsbury fatso was both easy and fun. He wonders how many guys it will take to get her body down from that third-floor apartment. He's guessing at least four. And think of the coffin! Jumbo size!

When he checks the website and finds it offline, his good mood collapses again. Yes, he expected Hodges would find a way to kill it, but he didn't expect it to happen so fast. And the phone number on the screen is as infuriating as the fuck-you messages Hodges left on Debbie's Blue Umbrella during their first go-round. It's a suicide prevention hotline. He doesn't even have to check. He *knows*.

And yes, Hodges will come. Plenty of people at Kiner Memorial know about this place; it's sort of legendary. But will he come straight in? Brady doesn't believe that for a minute. For one thing, the Det-Ret will know that many hunters leave their firearms out at camp (although few are as fully stocked with them as Heads and Skins). For another — and this is more important — the Det-Ret is one sly hyena. Six years older than when Brady first encountered him, true, undoubtedly shorter of wind and shakier of limb, but sly. The sort of slinking animal that doesn't come at you directly but goes for the hamstrings while you're looking elsewhere.

So I'm Hodges. What do I do?

After giving this due consideration, Brady goes to the closet, and a brief check of Babineau's memory (what's left of it) is all it takes for him to choose outerwear that belongs to the body he's inhabiting. Everything fits perfectly. He adds a pair of gloves to protect his arthritic fingers and goes outside. The snow is only a moderate fall and the branches of the trees are still. All that will change later, but for now it's pleasant

431

enough to go for a tramp around the property.

He walks to a woodpile whose surface is covered with an old canvas tarp and a few inches of fresh powder. Beyond it are two or three acres of old-growth pines and spruces separating Heads and Skins from Big Bob's Bear Camp. It's perfect.

He needs to visit the gun closet. The Scar is fine, but there are other things in there he can use.

Oh, Detective Hodges, Brady thinks, hurrying back the way he came. I've got such a surprise. Such a surprise for you.

23

Jerome listens carefully to what Hodges tells him, then shakes his head. 'No way, Bill. I need to come.'

'What you need to do is go home and be with your family,' Hodges says. 'You especially need to be with your sister. She had a close call yesterday.'

They are sitting in a corner of the Hilton's reception area, speaking in low voices although even the desk clerk has retired to the nether regions. Jerome is leaning forward, hands planted on his thighs, his face set in a stubborn frown.

'If Holly's going — '

'It's different for us,' Holly says. 'You must see that, Jerome. I don't get along with my mother, never have. I see her once or twice a year, at

432

most. I'm always glad to leave, and I'm sure she's glad to see me go. As for Bill . . . you know he'll fight what he's got, but both of us know what the chances are. Your case is not like ours.'

'He's dangerous,' Hodges says, 'and we can't count on the element of surprise. If he doesn't know I'll come for him, he's stupid. That's one thing he never was.'

'It was the three of us at the Mingo,' Jerome says. 'And after you went into vapor lock, it was just Holly and me. We did okay.'

'Last time was different,' Holly says. 'Last time he wasn't capable of mind control juju.'

'I still want to come.'

Hodges nods. 'I understand, but I'm still the wheeldog, and the wheeldog says no.'

'But — '

'There's another reason,' Holly says. 'A bigger reason. The repeater's offline and the website's shut down, but that leaves almost two hundred and fifty active Zappits. There's been at least one suicide already, and we can't tell the police all of what's going on. Isabelle Jaynes thinks Bill's a meddler, and anyone else would think we're crazy. If anything happens to us, there's only you. Don't you understand that?'

'What I understand is that you're cutting me out,' Jerome says. All at once he sounds like the weedy young kid Hodges hired to mow his lawn all those years ago.

'There's more,' Hodges says. 'I might have to kill him. In fact, I think that's the most likely outcome.'

'Jesus, Bill, I know that.'

433

'But to the cops and the world at large, the man I killed would be a respected neurosurgeon named Felix Babineau. I've wiggled out of some tight legal corners since opening Finders Keepers, but this one could be different. Do you want to risk being charged as an accessory to aggravated manslaughter, defined in this state as the reckless killing of a human being through culpable negligence? Maybe even Murder One?'

Jerome squirms. 'You're willing to let Holly risk that.'

Holly says, 'You're the one with most of your life still ahead of you.'

Hodges leans forward, even though it hurts to do so, and cups the broad nape of Jerome's neck. 'I know you don't like it. I didn't expect you would. But it's the right thing, for all the right reasons.'

Jerome thinks it over, and sighs. 'I see your point.'

Hodges and Holly wait, both of them knowing this is not quite good enough.

'Okay,' Jerome says at last. 'I hate it, but okay.'

Hodges gets up, hand to his side to hold in the pain. 'Then let's snag that SUV. The storm's coming, and I'd like to get as far up I-47 as possible before we meet it.'

24

Jerome is leaning against the hood of his Wrangler when they come out of the rental office with the keys to an all-wheel drive Expedition.

He hugs Holly and whispers in her ear. 'Last chance. Take me along.'

She shakes her head against his chest.

He lets her go and turns to Hodges, who's wearing an old fedora, the brim already white with snow. Hodges puts out a hand. 'Under other circumstances I'd go with the hug, but right now hugs hurt.'

Jerome settles for a strong grip. There are tears in his eyes. 'Be careful, man. Stay in touch. And bring back the Hollyberry.'

'I intend to do that,' Hodges says.

Jerome watches them get into the Expedition, Bill climbing behind the wheel with obvious discomfort. Jerome knows they're right — of the three of them, he's the least expendable. That doesn't mean he likes it, or feels less like a little kid being sent home to Mommy. He would go after them, he thinks, except for the thing Holly said in that deserted hotel lobby. *If anything happens to us, there's only you.*

Jerome gets into his Jeep and heads home. As he merges onto the Crosstown, a strong premonition comes to him: he's never going to see either one of his friends again. He tries to tell himself that's superstitious bullshit, but he can't quite make it work.

25

By the time Hodges and Holly leave the Crosstown for I-47 North, the snow is no longer just kidding around. Driving into it reminds

Hodges of a science fiction movie he saw with Holly — the moment when the Starship *Enterprise* goes into hyperdrive, or whatever they call it. The speed limit signs are flashing SNOW ALERT and 40 MPH, but he pegs the speedometer at sixty and will hold it there as long as he can, which might be for thirty miles. Perhaps only twenty. A few cars in the travel lane honk at him to slow down, and passing the lumbering eighteen-wheelers, each one dragging a rooster-tail fog of snow behind it, is an exercise in controlled fear.

It's almost half an hour before Holly breaks the silence. 'You brought the guns, didn't you? That's what's in the drawstring bag.'

'Yeah.'

She unbuckles her seatbelt (which makes him nervous) and fishes the bag out of the back seat. 'Are they loaded?'

'The Glock is. The .38 you'll have to load yourself. That one's yours.'

'I don't know how.'

Hodges offered to take her to the shooting range with him once, start the process of getting her qualified to carry concealed, and she refused vehemently. He never offered again, believing she would never need to carry a gun. Believing he would never put her in that position.

'You'll figure it out. It's not hard.'

She examines the Victory, keeping her hands well away from the trigger and the muzzle well away from her face. After a few seconds she succeeds in rolling the barrel.

'Okay, now the bullets.'

436

There are two boxes of Winchester .38s — 130-grain, full metal jacket. She opens one, looks at the shells sticking up like mini-warheads, and grimaces. 'Oough.'

'Can you do it?' He's passing another truck, the Expedition enveloped in snowfog. There are still strips of bare pavement in the travel lane, but this passing lane is now snow-covered, and the truck on their right seems to go on forever. 'If you can't, that's okay.'

'You don't mean can I load it,' she says, sounding angry. 'I see how to do that, a kid could do it.'

Sometimes they do, Hodges thinks.

'What you mean is can I shoot him.'

'It probably won't come to that, but if it did, could you?'

'Yes,' Holly says, and loads the Victory's six chambers. She pushes the cylinder back into place gingerly, lips turned down and eyes squinted into slits, as if afraid the gun will explode in her hand. 'Now where's the safety switch?'

'There isn't any. Not on revolvers. The hammer's down, and that's all the safety that you need. Put it in your purse. The ammo, too.'

She does as he says, then places the bag between her feet.

'And stop biting your lips, you're going to make them bleed.'

'I'll try, but this is a very stressful situation, Bill.'

'I know.' They're back in the travel lane again. The mile markers seem to float past with excruciating slowness, and the pain in his side is a hot jellyfish with long tentacles that now seem to reach everywhere, even up into his throat. Once, twenty years ago, he was shot in the leg by a thief cornered in a vacant lot. That pain had been like this, but eventually it had gone away. He doesn't think this one ever will. The drugs may mute it for awhile, but probably not for long.

'What if we find this place and he's not there, Bill? Have you thought about that? Have you?'

He has, and has no idea what the next step would be in that case. 'Let's not worry about it unless we have to.'

His phone rings. It's in his coat pocket, and he hands it to Holly without looking away from the road ahead.

'Hello, this is Holly.' She listens, then mouths *Miss Pretty Gray Eyes* to Hodges. 'Uh-huh . . . yes . . . okay, I understand . . . no, he can't, his hands are full right now, but I'll tell him.' She listens some more, then says, 'I could tell you, Izzy, but you wouldn't believe me.'

She closes his phone with a snap and slips it back into his pocket.

'Suicides?' Hodges asks.

'Three so far, counting the boy who shot himself in front of his father.'

'Zappits?'

'At two of the three locations. Responders at the third one haven't had a chance to look. They were trying to save the kid, but it was too late. He hung himself. Izzy sounds half out of her mind. She wanted to know everything.'

'If anything happens to us, Jerome will tell

Pete, and Pete will tell her. I think she's almost ready to listen.'

'We have to stop him before he kills more.'

He's probably killing more right now, Hodges thinks. 'We will.'

The miles roll by. Hodges is forced to reduce his speed to fifty, and when he feels the Expedition do a loose little shimmy in the slipstream of a Walmart double box, he drops to forty-five. It's past three o'clock and the light is starting to drain from this snowy day when Holly speaks again.

'Thank you.'

He turns his head briefly, looking a question at her.

'For not making me beg to come along.'

'I'm only doing what your therapist would want,' Hodges says. 'Getting you a bunch of closure.'

'Is that a joke? I can never tell when you're joking. You have an extremely dry sense of humor, Bill.'

'No joke. This is our business, Holly. Nobody else's.'

A green sign looms out of the white murk.

'SR-79,' Holly says. 'That's our exit.'

'Thank God,' Hodges says. 'I hate turnpike driving even when the sun's out.'

26

Thurston's Garage is fifteen miles east along the state highway, according to Holly's iPad, but it takes them half an hour to get there. The Expedition handles the snow-covered road easily, but now the wind is picking up — it will be blowing at gale force by eight o'clock, according to the radio — and when it gusts, throwing sheets of snow across the road, Hodges eases down to fifteen miles an hour until he can see again.

As he turns in at the big yellow Shell sign, Holly's phone rings. 'Handle that,' he says. 'I'll be as quick as I can.'

He gets out, yanking his fedora down hard to keep it from blowing away. The wind machine-guns his coat collar against his neck as he tramps through the snow to the garage office. His entire midsection is throbbing; it feels as if he's swallowed live coals. The gas pumps and the adjacent parking area are empty except for the idling Expedition. The plowboys have departed to spend a long night earning their money as the first big storm of the year rants and raves.

For one eerie moment, Hodges thinks it's Library Al behind the counter: same green Dickies, same popcorn-white hair exploding around the edges of his John Deere cap.

'What brings you out on a wild afternoon like this?' the old guy asks, then peers past Hodges. 'Or is it night already?'

'A little of both,' Hodges says. He has no time for conversation — back in the city kids may be jumping out of apartment building windows and swallowing pills — but it's how the job is done. 'Would you be Mr Thurston?'

'In the flesh. Since you didn't pull up at the

440

pumps, I'd almost wonder if you came to rob me, but you look a little too prosperous for that. City fella?'

'I am,' Hodges says, 'and in kind of a hurry.'

'City fellas usually are.' Thurston puts down the *Field & Stream* he's been reading. 'What is it, then? Directions? Man, I hope it's somewhere close, the way this one's shaping up.'

'I think it is. A hunting camp called Heads and Skins. Ring a bell?'

'Oh, sure,' Thurston says. 'The doctors' place, right near Big Bob's Bear Camp. Those fellas usually gas up their Jags and Porsches here, either on their way out or their way back.' He pronounces *Porsches* as if he's talking about the things old folks sit on in the evening to watch the sun go down. 'Wouldn't be nobody out there now, though. Hunting season ends December ninth, and I'm talking bow hunting. Gun hunting ends the last day of November, and all those docs use rifles. Big ones. I think they like to pretend they're in Africa.'

'Nobody stopped earlier today? Would have been driving an old car with a lot of primer on it?'

'Nope.'

A young man comes out of the garage bay, wiping his hands on a rag. 'I saw that car, Granddad. A Chev'alay. I was out front, talking with Spider Willis, when it went by.' He turns his attention to Hodges. 'I only noticed because there's not much the way he was headed, and that car was no snowdog like the one you've got out there.'

441

'Can you give me directions to the camp?'

'Easiest thing in the world,' Thurston says. 'Or would be on a fair day. You keep on going the way you were heading, about . . . ' He turns his attention to the younger man. 'What would you say, Duane? Three miles?'

'More like four,' Duane says.

'Well, split the difference and call it three and a half,' Thurston says. 'You'll be looking for two red posts on your left. They're tall, six feet or so, but the state plow's been by twice already, so you want to keep a sharp eye, because there won't be much of em to see. You'll have to bull your way through the snowbank, you know. Unless you brought a shovel.'

'I think what I'm driving will do it,' Hodges says.

'Yeah, most likely, and no harm to your SUV, since the snow hasn't had a chance to pack down. Anyway, you go in a mile, or maybe two, and the road splits. One fork goes to Big Bob's, the other to Heads and Skins. I can't remember which one is which, but there used to be arrow signs.'

'Still are,' Duane says. 'Big Bob's is on the right, Heads and Skins on the left. I ought to know, I reshingled Big Bob Rowan's roof last October. This must be pretty important, mister. To get you out on a day like this.'

'Will my SUV make it on that road, do you think?'

'Sure,' Duane says. 'Trees'll still be holding up most of the snow, and the road runs downhill to the lake. Making it out might be a little trickier.'

Hodges takes his wallet from his back pocket — Christ, even that hurts — and fishes out his police ID with RETIRED stamped on it. To it he adds one of his Finders Keepers business cards, and lays them both on the counter. 'Can you gentlemen keep a secret?'

They nod, faces bright with curiosity.

'I've got a subpoena to serve, right? It's a civil case, and the money at stake runs to seven figures. The man you saw go by, the one in the primered-up Chevy, is a doctor named Babineau.'

'See him every November,' the elder Thurston says. 'Got an attitude about him, you know? Like he's always seein you from under the end of his nose. But he drives a Beemer.'

'Today he's driving whatever he could get his hands on,' Hodges says, 'and if I don't serve these papers by midnight, the case goes bye-bye, and an old lady who doesn't have much won't get her payday.'

'Malpractice?' Duane asks.

'Don't like to say, but I'm going in.'

Which you will remember, Hodges thinks. That, and Babineau's name.

The old man says, 'There are a couple of snowmobiles out back. I could let you have one, if you want, and the Arctic Cat has a high windshield. It'd still be a chilly ride, but you'd be guaranteed getting back.'

Hodges is touched by the offer, coming as it does to a complete stranger, but shakes his head. Snowmobiles are noisy beasts. He has an idea that the man now in residence at Heads and

443

Skins — be he Brady or Babineau or a weird mixture of the two — knows he's coming. What Hodges has on his side is that his quarry doesn't know when.

'My partner and I will get in,' he says, 'and worry about getting out later.'

'Nice and quiet, huh?' Duane says, and puts a finger to his lips, which are curved in a smile.

'That's the ticket. Is there someone I could call for a ride if I do get stuck?'

'Call right here.' Thurston hands him a card from the plastic tray by the cash register. 'I'll send either Duane or Spider Willis. It might not be until late tonight, and it'll cost you forty dollars, but with a case worth millions, I guess you can afford that.'

'Do cell phones work out here?'

'Five bars even in dirty weather,' Duane says. 'There's a tower on the south side of the lake.'

'Good to know. Thank you. Thank you both.'

He turns to go and the old man says, 'That hat you're wearing is no good in this weather. Take this.' He's holding out a knit hat with a big orange pompom on top. 'Can't do nothing about those shoes, though.'

Hodges thanks him, takes the hat, then removes his fedora and puts it on the counter. It feels like bad luck; it feels like exactly the right thing to do. 'Collateral,' he says.

Both of them grin, the younger one with quite a few more teeth.

'Good enough,' the old man says, 'but are you a hundred percent sure you want to be driving out to the lake, Mr — ' He glances down at the

444

Finders Keepers business card — 'Mr Hodges? Because you look a trifle peaky.'

'It's a chest cold,' Hodges says. 'I get one every damn winter. Thank you, both of you. And if Dr Babineau should by any chance call here . . . '

'Wouldn't give him the time of day,' Thurston says. 'He's a snooty one.'

Hodges starts for the door, and a pain like none he's ever felt before comes out of nowhere, lancing up from his belly all the way to his jawline. It's like being shot by a burning arrow, and he staggers.

'Are you sure you're okay?' the old man asks, starting around the counter.

'Yeah, I'm fine.' He's far from that. 'Leg cramp. From driving. I'll be back for my hat.' With luck, he thinks.

27

'You were in there a long time,' Holly says. 'I hope you gave them a very good story.'

'Subpoena.' Hodges doesn't need to say more; they've used the subpoena story more than once. Everyone likes to help, as long as they're not the ones being served. 'Who called?' Thinking it must have been Jerome, to see how they're doing.

'Izzy Jaynes. They've had two more suicide calls, one attempted and one successful. The attempted was a girl who jumped out of a second-story window. She landed on a snowbank and just broke some bones. The other was a boy

445

who hung himself in his closet. Left a note on his pillow. Just one word, *Beth*, and a broken heart.'

The Expedition's wheels spin a little when Hodges drops it into gear and rolls back onto the state road. He has to drive with his low beams on. The brights turn the falling snow into a sparkling white wall.

We have to do this ourselves,' she says. 'If it's Brady, no one will ever believe it. He'll pretend to be Babineau and spin some story about how he was scared and ran away.'

'And never called the police himself after Library Al shot his wife?' Hodges says. 'I'm not sure that would hold.'

'Maybe not, but what if he can jump to someone else? If he could jump to Babineau, he could jump to someone else. We have to do this ourselves, even if it means we end up getting arrested for murder. Do you think that could happen, Bill? Do you do you do you?'

'We'll worry about it later.'

'I'm not sure I could shoot a person. Not even Brady Hartsfield, if he looks like someone else.'

He repeats, 'We'll worry about it later.'

'Fine. Where did you get that hat?'

'Swapped it for my fedora.'

'The puffball on top is silly, but it looks warm.'

'Do you want it?'

'No. But Bill?'

'Jesus, Holly, what?'

'You look awful.'

'Flattery will get you nowhere.'

'Be sarcastic. Fine. How far is it to where we're going?'

446

'The general consensus back there was three and a half miles on this road. Then a camp road.'

Silence for five minutes as they creep through the blowing snow. And the main body of the storm is still coming, Hodges reminds himself.

'Bill?'

'What now?'

'You have no boots, and I'm all out of Nicorette.'

'Spark up one of those joints, why don't you? But keep an eye out for a couple of red posts on the left while you do it. They should be coming up soon.'

Holly doesn't light a joint, just sits forward, looking to the left. When the Expedition skids again, the rear end flirting first left and then right, she doesn't appear to notice. A minute later she points. 'Is that them?'

It is. The passing plows have buried all but the last eighteen inches or so, but that bright red is impossible to miss or mistake. Hodges feathers the brakes, brings the Expedition to a stop, then turns it so it's facing the snowbank. He tells Holly what he sometimes used to tell his daughter, when he took her on the Wild Cups at Lakewood Amusement Park: 'Hold onto your false teeth.'

Holly — always the literalist — says, 'I don't have any,' but she does put a bracing hand on the dashboard.

Hodges steps down gently on the gas and rolls at the snowbank. The thud he expected doesn't come; Thurston was right about the snow not yet having a chance to pack and harden. It explodes away to either side and up onto the windshield, momentarily blinding him. He shoves the wipers into overdrive, and when the glass clears, the Expedition is pointing down a one-lane camp road rapidly filling with snow. Every now and then more flumps down from the overhanging branches. He sees no tracks from a previous car, but that means nothing. By now they'd be gone.

He kills the headlights and advances at a creep. The band of white between the trees is just visible enough to serve as a guide track. The road seems endless — sloping, switching back, then sloping again — but eventually they come to the place where it splits left and right. Hodges doesn't have to get out and check the arrows. Ahead on the left, through the snow and the trees, he can see a faint glimmer of light. That's Heads and Skins, and someone is home. He crimps the wheel and begins rolling slowly down the right-hand fork.

Neither of them looks up and sees the video camera, but it sees them.

28

By the time Hodges and Holly burst through the snowbank left by the plow, Brady is sitting in front of the TV, fully dressed in Babineau's winter coat and boots. He's left off the gloves, he wants his hands bare in case he has to use the Scar, but there's a black balaclava lying across one thigh. When the time comes, he'll don it to cover Babineau's face and silver hair. His eyes never leave the television as he nervously stirs the pens and pencils sticking out of the ceramic skull. A sharp lookout is absolutely necessary. When Hodges comes, he'll kill his headlights.

Will he have the nigger lawnboy with him? Brady wonders. Wouldn't that be sweet! Two for the price of —

And there he is.

He was afraid the Det-Ret's vehicle might get by him in the thickening snow, but that was a needless worry. The snow is white; the SUV is a solid black rectangle sliding through it. Brady leans forward, squinting, but can't tell if there's only one person in the cabin, or two, or half a fucking dozen. He's got the Scar, and with it he could wipe out an entire squad if he had to, but that would spoil the fun. He'd like Hodges alive.

To start with, at least.

Only one more question needs to be answered — will he turn left, and bore straight in, or right? Brady is betting K. William Hodges will choose the fork that leads to Big Bob's, and he's right. As the SUV disappears into the snow (with a brief flash of the taillights as Hodges negotiates the first turn), Brady puts the skull penholder down next to the TV remote and picks up an item that has been waiting on the end table. A perfectly legal item when used the right way . . . which it never was by Babineau and his cohorts. They may have been good doctors, but out here in the woods, they were often bad boys. He pulls this valuable piece of equipment over his head, and lets it hang against the front of his coat by the elastic strap. Then he pulls on the balaclava, grabs the Scar, and heads out. His heart is beating fast and hard, and for the time being, at least, the arthritis in Babineau's fingers seems to be completely gone.

Payback is a bitch, and the bitch is back.

29

Holly doesn't ask Hodges why he took the right-hand fork. She's neurotic, but not stupid. He drives at walking pace, looking to his left, measuring the lights to his left. When he's even with them, he stops the SUV and switches off the engine. It's full dark now, and when he turns to look at Holly, she has the fleeting impression that his head has been replaced by a skull.

'Stay here,' he says in a low voice. 'Text Jerome, tell him we're okay. I'm going to cut through those woods and take him.'

'You don't mean alive, do you?'

'Not if I see him with one of those Zappits.' And probably even if I don't, he thinks. 'We can't take the risk.'

'Then you believe it's him. Brady.'

'Even if it's Babineau, he's part of this. Neck-deep in it.' But yes, at some point he has become convinced that Brady Hartsfield's mind is now running Babineau's body. The intuition is too strong to deny, and has gained the weight of fact.

God help me if I kill him and I'm wrong, he thinks. Only how would I know? How could I ever be sure?

He expects Holly to protest, to tell him she has to come along, but all she says is, 'I don't think I can drive this thing out of here if something happens to you, Bill.'

He hands her Thurston's card. 'If I'm not back in ten minutes — no, make it fifteen — call this guy.'

'What if I hear shots?'

'If it's me, and I'm okay, I'll honk the horn of Library Al's car. Two quick beeps. If you don't hear that, drive the rest of the way to the other camp, Big Bob's Whatsit. Break in, find somewhere to hide, call Thurston.'

Hodges leans across the center console, and for the first time since he's known her, kisses her lips. She's too startled to kiss him back, but she doesn't pull away. When he does, she looks down in confusion and says the first thing that comes into her mind. 'Bill, you're in *shoes!* You'll *freeze!*'

'There's not so much snow in the trees, only a couple of inches.' And really, cold feet are the least of his worries at this point.

He finds the toggle switch that kills the interior lights. As he leaves the Expedition, grunting with suppressed pain, she can hear the rising whisper of the wind in the fir trees. If it were a voice, it would be mourning. Then the door shuts.

Holly sits where she is, watching his dark shape merge with the dark shapes of the trees, and when she can no longer tell which is which, she gets out and follows his tracks. The Victory .38 that Hodges's father once carried as a beat

451

cop back in the fifties, when Sugar Heights was still woodland, is in her coat pocket.

30

Hodges makes his way toward the lights of Heads and Skins one plodding step at a time. Snow flicks his face and coats his eyelids. That burning arrow is back, lighting him up inside. Frying him. His face is running with sweat.

At least my feet aren't hot, he thinks, and that's when he stumbles over a snow-covered log and goes sprawling. He lands squarely on his left side and buries his face in the arm of his coat to keep from screaming. Hot liquid spills into his crotch.

Wet my pants, he thinks. Wet my pants just like a baby.

When the pain recedes a little, he gathers his legs under him and tries to stand. He can't do it. The wetness is turning cold. He can actually feel his dick shriveling to get away from it. He grabs a low-hanging branch and tries again to get up. It snaps off. He looks at it stupidly, feeling like a cartoon character — Wile E. Coyote, maybe — and tosses it aside. As he does, a hand hooks into his armpit.

His surprise is so great he almost screams. Then Holly is whispering in his ear. 'Upsa-daisy, Bill. Come on.'

With her help, he's finally able to make it to his feet. The lights are close now, no more than forty yards through the screening trees. He can

452

see the snow frosting her hair and lighting on her cheeks. All at once he finds himself remembering the office of an antique bookdealer named Andrew Halliday, and how he, Holly, and Jerome had discovered Halliday lying dead on the floor. He told them to stay back, but —

'Holly. If I told you to go back, would you do it?'

'No.' She's whispering. They both are. 'You'll probably have to shoot him, and you can't get there without help.'

'You're supposed to be my backup, Holly. My insurance policy.' The sweat is pouring off him like oil. Thank God his coat is a long one. He doesn't want Holly to know he pissed himself.

'*Jerome* is your insurance policy,' she says. 'I'm your partner. That's why you brought me, whether you know it or not. And it's what I want. It's all I ever wanted. Now come on. Lean on me. Let's finish this.'

They move slowly through the remaining trees. Hodges can't believe how much of his weight she's taking. They pause at the edge of the clearing that surrounds the house. There are two lighted rooms. Judging by the subdued glow coming from the one closest to them, Hodges thinks it must be the kitchen. A single light on in there, maybe the one over the stove. Coming from the other window he can make out an unsteady flicker that probably means a fireplace.

'That's where we're going,' he says, pointing, 'and from here on we're soldiers on night patrol. Which means we crawl.'

'Can you?'

'Yeah.' It might actually be easier than walking. 'See the chandelier?'

'Yes. It looks all bony. Oough.'

'That's the living room, and that's where he'll probably be. If he's not, we'll wait until he shows. If he's got one of those Zappits, I intend to shoot him. No hands up, no lie down and put your hands behind your back. Do you have a problem with that?'

'Absolutely not.'

They drop to their hands and knees. Hodges leaves the Glock in his coat pocket, not wanting to dunk it in the snow.

'Bill.' Her whisper so low he can barely hear it over the rising wind.

He turns to look at her. She's holding out one of her gloves.

'Too small,' he says, and thinks of Johnnie Cochran saying, *If the glove doesn't fit, you must acquit*. Crazy what goes through a person's mind at times like this. Only has there ever in his life been a time like this?

'Force it,' she whispers. 'You need to keep your gun hand warm.'

She's right, and he manages to get it most of the way on. It's too short to get over all of his hand, but his fingers are covered, and that's all that matters.

They crawl, Hodges slightly in the lead. The pain is still bad, but now that he's off his feet, the arrow in his guts is smoldering rather than burning.

Got to save some energy, though, he thinks. Just enough.

It's forty or fifty feet from the edge of the woods to the window with the chandelier hanging in it, and his uncovered hand has lost all feeling by the time they're halfway there. He can't believe he's brought his best friend to this place and this moment, crawling through the snow like children playing a war game, miles from any help. He had his reasons, and they made sense back in that Airport Hilton. Now, not so much.

He looks left, at the silent hulk of Library Al's Malibu. He looks right, and sees a snow-covered woodpile. He starts to look ahead again, at the living room window, then snaps his head back to the woodpile, alarm bells ringing just a little too late.

There are tracks in the snow. The angle was wrong to see them from the edge of the woods, but he can see them clearly now. They lead from the back of the house to that stack of fireplace fuel. He came outside through the kitchen door, Hodges thinks. That's why the light was on in there. I should have guessed. I would have, if I hadn't been so sick.

He scrabbles for the Glock, but the too-small glove slows his grip, and when he finally gets hold of it and tries to pull it out, the gun snags in the pocket. Meanwhile, a dark shape has risen from behind the woodpile. The shape covers the fifteen feet between it and them in four great looping strides. The face is that of an alien in a horror movie, featureless except for the round, projecting eyes.

'*Holly, look out!*'

455

She lifts her head just as the butt of the Scar comes down to meet it. There's a sickening crack and she drops face-first into the snow with her arms thrown out to either side: a puppet with its strings cut. Hodges frees the Glock from his coat pocket just as the butt comes down again. Hodges both feels and hears his wrist break; he sees the Glock land in the snow and almost disappear.

Still on his knees, Hodges looks up and sees a tall man — much taller than Brady Hartsfield — standing in front of Holly's motionless form. He's wearing a balaclava and night-vision goggles.

He saw us as soon we came out of the trees, Hodges thinks dully. For all I know, he saw us *in* the trees, while I was pulling on Holly's glove.

'Hello, Detective Hodges.'

Hodges doesn't reply. He wonders if Holly is still alive, and if she'll ever recover from the blow she's just been dealt, if she is. But of course, that's stupid. Brady isn't going to give her any chance to recover.

'You're coming inside with me,' Brady says. 'The question is whether or not we bring her, or leave her out here, to turn into a Popsicle.' And, as if he's read Hodges's mind (for all Hodges knows, he can do that): 'Oh, she's still alive, at least for now. I can see her back going up and down. Although after a hit that hard, and with her face in the snow, who knows for how long?'

'I'll carry her,' Hodges says, and he will. No matter how much it hurts.

'Okay.' No pause to think it over, and Hodges

know it's what Brady expected and what Brady wanted. He's one step ahead. Has been all along. And whose fault is that?

Mine. Entirely mine. It's what I get for playing the Lone Ranger yet again . . . but what else could I do? Who would ever have believed it?

'Pick her up,' Brady says. 'Let's see if you really can. Because, tell you what, you look mighty shaky to me.'

Hodges gets his arms under Holly. In the woods, he couldn't make it to his feet after he fell, but now he gathers everything he has left and does a clean-and-jerk with her limp body. He staggers, almost goes down, and finds his balance again. The burning arrow is gone, incinerated in the forest fire it has touched off inside him. But he hugs her to his chest.

'That's good.' Brady sounds genuinely admiring. 'Now let's see if you can make it to the house.'

Somehow, Hodges does.

31

The wood in the fireplace is burning well and throwing a stuporous heat. Gasping for breath, the snow on his borrowed hat melting and running down his face in slushy streams, Hodges gets to the middle of the room and then goes to his knees, having to cradle Holly's neck in the crook of his elbow because of his broken wrist, which is swelling up like a sausage. He manages to keep her head from banging on the hardwood floor, and that's good. Her head has taken enough abuse tonight.

Brady has removed his coat, the night-vision goggles, and the balaclava. It's Babineau's face and Babineau's silvery hair (now in unaccustomed disarray), but it's Brady Hartsfield, all right. Hodges's last doubts have departed.

'Has she got a gun?'

'No.'

The man who looks like Felix Babineau smiles. 'Well, here's what I'm going to do, Bill. I'll search her pockets, and if I do find a gun, I'll blow her narrow ass into the next state. How's that for a deal?'

'It's a .38,' Hodges says. 'She's right-handed, so if she brought it, it's probably in the right front pocket of her coat.'

Brady bends, keeping the Scar trained on Hodges as he does so, finger on the trigger and the butt-plate braced against the right side of his chest. He finds the revolver, examines it briefly, then tucks it into his belt at the small of his back. In spite of his pain and despair, Hodges feels a certain sour amusement. Brady's probably seen badass dudes do that in a hundred TV shows and action movies, but it really only works with automatics, which are flat.

On the hooked rug, Holly makes a snoring sound deep in her throat. One foot gives a spastic jerk, then goes still.

'What about you?' Brady asks. 'Any other weapons? The ever-popular throwdown gun strapped to your ankle, perhaps?'

Hodges shakes his head.

'Just to be on the safe side, why don't you hoist up your pantslegs for me?'

Hodges does it, revealing soaked shoes, wet socks, and nothing else.

'Excellent. Now take off your coat and throw it on the couch.'

Hodges unzips it and manages to keep quiet while he shrugs out of it, but when he tosses it, a bull's horn gores him from crotch to heart and he groans.

Babineau's eyes widen. 'Real pain or fake? Live or Memorex? Judging from a quite striking weight loss, I'm going to say it's real. What's up, Detective Hodges? What's going on with you?'

'Cancer. Pancreatic.'

'Oh, goodness, that's bad. Not even Superman can beat that one. But cheer up, I may be able to shorten your suffering.'

'Do what you want with me,' Hodges says. 'Just let her alone.'

Brady looks at the woman on the floor with great interest. 'This would not by any chance be the woman who smashed in what used to be my head, is it?' The locution strikes him funny and he laughs.

'No.' The world has become a camera lens, zooming in and out with every beat of his laboring, pacemaker-assisted heart. 'Holly Gibney was the one who thumped you. She's gone back to live with her parents in Ohio. That's Kara Winston, my assistant.' The name comes to him from nowhere, and there's no hesitation as he speaks it.

'An assistant who just decided to come with

459

you on a do-or-die mission? I find that a little hard to believe.'

'I promised her a bonus. She needs the money.'

'And where, pray tell, is your nigger lawnboy?'

Hodges briefly considers telling Brady the truth — that Jerome is back in the city, that he knows Brady has probably gone to the hunting camp, that he will pass this information on to the police soon, if he hasn't already. But will any of those things stop Brady? Of course not.

'Jerome is in Arizona, building houses. Habitat for Humanity.'

'How socially conscious of him. I was hoping he'd be with you. How badly hurt is his sister?'

'Broken leg. She'll be up and walking in no time.'

'That's a shame.'

'She was one of your test cases, wasn't she?'

'She got one of the original Zappits, yes. There were twelve of them. Like the twelve Apostles, you might say, going forth to spread the word. Sit in the chair in front of the TV, Detective Hodges.'

'I'd rather not. All my favorite shows are on Monday.'

Brady smiles politely. 'Sit.'

Hodges sits, bracing his good hand on the table beside the chair. Going down is agony, but once he actually makes it, sitting is a little better. The TV is off, but he stares at it, anyway.

'Where's the camera?'

'On the signpost where the road splits. Above the arrows. You don't have to feel bad about missing it. It was covered with snow, nothing sticking out but the lens, and your headlights were off by then.'

'Is there any Babineau left inside you?'

He shrugs. 'Bits and pieces. Every now and then there's a small scream from the part that thinks it's still alive. It will stop soon.'

'Jesus,' Hodges mutters.

Brady drops to one knee, the barrel of the Scar resting on his thigh and still pointing at Hodges. He pulls down the back of Holly's coat and examines the tag. 'H. Gibney,' he says. 'Printed in indelible ink. Very tidy. Won't wash off in the laundry. I like a person who takes care of her things.'

Hodges closes his eyes. The pain is very bad, and he would give everything he owns to get away from it, and from what is going to happen next. He would give anything to just sleep, and sleep, and sleep. But he opens them again and forces himself to look at Brady, because you play the game to the end. That's how it works; play to the end.

'I have a lot of stuff to do in the next forty-eight or seventy-two hours, Detective Hodges, but I'm going to put it on hold in order to deal with you. Does that make you feel special? It should. Because I owe you so much for fucking me over.'

'You need to remember that *you* came to *me*,' Hodges says. 'You were the one who started the ball rolling, with that stupid, bragging letter. Not me. You.'

Babineau's face — the craggy face of an older character actor — darkens. 'I suppose you might have a point, but look who's on top now. Look who *wins*, Detective Hodges.'

'If you call getting a bunch of stupid, confused kids to commit suicide winning, I guess you're the winner. Me, I think doing that is about as challenging as striking out the pitcher.'

'It's *control*! I assert *control*! You tried to stop me and you couldn't! You absolutely couldn't! And neither could she!' He kicks Holly in the side. Her body rolls a boneless half a turn toward the fireplace, then rolls back again. Her face is ashen, her closed eyes sunk deep in their sockets. 'She actually made me better! Better than I ever was!'

'Then for Christ's sake, *stop kicking her*!' Hodges shouts.

Brady's anger and excitement have caused Babineau's face to flush. His hands are tight on the assault rifle. He takes a deep, steadying breath, then another. And smiles.

'Got a soft spot for Ms Gibney, do you?' He kicks her again, this time in the hip. 'Are you fucking her? Is that it? She's not much in the looks department, but I guess a guy your age has to take what he can get. You know what we used to say? Put a flag over her face and fuck her for Old Glory.'

He kicks Holly again, and bares his teeth at Hodges in what he may think is a smile.

'You used to ask me if I was fucking my mother, remember? All those visits you made to my room, asking if I was fucking the only person who ever cared a damn for me. Talking about how hot she looked, and was she a hoochie

462

mama. Asking if I was faking. Telling me how much you hoped I was suffering. And I just had to sit there and take it.'

He's getting ready to kick poor Holly again. To distract him, Hodges says, 'There was a nurse. Sadie MacDonald. Did you nudge her into killing herself? You did, didn't you? She was the first one.'

Brady likes that, and shows even more of Babineau's expensive dental work. 'It was easy. It always is, once you get inside and start pulling the levers.'

'How do you do that, Brady? How do you get inside? How did you manage to get those Zappits from Sunrise Solutions, and rig them? Oh, and the website, how about that?'

Brady laughs. 'You've read too many of those mystery stories where the clever private eye keeps the insane murderer talking until help arrives. Or until the murderer's attention wavers and the private eye can grapple with him and get his gun away. I don't think help is going to arrive, and you don't look capable of grappling with a gold-fish. Besides, you know most of it already. You wouldn't be here if you didn't. Freddi spilled her guts, and — not to sound like Snidely Whiplash — she will pay for that. Eventually.'

'She claims she didn't set up the website.'

'I didn't need her for that. I did it all by myself, in Babineau's study, on Babineau's laptop. During one of my vacations from Room 217.'

'What about — '

'Shut up. See that table beside you, Detective Hodges?'

It's cherrywood, like the buffet, and looks expensive, but there are faded rings all over it, from glasses that were put down without benefit of coasters. The doctors who own this place may be meticulous in operating rooms, but out here they're slobs. On top of it now is the TV remote and a ceramic skull penholder.

'Open the drawer.'

Hodges does. Inside is a pink Zappit Commander sitting on top of an ancient *TV Guide* with Hugh Laurie on the cover.

'Take it out and turn it on.'

'No.'

'All right, fine. I'll just take care of Ms Gibney, then.' He lowers the barrel of the Scar and points it at the back of Holly's neck. 'On full auto, this will rip her head right off. Will it fly into the fireplace? Let's find out.'

'Okay,' Hodges says. 'Okay, okay, okay. Stop.'

He takes the Zappit and finds the button at the top of the console. The welcome screen lights up; the diagonal downstroke of the red Z fills the screen. He is invited to swipe and access the games. He does so without being prompted by Brady. Sweat pours down his face. He has never been so hot. His broken wrist throbs and pulses.

'Do you see the Fishin' Hole icon?'

'Yes.'

Opening Fishin' Hole is the last thing he wants to do, but when the alternative is just sitting here with his broken wrist and his swollen, pulsing gut and watching a stream of high-caliber bullets divide Holly's head from her slight body? Not an option. And besides, he has read a person can't be hypnotized against his will. It's true that Dinah Scott's console almost put him under, but then he didn't know what was happening. Now he does. And if Brady thinks he's tranced out and he's not, then maybe . . . just maybe . . .

'I'm sure you know the drill by now,' Brady says. His eyes are bright and lively, the eyes of a boy who is about to set a spiderweb on fire so he can see what the spider will do. Will it scurry around its flaming web, looking for a way to escape, or will it just burn? 'Tap the icon. The fish will swim and the music will play. Tap the pink fish and add up the numbers. In order to win the game, you have to score one hundred and twenty points in one hundred and twenty seconds. If you succeed, I'll let Ms Gibney live. If you fail, we'll see what this fine automatic weapon can do. Babineau saw it demolish a stack of concrete blocks once, so just imagine what it will do to flesh.'

'You're not going to let her live even if I score five thousand,' Hodges says. 'I don't believe that for a second.'

Babineau's blue eyes widen in mock outrage. 'But you should! All that I am, I owe to this bitch sprawled out in front of me! The least I can do is spare her life. Assuming she isn't suffering a brain bleed and dying already, that is. Now stop playing for time. Play the game instead. Your one hundred and twenty seconds start as soon as your finger taps the icon.'

With no other recourse, Hodges taps it. The screen blanks. There's a blue flash so bright it makes him squint, and then the fish are there, swimming back and forth, up and down, crisscrossing, sending up silvery trails of bubbles. The music begins to tinkle: *By the sea, by the sea, by the beautiful sea* . . .

Only it isn't *just* music. There are words mixed in. And there are words in the blue flashes, too.

'Ten seconds gone,' Brady says. 'Tick-tock, tick-tock.'

Hodges taps at one of the pink fish and misses. He's right hand-dominant, and each tap makes the throbbing in his wrist that much worse, but the pain there is nothing compared to the pain now roasting him from groin to throat. On his third try he gets a pinky — that's how he thinks of them, as pinkies — and the fish turns into a number 5. He says it out loud.

'Only five points in twenty seconds?' Brady says. 'Better step it up, Detective.'

Hodges taps faster, eyes moving left and right, up and down. He no longer has to squint when the blue flashes come, because he's used to them. And it's getting easier. The fish seem bigger now, also a little slower. The music seems less tinkly. Fuller, somehow. *You and me, you and me, oh how happy we'll be.* Is that Brady's voice, singing along with the music, or just his imagination? Live or Memorex? No time to think about it now. *Tempus is fugiting.*

He gets a seven-fish, then a four, and then — jackpot! — one turns into a twelve. He says, 'I'm up to twenty-seven.' But is that right? He's losing count.

Brady doesn't tell him, Brady only says,

'Eighty seconds to go,' and now his voice seems to have picked up a slight echo, as if it's coming to Hodges from the far end of a long hallway. Meanwhile, a marvelous thing is happening: the pain in his gut is starting to recede.

Whoa, he thinks. The AMA should know about this.

He gets another pinky. It turns into a 2. Not so good, but there are plenty more. Plenty, plenty more.

That's when he starts to feel something like fingers fluttering delicately inside his head, and it's not his imagination. He's being invaded. *It was easy*, Brady said of Nurse MacDonald. *It always is, once you get inside and start pulling the levers.*

And when Brady gets to *his* levers?

He'll jump inside me the way he jumped inside Babineau, Hodges thinks . . . although this realization is now like the voice and the music, coming from the far end of a long hallway. At the end of that hallway is the door to Room 217, and the door is standing open.

Why would he want to do that? Why would he want to inhabit a body that's turned into a cancer factory? Because he wants me to kill Holly. Not with the gun, though, he'd never trust me with that. He'll use my hands to choke her, broken wrist and all. Then he'll leave me to face what I've done.

'You're getting better, Detective Hodges, and you still have a minute to go. Just relax and keep tapping. It's easier when you relax.'

The voice is no longer echoing down a

hallway; even though Brady is now standing right in front of him, it's coming from a galaxy far, far away. Brady bends down and stares eagerly into Hodges's face. Only there are fish swimming between them. Pinkies and blueies and reddies. Because Hodges is in the Fishin' Hole now. Except it's really an aquarium, and he's the fish. Soon he will be eaten. Eaten alive. 'Come on, Billy-boy, tap those pink fish!'

I can't let him inside me, Hodges thinks, but I can't keep him out.

He taps a pink fish, it turns into a 9, and it isn't just fingers he feels now but another consciousness spilling into his mind. It's spreading like ink in water. Hodges tries to fight and knows he will lose. The strength of that invading personality is incredible.

I'm going to drown. Drown in the Fishin' Hole. Drown in Brady Hartsfield.

By the sea, by the sea, by the beautiful s —

A pane of glass shatters close by. It's followed by a jubilant chorus of boys shouting, *'That's a HOME RUN!'*

The bond binding Hodges to Hartsfield is broken by the pure, unexpected surprise of the thing. Hodges jerks back in the chair and looks up as Brady wheels toward the couch, eyes wide and mouth open in startlement. The Victory .38, held against the small of his back only by its short barrel (the cylinder won't allow it to go deeper), falls out of his belt and thumps to the bearskin rug.

Hodges doesn't hesitate. He throws the Zappit into the fireplace.

468

'*Don't you do that!*' Brady bellows, turning back. He raises the Scar. '*Don't you fucking da* — '

Hodges grasps the nearest thing to hand, not the .38 but the ceramic penholder. There's nothing wrong with his left wrist, and the range is short. He throws it at the face Brady has stolen, he throws it hard, and connects dead center. The ceramic skull shatters. Brady screams — pain, yes, but mostly shock — and his nose begins to gush blood. When he tries to bring up the Scar, Hodges pistons out his feet, enduring another deep gore of that bull's horn, and smashes them into Brady's chest. Brady back-pedals, almost catches his balance, then trips over a hassock and sprawls on the bearskin rug.

Hodges tries to launch himself out of the chair and only succeeds in overturning the end table. He goes to his knees as Brady sits up, bringing the Scar around. There's a gunshot before he can level it on Hodges, and Brady screams again. This time it's all pain. He looks unbelievingly at his shoulder, where blood is pouring through a hole in his shirt.

Holly is sitting up. There's a grotesque bruise over her left eye, in almost the same place as the one on Freddi's forehead. That left eye is red, filled with blood, but the other is bright and aware. She's holding the Victory .38 in both hands.

'*Shoot him again!*' Hodges roars. '*Shoot him again, Holly!*'

As Brady lurches to his feet — one hand

clapped to the wound in his shoulder, the other holding the Scar, face slack with disbelief — Holly fires again. This bullet goes way high, ricocheting off the fieldstone chimney above the roaring fire.

'Stop that!' Brady shouts, ducking. At the same time he's struggling to raise the Scar. 'Stop doing that, you bi — '

Holly fires a third time. The sleeve of Brady's shirt twitches, and he yelps. Hodges isn't sure she's winged him again, but she at least grooved him.

Hodges gets to his feet and tries to run at Brady, who is making another effort to raise the automatic rifle. The best he can manage is a slow plod.

'You're in the way!' Holly cries. '*Bill, you're in the fracking way!*'

Hodges drops to his knees and tucks his head. Brady turns and runs. The .38 bangs. Wood splinters fly from the doorframe a foot to Brady's right. Then he's gone. The front door opens. Cold air rushes in, making the fire do an excited shimmy.

'I missed him!' Holly shouts, agonized. 'Stupid and useless! Stupid and useless!' She drops the Victory and slaps herself across the face.

Hodges catches her hand before she can do it again, and kneels beside her. 'No, you got him at least once, maybe twice. You're the reason we're still alive.'

But for how long? Brady held onto that goddam grease gun, he may have an extra clip or two, and Hodges knows he wasn't lying about the SCAR 17S's ability to demolish concrete blocks. He has seen a similar assault rifle, the HK 416, do exactly that, at a private shooting facility in the wilds of Victory County. He went there with Pete, and on the way back they joked about how the HK should be standard police issue.

'What do we do?' Holly asks. 'What do we do now?'

Hodges picks up the .38 and rolls the barrel. Two rounds left, and the .38 is only good at short range, anyway. Holly has a concussion at the very least, and he's almost incapacitated. The bitter truth is this: they had a chance, and Brady got away.

He hugs her and says, 'I don't know.'

'Maybe we should hide.'

'I don't think that would work,' he says, but doesn't say why and is relieved when she doesn't ask. It's because there's still a little of Brady left inside of him. It probably won't last long, but for the time being, at least, Hodges suspects it's as good as a homing beacon.

32

Brady staggers through shin-deep snow, eyes wide with disbelief, Babineau's sixty-three-year-old heart banging away in his chest. There's a metallic taste on his tongue, his shoulder is burning, and the thought running through his head on a constant loop is *That bitch, that bitch, that dirty sneaking bitch, why didn't I kill her*

471

while I had the chance?

The Zappit is gone, too. Good old Zappit Zero, and it's the only one he brought. Without it, he has no way to reach the minds of those with active Zappits. He stands panting in front of Heads and Skins, coatless in the rising wind and driving snow. The keys to Z-Boy's car are in his pocket, along with another clip for the Scar, but what good are the keys? That shitbox wouldn't make it halfway up the first hill before it got stuck.

I have to take them, he thinks, *and not just because they owe me. The SUV Hodges drove down here is the only way* out *of here, and either he or the bitch probably has the keys. It's possible they left them in the vehicle, but that's a chance I can't afford to take.*

Besides, it would mean leaving them alive.

He knows what he has to do, and switches the fire control to FULL AUTO. He socks the butt of the Scar against his good shoulder, and starts shooting, raking the barrel from left to right but concentrating on the great room, where he left them.

Gunfire lights up the night, turning the fast-falling snow into a series of flash photographs. The sound of the overlapping reports is deafening. Windows explode inward. Clapboards rise from the façade like bats. The front door, left half-open in his escape, flies all the way back, rebounds, and is driven back again. Babineau's face is twisted in an expression of joyful hate that is all Brady Hartsfield, and he doesn't hear the growl of an approaching engine or the clatter of steel treads from behind him.

33

'*Down!*' Hodges shouts. '*Holly, down!*'

He doesn't wait to see if she'll obey on her own, just lands on top of her and covers her body with his. Above them, the living room is a storm of flying splinters, broken glass, and chips of rock from the chimney. An elk's head falls off the wall and lands on the hearth. One glass eye has been shattered by a Winchester slug, and it looks like it's winking at them. Holly screams. Half a dozen bottles on the buffet explode, releasing the stench of bourbon and gin. A slug strikes a burning log in the fireplace, busting it in two and sending up a storm of sparks.

Please let him have just the one clip, Hodges thinks. And if he aims low, let him hit me instead of Holly. Only a .308 Winchester slug that hits him will go through them both, and he knows it.

The gunfire stops. Is he reloading, or is he out? Live or Memorex?

'Bill, get off me, I can't breathe.'

'Better not,' he says. 'I — '

'What's that? What's that sound?' And then, answering her own question, 'Someone's coming!'

Now that his ears are clearing a little, Hodges can hear it, too. At first he thinks it must be Thurston's grandson, on one of the snowmobiles the old man mentioned, and about to be slaughtered for trying to play Good Samaritan. But maybe not. The approaching engine sounds too heavy for a snowmobile.

Bright yellow-white light floods in through the

shattered windows like the spotlights from a police helicopter. Only this is no helicopter.

34

Brady is ramming his extra clip home when he finally registers the growl-and-clank of the approaching vehicle. He whirls, wounded shoulder throbbing like an infected tooth, just as a huge silhouette appears at the end of the camp road. The headlamps dazzle him. His shadow leaps out long on the sparkling snow as the whatever-it-is comes rolling toward the shot-up house, throwing gouts of snow behind its clanking treads. And it's not just coming at the house. It's coming at *him*.

He depresses the trigger and the Scar resumes its thunder. Now he can see it's some kind of snow machine with a bright orange cabin sitting high above the churning treads. The windshield explodes just as someone dives for safety from the open driver's side door.

The monstrosity keeps coming. Brady tries to run, and Babineau's expensive loafers slip. He flails, staring at those oncoming headlights, and goes down on his back. The orange invader rises above him. He sees a steel tread whirring toward him. He tries to push it away, as he sometimes pushed objects in his room — the blinds, the bedclothes, the door to the bathroom — but it's like trying to beat off a charging lion with a toothbrush. He raises a hand and draws in breath to scream. Before he can, the left tread of the Tucker Sno-Cat rolls over his midsection and chews it open.

35

Holly has zero doubt concerning the identity of their rescuer, and doesn't hesitate. She runs through the bullet-pocked foyer and out the front door, crying his name over and over. Jerome looks as if he's been dusted in powdered sugar when he picks himself up. She's sobbing and laughing as she throws herself into his arms.

'How did you know? How did you know to come?'

'I didn't,' he says. 'It was Barbara. When I called to say I was coming home, she told me I had to go after you or Brady would kill you . . . only she called him the Voice. She was half crazy.'

Hodges is making his way toward the two of them at a slow stagger, but he's close enough to overhear this, and remembers that Barbara told Holly some of that suicide-voice was still inside her. Like a trail of slime, she said. Hodges knows what she was talking about, because he's got some of that disgusting thought-shot in his own head, at least for the time being. Maybe Barbara had just enough of a connection to know that Brady was lying in wait.

Or hell, maybe it was pure woman's intuition. Hodges actually believes in such a thing. He's old-school.

'Jerome,' he says. The word comes out in a

dusty croak. 'My man.' His knees unlock. He's going down.

Jerome frees himself from Holly's deathgrip and puts an arm around Hodges before he can. 'Are you all right? I mean . . . I know you're not all right, but are you shot?'

'No.' Hodges puts his own arm around Holly. 'And I should have known you'd come. Neither one of you minds worth a tinker's damn.'

'Couldn't break up the band before the final reunion concert, could we?' Jerome says. 'Let's get you in the — '

There comes an animal sound from their left, a guttural groan that struggles to be words and can't make it.

Hodges is more exhausted than ever in his life, but he walks toward that groan anyway. Because . . . Well, because.

What was the word he used with Holly, on their way out here? Closure, wasn't it?

Brady's hijacked body has been laid open to the backbone. His guts are spread out around him like the wings of a red dragon. Pools of steaming blood are sinking into the snow. But his eyes are open and aware, and all at once Hodges can feel those fingers again. This time they're not just probing lazily. This time they're frantic, scrabbling for purchase. Hodges ejects them as easily as that floor-mopping orderly once pushed this man's presence out of his mind.

He spits Brady out like a watermelon seed.

'Help me,' Brady whispers. 'You have to help me.'

'I think you're way beyond help,' Hodges says.

'You were run down, Brady. Run down by an extremely heavy vehicle. Now you know what that feels like. Don't you?'

'Hurts,' Brady whispers.

'Yes,' Hodges says. 'I imagine it does.'

'If you can't help me, shoot me.'

Hodges holds out his hand, and Holly puts the Victory .38 into it like a nurse handing a doctor a scalpel. He rolls the cylinder and dumps out one of the two remaining bullets. Then he closes the gun up again. Although he hurts everywhere now, hurts like hell, Hodges kneels down and puts his father's gun in Brady's hand.

'You do it,' he says. 'It's what you always wanted.'

Jerome stands by, ready in case Brady should decide to use that final round on Hodges instead. But he doesn't. Brady tries to point the gun at his head. He can't. His arm twitches, but won't rise. He groans again. Blood pours over his lower lip and seeps out from between Felix Babineau's capped teeth. It would almost be possible to feel sorry for him, Hodges thinks, if you didn't know what he did at City Center, what he tried to do at the Mingo Auditorium, and the suicide machine he's set in motion today. That machine will slow down and stop now that its prime operative is finished, but it will swallow up a few more sad young people before it does. Hodges is pretty sure of that. Suicide may not be painless, but it *is* catching.

You could feel sorry for him if he wasn't a monster, Hodges thinks.

Holly kneels, lifts Brady's hand, and puts the

muzzle of the gun against his temple. 'Now, Mr Hartsfield,' she says. 'You have to do the rest yourself. And may God have mercy on your soul.'

'I hope not,' Jerome says. In the glare of the Sno-Cat's headlights, his face is a stone.

For a long moment the only sounds are the rumble of the snow machine's big engine and the rising wind of winter storm Eugenie.

Holly says, 'Oh God. His finger's not even on the trigger. One of you needs to help me, I don't think I can — '

Then, a gunshot.

'Brady's last trick,' Jerome says. 'Jesus.'

36

There's no way Hodges can make it back to the Expedition, but Jerome is able to muscle him into the cab of the Sno-Cat. Holly sits beside him on the outside. Jerome climbs behind the wheel and throws it into gear. Although he backs up and then circles wide around the remains of Babineau's body, he tells Holly not to look until they're at least up the first hill. 'We're leaving blood-tracks.'

'Oough.'

'Correct,' Jerome says. 'Oough is correct.'

'Thurston told me he had snowmobiles,' Hodges says. 'He didn't mention anything about a Sherman tank.'

'It's a Tucker Sno-Cat, and you didn't offer him your MasterCard as collateral. Not to mention an excellent Jeep Wrangler that got me out here to the williwags just fine, thanks.'

'Is he really dead?' Holly asks. Her wan face is turned up to Hodges's, and the huge knot on her forehead actually seems to be pulsing. 'Really and for sure?'

You saw him put a bullet in his brain.'

'Yes, but is he? Really and for sure?'

The answer he won't give is no, not yet. Not until the trails of slime he's left in the heads of God knows how many people are washed away by the brain's remarkable ability to heal itself. But in another week, another month at the outside, Brady will be all gone.

'Yes,' he says. 'And Holly? Thanks for programming that text alert. The home run boys.'

She smiles. 'What was it? The text, I mean?'

Hodges struggles his phone out of his coat pocket, checks it, and says, 'I will be goddamned.' He begins to laugh. 'I completely forgot.'

'What? Show me show me show me!'

He tilts the phone so she can read the text his daughter, Alison, has sent him from California, where the sun is no doubt shining:

HAPPY BIRTHDAY, DADDY! 70 YEARS OLD AND STILL GOING STRONG! AM RUSHING OUT TO THE MARKET, WILL CALL U LATER. XXX ALLIE

For the first time since Jerome returned from Arizona, Tyrone Feelgood Delight makes an appearance. 'You is sem'ny years old, Massa

479

Hodges? Laws! You don't look a day ovah sixty-fi'!'

'Stop it, Jerome,' Holly says. 'I know it amuses you, but that sort of talk sounds very ignorant and silly.'

Hodges laughs. It hurts to laugh, but he can't help it. He holds onto consciousness all the way back to Thurston's Garage; is even able to take a few shallow tokes on the joint Holly lights and passes to him. Then the dark begins to slip in.

This could be it, he thinks.

Happy birthday to me, he thinks.

Then he's gone.

AFTER

Four Days Later

Pete Huntley is far less familiar with Kiner Memorial than his old partner, who made many pilgrimages here to visit a longterm resident who has now passed away. It takes Pete two stops — one at the main desk and one in Oncology — before he locates Hodges's room, and when he gets there, it's empty. A cluster of balloons with HAPPY BIRTHDAY DAD on them are tethered to one of the siderails and floating near the ceiling.

A nurse pokes her head in, sees him looking at the empty bed, and gives him a smile. 'The solarium at the end of the hall. They've been having a little party. I think you're still in time.'

Pete walks down. The solarium is skylighted and filled with plants, maybe to cheer up the patients, maybe to provide them with a little extra oxygen, maybe both. Near one wall, a party of four people is playing cards. Two of them are bald, and one has an IV drip running into his arm. Hodges is seated directly under the skylight, doling out slices of cake to his posse: Holly, Jerome, and Barbara. Kermit seems to be growing a beard, it's coming in snow-white, and Pete has a brief memory of going to the mall with his own kids to see Santa Claus.

'Pete!' Hodges says, smiling. He starts to get

481

up and Pete waves him back into his seat. 'Sit down, have some cake. Allie brought it from Batool's Bakery. It was always her favorite place to go when she was growing up.'

'Where is she?' Pete asks, dragging a chair over and placing it next to Holly. She's sporting a bandage on the left side of her forehead, and Barbara has a cast on her leg. Only Jerome looks hale and hearty, and Pete knows the kid barely escaped getting turned into hamburger out at that hunting camp.

'She went back to the Coast this morning. Two days off was all she could manage. She's got three weeks' vacation coming in March, and says she'll be back. If I need her, that is.'

'How are you feeling?'

'Not bad,' Hodges says. His eyes flick up and to the left, but only for a second. 'I've got three cancer docs on my case, and the first tests came back looking good.'

'That's fantastic.' Pete takes the piece of cake Hodges is holding out. 'This is too big.'

'Man up and chow down,' Hodges says. 'Listen, about you and Izzy — '

'We worked it out,' Pete says. He takes a bite. 'Hey, nice. There's nothing like carrot cake with cream cheese frosting to cheer up your blood sugar.'

'So the retirement party is . . . ?'

'Back on. Officially, it was never off. I'm still counting on you to give the first toast. And remember — '

'Yeah, yeah, ex-wife and current squeeze both there, nothing too off-color. Got it, got it.'

'Just as long as we're clear on that.' The too-big slice of cake is getting smaller. Barbara watches the rapid intake with fascination.

'Are we in trouble?' Holly asks. 'Are we, Pete, are we?'

'Nope,' Pete says. 'Completely in the clear. That's mostly what I came to tell you.'

Holly sits back with a sigh of relief that blows the graying bangs off her forehead.

'Bet they've got Babineau carrying the can for everything,' Jerome says.

Pete points his plastic fork at Jerome. 'Truth you speak, young Jedi warrior.'

'You might be interested to know that the famous puppeteer Frank Oz did Yoda's voice,' Holly says. She looks around. 'Well, I find it interesting.'

'I find this cake interesting,' Pete says. 'Could I have a little more? Maybe just a sliver?'

Barbara does the honors, and it's far more than a sliver, but Pete doesn't object. He takes a bite and asks how she's doing.

'Good,' Jerome says before she can answer. 'She's got a boyfriend. Kid named Dereece Neville. Big basketball star.'

'Shut up, Jerome, he is not my boyfriend.'

'He sure visits like a boyfriend,' Jerome says. 'I'm talking every day since you broke your leg.'

'We have a lot to talk about,' Barbara says in a dignified tone of voice.

Pete says, 'Going back to Babineau, hospital administration has some security footage of him coming in through a back entrance on the night his wife was murdered. He changed into maintenance-worker duds. Probably raided a locker. He leaves, comes back fifteen or twenty minutes later, changes back into the clothes he came in, leaves for good.'

'No other footage?' Hodges asks. 'Like in the Bucket?'

'Yeah, some, but you can't see his face in that stuff, because he's wearing a Groundhogs cap, and you don't see him go into Hartsfield's room. A defense lawyer might be able to make something of that stuff, but since Babineau's never going to stand trial — '

'No one gives much of a shit,' Hodges finishes.

'Correct. City and state cops are delighted to let him carry the weight. Izzy's happy, and so am I. I could ask you — just between us chickens — if it was actually Babineau who died out there in the woods, but I don't really want to know.'

'So how does Library Al fit into this scenario?' Hodges asks.

'He doesn't.' Pete puts his paper plate aside. 'Alvin Brooks killed himself last night.'

'Oh, Christ,' Hodges says. 'While he was in County?'

'Yes.'

'They didn't have him on suicide watch? After all this?'

'They did, and none of the inmates are supposed to have anything capable of cutting or stabbing, but he got hold of a ballpoint pen somehow. Might have been a guard who gave it to him, but it was probably another inmate. He drew Zs all over the walls, all over his bunk, and all over himself. Then he took the pen's metal

484

cartridge out of the barrel and used it to — '

'Stop,' Barbara says. She looks very pale in the winterlight falling on them from above. 'We get the idea.'

Hodges says, 'So the thinking is . . . what? He was Babineau's accomplice?'

'Fell under his influence,' Pete says. 'Or maybe both of them fell under someone else's influence, but let's not go there, okay? The thing to concentrate on now is that the three of you are in the clear. There won't be any citations this time, or city freebies — '

'It's okay,' Jerome says. 'Me n Holly have still got at least four-years left on our bus passes, anyway.'

'Not that you ever use yours now that you're hardly ever here,' Barbara says. 'You should give it to me.'

'It's non-transferrable,' Jerome says smugly. 'I better hold onto it. Wouldn't want you to get in any trouble with the law. Besides, soon you'll be going places with Dereece. Just don't go too far, if you know what I mean.'

'You're being childish.' Barbara turns to Pete. 'How many suicides were there in all?'

Pete sighs. 'Fourteen over the last five days. Nine of them had Zappits, which are now as dead as their owners. The oldest was twenty-four, the youngest thirteen. One was a boy from a family that was, according to the neighbors, fairly weird about religion — the kind that makes fundamentalist Christians look liberal. He took his parents and kid brother with him. Shotgun.'

The five of them fall silent for a moment. At

the table on the left, the card players burst into howls of laughter over something.

Pete breaks the silence. 'And there have been over forty attempts.'

Jerome whistles.

'Yeah, I know. It's not in the papers, and the TV stations are sitting on it, even Murder and Mayhem.' This is a police nickname for WKMM, an indie station that has taken *If it bleeds, it leads* as an article of faith. 'But of course a lot of those attempts — maybe even most of them — end up getting blabbed about on the social media sites, and that breeds still more. I hate those sites. But this will settle. Suicide clusters always do.'

'Eventually,' Hodges says. 'But with social media or without it, with Brady or without him, suicide is a fact of life.'

He looks over at the card players as he says this, especially the two baldies. One looks good (as Hodges himself looks good), but the other is cadaverous and hollow-eyed. One foot in the grave and the other on a banana peel, Hodges's father would have said. And the thought that comes to him is too complicated — too fraught with a terrible mixture of anger and sorrow — to be articulated. It's about how some people carelessly squander what others would sell their souls to have: a healthy, pain-free body. And why? Because they're too blind, too emotionally scarred, or too self-involved to see past the earth's dark curve to the next sunrise. Which always comes, if one continues to draw breath.

'More cake?' Barbara asks.

'Nope. Gotta split. But I will sign your cast, if I may.'

'Please,' Barbara says. 'And write something witty.'

'That's far beyond Pete's pay grade,' Hodges says.

'Watch your mouth, *Kermit.*' Pete drops to one knee, like a swain about to propose, and begins writing carefully on Barbara's cast. When he's finished, he stands up and looks at Hodges. 'Now tell me the truth about how you're feeling.'

'Damn good. I've got a patch that controls the pain a lot better than the pills, and they're kicking me loose tomorrow. I can't wait to sleep in my own bed.' He pauses, then says: 'I'm going to beat this thing.'

★ ★ ★

Pete's waiting for the elevator when Holly catches up to him. 'It meant a lot to Bill,' she says. 'That you came, and that you still want him to give that toast.'

'It's not so good, is it?' Pete says.

'No.' He reaches out to hug her, but Holly steps back. She does allow him to take her hand and give it a brief squeeze. 'Not so good.'

'Crap.'

'Yes, crap. Crap is right. He doesn't deserve this. But since he's stuck with it, he needs his friends to stand by him. You will, won't you?'

'Of course I will. And don't count him out yet, Holly. Where there's life, there's hope. I know it's a cliché, but . . . ' He shrugs.

487

'I *do* have hope. I have Holly hope.'

You can't say she's as weird as ever, Pete thinks, but she's still peculiar. He sort of likes it, actually. 'Just make sure he keeps that toast relatively clean, okay?'

'I will.'

'And hey — he outlived Hartsfield. No matter what else happens, he's got that.'

'We'll always have Paris, kid,' Holly says in a Bogart drawl.

Yes, she's still peculiar. One of a kind, actually.

'Listen, Gibney, you need to take care of yourself, too. No matter what happens. He'd hate it if you didn't.'

'I know,' Holly says, and goes back to the solarium, where she and Jerome will clean up the remains of the birthday party. She tells herself that it isn't necessarily the last one, and tries to convince herself of that. She doesn't entirely succeed, but she continues to have Holly hope.

Eight Months Later

When Jerome shows up at Fairlawn, two days after the funeral and at ten on the dot, as promised, Holly is already there, on her knees at the head of the grave. She's not praying; she's planting a chrysanthemum. She doesn't look up when his shadow falls over her. She knows who it is. This was the arrangement they made after she told him she didn't know if she could make it all the way through the funeral. 'I'll try,' she said, 'but I'm not good with those fracking things. I may have to book.'

'You plant these in the fall,' she says now. 'I don't know much about plants, so I got a how-to guide. The writing was only so-so, but the directions are easy to follow.'

'That's good.' Jerome sits down crosslegged at the end of the plot, where the grass begins.

Holly scoops dirt carefully with her hands, still not looking at him. 'I told you I might have to book. They all stared at me when I left, but I just couldn't stay. If I had, they would have wanted me to stand up there in front of the coffin and talk about him and I couldn't. Not in front of all those people. I bet his daughter is mad.'

'Probably not,' Jerome says.

'I *hate* funerals. I came to this city for one, did you know that?'

Jerome does, but says nothing. Just lets her finish.

'My aunt died. She was Olivia Trelawney's mother. That's where I met Bill, at that funeral. I ran out of that one, too. I was sitting behind the funeral parlor, smoking a cigarette, feeling terrible, and that's where he found me. Do you understand?' At last she looks up at him. 'He *found* me.'

'I get it, Holly. I do.'

'He opened a door for me. One into the world. He gave me something to do that made a difference.'

'Same here.'

She wipes her eyes almost angrily. 'This is just so fracking poopy.'

'Got that right, but he wouldn't want you to go backward. That's the last thing he'd want.'

'I won't,' she says. 'You know he left me the company, right? The insurance money and everything else went to Allie, but the company is mine. I can't run it by myself, so I asked Pete if he'd like to work for me. Just part-time.'

'And he said . . . ?'

'He said yes, because retirement sucked already. It should be okay. I'll run down the skippers and deadbeats on my computer, and he'll go out and get them. Or serve the subpoenas, if that's the job. But it won't be like it was. Working for Bill . . . working *with* Bill . . . those were the happiest days of my life.' She thinks that over. 'I guess the only happy days of my life. I felt . . . I don't know . . . '

'Valued?' Jerome suggests.

'Yes! Valued.'

'You should have felt that way,' Jerome says, 'because you were very valuable. And still are.'

She gives the plant a final critical look, dusts dirt from her hands and the knees of her pants, and sits down next to him. 'He was brave, wasn't he? At the end, I mean.'

'Yes.'

'Yeah.' She smiles a little. 'That's what Bill would have said — not yes, but yeah.'

'Yeah,' he agrees.

'Jerome? Would you put your arm around me?'

He does.

'The first time I met you — when we found the stealth program Brady loaded into my cousin Olivia's computer — I was afraid of you.'

'I know,' Jerome says.

'Not because you were black — '

'Black is whack,' Jerome says, smiling. 'I think we agreed on that much right from the jump.'

' — but because you were a stranger. You were from *outside*. I was scared of outside people and outside things. I still am, but not as much as I was then.'

'I know.'

'I loved him,' Holly says, looking at the chrysanthemum. It is a brilliant orange-red below the gray gravestone, which bears a simple message: KERMIT WILLIAM HODGES, and, below the dates, END OF WATCH. 'I loved him so much.'

'Yeah,' Jerome says. 'So did I.'

She looks up at him, her face timid and hopeful — beneath the graying bangs, it is almost the face of a child. 'You'll always be my friend, won't you?'

'Always.' He squeezes her shoulders, which are heartbreakingly thin. During Hodges's final two months, she lost ten pounds she couldn't afford to lose. He knows his mother and Barbara are just waiting to feed her up. 'Always, Holly.'

'I know,' she says.

'Then why did you ask?'

'Because it's so good to hear you say it.'

End of Watch, Jerome thinks. He hates the sound of that, but it's right. It's right. And this is better than the funeral. Being here with Holly on this sunny late summer morning is much better.

'Jerome? I'm not smoking.'

'That's good.'

They sit quiet for a little while, looking at the chrysanthemum burning its colors at the base of the headstone.

'Jerome?'

'What, Holly?'

'Would you like to go to a movie with me?'

'Yes,' he says, then corrects himself. 'Yeah.'

'We'll leave a seat empty between us. Just to put our popcorn in.'

'Okay.'

'Because I hate putting it on the floor where there are probably roaches and maybe even rats.'

'I hate it, too. What do you want to see?'

'Something that will make us laugh and laugh.'

'Works for me.'

He smiles at her. Holly smiles back. They leave Fairlawn and walk back out into the world together.

August 30, 2015

AUTHOR'S NOTE

Thanks to Nan Graham, who edited this book, and to all my other friends at Scribner, including — but not limited to — Susan Moldow, Roz Lippel, and Katie Monaghan. Thanks to Chuck Verrill, my longtime agent (important) and longtime friend (more important). Thanks to Chris Lotts, who sells the foreign rights to my books. Thanks to Mark Levenfus, who oversees such business affairs as I have, and keeps an eye on the Haven Foundation, which helps freelance artists down on their luck, and the King Foundation, which helps schools, libraries, and small-town fire departments. Thanks to Marsha DeFilippo, my able personal assistant, and to Julie Eugley, who does everything Marsha doesn't. I'd be lost without them. Thanks to my son Owen King, who read the manuscript and made valuable suggestions. Thanks to my wife, Tabitha, who also made valuable suggestions . . . including what turned out to be the right title.

Special thanks to Russ Dorr, who has traded in his career as a physician's assistant to become my research guru. He went the extra mile on this book, patiently tutoring me on how computer programs are written, how they can be rewritten, and how they can be disseminated. Without Russ, *End of Watch* would have been a far lesser book. I should add that in some cases I eliberately changed various computer protocols to serve my fiction. Tech-savvy individuals will see that, which is fine. Just don't blame Russ.

One last thing. *End of Watch* is fiction, but the high rate of suicide — both in the United States and in many other countries where my books are read — is all too real. The National Suicide Prevention Hotline number given in this book is also real. It's 1-800-273-TALK. If you are feeling poopy (as Holly Gibney would say), give them a call. Because things can get better, and if you give them a chance, they usually do.

Stephen King.